RETURN TO SENDER

Stephanie Parente

**SIMON &
SCHUSTER**

London · New York · Amsterdam/Antwerp · Sydney/Melbourne · Toronto · New Delhi

First published in Great Britain by Simon & Schuster UK Ltd, 2026

Copyright © Stephanie Parente, 2026

The right of Stephanie Parente to be identified as author of this work has been asserted in accordance with the Copyright, Designs and Patents Act, 1988.

1 3 5 7 9 10 8 6 4 2

Simon & Schuster UK Ltd, 7th Floor,
199 Bishopsgate, London EC2M 3TY

Simon & Schuster Australia, Sydney
Simon & Schuster India, New Delhi

www.simonandschuster.co.uk
www.simonandschuster.com.au
www.simonandschuster.co.in

The authorised representative in the EEA is Simon & Schuster Netherlands BV, Herculesplein 96, 3584 AA Utrecht, Netherlands. info@simonandschuster.nl

Simon & Schuster strongly believes in freedom of expression and stands against censorship in all its forms. For more information, visit BooksBelong.com

A CIP catalogue record for this book is available from the British Library

Paperback ISBN: 978-1-3985-5609-6
eBook ISBN: 978-1-3985-5610-2
Audio ISBN: 978-1-3985-5611-9

Printed and Bound in the UK using 100% Renewable Electricity
at CPI Group (UK) Ltd

Praise for *Return to Sender* from Authors and Reviewers

'I read it in one joyous, tear-filled day. Savor it, devour it,
come to this book with open arms and it will love you back.
Steph Parente has done something truly special'
CARA BASTONE, author of *Promise Me Sunshine*

'From the first page, I was hooked … My god, the romance.
Dex is peak swoon. The things he says? I highlighted half his
dialogue. And the slow burn absolutely killed me – in the best way.
The tension and chemistry were so palpable I kept telling myself
"one more chapter" until I realized I had finished the book'
READER REVIEW, 5 stars

'I laughed. I cried. I blushed hard on a park bench,
but most importantly, I fell hard and fast for our unlikely
trio. Violet and Dex stole my heart, and Stephanie Parente
has a firm forever fan in me'
CATHERINE WALSH, author of *One Night Only*

'Absolutely incredible – heartfelt and genuine and romantic. If
you like romances that truly puts the character work in and deals
with grief in such a nuanced and careful way, pick this up I BEG'
READER REVIEW, 5 stars

'Three things: The banter, the originality, and the miles of hope.
Return to Sender illuminates the power of love and loss with a
deft hand, sharp eye, and sharper tongue. I lost count of how
many times I laughed and teared up on the same page'
BECK DOREY-STEIN, author of *Spectacular Things*

'Even though I spent the last six hours crying, it's the thought
that I could have missed this book entirely that makes me feel
truly sick. *Return to Sender* is my favorite story I've read this year'
READER REVIEW, 5 stars

For Mom, Samantha, and Luca
Every tomorrow is better because of you

RETURN
TO
SENDER

One

Someone once told me optimism was genetic. My dad forged a path to the bright side and I followed close behind, nearly sunburned from the glare. I lived in everlasting warmth, naïvely believing it belonged to me.

After nine months in the dark, it felt like maybe I'd never seen the sun at all.

I felt furthest from my dad's optimism walking through the doors of Farnum High School. The scent—an amalgam of cheap perfume, body spray, and cleaning product—stung the back of my throat. My footsteps echoed, synchronizing with disembodied squeaking sneakers from the nearby gymnasium. I'd memorized the way by my third visit.

The office had to be a solid ten degrees warmer than the rest of the school, even with open windows.

"Violet," the woman behind the front desk, Gloria, crowed. She gestured to the visitors' log, as if I hadn't done this a dozen times. "How are you doing, sweetheart?"

I bent to scribble my and Phoebe's names. My smile didn't fit right. "Oh, you know."

"Boy, do I." Hers was more convincing. "Have a seat. Principal Chambers will be with you in a jiff."

Phoebe sat alone in a row of stiff chairs, isolating and far enough from the windows to be both embarrassing and unbearable, scowling at her lap instead of meeting my eyes. I veered for her. Her choppy pink hair spilled from a short ponytail, messily framing her face; multicolored fingernails picked at a rip in her jeans; her face was scrubbed clean of the usual raccoon makeup, eyes red. Dry blood stained the front of her—*my*—Fleetwood Mac tee.

I sat beside her. "Seriously?"

"He started it," she fired at once, though her tone lacked the usual flames.

"You have two weeks left of school."

"*He started it.*"

I pressed my fingers into my eyes, exhaling sharply. "I had to leave work again, Phoebe. This can't keep happening."

The bell rang overhead, sharp and deafening, but Phoebe didn't flinch. I resisted the urge to ask for details. I'd been stuck on the outside of her life for nine months, desperate for a way in; you can't force a fourteen-year-old to practice healthy communication if they're hell-bent on staying inside their own head.

Three things: *We have each other, you have a job to provide for her, a roof over your heads.*

Three positives to combat the rest. It had become a mantra, something keeping me afloat when the rest of my world took on water. Lately, I struggled with three. Not great, seeing as I'd cut it down from five.

I decided to risk a question: "Are you okay?"

Phoebe's scowl deepened, so I pointed to her bloody shirt. She spared it a quick glance. "It's not mine," she said.

"The blood or the shirt?"

The corner of her mouth twitched. "Sorry."

"That's what you're sorry about?"

"Well, I know how much you like this shirt."

I blew out a sharp breath, relenting to the urge. "What happened?"

"Don't worry about it," she replied. I sank farther into the stiff seat, defeat inching up my neck in a warm flush. Still, I knew I'd keep trying. Even if it wore me to dust, I'd make the effort. I cared as loudly as possible and she pushed me away in equal measure. On bad days, I'd think it would be nice if she reciprocated in a way I understood, but then the unfairness would sneak up on me and I'd shove the thought to the furthest corner of my mind. Grief has no room for selfishness, especially when teenagers are involved.

I wanted to keep poking. The relentless bright side in me insisted I could get through somehow, but the logical side of my brain reached for the advice from my best friend, Arden, or my therapist, or Phoebe's therapist—*give her space to grieve and trust the process.* If her process was anywhere near as nightmarish as mine, I wouldn't hold my breath.

We sat in silence. Phoebe inspected her chipped nail polish and cast an apathetic glance toward the clock on the wall. I bit my tongue so hard, I tasted blood.

The door directly across from us swung open and out swept Principal Chambers, all long legs, blond curls, and the Reformation dress I'd had bookmarked on the website for over a year. Meanwhile, my hair was windblown because the AC in my car didn't work, and my outfit cost a whopping thirty bucks from TJ Maxx. I did my best not to shrink in her presence, but as an elementary school teacher and former honor roll student, principals were my kryptonite.

"Violet," she said, offering a breezy smile. "Nice to see you again. And so soon."

Phoebe bristled. I forced a smile and said, "Hi."

"Come on in. Let's chat." Her tone sent a shiver down my spine. Phoebe and I both stood. Principal Chambers said, "Oh, no. You stay, Phoebe. I'd like to speak to your sister alone."

Phoebe spun to me, panic flashing in her eyes. I swallowed hard and curled my hands into fists so they'd stop shaking.

"I'll be right back," I said. She wiped her face clear of emotion and sat, folding her arms tightly over her chest. "It'll be okay."

Principal Chambers's office burned itself into my memory eight months ago, but since then I'd spent so much time here, the lightly padded chair had practically formed to my ass and I knew to avoid eye contact with the framed photo of her city council husband who stole a parking spot from me at the grocery store last year.

The air-conditioning was new. Thinking of Phoebe sitting in the stifling heat just outside the door, my contempt skyrocketed.

"So," Principal Chambers said, easing into her desk chair. She folded her hands, eyes swimming with performative pity. "How are you doing, Violet?"

"Great," I answered. The nearly imperceptible flick of her eyebrow had me backtracking. "I mean, fine."

"I can't imagine what you're going through. Both of you." My fingernails dug into the arms of the chair. I forced another smile. "Losing a parent is tragic."

My uvula tied itself in a knot. Swallowing over it, I said, "We're getting through it."

"Hmm." She leaned back in her chair, eyeing me. "I understand this hasn't been an easy transition. But this is the twelfth time I've had to call you this year."

I flinched. "I don't think it's twelve."

"Twelve," she said, tone clipped. "Phoebe's behavior has become increasingly erratic. Today, she nearly broke a boy's nose. The only reason she's not suspended is because several eyewitnesses claim she was defending herself."

My fingers dug farther into the chair at that word: *claim*. As if she didn't believe it, even slightly.

"She was defending herself?" I repeated. Phoebe's words flitted through my head: *Don't worry about it*. As if I'd be able to think about anything else. "What happened?"

"You know kids," Principal Chambers replied. Her flippant tone rankled and I had to grind my teeth so I wouldn't lash out. "Words were said—it remains unclear exactly what these words were. However, Phoebe was the one to resort to violence."

"Okay," I said. "So, what happens to him?"

"Don't worry. He's fine."

"I'm not worried. I want to know he won't mess with my sister again."

"Violet." Never had my name sounded so condescending. "Let's focus on Phoebe."

I clenched my jaw and tried to come up with three things, but my mind indulged in how good it would feel to slash her tires. I'd had the problematic child conversation with a number of parents and it was always a minefield, so I kept things gentle with them. Meanwhile, Principal Chambers looked about ready to break into villainous laughter. She *relished* this.

"Her behavior is beyond concerning and has only been escalating," she said. My vision drifted over her shoulder, focus locking on the soft hum of the air conditioner. "Have you considered seeking professional help?"

My eyes snapped to hers. "Excuse me?"

"I have the names of some wonderful psychiatrists in the

area," she charged on. I released my grip, fingers throbbing, heat surging up my neck.

"Is this a joke?"

"I can assure you, there is nothing funny about this situation."

"Oh, I don't know about that. The audacity alone is hilarious."

Her eyes narrowed to slits. "I apologize if I offended you, Ms. St. Clair, but you know as well as I do that Phoebe is out of control. Her grades are slipping. She's starting fights. Phoebe will scrape through this year. We'll give her that, all things considered. But her behavior is unacceptable and if it continues into the next school year, she *will* be expelled."

A war of emotions broke out in my brain. Fury triumphed. I stood, not bothering to fake another smile. "Are we done?"

She folded her hands over her desk and offered a stiff nod. "Keep what I said in mind, Violet. There are options," she said, fixing me with an unfriendly smile. "Have a great day."

I stalked out of her office, leaving the door open behind me. Equal parts bitter and immature. I worked with nine-year-olds— every once in a while, the childish whims won. Phoebe leapt to her feet, her expression shifting from curiosity to dread as she registered my anger. I was halfway out the door when Gloria called out a goodbye. Phoebe jogged to keep up.

"Stupid bitch," I grumbled.

"Are they kicking me out?" Phoebe asked breathlessly. We turned the corner and pushed through the doors, out of the building. A warm breeze curled around us, the smell of impending summer permeating the air—gasoline, hot asphalt, a savory drift from the food trucks setting up shop in the park down the street. This would be Phoebe's first summer in the city and I had no idea if she missed the salt of the ocean or the sweetness of the magnolia tree Dad planted in the yard when she was born.

"No," I said. I paused at the edge of the sidewalk, hands on my hips. The tension in Phoebe's shoulders ebbed slightly. "They're giving you the year. But if you keep it up, you're done."

"Well, that's good, right?"

"No, Phoebe. It's not good."

"What? You'd rather I get expelled for breaking some asshole's nose?"

"No! I'd rather you didn't break anyone's nose!" I tipped my head back, closing my eyes. The sun warmed my face. Somewhere close by, a bird sang its song. When I looked back at my sister, her eyes hardened, daring me to throw down the guardian card. It was overdue and completely worthless.

Some of the girls from high school I followed on Instagram *chose* to become parents at twenty-six. I hated every single one of them.

"You didn't break his nose," I said. She furrowed her brow. "Nearly, but no dice."

Her lip twitched. "Damn. Guess I'll try harder next time."

Together, we crossed the lot. My car had only been parked in the sun for a few minutes, but the inside already tipped from uncomfortable to sweltering. I made sure Phoebe had her seatbelt on before driving off. She stuck her head out the window like a dog, effectively cooling off and delaying the rest of this unpleasant conversation. I didn't mind. I stuck my hand out the window, letting the breeze rush through my fingers, wondering how our dad managed to get through the tough talks with a smile on his face.

My eyes burned. I pretended it was sweat.

Once we reached our apartment building, Phoebe was out of the car before I even put it in park. I stepped out, watching her dart across the lot.

"Outrunning me? That's your plan?"

She flipped me off over her shoulder.

I trailed behind, wincing as she stomped through the ring of flowers near the entrance of our building. The only reason we managed to nab a unit in such a coveted area was my best friend's boyfriend, Noah, and the endless list of Guys He Knew—when the apartment across the hall opened up a few months ago, it was ours before it officially hit the market. The rent was expensive, but utilities were included, and I could walk to work.

Plus, it wasn't our dead dad's house.

Phoebe slammed the Door Close button repeatedly as I collected our mail and approached the elevator, but as the doors slid shut, a hand slipped out, stopping them. She groaned.

"Goddammit."

I stepped into the elevator, shooting our elderly neighbor a smile. To Phoebe, I said, "You should've taken the stairs."

She rolled her eyes.

It was supposed to get easier, wasn't it? Nine months of backbreaking effort and yet I could've been standing in the teachers' lounge in September, answering a phone call from the hospital, understanding the nurse's grim tone before anyone had to say the words out loud.

Phoebe bolted when the doors opened. With a sigh, I made my way down the hall, surprised to find her waiting outside the apartment door for me. She shrugged.

"Lost my key."

"Of course you did." I handed her mine, along with the mail. "Go ahead. I'll be there in a minute."

She let herself into the apartment without a word. In the months after our dad's death, I read several parenting books in a desperate attempt to feel in control of an uncontrollable situation. Phoebe had been drifting fast, her moods souring, patience thinning, and each book assured nothing I said would be right in a teenager's eyes. I didn't find it quite as comforting when I used to be Phoebe's hero. Now, sometimes it felt like I hadn't done anything right since taking her in, and even that might've been a mistake. I couldn't imagine her anywhere else. But maybe *she* could.

I drifted across the hall and banged my forehead against the door three times. A beat later, Arden opened it, her presence illuminating something in me. Even when everything else caught fire and burned to ash, I had her, so things could never be irreversibly bad.

"Hey," she said cautiously, dark eyes studying my face. I should've been at work, not barging in on her day off. But she'd been my rock for years, especially since Dad died, and it would be a disservice to her if I held off on a vent session when I needed one.

"I used to be a happy person, right?" I asked. She winced.

"Uh-oh."

I swept past her, plunking down on the green velvet chaise. "I was joyful at one point. Fun to be around. A good person," I continued, looking to her for verification. She folded her arms, eyebrows pinched thoughtfully.

"You are a good person," she said. "Present tense."

"But not a *happy* one."

"Well, life screwed you over. It takes a while to bounce back after something like that."

She sat beside me, crossing her legs at the ankles; the girl drew eyes by simply existing with her curly black hair and pink apple cheeks, though being perceived was her worst nightmare. When she found out a majority of pharmacy patrons referred to her as the hot pharmacist, she called in sick for three days straight.

"What happened?" she asked. I dropped my face into my hands, letting out a short laugh, and delved into the story.

I wasn't proud of how often I showed up at Arden's to vent. By some miraculous twist of fate, Northeastern paired us up freshman year and we imprinted on each other like baby ducks. Over the years, we moved into a crappy apartment, worked crappy part-time jobs to pay rent while finishing our degrees, and spent a lot of time lamenting terrible dates. She fell in love with Noah the same week she was accepted into her doctorate program and within six months, I met Shawn. It felt like we were meant to experience life in unison until my dad died, I took custody of my sister, and my boyfriend bailed because it was too much. Now, Noah had recruited me to help pick an engagement ring, and I hadn't moved an inch. I hated the jealousy I felt toward my best friend for having her shit together. More than that, I hated mourning my father *and* the life I would've lived if a pickup truck hadn't run a red light.

No amount of positives could lift me up from that.

"First thing's first," Arden said once I finished the recap. "That principal is a bitch."

"Yes."

"And she deserves to be fired."

"Yes."

"And for her house to burn down with her husband still inside it."

"Well—"

"Too far. I take it back. But they both suck." She brushed a curl out of her eyes, her expression softening as she studied my face. "*She* sucks. Has Phoebe been a little unhinged? Sure. But she was defending herself, so the expulsion conversation was out of bounds."

I dug the heels of my hands into my eyes until I saw stars. "Yeah."

"Phoebe will be fine. She's strong. Once she's past the angry phase, things will go back to normal," she said. "Well, not normal. But a new normal where things are okay."

"That's a nice thought. Maybe in this alternate universe, Phoebe tells me why she has to defend herself at school. Maybe she likes me again. Maybe I don't cry in the shower."

Arden's fingers wrapped around my wrist, squeezing gently. I lowered my hands to meet her gaze. "You're not failing, Vi," she said. "That's not what this is."

"I have no idea what I'm doing," I replied, throat tightening against the words. "Feels like failing to me."

"You're allowed to tread water for a while."

"It's been *nine months*."

"Grief doesn't have a time limit."

"It does when you're in charge of a kid."

She bit her lip and looked toward the kitchen, unable to dispute this. My dad never fell apart in front of us—he always had his shit together, even if he was pretending for our benefit. I needed to do the same for Phoebe. I just had no idea *how*.

"So, what are you gonna say?" she asked. "To Phoebe."

I groaned. "God. I don't know."

"You have to stop giving her the power, Vi," she said. "She's a kid. She needs an authority figure."

"She needs our dad." I swallowed over the tightness in my throat. "I was the cool older sister. She's never going to see me differently."

"She will if you make her."

Like it was *easy*. I climbed to my feet, emitting a heavy sigh. "I should go. Hopefully she hasn't bolted down the fire escape."

Arden stood, wiping her hands on her shorts. "Why don't you guys come over for dinner? We're ordering pizza. Phoebe can play video games with Noah and we can talk shit in the kitchen."

A rush of love swept through me. As jealous as I was of Arden, I couldn't have been more grateful to have her in my life. I would quite literally die without her.

"That sounds great," I said. She pulled me into a tight hug.

"Three things," she prompted, her voice soft in my ear. I squeezed my eyes shut.

"You. Noah. Pizza."

"There you go."

A little lighter on the dread, I returned to my apartment, reveling in the tiny bursts of comfort: the air-conditioning, the "cashmere woods" air freshener plugged in the wall, the message etched into the center of the steel door: *At least tomorrow.* Those words were the last thing I saw before leaving each morning. The building owner had offered to replace the door when we moved in, but something about it clutched my heart, calling to the optimist in me.

The apartment was sparse. We still lived out of boxes, despite having moved in three months ago. After packing up our childhood home and selling it off to the highest bidder, neither of us was up for the task of settling in somewhere new. A coffee maker and a toaster sat on the counter, mugs filled the sink, a trash can in the corner overflowed with paper plates and plastic cutlery. Our only piece of furniture, a purple velvet couch, was given to us by Arden and Noah when they decided to invest in a sectional. Still, it was a relief to have a place untouched by the past.

I nearly tripped on Phoebe's backpack on my way in. I expected her to be locked away in her room, but she was lounging on the couch, absorbed in a piece of paper.

"Hey," I said. Her head snapped up. "Arden invited us over for dinner. They're ordering pizza."

"Cool." Her eyes darted to the paper clutched in her hands. "Yeah, cool. Sounds good."

"So, we should probably talk about what happened."

"No, yeah. For sure."

I narrowed my eyes. Her acquiescence was more than a little suspicious. "I know you don't want to explain what happened today, but Principal Chambers said it was self-defense," I said, taking note of the lack of reaction. Normally, she would've tensed up or shrugged this off. "You don't have to tell me what happened, and I'm not mad. I always want you to defend yourself. I'll punch the little prick myself, if you want."

"No, yeah," she repeated, eyes on the paper. "I won't do it again. Promise."

"That's not—" I scowled. "*Phoebe.*"

She glanced up. "Huh? Sorry. I was maybe not totally listening," she said, and to her credit, she sounded genuine. "But, uh, I'll be on my best behavior from now on."

Okay, now I really was suspicious. "What's going on, Phoebe?"

She sprang to her feet, sliding across the wood floor in her socks, and thrust the paper into my hands. "This came."

A neatly written letter, along with a torn envelope addressed to someone named Catalina Arroyo in Hartford. *RETURN TO SENDER* was stamped across it in bright red ink. My eyes flicked to the return address.

Our address. As in this apartment.

I double-checked to make sure one of us hadn't sent the letter. Instead, the name *Benji Dexter* was scrawled in blocky handwriting.

"What is this?" I asked, turning the envelope over to inspect the back, as if it might hold the answer. Phoebe bounced on her heels, showcasing more life than I'd seen since last year.

"It was written by the dude who lived here before us," she told me. I lifted my eyes to hers, raising my eyebrows.

"You opened it?"

"Yeah. It was sent to us."

"It was sent to *him*."

"And where is he, Vi? Not here. Fair game."

The teenage mind was truly a wonder to behold. "Phoebe," I said slowly, lifting the torn envelope. "This is a felony."

"Barely," she replied. I shot an imploring look to the ceiling, wishing my dad would take a break from the afterlife to knock some sense into his youngest daughter. "Vi, you have to read it."

"What?" I blinked at her. "I'm not reading it."

"It's so good, Vi—you have to!"

"It's not for me! It's for Catalina!"

"Well, she clearly never got it! Or if she did, she wasn't interested in whatever this Benji guy had to say," she said, hopping over to stand at my side. "Read it. Seriously. Read it."

Despite myself, curiosity burned. Months and months of apathy, of bad moods and rolled eyes, of sitting on the couch when she once would've been doing something, everything, *any-thing* to fend off boredom—here, suddenly, a *spark*. All because of a misaddressed letter.

Seeing Phoebe come alive awoke something in me. I would've done anything to help that spark ignite into something real.

"Fine," I relented. Her eyes lit up. "Since you already opened it."

Unfolding the letter revealed a single page of neat, tightly scrawled handwriting.

Cat,

I'm sorry. I need that said before everything else because I love you and you were right and I will regret letting you walk away for the rest of my life.

I knew I was fucking it up as I was fucking it up. I remem-

ber every second. I've been going over it again and again, hating myself for the things I said. You were right. I pushed you away on purpose. I'm used to working shit out on my own and not having to explain myself to anyone else, and my issues not affecting anyone but me. But we were partners. And in hurting myself, I hurt you, and I couldn't stand it. I didn't want to hurt you anymore, so I told you to go instead of asking how you felt about it. I think I was afraid of the answer.

I regretted it during the fight. I regretted it when I told you to go. I regretted it when you walked out the door. And that goddamn message stared back at me, mocking me. At least tomorrow . . . nothing. Tomorrow wasn't worth waking up to if you weren't beside me.

I'm sleepwalking through these days, Cat. I miss you so much, I'm sick. I can feel my sadness poisoning everyone around me. I thought leaving you would save us both from the hurt, but this is so much worse. I can't imagine a worse life than this. Me without you. It doesn't make sense, and I can't believe I ever thought it would.

I'm so sorry, Cat. I will do anything to make up for what I've done. I love you. I love you. I love you. Please come home.

Maybe it's not fair for me to send this. Maybe I should leave well enough alone. I hurt you, I hurt me, the end. I should let things heal. But I want to lay my cards on the table. I want you to have a beautiful life, Cat. You deserve it, with or without me. I want you to keep dancing. I want you to sing while loading the dishwasher. I want you to pet every dog you pass on the street and cry during happy movies. Be with someone who will treasure all that you are.

I do. I would. I want to be that person for you, if you'd have me. I'll do my best to make sure I don't spiral like that again. I made an appointment with my old therapist. I called my mom.

I want to be okay. I won't make you carry me. I just want to walk beside you.

You're everything, Cat. I'll love you forever.

Love,

Benji

"Wow," I said, scanning the words a second time. "We just read something we weren't ever supposed to read."

"I know, right?" Phoebe shuffled her feet, as if physically unable to contain the excitement. She couldn't wipe the smile off her face, and despite the federal crime we'd just committed, anger wasn't an option. Watching her, a pulse of joy radiated through my chest, so reminiscent of the day she was born that I nearly lost my breath. *Hi, Bumble Bee,* I'd whispered to the tiny pink face snuffling against a cocoon of blankets. *I can't believe you're real.*

She was perfect then, and perfect now.

"What do we do with it?" I asked, turning the letter over in my hands. "Take it to the post office? Throw it away?"

"No!" Phoebe moved to snatch the letter, but I whipped it out of her reach. "It's not our letter to throw away."

"It's not our letter to *read.* This was a mistake."

Her smile wobbled. Every nerve in my body clenched, desperate to put it back in its place.

"We'll take it to the post office tomorrow," I said swiftly. *I take it back,* I wanted to say. *We can do whatever you want, forever.* "They must have a current address for Benji or Catalina."

"If they had a current address," she replied, unsmiling, "why would they send it here?"

"Good point." I brushed my thumb over Catalina's address, noting how Benji wrote it with so much more precision than his own. "Noah knows everyone. And if he used to live across from this guy, he might know where he is now."

Phoebe perked up. "Can we go ask?"

"Noah's at work," I said. "Kind of like I should be."

She smiled sheepishly. "Oh. Right."

"You might get to skate through the year, but my boss isn't so bereavement-friendly. I can't keep leaving early."

"Your boss sounds like a bitch."

"Not the point."

Phoebe shifted her weight between her feet. "I know. You can go back to work, if you want."

Her contrition pinched somewhere beneath my ribs. "Also not the point. Today doesn't count. But this was the twelfth time I've had to talk to the principal. That's a problem, Bee."

She scrunched up her face. "It's so not twelve." She reached for the letter again. This time, I let her take it. "I get it, okay? I'll be better."

"I'm not asking you to be better," I replied. "I'm asking you not to break anyone's nose on school property."

She offered a salute and returned to the couch, tossing herself over the side to land with a soft *flump,* scanning the letter again. I exhaled, feeling like I'd finished dead last in a marathon. Maybe somewhere my dad was beaming with pride and giving me a corny thumbs-up—*You're a star, Vi, I knew you could do it!*

The glittering fragments of my heart jostled inside my chest as I made my way to my nearly empty bedroom and plopped face down on the mattress.

Two

I forgot about the letter until Noah answered the door and Phoebe shoved it in his face, shouting, "WHO LIVED HERE BEFORE US?"

"Jesus," Noah said, blinking rapidly. He and I were the two most important people in Arden's life, but I was the one talking her down after their parents set them up. Originally from Seoul, her parents had a lot of expectations when it came to a partner for Arden, and she revolted at every opportunity until they shipped her off to dinner with a sharp-jawed future pediatrician.

Four years later, Arden remained sore about it.

"Phoebe," I said. "When I said to ask Noah, I didn't mean the second we got here."

Ignoring me, she brandished the letter. "This came today. Do you know anything about this guy?"

Noah glanced at me, raising his eyebrows. He'd spent enough evenings playing the buffer between us to recognize the shift in Phoebe—something illuminated for the first time in months—that I didn't have to say a word. He delicately turned the envelope over in his hands, studying it.

"You opened it?"

"Not the point."

His eyes cut to me. "Might be kind of the point."

I shrugged helplessly. "She's fourteen, man. I don't know."

"Okay, let's check this out," he said, stepping aside to let us in. Phoebe herded him to the couch like a border collie; I could practically hear her nerves revving. I didn't know why she was so invested in this, but the relief of it doused me in a warmth that had me wondering if I'd been living in a permanent winter since September.

"Do you remember him?" Phoebe asked, bouncing on the cushion beside Noah. A line appeared between his eyebrows as he inspected the envelope again and then carefully slipped the letter out.

"When we moved in, a woman lived there. Shawna."

Phoebe slumped. "Oh."

"She had just moved in when we did, so Benji must've moved out a year, year and a half ago." He rubbed his chin, eyes skimming the letter. "Strange that it would show up now."

"It's weird, right?" Phoebe scooted closer, reading over his shoulder. "I wonder if this Catalina chick held on to it for a while and was finally like, 'Bye bitch!' And sent it back."

"That or it got lost somewhere and she moved from this address before it reached her."

"So, we're all invested in this now," I said, looking between them. Noah didn't lift his attention from the letter, brow furrowing. Behind me, the door opened and Arden waltzed in, carrying two pizza boxes along with a smaller box on top.

"Antonio gave us free garlic bread!" she declared, kicking the door shut. "I was totally right about his thing for me."

I perked up—I knew Antonio from Antonio's Pizza was into Arden, but this was the first time his crush resulted in a free appetizer. Meanwhile, Noah and Phoebe were too engrossed to notice.

"Man," Noah said. "There is some serious groveling going on here."

"Groveling?" Arden deposited the boxes on the kitchen counter, scrunching her face up in confusion. "What do you mean? What'd I miss?"

"We got a letter in the mail written by the dude who used to live in our apartment. Phoebe, being Phoebe, opened it."

Arden's eyes lit up and she veered for the sofa. "Ooh. Let me see."

Checking back into reality, Noah glanced at me with a smirk. "Notice how she has no issue with the felony."

"Opening someone's mail is barely a felony," she said, leaning over the back of the couch to get a closer look. Phoebe threw me a victorious smile. And *dammit,* I couldn't muster a lick of irritation; that smile was too nice to see.

"They were hoping we knew him," Noah mentioned. "But Shawna lived there when we moved in, right?"

Arden nodded absently. I stood off to the side and rolled up the sleeves of my oversized flannel, watching as the three most important people in my life read and reread that letter with mounting interest. I mean, it *was* interesting. But it didn't necessarily deserve more attention than hot pizza.

"That's *crazy,*" Arden said, tearing her gaze from the letter. "That's some true love shit. I don't think Noah loves me that much."

"I love you more," he protested. "If we broke up, I wouldn't write a sad letter. I would *do* something."

She ignored this and drew her phone out of her pocket. "We have to look this guy up."

"Already did," Phoebe said. I raised my eyebrows.

"You did?"

"Yeah, but there's literally nothing." She pushed up on her knees, leaning toward Arden to get a look at her phone. "See? No Benji Dexters. There are Benjamin Dexters, but no one in Boston. And all the ones I found are, like, elderly."

"How do you know this guy isn't elderly?" Noah asked. Phoebe rested her elbow along the back of the couch, twisting to face him.

"I found Catalina."

I recoiled. "How?"

She waved this off. "Her social media is private. But you can tell from her profile pictures she's pretty young. Late twenties, early thirties maybe," she explained, her voice rising an octave from the excitement.

I stared at her, dumbfounded. "Who *are* you?"

Arden quickly tapped something new into the Google search bar. "Which one?"

Phoebe scanned the screen, then pointed. "Her."

"Holy shit."

"Right? She's hot."

"I wanna see," Noah said. Arden shot him a look. "I mean, I'm also looking at a hot girl, so I don't need to see."

She turned back to her phone, shifting closer to Phoebe. "We should create a burner account and request to follow her."

"I thought about it, but that might cross the line from curiosity to stalker," Phoebe replied.

"What is happening?" I said to no one in particular. Phoebe glanced at me, her expression inscrutable.

"How are you not interested?"

"I am interested. This"—I gestured toward them—"isn't interest. It's something else."

"Obsession," Arden said, spinning to face me. "I'm obsessed, and you should be, too. Your apartment has lore, Vi! Lore that doesn't include haunting!"

"It might include a little haunting," Phoebe said. "My bedroom door shut on its own the other day."

"You left your window open." I turned, heading to the counter to grab a slice of pizza. "Isn't this the end of the road? The guy doesn't exist and the girl doesn't want to be found. The end."

"Or," Phoebe said, "we could break into the building manager's office and find Benji's old files."

My mouth dropped open. Even Arden balked.

"Please tell me you're joking," I said as Principal Chambers's warnings about escalation swam through my head. Broken rules graduating into broken laws. Phoebe dipped her toe in with mail fraud—the only thing standing in her way of a life of crime was me, the woman with a hidden stash of Twinkies in her underwear drawer.

"They must have them, right?" Phoebe pressed, looking to Noah for reassurance. His lips pressed into a line, eyes darting to me and back again.

"Probably not. I doubt a place like this holds on to tenant information that long."

"But you don't *know.*"

"We're not breaking in anywhere," I cut in, earning my tenth eye roll of the day. "What are you doing right now, Phoebe? What is this?"

"I'm trying to return someone's private property, no thanks to you."

"You're trying to break the law. Again."

"Reading someone's mail is barely illegal, Vi! And it was sent to us!"

"It was sent to him!"

"*Our* apartment."

"*His* name."

Noah and Arden watched us go back and forth like Venus and Serena at Wimbledon, but then Arden caught my eye, something twinkling. She could see the difference in Phoebe too. My best friend and Noah had been with us through the entire hellish ride, diffusing tension when things got too sour by inviting us over for dinner or out to a movie. And now, finally, Phoebe's permanent scowl had fled, smiling like the kid Arden and I would make peanut butter and fluff sandwiches for when we were on break from college.

Maybe I wasn't invested in the letter, but I was invested in *that*.

"Fine," I said, and Phoebe straightened. "If you can figure out a way—a *legal* way—to find Benji Dexter, I will do everything in my power to get that letter to him."

She considered this. "Define 'legal.'"

Noah snorted.

"I'm kidding," she said, sending me a reassuring smile. "All my research will be aboveboard. Promise."

Phoebe padded over to the pizza. I watched her, the anxiety in my chest flaring as her smile dimmed a few watts. I wanted her to be happy. I *needed* her to be happy. My reckless, wonderful childhood had shifted irrevocably with the birth of my sister; even at twelve, I found myself protective to a vicious degree, and that part of me grew along with her, exploding into an inferno when she came out to me last summer. I'd never forget the shake in her voice, as if she truly believed something would change between us because she liked girls, or the joyful tears in her eyes when I'd told her I was bisexual.

It was scary, loving someone that much. I wanted to warp the world into a softer, more palatable place for her. Maybe, somehow, this was the first step.

Arden sidled up beside me, her fingers wrapping around my arm. "She's *smiling*," she hissed in my ear. I nodded stiffly.

"I know."

"That's *big*."

"I know."

"We have to pursue this."

I shut my eyes, Phoebe's smile seared into my memory, my eyelids, my very being.

"I know," I said.

Three

Two days after the letter arrived, I found Phoebe waiting on the sidewalk outside our apartment when I got home from work, a storm of emotions brewing in her features.

"You're late!" she cried as soon as I was within earshot. Her backpack sat on the pavement at her feet, meaning she hadn't bothered dropping it off upstairs. I knew something was up this morning when she wolfed down a bowl of cereal and told me to have a great day before rushing out the door. A stark difference to the silent stompings of mornings past. I floated through most of the day, keenly aware my phone *wasn't* ringing (we weren't supposed to keep our volume on at work, but considering how often Phoebe's school called, it had become a necessity, and my students danced along to the ringtone whenever it chimed). The optimistic part of me hoped we'd simply turned a corner and she liked me again, but I knew better than to trust it by now.

She'd been sleuthing. Hopefully the nice, legal kind of sleuthing that takes place in a public library, but I had my doubts.

"Hello to you, too," I said, keeping my pace leisurely to piss her off. As much as I wanted her happy, sometimes the older sister gene won out. "And I'm not late. This is the time I get home. You'd know that if you didn't have detention every day."

She sneered. "Not today."

"Not today or you skipped it today?"

"Vi," she said, ignoring the question, "I found him."

I sighed. "Of course you did."

"I didn't do anything illegal," she told me in a breathless rush, eyes bright.

"Okay," I said. "Then how'd you find him?"

"Can't you just be like, 'Wow, Bee, you are so beautiful and impressive. Let's hit the road.'"

"Wow, Bee, you are so beautiful and impressive," I echoed. "Before we hit the road, though, I need to know how you managed to track this guy down."

She scrunched her nose up, which always preceded something I wouldn't approve of. Barbies flushed down the toilet, an abandoned baby bunny living in a box in her closet, something terrifically illegal to find a man who didn't want to be found.

"Remember when Noah said our apartment building probably doesn't keep records?" She smiled with all her teeth. "Well . . ."

A breath wheezed out of me like an old balloon. "Phoebe."

"I didn't break into anything," she added quickly. "Rhonda, the lady who works in the office? I just asked her some questions."

"What kind of questions?"

"Does it matter?"

"Yes. Very much."

"Just, like, how her day was going and what she likes most about her job." She bit her thumbnail. "If she'd be interested in letting me man the desk for a bit while she has a long lunch with her boyfriend."

"So, bribery," I said flatly. I shouldn't have expected anything less when she was so hell-bent on answers. "Which is illegal."

"It's not bribery. There was no exchange of goods. Just information."

I groaned.

"It's fine," she insisted. "I didn't break into anything, either. Rhonda looked up Benji for me and told me he lived here for two years, he has fantastic credit, and he works at Sequest. You know Sequest, right?"

I did. Sequest was a small nonprofit organization that supported LGBT+ youth, particularly those who'd been displaced, and I passed it every morning on my walk to work. Multiple laws broken in an effort to find a man ten minutes down the road.

"Sequest," I repeated, trying to wrap my head around it. I hadn't imagined much about Benji Dexter, but this certainly felt a bit out of left field; if I had to guess, I would've said he was some sort of writer, considering the yearning letter.

"Right?" Phoebe said. "I have a good feeling about it. Do you?"

The opposite. If not for Phoebe, I would've put the letter in a drawer and forgotten about it. But we were in this together, somehow. Our first adventure since Dad died. I had no idea how it turned into this, but I wouldn't complain.

"I haven't decided, yet," I replied. She studied my face, her expression growing wary.

"You said if I found him, we would take him the letter."

"I know what I said."

"So . . . ?" She tilted her head, fixing me with one of the sparkly, hopeful looks she used to wear when the tinkling sound of the ice cream truck swung around the corner. My heart dipped, and frankly, I'd let it drown if it meant this budding bond between us could bloom.

"Yeah," I said. "Yeah. We can go."

A bright grin overtook her face.

"But we have to bring Arden," I added. "She'll kill me if we don't."

Phoebe snatched her backpack off the sidewalk and bolted for the entrance of our building. It wasn't until the elevator doors slid shut, revealing our reflections, that I realized I was smiling too.

Two and a half minutes into the walk to Sequest, Phoebe and Arden had already lost their minds.

"This is so exciting," Arden said, clapping her hands over her cheeks. "Do you know what this could mean?"

"We go to jail for breaking the law?" I muttered, sidestepping a jogging woman. The beaming sun had the sidewalks bustling. Boston was at its very best on the cusp of summer, an almost electric feel in the air. A steady stream of traffic emitted the stench of exhaust and gasoline, mingling with the smells coming from Antonio's Pizza and the quaint café next door. I loved the orange hue painting the tippy tops of high-rises and strategically planted trees, but I couldn't bring myself to appreciate it with the tittering behind me.

"Think of the possibilities," Arden said. "What if this is what reunites them? We could bring true love back together!"

"Imagine if that letter never got to Catalina," Phoebe agreed wistfully. "I would forgive someone if they wrote me a letter like that. Wouldn't matter what they did."

I kept my mouth shut so I wouldn't unleash the pessimistic

thoughts rolling through my head. Phoebe needed me to be on board with this. She needed me to be the Violet who was optimistic and fun, even though that version of me had been struggling to scratch the surface since September.

Three positives: *Phoebe was smiling, Noah gave us a quart of chicken noodle soup, I avoided stepping in a huge pile of dog shit someone left on the sidewalk.*

"We could have a part in this couple's love story." Arden burst forward to throw her arms around my shoulders. "Isn't that *exciting?*"

"You guys need to calm down," I replied. "You're gonna freak everyone out. This whole thing is weird enough without imagining a reconciliation."

Arden released me at once, turning to Phoebe. "She's right. They'll see the mania in our eyes."

My sister, not listening, said, "Do you think Benji's bi? Or trans? And that's why he works at Sequest?"

Arden covered her heart with her hands. I turned to walk backward, pointing between them as I said, "Stop. That's none of our business. None of this is any of our business. We are returning a letter to its rightful owner, that's all. If he's even there."

"He's there," Arden said confidently. "I can feel it. My gut feelings are getting way more accurate lately. Remember Antonio?"

"Anyone with half a brain knows Antonio has a thing for you," I rebuffed, facing forward. "Just chill out. Both of you."

"Maybe you should do the talking," Phoebe said. I stopped on the sidewalk to meet her challenging gaze. "Since this doesn't matter to you whatsoever."

"Okay," Arden cut in, placing a hand on Phoebe's shoulder. She shrugged her off. "We're doing something cool right now, remember? Can we focus on that?"

Phoebe continued staring me down, smile gone. I took a small step toward her. "I care," I said. "I'm keeping my expectations low. It's not so easy to be optimistic these days. But I *do* care."

Her expression softened imperceptibly. "Fine. Whatever. Let's go."

The broody stomping briefly returned, but by the time the small brick building came into view, Phoebe was smiling and any semblance of doubt fled my head.

The building itself was fairly bland, save for the Pride flag twitching in the breeze. Phoebe quickened her pace to reach the door first. Inside, warm lighting and inviting velvet furniture filled the lobby, the walls adorned with paintings, as well as drawings done by children. It smelled like lemon and honey. An immediate sense of calm drifted through me, and I realized that was exactly the point of a place like this.

An older woman sat behind a mahogany desk, glasses perched at the tip of her nose. She looked up at our arrival, smiling. "Hello. What can I do for you?"

I glanced at Phoebe and Arden, who stared at me expectantly. So, I was actually doing the talking here.

"Hi," I said, stepping up to the counter. "Um, we have a question. Sort of."

"I'm happy to answer any questions you have."

"It's about someone who works here. Or worked here." I winced. Years of parent-teacher conferences hadn't prepared me for interrogating a stranger about her co-worker's whereabouts. "Basically, we're looking for someone, and we were hoping he might be here. Benji Dexter."

The woman's smile dropped. "I'm sorry," she said, blinking several times. "You're looking for Benji Dexter?"

"We have something for him," I added quickly, casting a

glance to Phoebe and Arden. They looked on, engrossed. "Mail. It came to our apartment by mistake. Or, not by mistake, but . . ." I cleared my throat, wishing this woman would stop looking at me like I'd asked to speak with a ghost. "We just want to make sure the letter gets to him."

She threw an anxious glance over her shoulder. "Let me . . . One moment, please."

She stood up and approached an open door to her right, ducking her head in and lowering her voice so we couldn't hear. A different voice shrieked "WHAT? WHY?" loud enough to echo in the lobby.

"That's foreboding," Arden said. I cleared the tangle of nerves from my throat.

"We don't know they're talking about us."

On cue, a blond woman appeared in the doorway with the receptionist, and both looked at us, expressions grim. My fingernails dug into my palms.

"This is weird." Arden looked at me, anxiety overtaking the exhilaration. "It's weird, right? I think I'm having a gut feeling. We're about to be true crimed."

"Stop," I hissed.

"I mean," Phoebe said, catching my eye. "It's not *not* weird."

It was extremely weird. But I had to keep my shit together, so I rolled my shoulders and donned what I hoped was a casual, cool smile. *Phoebe. This is for Phoebe.*

The receptionist slipped away, veering to the other end of the building. Flashing us a tight smile, she held up a finger and disappeared through a blue door. The blonde remained in the doorway, watching us with wide eyes, and said, "She'll be right back."

Arden leaned to whisper in Phoebe's ear, "They're going to eat us, aren't they?"

I took a step backward to join their huddle. "So, he's here, right?"

"That or his name is a code for terrorism," Arden replied.

"They're, like, *afraid*," Phoebe murmured, attention locked on the second door, waiting for the receptionist to emerge with or without Benji Dexter. "Maybe he's a huge piece of shit."

Arden hummed thoughtfully. "Would a huge piece of shit work for a nonprofit?"

"Uh, yeah. Absolutely," Phoebe said.

"I don't know. I think—"

A man emerged from the blue door, effectively sucking every decibel from the room. He had the kind of face that shuts down the possibility of a double take—a glance mindlessly shifted into an open-mouthed stare.

I decided he was 40 percent gorgeous, 60 percent intimidating. Olive skin, broad shoulders taut against a crisp white button-up tucked into slim charcoal trousers. I liked the juxtaposition of a polished outfit against the five o'clock shadow coating his angular jaw, crooked nose against a perfect face, thick brown hair finger combed carelessly. Dark, distrustful eyes pinned me into place. It was like a young Harrison Ford opted to go into the CIA instead of acting.

He stopped halfway to us, glowering. Suddenly, Arden's theory about cannibalism didn't seem so far off. It wasn't until Phoebe pressed the letter into my palm that I remembered what we were doing here. Who this *was*.

I took a tentative step forward. "Benji Dexter?"

A muscle in his jaw jumped.

"I'm Violet. This is kind of weird, but, um, I live in your old apartment. On Bluebird Street?" His eyes narrowed. I took that as confirmation. "We got this in the mail," I plowed on, moving toward him, brandishing the envelope. His eyes snapped to it, and this time the recognition was unmistakable—the hardness in his eyes dimmed, his lips parting ever so slightly. "I'm sorry if this is an invasion of privacy, but . . . I don't know. We thought you should have it."

Without lifting his gaze from the envelope, he reached for it, plucking it from my grasp with enough care that my heart did a little flip—this was important to him, and Phoebe had been right in her determination to track him down.

His eyes flashed to me. "You opened it?"

His voice was low, rough, distracting enough that I nearly missed the question. Shame ripped up my neck. "What? No."

"It came that way," Arden blurted.

"It's your word against ours," Phoebe said.

He kept his eyes on me, sharp and accusatory.

"I . . ." I dropped the act, exhaling roughly. "I'm sorry. I figured if it was unimportant, we wouldn't bother tracking you down. But it's not. Unimportant."

His expression didn't change. And I got it: We had seen a deeply private message intended only for Catalina. It was like we'd read his diary. If anyone read my journal entries from my worst days, I'd put myself into witness protection, so I didn't expect Benji to shrug this off. Phoebe had so many questions for him. So did I. When did he send that letter? Had he spoken to Catalina since? What happened between then and now to make a tenderhearted person stare at three strangers with such derision?

We had no right to ask, and I knew he wouldn't give us the chance even before he turned and stalked back to the blue door, letting it slam behind him.

"Wow," Arden said, her voice loud against the echo of silence in Benji's wake. "That was anticlimactic."

I didn't want to look at Phoebe. I could feel her disappointment, as if the sheer volume of it shrank the room, closing every wall in.

"Yeah," I said, willing the door to open again. For him to emerge and give us something, anything that might satisfy Phoebe's curiosity. I was tempted to bolt forward and knock until my knuckles bled.

It opened again, but only the receptionist appeared, looking troubled. She offered a small smile. "Thanks for stopping by."

Dismissed. I chewed my lip and cast Phoebe a glance. She stared at the blue door, eyes glassy, shoulders low, the illumination of excitement extinguished in five minutes or less.

Arden and I led Phoebe out of Sequest. The sky had darkened marginally and mosquitoes were out in full force. We headed down the sidewalk toward home.

"He didn't even say thank you," Arden muttered. I raised my eyebrows at her.

"What did you expect him to say? 'Thanks for reading this deeply personal letter that was only meant to be read by one person'?"

"Not those words exactly."

"He didn't seem like a man of many words. Or emotions." I tilted my head, gazing at the sky. The moon hung low, just a sliver glowing against the fading blue. "The fact that he wrote that letter is mind-blowing."

"Right?" Arden agreed. "No way is he a romantic."

"At least not anymore."

"Do you think he'll send it?" Phoebe asked, breaking her silence. She was walking a beat behind us, frowning.

Arden and I exchanged a look. No way would that dude send a love letter to anyone, least of all someone who potentially Return to Sender–ed him.

"Oh. I don't know," I said. "Maybe? Probably not?"

"But he obviously still loves her," she protested, dropping her arms to her sides. "That's why he's so mad. He lost the love of his life and he thinks she's fine with that because she never responded to his letter. But she never *got* his letter. Now that he knows it, he could find her and give it to her."

Arden bit her lip. "I mean, it's a nice thought."

"Did you see the way he looked at it?" Phoebe looked between us, eyes full of emotion. "It *means* something to him."

"We don't know how long ago he sent that letter," Arden said gently. "Maybe they both moved on."

"That dude was, like, the loneliest human being I have ever seen in my life."

"You can't decide someone's lonely to fit a narrative in your head," I said. She shot me a look. "I hope he sends it, Bee. But we did our part. We're not entitled to the rest of the story."

The light drained from Phoebe's eyes and she moved briskly ahead of us, head ducked against the breeze. A backward sprint after so many steps forward.

I could've sunk through the pavement from the defeat. Arden squeezed my shoulder and steered me forward. She was always good at keeping me going when it felt like the world collapsed around me.

Phoebe was miserable, and I was clueless, and despite the last forty-eight hours, nothing had changed at all.

Four

My dad died on a Tuesday.

I'd been conditioned to believe if I was good and polite, nothing bad could happen to me. As if a halo deterred misfortune. Happy in my mindless optimism, swimming in an endless belief that life was full of beauty and wonder, and anything less couldn't reach me if I did my chores and smiled at strangers.

Two weeks into the school year, the sky was gray, air crisp. I wore a daisy-printed sweater that one of my students told me looked like summer. It was my second year working full-time at Spencer Elementary and the imposter syndrome raged, whispering that I wasn't ready, or good enough. But the kids liked me, and my fellow teachers welcomed me warmly. I'd fallen in love with teaching while helping raise my sister; I couldn't imagine wanting to do anything else. My life had fallen into place, surely because I'd done everything I was supposed to do.

Three other teachers sat around the lounge during lunch, making small talk. My phone vibrated. I almost didn't answer it.

When the voice on the other end mentioned the hospital, the world skidded to a stop.

A few words stuck. *Emergency contact. Accident. ICU.*

And I knew. She gave almost nothing away, but the slightest edge of sympathy digging into the nurse's tone told me my dad was dead before I hung up the phone. Hands shaking, vision blurry, a colleague led me out of the lounge and walked me outside for some fresh air while she called my boyfriend. Gray sky. Cool breeze. Dead dad.

And that simply made no sense because I'd seen him Sunday night. We had dinner, eating our weight in clam cakes and chowder, laughing at how bitchy the contestants were in an old season of *MasterChef.*

Later, I'd learn someone ran a red light. That his heart stopped in the ambulance and doctors worked for nearly half an hour to save him. That by the time his heart miraculously restarted, his brain couldn't follow through.

I was a ghost, barely in my body. Shawn arrived and held me in the parking lot, whispering the same thing over and over. *He's okay. He'll be okay.* And I already knew he wouldn't, but I let Shawn keep saying it, as if the repetition might sink in and tattoo the words into truth. I needed him to keep saying it, especially once we made it to Rhode Island to pick up Phoebe.

She believed it. I hated him a little for that.

A blurry nightmare in which an open gray sky danced overhead as we sped to the hospital. Stepping out of the elevator, we were met by the ICU waiting room decorated for Halloween, and a nurse who knew who we were. Eyes tracked us down the hall, heads turning, as if grief and fame bore the same face. We passed rooms of people in white beds hooked up to various machines. The ceiling tiles were the same as my classroom's.

He looked the same, save for a few cuts and bruises. He could've been asleep. But a machine breathed for him, wires protruded from his chest, and ominous beeping came from the machines around him.

The doctor sat us down and told us what I already knew. Shawn wrapped me in his arms, holding me tight. Phoebe clutched our dad's hand and kept asking the doctor if there was any chance at all, and they never gave her a straight answer.

Nurses moved around us and we were supposed to pretend they weren't there.

It felt imperative to keep my hands in my pockets.

Nurses discussed his condition around us, not to us.

A social worker dropped in to express her condolences and gave us her card, assuring us she'd be around.

I sat in a stiff chair beside the hospital bed, watching the pointless heart monitor. My shoulder was squeezed by everyone who entered the room, whether they made eye contact or not.

When a different doctor arrived to check whether my dad's organs were viable for donation, I quietly excused myself and threw up in the restroom. On my way back, the social worker stopped me to ask if my mother was in the picture, and suddenly trauma gave way to something bigger.

Dad loved us so wholly, it never felt like we were missing out. And now, for the first time in the fourteen years since his decades-long situationship admitted she wasn't cut out to be a mother and signed over all parental rights, I felt the absence. I felt fucking unmoored.

Phoebe didn't have anyone else. Just me.

I couldn't fall apart.

We pulled the plug the next morning, because he would've hated living like that. My dad's boss paid for the funeral. I took a leave from work for bereavement, technically, because there's not an official term for taking custody of your sister when your father dies.

Phoebe spent a few nights at the apartment I shared with Shawn, crashing on the couch. Neither of us could stomach going back to Dad's. I knew it would be hard for Shawn, but it wore on him faster than I anticipated. Maybe it was the grief, or the sudden responsibility of caring for a teenager, or maybe there were underlying problems my dad's death merely brought to light. Within a week, Phoebe and I moved into our dad's house, and Shawn ended things six days after that.

"I'm sorry," he'd said after driving all the way from Boston. "It's just too much. I love you. You know I love you. But this isn't what I signed on for."

Every good thing in my life vanished, leaving me with shattered remains. My sister who wouldn't even look at me. The house I grew up in, haunted. My best friend texting every hour to check in. My dad's wisdom, smile, silly jokes, every ounce of kindness and light he saved for me at any given moment, gone forever.

I felt like a husk of a person, every morning spent sitting at the kitchen island where my dad or I used to pour Phoebe cereal, staring out the window to the creek where we used to play, listening to my sister's sobs turn into stomped feet and slammed doors. Desperate measures didn't seem like enough, but one night I asked Phoebe how she felt about selling the house. I'd been living in Boston since college; Arden and Noah were there, my job, a life that wasn't full of ghosts. I would've stayed in Rhode Island if Phoebe asked. I would've lived in that haunted house and driven around the city where my father's heart stopped beating and I would've died inside every day, but if Phoebe had the slightest hesitation, I would've done it. Instead, I saw a spark of relief in her eyes.

I never saw that relief again. Phoebe only seemed angrier in Boston. I tried so hard and she drifted further and further from me.

Dad was gone. Phoebe was running.

My life split in two on a Tuesday. You don't come back from that.

Nearly a week after Phoebe's last indiscretion, I began wishing for angry calls from Principal Chambers. At the very least, acting out meant Phoebe felt *something*.

Work became excruciating. All day, my body tensed in anticipation, waiting for my phone to blare with another complaint from Phoebe's principal. My brain began throwing out terrible ideas on an hourly basis, like *start a fire* or *slash a tire*. It was bad. I knew that. But I had to believe it was forgivable because dammit, I just wanted my sister to be okay, and she *wasn't*.

I'd get home from work and Phoebe would be in her room doing homework in silence. Considering our dad routinely wore earplugs around the house to block out the sound of her music, this was more than a little concerning. I overcorrected. Since we returned the letter, Phoebe had sulked her way through Ice Cream Sunday, Chinese Takeout Night, and Surprise Gift of the Month. Growing more desperate, I recruited Arden and Noah to pool together enough money for tickets to see Phoebe's favorite band. She barely managed a smile.

I knew my sister. After nine months, I could tell the difference between apathy and genuine depression. We'd reached the latter, and it scared the shit out of me.

Her therapist told me we had to wait it out. Everyone goes through rough patches, grief isn't linear. But the thing is, I'd seen a difference in Phoebe for a minute there. A noticeable difference after nine months of stagnancy. Joy that was snuffed out before it got the chance to spark. And as much as I agreed only time healed wounds, a nagging thought kept insisting there might be a shortcut.

The idea flitted around my head all week, growing wilder each time I passed Sequest on my way to and from work. Somewhere inside that building sat the answer to my problems. Or at least half an answer. Phoebe wouldn't magically cheer up if I managed to coax information out of Benji Dexter, but at least she wouldn't be left wondering.

Would he get the letter to Catalina? Did he know where she was? Did he still care?

I missed Phoebe's smile so much, I burned through a jumbo pack of TUMS. Stress raged, my esophagus was eating itself, and the only thing I could think to do was beg a stranger for information about his love life. Nothing had ever felt so pathetic.

By the end of the week, I anticipated the quiet upon walking into the apartment. I dropped my bag by the door and slipped off my shoes, then padded to Phoebe's bedroom, racking my brain for something that might cheer her up. My list of things that wouldn't work had grown longer than what would.

Three things might have to get downgraded again.

I knocked softly, only pushing the door open once she grunted. Her room was like mine: mostly empty, boxes everywhere, her backpack unzipped with books strewn across the floor, her bare mattress sending a tiny shock of guilt through me—I'd buy sheets and put them on myself, if I had to. This, I could control.

Phoebe sat at the edge of the mattress, laptop balanced on her lap as she typed furiously.

"Hey," I said. "I'm back."

She kept typing.

"Any idea what you want for dinner?" I chewed my lip, aching for something more than the head shake she offered. "That new Thai place opened, if you wanna try it."

"Sure."

"It's supposed to be really good."

"Just get me whatever," she muttered without looking up. I shoved down the muddle of anxiety and disappointment dancing in my chest and eased her bedroom door shut. Sun streamed through the windows, warming the living room. This time last year, I would've basked in the light. Now, I drew the curtains shut and plunked down on the couch to pull up the restaurant menu on my phone.

A text from Arden pinged: How are Things?

Miserable, I replied. But we're getting Thai food so. Silver linings.

She reacted to my text with a heart and proceeded to type for a solid two minutes, finally sending, Phoebe will inevitably catch on to the shower of gifts and treats and when she does, she will weasel a puppy out of you. Do NOT fall for it!!! You'll be the one who has to house-train it!!!

I would've done anything to put a smile on Phoebe's face; I'd find an entire litter of puppies if it would make her happy. But she wasn't asking for *things*. Anything material was shrugged off or ignored, and I couldn't blame her since the last *thing* that brought me immeasurable joy in the last nine months was a really good burrito. Phoebe's tunnel vision cured her and broke her just as quickly. The only thing she cared about—*one* thing— was that letter.

Fuck it.

I sent another text to Arden: Can I borrow the red dress that makes my boobs look great?

She replied immediately: YES??? WHO ARE YOU TRYING TO IM-PRESS????????

She wouldn't believe me if I told her, so I slipped my phone in my pocket and rifled through boxes in my room until I found my makeup bag buried under the Sherpa throws I got custody of in the breakup. Makeup didn't register as important when my dad was dead and my sister was depressed. On the bright side, nine months without foundation and my skin had never looked better.

As I brushed blush over the apples of my cheeks, it occurred to me that years separated me from the last time I dolled myself up to impress someone. First dates were never my forte, but Shawn had made it easy. My nerves gave way to molten excitement and I didn't excuse myself from the table to check my makeup once. And then we were together. Three years of stability, comfort, and safety undone in two weeks, and now I would have to suffer through dating apps and painful first dates, only it would be a million times more awkward because Phoebe would be at home waiting.

The idea of dipping my toe into the dating pool again made my stomach turn. I hadn't felt remotely inclined over the last eight months, and even now, gazing at my reflection in the mirror—auburn hair loose over my shoulders, gold eye shadow to enhance the green of my eyes, skin clear and freckled; someone pretty and fun and optimistic, not me at all—I couldn't picture it.

This was for Phoebe. And then I'd shove the makeup back to the bottom of the box it came from.

I rapped on her bedroom door to tell her I was heading out to pick up the food. She didn't respond. I threw on my favorite pair of black mules and slipped out the door, making the quickest pit stop at Arden's for the last piece of this shameless puzzle.

The red dress. Short and flippy with an open back and a low neckline, it looked amazing on both Arden and me, but her boobs were smaller, so it fit her better. I filled it out.

I parked in front of Sequest, knowing damn well this was an embarrassing, futile idea, and yet I stepped onto the sidewalk without giving myself the opportunity to second-guess it. I would do anything for Phoebe, including this.

The same woman sat behind the desk when I walked in, only this time she wasn't alone; Benji Dexter stood at her side, bent to inspect the computer screen, one hand braced on the desk. I froze in the doorway. I hadn't expected him to be front and center and was immediately thrown off what little game I had.

"—just don't see how it could work," the receptionist was saying. She glanced over, her polite smile flattening in a blink. Benji, either oblivious to my presence or ignoring it, rubbed his scruffy chin thoughtfully.

"I'll cover the surplus."

The receptionist sighed and murmured something I couldn't hear. He straightened, folding his arms over his chest, eyes flashing to me.

"Hi," I said. Stupidly, I pointed to myself and added, "Violet. I was here last week. You remember me. I can tell by the withering look."

Withering might've been an understatement. He looked about ready to throw flaming darts at my face.

"Oh," the receptionist said, jumping to her feet. "Did you hear that? The phone."

With that, she bolted out of the room.

I cleared my throat, reminding myself that I looked awesome, that this was for Phoebe, and if I ended up cannibalized by humanitarians, at the very least she might find it funny.

"Hi," I said again. I was 90 percent sure he wasn't blinking as he stared me down. "Um, it was nice meeting you the other day.

I was in the neighborhood. You know that. You know where I live." I coughed out an uncomfortable laugh. Benji remained statuesque. "Um, I actually—I work at the elementary school. I'm a teacher. Third grade."

Why was I telling him where I worked? Why was I making it easier for this guy to make it look like an accident?

"So, I, uh, I walk by pretty much every day," I pressed on, my voice heightening an octave. "Weird that this whole time, you were in here. And we, you know. Have lived in the same apartment. Some might call it fate or . . . something."

The withering look gave way to confusion. *You and me both, dude.*

"Are you . . ." He furrowed his brow and I wished with all my might for a freak tornado to touch down on top of us and take me away from this unbearable situation. "Are you trying to flirt with me?" he asked incredulously. My face flamed, the mortification pooling in my chest like molten lava.

"What? No. Obviously—No."

His gaze slipped down, taking in the dress and the way it accentuated my curves in what was suddenly the worst way. The lava erupted, spreading to my gut, down my limbs.

"You're all dressed up," he said. "You going somewhere?"

"I . . . I'm picking up takeout. From that new Thai place down the road."

"That's a hell of a dress for cheap pad Thai."

"I like to look nice," I replied, a breathless note in my voice. His throat worked tightly and *damn,* this might've worked if I was even marginally smoother. "It makes me feel good."

"The last time you were here," he said, "you were in leggings and a big flannel shirt."

I shrank back. "Okay. That's pretty uncalled for. Those are my normal clothes."

His expression hardened and I winced, realizing too late I'd played right into his hand.

"Fine!" I huffed. "You win. Yes, I'm trying to flirt with you."

"Why?"

I inhaled deeply through my nose, brain searching for the right combination of words to unlock the vault surrounding this guy. "Do you have siblings?"

His expression slipped—horror, or something close to it blooming and rotting in the span of half a second. "What does that have to do with anything?"

A frustrated sound tore from me. "I don't know how to respond to your responses. You're not following proper conversation protocol."

"What is happening right now?" Whether he was asking himself or the universe, I had no idea. All I knew was that I'd made an ass of myself and we were so offtrack, the chances of salvaging this interaction shriveled to nothing. I should've just come out with it—he might've respected the blunt honesty.

"I'm sorry," I said, rubbing the bridge of my nose. "This turned into something so weird. I just . . . I need to know if you sent the letter."

He straightened, his mouth actually falling open. Clearly, he expected another Return to Sender–stamped envelope from the USPS, or for me to plead my case about not pressing charges. Nope. I was a girl with audacity up to her eyeballs and very little self-preservation left.

"It's none of my business," I continued, talking fast. "I know that. But my sister, Phoebe—she was here with me last week—I love her more than anything in the world and she is so far gone right now. I don't know what to do. I've been in over my head for months, and then suddenly she finds your letter and she was *smiling* again. She needs to know how it ends," I pleaded. Benji studied me, arms crossed, jaw set. But he was listening. "This is the first thing that has brought her a semblance of joy since our dad died, and now I'm spouting off my business to a complete stranger, so maybe we're a little bit even. She needs this. So, please tell me if you sent the letter or if you're going to, and you will never see me again."

He tilted his head, studying me with those dark eyes. A last bit of self-preservation kicked up and told me to run, fast and far.

"So, your plan was to seduce me into revealing this information?"

I crossed my arms. "Well, it sounds silly when you say it like that."

He quirked an eyebrow, as if to say, *Sure, it was* me *doing the heavy lifting.*

"Okay, look," I said, letting my arms fall to my sides. Opening up, allowing myself to be semivulnerable. "It was a really beautiful letter. It deserves to be read by the person it was meant for."

"You read it," he pointed out flatly. "And your sister, apparently."

"That's irrelevant."

"It's a felony."

"My intentions were honorable."

"That argument won't hold up in court."

"I think it will." I lifted my chin in defiance, meeting his dark eyes, refusing to fall victim to the intimidation tactic. I bet it worked on everyone and they left him to steep in his miserable little bubble alone. Unfortunately for him, I worked with kids, so I was well-equipped to deal with the emotionally stunted equivalent of a hissy fit. "I'm very popular. I could get a lot of character witnesses."

The air conditioner hummed against the silence, and it was only then that my skin had the sense to feel the chill in the air.

Goosebumps raised along my arms. Under Benji's gaze, I shivered.

It was reckless, coming here. Prying into a stranger's personal life made my skin crawl, but it would be worth it to help Phoebe.

He blinked then looked down, rearranging a few loose papers on the desk in front of him. "I haven't sent it," he said.

Disappointment flooded my stomach. Not just for Phoebe, but my own; I hadn't realized how invested I'd become in this saga, until it was ending too soon.

"Why?" The word rushed out before I could give it any thought. "I mean, it's none of my business, but *why?*"

"You said I'd never see you again if I told you the end of the story." He wouldn't look at me. "You never said anything about follow-up questions."

"That's not an ending. You're leaving it unfinished."

He plucked up a paper from the desk and headed toward the blue door at the opposite end of the room. Desperation clutched my heart. He said, "You can go."

I sped after him. "Sending the letter would be brave," I told him. "It would be brave and real and a showcase of *growth.* That's what you wanted Catalina to see, right? That you've changed? You have the opportunity to make things right, Benji. That doesn't come around very often."

He wheeled around, eyes fiery, and I stumbled to a halt. "Don't call me that," he growled. "You don't know anything about me or Catalina. I've been more than amenable, but this is fucking ridiculous."

I exhaled sharply. Embarrassment sizzled through my veins. "God. I'm sorry. I'm not this person. I'm a mess right now and I have no idea what I'm doing. I'm sorry. I'm so sorry."

I spun around and hurried toward the door, eyes stinging. Behind me, I heard a sigh. Then, "Sorry about your dad."

I jolted to a stop. I'd heard it so many times over the last nine months, yet it never got less jarring. A wrecking ball to the soul from the moment the doctor looked me in the eye and said exactly what I expected her to say.

"And your sister," he added. I turned, swallowing over the humongous knot his words left in my throat. Our eyes met across the room, exhaustion seeming to replace the fury. "But giving this letter to Cat won't change anything. It's not an answer to her problems, or my problems, or yours. No matter how badly you want it to be."

Obviously, the letter wouldn't fix everything broken in our lives. Maybe it had already done its job in reminding Phoebe there were things worth looking forward to, things that would bring her joy. Maybe, instead of finding Phoebe her ending to this story, all we could do was wait for time to do its thing.

"I know," I said softly, and a tear slipped out. I wiped it away, turning my head in the pathetic hope that he might not notice, as if he hadn't clocked my plan the second I walked in here. "I just . . . I don't know what to do anymore." The tears kept coming and I dropped my face into my hands. "I don't know what I'm doing and it's ruining her. I'm ruining her."

A moment later, featherlight fingers wrapped around my elbow, gently guiding me into a soft chair, a box of tissues on my lap. When I lowered my hands from my face, he had retreated behind the front desk, as if we needed something solid between us. Maybe he thought emotions were contagious.

"Sorry," I croaked, pulling several tissues from the box. He watched me uneasily, his hands in the pockets of his dark trousers. "This is so pathetic. I'm sorry."

"When, uh . . ." He squirmed, clearly uncomfortable, yet his eyes remained fixed on me. "When did it happen? Your dad."

I sniffled, wiping my eyes again. "September."

He shut his eyes, nodding, and his expression struck me somewhere behind my rib cage, the familiarity of it. Loss. I imagined him thinking back to Catalina leaving. Maybe he'd remember how out of his mind he was back then and it would be easier to see where Phoebe and I were coming from when we opened that letter and proceeded to turn his life sideways.

"It's still new. Raw," he said. I clutched the bunch of tissues in my fist a bit harder as his eyes met mine again. "I see it all the time with the kids who come in here. There's no magic fix. It's just . . . time. It takes time."

"I know that. But it's hard to sit here and wait when a week ago, Phoebe was smiling." I stood, still wobbly on my feet. He removed a hand from his pocket to rub his jaw, that penetrating gaze less intimidating. Something in there wasn't calcified and cold; a glimmer in that gentle touch, a willingness to listen. "Can I . . . What can I call you?"

He tugged anxiously at his hair. "What?"

"You told me not to call you that name. What should I call you?"

"I don't . . ." He broke off with a sigh, dropping his gaze to the desk. I shouldn't be calling him anything, he meant. I should be walking out the door and making a point to never see him again. I'd read his deepest thoughts and feelings without consent— I was not entitled to his name. But then he dropped his hand to his side and said, "Dex."

Dex. It certainly fit him. A little more mysterious.

"Dex," I said and he immediately lifted his head, eyes meeting mine. "Thank you for giving me the time of day. You have no idea how much I appreciate it."

He offered a stiff nod, and it felt something like a truce. He made his way around the desk, toward the blue door without another word, and my eyes snagged on the slope of his shoulder blades beneath the crisp gray button-up. Fleetingly, I wondered what made him the kind of person who ironed his clothes, but neglected combs and razors. I understood the desire my sister felt to unravel it, solve it, tie each end neatly. But if he wanted those ends tied, he would've tied them. That same apathy probably kept him from combing his hair.

Or maybe it wasn't apathy. Maybe it was a level of self-preservation I'd lost a long time ago.

I returned to the apartment with two bags of Thai food and a supremely bruised ego. Phoebe popped her head over the side of the couch, interest piqued by the arrival of food, but sat bolt upright upon noticing my outfit.

"Are you going out?" she demanded. I piled the bags on the counter, wishing with everything in me that I'd left well enough alone.

"Nope." I unloaded the take-out containers, ignoring her eyes piercing a hole in my back. "Food's hot."

"Then why are you—"

With a sigh, I turned. "He didn't send it."

I braced for visceral disappointment, for Phoebe to crash, shut down, spiral out. Instead, she hurled herself over the edge of the couch.

"Oh my god! You went back?"

"I was curious."

"You went back dressed like *that*?" She smirked. "Vi."

"Gotta work with what you got, right?" I replied, keeping my tone neutral. She'd transformed into a curious shelter cat who'd finally moved in to sniff my extended hand. I didn't want to make any sudden movements. "It was pointless, though. He didn't send the letter and doesn't plan to."

"How did you even get him to talk?" She moved closer, eyes wide, rapt. I began distributing our food onto the cheap-ass paper plates I kept buying so I wouldn't have to do dishes. "He looked like he might call the cops if he ever saw us again."

"Yeah, I got that vibe. But I got lucky and he was right there when I walked in."

"Okay, but how did you get him to tell you anything? Was it the dress?"

"Uh. No." I offered a plate to her and she took it, immediately shoveling some pad Thai in her mouth while maintaining eye contact. "I may have gone the dead dad route?"

She nodded thoughtfully. "Even assholes are moved by the dead dad bit."

I put together my own plate and motioned for her to follow me into the living room. We sat side by side on the couch, plates balanced on our laps, and she kept her eyes on me, waiting for details. I expected her to be disappointed, but even an insufficient ending was an ending. She didn't have to wonder anymore.

I resisted the urge to beg for validation. The light had returned to her eyes, so clearly I'd done something right. It wasn't fair to ask for more.

Five

"I still can't believe the dress didn't work," Arden said, weighing two identical peaches in her hands. I grabbed a random one and sniffed it—peachy—then added it to my own bag. "It would work on me if you looked at me right."

"Well, you're only human," I replied. We moved away from the stone fruits, Arden pushing our cart while I punched numbers into my calculator app. "Benji Dexter is some sort of cyborg programmed to write yearning love letters and shoot lasers out of his eyes."

"If anyone could kill with a look, it's him. I can't believe you went back."

I groaned. "He's probably filing a restraining order as we speak."

"You can't hold questionable actions against someone who's grieving." She pointed at me, her expression growing serious. "It's basically a form of self-defense, but, like, against yourself."

"What the hell are you talking about?"

"I don't know. I'm so hungry. I might be a little delirious. But I think my point stands."

"It does not."

She moved to the leafy greens. I chewed my lip, gazing at the fresh spinach, heads of lettuce, collards, broccoli. My dad sparked our shared hobby when he accidentally signed up for a couples cooking class and invited me to tag along—we had a blast and made a point to get together at least once a month to try out a new recipe. Now, it had been months since I'd cooked anything other than instant ramen or microwave meals. I hadn't felt the urge to scour the internet for new recipes in a hot minute, but with a fourteen-year-old to feed and sole responsibility for bills, I couldn't afford much of anything except frozen meals and cheap takeout anyway. The ache in my chest reminded me of how much I missed it.

I had twenty-six dollars left. Frozen broccoli would be cheaper.

"Is Phoebe bummed?" Arden asked, loading the cart with all sorts of green goodies. "About him not sending the letter?"

"Not really? I think she's happy to know."

"Shitty end to the story, though."

"That's what I told him."

She snorted. "Lucky he didn't zap you out of existence with his laser eyes."

We moved out of the produce section into the natural foods. I didn't bother looking at the shelves, knowing it was out of my price range.

I missed having my shit together. Every time I went grocery shopping with Arden, I couldn't help the surge of bitterness as I watched her shop around not just for necessities, but little luxuries like a new pan or candle. I'd shove the thoughts down deep before I had the chance to decipher if I was jealous of her disposable income or lack of responsibility.

I wanted to give Phoebe a good life. Instead, I was scraping by with teaching and an upcoming bartending gig at Noah's friend's restaurant for the summer. Possibly a future in selling feet pics on the internet, if there was still a market for that kind of thing.

(Arden assured me there was always a market for that kind of thing.)

"You would tell me if Noah was proposing, right?" she asked, snapping me into grocery store reality. Inspecting the back of a box of Annie's mac and cheese, she didn't bother meeting my eyes. Of course she knew. She was the smartest person in the entire world.

"No," I said. "Why?"

Now she did look at me. "I hate surprises."

"You've been talking about getting married for two years. It wouldn't be a surprise."

She widened her eyes meaningfully. "He wants to make me dinner tonight."

"Doesn't he always make dinner on Tuesdays?"

She pointed the box of mac and cheese at me. "*Exactly*. But he made a point of saying it to me. That's weird."

It *was* weird. Total slipup on Noah's part.

"You think you'd want me to tell you . . ." I said, guiding the shopping cart toward me. She narrowed her eyes, brandishing the box as if she might throw it at my head. "But if it was actually happening, you'd love being surprised."

"Wrong. I hate surprises in every capacity and if Noah doesn't understand that, maybe I shouldn't marry him."

I shrugged. "Maybe."

"What?" Her eyes bugged. "Are you serious? How can you be so blasé about me saying something like that. It's *Noah*. He's the love of my life. If I start talking like that, you need to run me down in the parking lot."

I tilted my head, offering a wry smile, and her incredulous expression shifted into irritation. "I know you," I said. "And Noah knows you. If he's proposing, he's not going to do it in a way you'll hate."

She bent to press her forehead against my shoulder. "I just want to know! I want to be engaged! I want a diamond on my finger, and I want to buy bride magazines instead of sneakily flipping through them on my lunch break," she moaned, voice muffled. I wrapped my arms around her, resting my chin on her head.

"You will. At some point."

"Just tell me."

"This conversation never happened."

"Use 'ketchup' casually in a sentence if he's proposing."

I released her and drifted to the deli, biting my cheek to resist laughter. My best friend had dreamt about her wedding since childhood. I couldn't relate, having spent most of my time exploring the creek behind my house with my dad in search of crawfish and salamanders—but it was a stereotype for a reason. Weddings are supposedly the most important day of our lives, and Arden yearned for it. Tonight, Noah would put it into motion.

I couldn't have been happier for her. But that tiny, jagged piece of resentment drove its way through my rib cage, taunts of how far behind I'd fallen. A year ago, Shawn and I were talking about marriage. We looked at rings. Arden would send me photos from those magazines of dresses she thought I'd like. Every week we had a standing double date and while Noah and Shawn discussed their latest video game obsession, Arden and I would beam at each other because we'd found something that felt like a daydream. And now, my best friend's life was flourishing while I couldn't afford to buy spinach.

The three things my mind whispered to me now: *Pathetic. Pathetic. Pathetic.*

It was harder than I would have liked to believe that it wasn't pathetic for life to stagnate in response to grief. My brain had simply turned on me in the same way the universe had.

"Okay, how about this." Arden caught up to me, blowing a piece of dark hair out of her face. "Not saying I'm getting engaged tonight, but should I wear my floral halter dress or the black mini?"

I considered this, pretending to study the slabs of meat beneath the glass counter. "You might want to think about the silky green dress," I said. She inhaled sharply.

"Oh my god."

"Because it's so pretty."

"Vi."

"And it has that backless thing going on."

"Did you help pick the ring? He has such bad taste in jewelry. Blink once if he made you pick the ring."

I cackled and looped my arm through hers, dragging her along. She would die for the 1920s art deco style I'd directed Noah to. "I think it's gonna be a great night."

I blew seventy-five bucks on two bags of groceries, my Check Engine light pinged on the way home, and one of the bags split the moment I stepped into the apartment. So my night wouldn't be as great as Arden's.

I knelt to gather the mess, noting the silence. It had been three days since I'd gone back to Sequest, and Phoebe had slightly cheered up—she'd get home from school and make camp on the couch, music blasting. It was the first time in nine months things felt relatively okay. Not good, but maybe, possibly, on the way there. Now, though, an empty couch welcomed me and Phoebe's bedroom door was wide open, lights out.

She wasn't here.

Most days, I arrived home before Phoebe because she had detention or cross-country. Today I ran a little late at work, and then met Arden at the grocery store. I glanced at the oven clock: 5:26. Phoebe was always home by five.

I checked my phone for messages—none. I called her, telling myself everything was normal until her voicemail picked up. Anxiety clutched my throat and I dropped the rest of the groceries on the floor, not bothering to put away perishables, then bolted across the hall, nearly banging down the door.

Noah opened it, brow creased in concern. "What's up?"

I pushed past him into the apartment. "Is Phoebe here?"

"No." In the kitchen, Arden turned away from the half-empty bags of groceries littering the countertops and gave me her full attention. "Why? She's not home?"

I dragged a hand through my hair, letting out a slow breath. "She's always home by now. I called her, but she didn't answer."

"She's fine," Noah said. He placed a hand on my shoulder, squeezing gently. "She's probably with friends."

Arden and I exchanged a look. Phoebe hadn't made friends since the move, and it was something I carried tremendous guilt over.

"Or," Noah added quickly, "cross-country ran late."

"Cross-country ended for the year." I pressed my palms into my eyes. "God. Where is she?"

"Try calling again," Arden suggested. "I'm gonna go downstairs and see if she stopped by the office to work with Rhonda."

"Don't panic until there's something to panic about," Noah said. "If she's not home by six and you still haven't heard from her, we'll go from there."

I swallowed hard, unsure of whether I'd make it to six without losing my mind. But he had a point; half an hour wasn't the end of the world, or a call to action. Time to settle into a happy medium of realism: In all likelihood, Phoebe was fine and simply late, not stuffed in the trunk of someone's car.

Alone in the apartment, my throat grew tight again. I checked my phone in case Phoebe had responded while I was distracted. She hadn't.

Things had been so shitty recently, I forgot they could get worse.

I sat on the couch, fingers clutching my phone so tightly they turned white. 5:35 and still waiting. 5:40 and my dad was dead and my sister still hadn't called me back. 5:45 and the walls began to close in when a new text from Arden popped up: Not downstairs but don't worry!!!!! She'll be home soon.

I squeezed my eyes shut and tossed my phone onto the opposite side of the couch. If I ignored it, Phoebe would call. That's how the world worked, right?

Anything, I thought. *You can do anything you want to me, just let her be okay.*

My ringtone blasted and I dove for my phone, heart stuttering at the words *Unknown Number.* There was a nonzero chance the dude from *Taken* would be on the other end, but I didn't hesitate.

"Hello?"

"Violet St. Clair?" a woman's voice said, and my hand shot to my chest, lungs collapsing, anticipating the words *hospital* and *ICU* and *critical condition.* "This is Mary from Sequest."

I doubled over, gasping like a drowned man breathed back to life. "Oh my god."

Recognizing my panic, Mary said, "She's here. She's fine. She stopped by after school and has been holed up in Mr. Dexter's office ever since. He asked me to call you."

"Thank you." I shut my eyes. My hands were trembling. "Thank you. I'm on my way."

I fired off an update to Arden and Noah and got the hell out of Dodge. Pouring rain and rush hour traffic, the scent of gasoline and wet pavement; I was running down the sidewalk before my brain caught up. Soaked to the bone, hair plastered to my face. More than a few passing drivers stared—the panic must've haunted my features, lingering despite the knowledge that Phoebe was ten minutes away.

I couldn't trust it until she was right in front of me.

Though it was nearly a year since my last round of cardio, I managed a fairly impressive time, despite the rain and my lungs an inch from bursting in my chest. I threw myself through the door of Sequest. The same woman sat behind the front desk, eyes popping at the sight of me.

"Where is she?" I gasped, moving a hand to my side to rub away a cramp.

"Right through there," she said, pointing to the blue door. "Do you want some water? Or a towel? I think we have towels in the back."

"No. No. I . . ." I focused on my breathing for a second so I wouldn't pass out. "I'm sorry about this."

"Oh, don't be. That girl is a riot."

She was something, all right.

I pushed through the door, unsure of what to expect, but the floor-to-ceiling bookshelves flanking the walls and several huge beanbags were certainly not it. Dark wooden floors and a massive colorful rug covered the expanse of a reading nook. At the end of the room sat a sky-blue desk thoroughly covered in writing, doodles, and stickers. I would've guessed it belonged to anyone other than the man sitting behind it with his arms folded over his chest, hair standing on end, five o'clock shadow gradu-ating into beard territory. He shot to his feet when I walked in.

And across from the desk, debilitating relief in the form of a pink head of hair.

"Phoebe," I exhaled. The chair spun and there she was, per-fect and unharmed, sporting a Front Bottoms T-shirt big enough to hang like a dress, snacking from a small bag of chips.

"Vi!" Her face broke into a grin, the happiest she'd been to see me since the weekends I'd come home from college. "Wanna take a trip?"

Six

"Did you run here?"

My heartbeat in my ears mostly drowned out Dex's question. I shuffled forward, eyes locked on my sister, and wrapped my arms around her, tucking her head under my chin.

"Ew. Why?" she said, trying to squirm out of my grasp. I held on tighter.

"You can't do that," I whispered, voice catching. Phoebe went still. "I have to know where you are. You can't just disappear."

I breathed in the smell of her coconut shampoo and the panic started to subside. The stark silence of the room caught me off-guard. No air-conditioning.

"Sorry," Dex said quietly. I glanced at him as Phoebe resumed her attempts to wiggle out of my hug. His expression was solemn, arms at his sides, his hair slightly less Einstein-ish, as if he'd attempted to tame it since I walked in. "I thought—I assumed you knew she was here. When she mentioned you didn't, I had Mary call you."

I mouthed the words *Thank you*. I didn't trust myself not to burst into tears and I wasn't about to cry in front of this guy again.

"It's not a big deal," Phoebe mumbled, successfully extracting herself from my arms. I resisted the urge to brush a pink piece of hair out of her face. "Can we forget about the momentary panic? We have exciting news."

My eyes shot back to Dex. "'We'?"

He shook his head. Phoebe hopped to her feet, her energy vibrating the room. "I found Catalina," she declared, that bright grin appearing once again. I nearly returned the gesture before her announcement struck me somewhere in the throat.

"You what?"

"Remember when I said I wouldn't create a burner account to follow her on Insta because it was weird? Well, I did it anyway." I sank into the seat she'd inhabited moments earlier, my legs on the verge of giving out. I was pretty sure Phoebe's smile was the only thing keeping me conscious. "And last week, she posted this picture with a friend and tagged the restaurant they were at," she continued, gesturing wildly, the same way I did mid-rant. "Bend, Oregon. I checked a few more geotags from over the last year, and they're all there. She moved to Oregon."

"I told you," Dex said with a surprising level of patience, "this is not new information."

"It is to *me*."

"What—" The word slipped out unwittingly and I cut myself off, trying to catch up. "What does this have to do with anything? I don't understand."

"You said Dex told you he wasn't gonna send the letter," Phoebe said. "So, I obviously had to come here and tell him he's wrong."

I let out a soft groan, too exhausted to get into this. It was too big a conversation to have under the circumstances. A week ago, I might've assumed my sister was old enough to respect other people's business, but hey, I'd been wrong about a lot of things lately.

"It's fine." Phoebe's hands found my shoulders and when I met her electric gaze my own energy seemed to lift from the proximity. "I'm right. He knows I'm right. He said so. But it's not enough to just send it at this point, right?"

I shook my head and a drop of rain fell from my eyelashes. "I'm not following. This is all going over my head."

"He needs to *give* her the letter," she explained, no less enthusiastic in the face of my confusion. "And he needs to apologize. In person."

"What does this have to do with us?"

"Good question," Dex muttered.

Phoebe spun to face him. "It has everything to do with us and you know it. We spent like an hour talking about it."

My mind pushed hard to keep up, snagging briefly on that time frame; I couldn't believe Dex humored my sister for an hour and the building was still standing.

"Vi," Phoebe said, tearing my attention back to her. The grin faded, but fireworks burst in her eyes. "Dex is going to Oregon to see Catalina. We should go with him."

My lips pulled into a smile against my will. "I'm sorry, *what?*"

"Your sister has it all figured out," Dex said, deadpan, and whatever emotion was swirling ominously through my chest weakened.

"Figured what out?"

"Hear me out," Phoebe said. Her eyes locked on me, determined. I'd seen that look before. A blond toddler taking a running leap into an in-ground pool; an eight-year-old reaching for the scariest book in the horror section at Barnes & Noble.

Phoebe's mind was a trap, and when it latched on to something, the end. All I could do was deal with the aftermath: jumping into a freezing pool after her, snuggling in bed with the lights on until she fell asleep.

Or whatever *this* was going to be.

"We need this," she said. "Things suck right now. Everything has sucked since Dad died. We needed something to pull us out of it and suddenly that letter shows up . . . We were *meant* to get that letter, Vi. We were meant to find Dex. And we're meant to go to Oregon to give it to Catalina."

A humorless laugh escaped me. "What? No."

"Don't say no, yet!" Phoebe's eyes darted from me to Dex and back again. He surveyed the scene, arms crossed, expression pinched, like maybe I wasn't following the script. "I know it sounds crazy. Maybe it is. But ever since Dad died, everything has been warped. Like it's not even real. Sometimes it's like . . . like nothing even matters." She winced, noticing the panic rising in my eyes, and added, "Don't read into that. I'm not explaining this right."

"Tell her what you told me," Dex offered. My eyes snapped to him, the contents of my stomach lurching like we'd hit the loop of a roller coaster.

Tell her what you told me.

Not only had she graced him with an hour of her time—something I was only awarded if I supplied take-out—but she'd *talked* to him. Given the fact that Dex seemed softer in her presence, I'd wager she'd delved into the things she reserved for her therapist. Maybe deeper.

Phoebe bit her lip, shifting her weight from one foot to the other, reluctant to share what she'd offered Dex. Her resistance to let me in cut to the bone. In her desperation to get what she wanted, she'd unraveled a little bit. But not for me. Never for me.

"It's not important," she said, waving this off. I scraped some damp hair out of my face, hoping neither of them could detect the pain reverberating in my chest. "School sucks. Grief sucks. Whatever. We need this, Vi. We *need* to see this through."

"Haven't we?"

"No! This is the most important part. We can't miss it!"

"We're not a part of it, Bee. This has nothing to do with us."

"The postal service got us involved," she insisted. Dex turned his gaze to the ceiling. "And now we're here. It's all of our thing. We have to do this. Together."

My mind scrambled for three things, came up empty. I was at a complete loss. I couldn't give in to everything Phoebe wanted purely because our dad died, but the temptation to agree wasn't even about that, really. It was the look on her face, the wondrous light, the long-dormant smile. Dex's letter had brought my sister back to life, and I'd already made a fool of myself ensuring we had the chance to see this through.

"What are you doing?" Dex demanded, snapping me out of my head. His attention was back on me, eyes fiery. "You're considering this, aren't you?"

"No," I lied.

"You are. It's written all over your face."

"You don't know me well enough to read my face."

"You're an open book." He dragged a hand through his hair. "It's not happening. No."

Phoebe wheeled around. "What the hell? You said you'd consider it if Violet said yes!"

"I didn't think she would," he muttered. "That's on me. I should've known how this would go after that fucking dress."

My cheeks flushed fever hot. I stood up. "What kind of asshole makes a kid promises and immediately rips the rug out from under them?"

At my side, Phoebe stared him down, and he looked between us emotionlessly; the only indication this meant anything to him were his clenched fists.

"How do you live with yourself?" Phoebe added, piling on in that voice she used when issuing a challenge. As if this was a game, not some life-altering fork in the road.

"I live with myself just fine," Dex said. "I haven't completely lost myself in entertaining the every whim of a child."

His accusation hit hard. He meant it to. It was my worst fear, spoken aloud: I had accepted the role of Phoebe's guardian without taking into account the work and wisdom it takes to raise a child, and in my failure, I'd overcompensated. I let her run wild. We were both flailing, searching for something solid to hang on to, because I had no idea what I was doing.

You didn't even take time to consider the options, Shawn had said two days after the accident. But Phoebe and I were crushed and we needed each other—there *were* no other options.

I felt Phoebe look at me, but I couldn't bring myself to see her reaction to Dex's words. My eyes stung and everything in my body grew heavy; I wanted to lie on the floor and cry. I'd done everything wrong. My own grief muddled the clarity of the situation and now, here we were. Drowning.

How am I supposed to take care of a kid when I can barely take care of myself?

The question had been haunting me for nine months and I still didn't have a good enough answer.

As gutting as it was to hear Dex's words out loud, something else emerged with that pain—*relief.* It had been so long since anyone spoke to me with unabashed honesty. Phoebe held so much in. Arden's compulsive sugarcoating nearly gave me a cavity. Shawn was the last one to look me in the eyes and say what he felt, even though it hurt us both.

Dex saw my fragility, my failure, and refused to go easy on me. Part of me wanted him to keep talking. To hurt me more, until I felt like me again.

I placed my hand on Phoebe's shoulder and murmured, "Let's go."

"No!" she cried. "That's what he wants. He's only insulting us so we'll leave and he'll be off the hook."

"I'm not on a hook," Dex said, a sharpness edging into his tone. "I can sympathize with your situation, but that's the end of it. This is none of your business. You weren't supposed to read that letter. I'll get it to Cat one way or another, but I don't owe you anything, especially something you took."

Phoebe opened her mouth to argue, then snapped it shut. Another gut-punch truth out in the open. I admired Dex's ruthless honesty. I'd been playing pretend for so long, I couldn't tell genuine optimism from the façade anymore.

"Fine," Phoebe said softly, hammering a crack into my heart. She bent down to grab her backpack. "Whatever. Let's go."

Thunder rumbled through the building, rattling the bookshelves as we left Dex's office. I'd run here in a blind panic and now we'd be walking home in a thunderstorm. Great. Just another thing I screwed up.

Rain pounded the windows in the lobby. The woman behind the front desk, Mary, smiled when she saw us. Phoebe walked right over and said, "So, is he a serial killer or what?"

Mary guffawed. "You're a hoot, Miss Phoebe," she said. "But no, Mr. Dexter is a good man, if a bit rough around the edges." She leaned in conspiratorially, adding, "*Very* rough around the edges."

Phoebe knocked her knuckles twice on the desk. "Tell him I hate him and he's an asshole."

Mary's face blanched. "I'll paraphrase."

With that, we ventured into the storm.

Phoebe muttered something about not bringing an umbrella but left it at that, aware she'd scared me to death. I should've been lecturing her, grounding her. Instead, I walked alongside her in silence, wincing when the sky lit up overhead. I didn't bother calling her out or apologizing, rather floating in this aimless purgatory we'd found ourselves in without Dad. Without each other.

For a split second, I wished I could go back in time. Five minutes. I'd do whatever it took to convince Dex to take that trip, fallout be damned. I'd sell my soul for Phoebe's smile.

Then a pair of headlights cut through the blanket of rain. A sleek SUV pulled up beside us. Phoebe stopped short, as if she knew it was Dex before the window slid down.

"Get in," he shouted over the rain. Phoebe crossed her arms. Mascara spilled down her cheeks, yet she held herself tall. I'd never had that confidence, even when I had everything else.

"Why?"

"I can't afford your deaths on my conscience when you get struck by lightning."

"Maybe we *want* that on your conscience."

"I don't doubt it." He leaned over, pushing the passenger-side door open. "Come on."

Phoebe dove for the back seat, probably under the impression I'd decline the ride. As if a bone-deep exhaustion hadn't taken over the second Phoebe was safely in front of me. I had no fight left.

As I climbed into the front seat, Phoebe poked her head through the center console. "A Mercedes, huh?" she said and threw me a look. *What kind of nonprofit pays enough for a luxury car?* it seemed to say, and I would've thought the same thing if my brain hadn't short-circuited somewhere on the sidewalk.

Dex's long fingers drummed the wheel at an incessant, almost anxious rate. Rain pelted the car from every angle, wind whistling outside the closed windows; it reminded me of my dad's old white noise machine, and I sank into the buttery leather seat, shutting my eyes, pretending I was there, back in the hallway of the house I grew up in, padding to his bedroom to wake him up when he overslept on weekends.

This was my life, now. Reminders of my father breaking my heart, over and over.

"I don't hate you, you know." Phoebe's voice wrenched me out of my whirlpool of grief. Lightning flashed overhead.

"Oh, good," Dex muttered. "I was losing sleep."

"I know that was your whole plan," Phoebe continued conversationally. "To make us hate you."

He squinted through the windshield, the wipers on full blast and barely making a dent in the flow. "Am I supposed to ask why?"

"Nah, it's obvious. You have trust issues."

He scoffed. "Sure."

"You push people away because it's better to be the one to leave than to be the one left behind," she explained. "Plus, you're pissed we reminded you of something you want to forget. Maybe if you, like, actually dealt with your issues, you could move on."

I resisted the painful urge to laugh. How fucking ironic.

"Is that what you're doing?" Dex countered, voicing my own thoughts. "Hounding a stranger about a letter you had no business reading? This is you dealing with your issues?"

"I'm fourteen. You're middle-aged. You do the math," she said.

His grip on the wheel loosened and a soft sound whooshed out of him, something almost like a laugh. "I'm thirty-one."

"That's too old to be arguing with a teenager." I could hear the smile in her voice. I stopped myself before glancing over my shoulder to see it. I didn't want to intrude on whatever was happening here; Phoebe and Dex going tit for tat with ease, as if they'd known each other forever. How was it so easy for her to talk to this man? Why was it so impossible for her to talk to *me*?

"Look," she said, her voice dipping into something softer, sympathetic. "You're right. We don't know you. But we *did* read that letter, so we know how you felt. And it seems like you're still kinda steeping in that."

The car slowed, blinker ticking. Dex turned into the parking lot of our building, pulling right up to the entrance. Another roll of thunder filled the air.

"Why did that letter show up now?" she pressed. "You haven't lived here in, what? A year? Don't you think there's a reason this happened?"

"I don't believe in fate."

"Fate or not, that letter showed up. You cared so much that you wrote it, once. You *sent* it. How does that not mean something to you?" That muscle in his jaw jumped, but he didn't respond. "All this time," Phoebe said softly. "Don't you think she deserves to know you were sorry?"

Dex winced and hunched over to press his forehead against the steering wheel. He'd been so careful to remain stoic, it struck me somewhere tender.

Two things occurred to me at once: *I like him better like this* and *He's going to give in.*

"Whoa," Phoebe said, popping up between the center console again. "I think I broke him."

Outside, the rain picked up, blurring out the rest of the world.

"Dex." My voice was quiet, but he straightened and looked at me, those dark eyes wide and wild, searching mine. I didn't know what he was looking for and it made me want to cover my entire body in bubble wrap.

"Why?" he asked. "Why should we do this?"

"Because—" Phoebe started, but he held up his hand to stop her.

"I know why you want to. I know why I should. I want to know her reason." He tilted his head in my direction. I could feel Phoebe's sharp gaze on me, but I couldn't tear my eyes away from Dex. "Is there anything in this for you that has nothing to do with your sister?"

They both expected a knee-jerk answer and I almost complied. It would be so easy to lean into the desperation to make Phoebe happy, to let it consume me, to let that be my purpose. Isn't that what I'd done for the last nine months? But three stories above us, my best friend's life tumbled forward at a steady clip without me.

I was *so* happy for Arden and Noah. I was so fucking devastated for myself.

"My best friend is getting engaged tonight," I heard myself say. Phoebe slowly drew back in her seat. Dex kept staring, his expression inscrutable. "I love her and I'm happy for her, but now I am excruciatingly aware of the gap between us. How far she's moved in a year and how I've been standing still, hiding from everything. I'm sick of standing still. I need to do something. And yeah, this is probably a bad idea and everyone is going to think we're batshit crazy, but hey! Maybe I am. Grief is fucked!"

Phoebe leaned forward. "Admitting you're crazy is not the way to get him on board."

"What do you want me to do? Pay him? We're broke."

Dex's face twisted into a scowl. "I don't want your money. I want this done. I want it over with as soon as possible." He scrubbed a hand over his eyes, nodding jerkily. "Okay, yeah," he said, dropping his hand to his lap. Thunder crashed over us; Phoebe and I both jumped, but Dex didn't flinch. "Yeah. What the hell. Let's do it."

Phoebe's hand shot out, gripping my elbow so tightly, it would leave a mark. I swallowed hard over the dread pressing into my throat.

"Oh," I said. Phoebe's grip tightened further, a futile attempt to silence my next question. "Are you sure? I mean, this is . . ." I trailed off. *Crazy* was the word that came to mind. A crazy, impulsive decision neither of us even had the chance to wrap our brains around. The only person in the car who knew what they were doing was the fourteen-year-old, and that didn't bode well.

"Are you?" Dex challenged. My posture straightened, eyes narrowing. I didn't consider myself a spiteful person, but something about this man coaxed the worst out of me.

"Yes," I replied without hesitation. "Never been more sure about anything."

"Great."

"Awesome."

"Fan-*fucking*-tastic."

Phoebe's face appeared between us, her smile eliminating every ounce of doubt in my mind. Crazy, impulsive, thoughtless, whatever. I would do anything to keep her happy. Even this.

"Chill out," she said, placing a hand on either of our shoulders. "Road trips are supposed to be fun."

I swiveled in my seat, darkness edging into my vision. Spots. So many spots. "I'm sorry," I said. "Did you just say *road trip*?"

Phoebe's smile didn't falter. "Oh, oops. Did I not mention that part?"

Seven

I could listen to every iteration of Arden's engagement recap on repeat for the next sixty years, but it took seventeen minutes for Phoebe to start with the *please-for-the-love-of-god* looks.

"You were so right about the green dress," Arden gushed, starry-eyed and glowing in her drab pharmacist uniform, her smile nearly as sparkling as the diamond on her finger. She'd burst into the apartment minutes after Noah popped the question last night—we hugged and cried for a solid five minutes before she went back home to celebrate privately. I'd been so thrilled for her, my own news fell to the wayside. Now, though, our packed bags were hidden behind bedroom doors and I was crawling out of my skin with every passing second.

I had to tell Arden. I had no idea how.

"You look amazing in the pictures," I said. Phoebe shot me another pointed look and my fingernails dug further into my palms.

Arden let out a dreamy sigh. "It was perfect. Noah's original plan was to do it at the botanical garden and invite our friends and family, which is a sweet thought, but he said you told him if I got engaged in front of my mother, I'd kill myself. You're my hero."

I shot a finger gun at her. "I got you."

"Have you given any thoughts to your honeymoon?" Phoebe interjected with a placid smile. I stiffened.

"Well, you know Noah hates sand."

"I've been seeing a lot of honeymoon road trips," Phoebe went on, her gaze snapping to me, challenging me to take this opening.

"Ooh, yeah I've seen that! It's big with travel influencers right now," Arden said. She held out her hand, gazing at her ring, and a goofy smile bloomed. "I don't know. I think we're gonna focus on being engaged for a bit. It's so fun."

Taking advantage of Arden's distraction, Phoebe caught my eye and mouthed, *Coward.*

Considering my inability to say no to a cross-country road trip with a complete stranger, I was in no position to argue.

I could still call it off. That thought was the only thing keeping me upright; three things disappeared, replaced by this thought, a pathetic possibility revolving around my brain since the moment Dex and I exchanged numbers. *I can call it off,* as I stuffed random things into bags. I kept my phone within view at all times, ready to fire off a text that would ease the anxiety roaring in my gut.

A road trip with Benji Dexter.

I'd sat dumbstruck in the passenger seat as Phoebe breathlessly explained Dex's fear of flying and his excellent driving record. The word *no* played on a constant loop in my head, even as my mouth asked pointless questions like *What about work?* and *Shouldn't someone tell Catalina so we don't just barge into her life unannounced?* Dex's noncommittal answers led me to believe he had no way to contact Catalina (which made sense, considering his usage of the postal service rather than, like, an *email*). Phoebe didn't have all the answers, but she did have a locked and loaded manipulation tactic: *I have Dad's Polaroid camera,* she'd told me. *I could take pictures, Vi. Just like he used to on his trips.*

I warmed to the idea at once, remembering my sister discovering that clunky old camera in the back of Dad's closet and taking photos of everything and how Dad had covered the fridge with them. They'd shared that curiosity for the world around them, the urge to document and return to the memories. There was a bookshelf in the living room dedicated to photo albums from his touring days, and another to the photo albums of Phoebe and me growing up; every single one lived in a storage unit now.

I *could* call this off.

But I wouldn't.

"Vi!" Arden's voice jolted me out of my head, her concern palpable before I even met her eyes. "Is everything okay?" she asked, studying me closely. "Where were you just now?"

Phoebe jumped to her feet. "I'm gonna do homework," she said, veering for her bedroom. Arden furrowed her brow, looking between us. "Or something. Later!"

I watched the traitor disappear into her room, gnawing my lip. Arden shifted her gaze to me, sharper, more suspicious.

"What was that?"

"She's fourteen. I don't know."

"Violet. What's going on?"

"Nothing."

"Am I talking about the engagement too much?" she asked, wincing. "Oh god. I am, aren't I? You're already picturing me as Bridezilla and you want to rip my face off."

"Arden, no. I want to hear about the engagement. We've barely scratched the surface." I took a breath, wiping my palms on my sweatpants. "Sorry. I'm not trying to be weird. I just . . . I have to talk to you about something."

Her hand flew to her chest. "You're sick."

"What? Obviously not."

"Oh, thank god. Sorry. My mind goes to the worst-case scenario when someone says they have to talk to me." Her eyes widened. "Noah. *Phoebe*."

"Arden."

"Sorry. I'll stop guessing."

The catastrophic guesses softened the blow, so I took a breath and forced the words out.

"Phoebe and I are going on a trip."

She pushed a curl out of her face, her ring glinting in the sunlight. "Since when?"

"Yesterday."

"Does this have to do with where she was?" Her expression went grim. "I got so distracted, I never asked after you told us she was okay. Where was she?"

"She went to Sequest," I said quietly. Arden's eyes sharpened, as if she read ahead in my face to see exactly what the future held. "She, uh, found Catalina."

Her jaw dropped. "*What?*"

"She basically stalked her way to the information. I don't know." I sighed, rubbing my eyes. "Phoebe went to Sequest to convince Dex to give Catalina the letter and, somehow, it snowballed into this."

"This?"

I winced at the edge in her tone. "The road trip."

"Trip where?" she demanded.

"Oregon," I told her. She blinked.

"Oregon." Another blink. "To . . . what? Give Catalina the letter?"

"Yeah." I hesitated. "With Dex."

Arden fell back in her chair with a humorless laugh. "I'm sorry," she said. "You're going across the country with the robot who shoots lasers out of his eyes? That's what you're telling me right now?"

"He's not that bad," I muttered. "We read his mail. Of course he was mad."

"Violet." She widened her eyes at me. "What are you *doing?*"

Something, my mind whispered. *Finally, something.*

"I know it doesn't make sense to you," I said, and she let out another short laugh.

"Yeah, no shit it doesn't make sense to me. What the fuck, Violet?"

It had been so long since she'd spoken to me like this, like I wasn't a fragile, broken thing. That same relief sparked by Dex's unabashed honesty coursed through my veins, shouting that as strange and awful as this felt, it *was* the right decision.

"Phoebe needs this," I said. She opened her mouth to argue—no doubt another plea to stop giving in to my sister on the tip of her tongue. I cut her off before she could. "I think I need this, too. A change of scenery. Something else. Just . . . something. You know?"

"No! I don't know!" She scrambled to her feet and paced the length of the couch for a solid ten seconds. "I've been trying to be cool. I really have. I don't sneak fresh produce in your fridge or slip twenty dollars in your purse. I don't force you to go out on weekends. You are stubborn and proud and that's fine because you let me help even when you're not letting me step in.

But a road trip with a stranger is going too far, Violet. This is me officially intervening."

"Intervening in what?"

She waved her hand wildly at me. "This! You! This whole situation!"

"It's not about you," I said. "You don't get a say."

"Like hell I don't. This isn't happening." She folded her arms over her chest, drenched in conviction. "It's just not."

"It is happening," I replied softly. "We're packed. We leave tomorrow."

A thud came from Phoebe's door, followed by a soft curse. The absurdity of the situation could've set me off—my best friend standing before me, dumbstruck, while my sister eaves-dropped from the next room, and somewhere across the city, a stranger packed his bags to escort us across the country. My dad would've been in hysterics, as in actual knee-slapping and tears.

Arden sank down on the couch. "No," she whispered. "No, but . . . No. You can't just *leave,* Violet. What is going on?"

I scooted closer to her, wrapping my fingers around her trembling hands. "I love you. I am so happy for you. No one in the world deserves happiness and love more than you," I told her earnestly. She looked at me, eyes glassy. "As happy as I am for you, it's also this huge neon sign of how far behind I am. A year ago, Shawn and I were looking at rings and now . . ."

"Your dad died," she said, folding her hands over mine, hold-ing on tightly. "You're grieving. That's not falling behind."

"I'm stuck, Arden." My eyes stung. "I'm so terrified of what happens next, I stopped living. So maybe this trip is a terrible idea and I'll regret it two seconds in, but at least it's *something.*"

She let out a tortured groan. "I hate this. I hate this so much. I know growth is supposed to be scary, but I don't think they meant traveling across the country with a potential serial killer scary."

"He's not a serial killer," I said, comforted by both Mary's assurance and the frankly bizarre phone call I'd received from a friend of Dex's named Gavin who proceeded to vet *me*, as if I was the threat. Dex had people who were as worried about his decision as Arden was about mine: It didn't carry enough weight for unconditional trust, but enough to move forward. "He's just a guy."

"No one," she said gravely, "is just a guy."

"I know you hate this," I said, sounding marginally more confident than I felt. Which was not at all. "But I need you to be on my side."

"I am on your side. Even when you're batshit crazy. Which is right now, by the way. You're being batshit crazy."

"I'm aware."

Chances were, I *was* making a terrible mistake, and I'd regret involving Phoebe in something so dicey. With the odds stacked high against me, I let the ball keep tumbling down the hill on the off chance optimism might stick to it like moss along the way.

Even as anxiety ballooned in my chest, I fixed my face into what I hoped was a convincing smile and said, "I feel good about this, Arden. It's okay."

"How is this okay to you?" Arden asked. "I've been telling you that you deserve a life for months, but I meant going on dates or a new hobby. Not taking a road trip with a stranger."

Arden could say I needed a life all day long, but she'd never understand. This was my life. I didn't have the luxury of being a normal twenty-six-year-old, and I couldn't be *not* okay with that.

"I wouldn't be doing this if I wasn't one hundred percent on board," I lied. "Phoebe is more excited than I've ever seen her. I trust Dex, I think. At the very least, he's not a murderer."

"That you know of," Arden replied darkly.

"We can change our minds at any time," I said, lowering my voice in case Phoebe was still eavesdropping. "If it's awful, we'll come home. No harm, no foul."

"And crush Phoebe?" Arden raised her eyebrows. "No, you won't. You'll suffer for her."

"You keep telling me to be the guardian. I'll put my foot down."

She looked at me like my nose had grown by the end of the sentence.

"It'll be fine," I insisted. And I mostly believed it, because Phoebe hadn't stopped smiling since Dex dropped us off last night.

Phoebe's door squeaked open and she slipped out, angel-faced and armed with Dad's Polaroid camera. "Heeey," she said, dragging out the word. Arden narrowed her eyes at her. "Are you mad?"

"Am I *mad*?"

"Don't be mad." Phoebe shuffled over, dropping onto the cushion between us. "It'll be fine. This is gonna be good for us."

"It won't be fine. Want to know why?" Arden made a show of drawing her phone out of her pocket and opening the search engine. I sighed.

"Are you googling gruesome statistics?"

She held up her phone, eyes wild. "Eighty-eight percent of woman die while traveling with strangers!"

"That *cannot* be true," I said.

Phoebe snatched her phone. "What did you even look up? God."

"You can't do this," Arden pressed. "It's not safe."

"First of all, don't trust the AI function," Phoebe said, handing her back the phone. "Second, that's not even what the statistic is. It says eighty-eight percent of women feel unsafe while traveling alone."

"I'm panicking!" Arden cried. "You can't unload this information on me and expect me to be like, 'Bon voyage!'"

"No one says 'bon voyage' anymore," Phoebe said. "It's cringe."

Arden recoiled. "It's *French*."

"I don't expect you to be okay with this," I cut in, earning their undivided attention. I hated being the reason Arden's eyes were swimming, but Phoebe sat between us, beaming, and I couldn't let that go for anything. "I'll keep you updated every step of the way. I'll even get the creepy Find My Friends app if you want me to. But this is happening."

Arden fell into our scratchy three-dollar throw pillow, flinging her arm over her face. "Fine. You win," she said. Phoebe threw me a victorious smile, but I couldn't bring myself to return the gesture. None of this felt like winning.

"It'll be fine," Phoebe insisted, patting Arden's leg. "Right, Vi?"

"Of course it will," I said. Phoebe glanced at me, hope sparking in her eyes. My words meant something to her; she'd done her best to keep it buried, but here was a tiny hint of that adoration she used to showcase without a second thought. I still mattered.

And I guess I knew it all along, but it was nice to see.

Arden sat up, eyes sharp, and pointed right in my face. "You're getting the Find My Friends app."

"I said I would."

"And I want hourly updates."

"Yeah, that's not happening."

"Do you *want* me to go crazy?"

"As if we're not already there," Phoebe muttered under her

breath. I jabbed her with my elbow and she stifled a smile, turning her attention to the camera in her lap.

"You have to trust us, Arden. We can handle ourselves."

"I do trust you," she said. "It's *him*."

"He's harmless," Phoebe said, waving this off. "Before Vi picked me up yesterday, he offered to drive me home because I had a blister. Dude's a total softie."

Arden shot me a dubious look. I wouldn't categorize Dex as a softie, by any means, but he'd revealed small, softer factions of himself in the short time we'd known him. A tissue, a ride home in the rain, a Sorry for Your Loss that didn't feel like obligation so much as understanding. He remained a mystery, but something deep in my bones whispered we were the same.

"Sure. Harmless," Arden said. "But we definitely need a code word. Use 'papaya' in a sentence if he's holding a gun to your head."

"How would we use 'papaya' in a normal sentence?" I asked. She rolled her eyes.

"'I've been craving some juicy papaya.'"

"Ew. I'm not going to say that."

"I hope to God you won't have to."

I opened my mouth to argue and Phoebe held the camera out, angled toward us, a flash immediately blinding us.

"My eyes!" Arden wailed as I rubbed the stars from my eyes.

"Whoops," Phoebe said. "Is there a way to turn the flash off?"

I dropped my hands, squinting at her blurry form on the couch wielding the Polaroid camera. "Why would you choose that moment?"

"This is the beginning of the trip. I want to remember it." She held the camera up to her eye, angling it around the room before setting it down on the couch cushion beside her. She pinched the photograph of Arden and me between her fingers and shook it. "Plus, your face was really funny when Arden said 'juicy papaya.'"

"She's not wrong," Arden said. "But you're not supposed to shake Polaroids."

Phoebe froze. "What? Really?"

"Yeah. It could alter the chemicals and make the picture all wonky," I mentioned. Phoebe studied the photo, tilting her head slightly.

"Huh. Doesn't look wonky to me. Except your face."

I rolled my eyes. "Nobody is photogenic when they're blinded."

"You look like you're about to sneeze. Arden looks like a goddess."

Arden beamed. "I was discovered at a mall in high school by a modeling agent. My absolute nightmare, of course, but it was so flattering."

"From what you've told me about that interaction," I said, "that guy was not a modeling agent."

Phoebe gasped. "Oh my god, Arden. You were almost true crimed in high school?"

"He was an agent! He said I could be the next Kate Moss!"

"He asked if you'd ever do tasteful nudes."

Arden threw up an exasperated hand. "I looked older than I was at sixteen!"

"Gross." Phoebe hopped to her feet, weighing the camera in her hands. "So, do we think we're staying in, like, hotels? Or Airbnbs?"

Arden leveled her gaze on me, awaiting the answer to this question. I drummed my fingers on my thigh, scrunching up my nose. I'd texted Dex last night telling him I had a tiny bit of savings I could contribute to the budget, to which he replied: *There's no budget. Don't worry about it.*

The nonprofit had to be a front for some Heisenberg-level shit.

"No idea," I said, hoping I sounded more confident than I felt. "But Dex seems to have pretty high standards, so I would guess hotels."

"Swanky," Arden said, lifting a brow. I shrugged. "Tomorrow, huh?"

Anxiety rolled through my stomach like thunder. "School's out on Monday and nothing was official with the bartending job, so . . . Why not, right?"

"We wanted to get going ASAP," Phoebe said with a grin. This was true for her, but I had a feeling Dex and I agreed on the early departure so we wouldn't lose our nerve. Every minute between now and eight o'clock tomorrow morning was an opportunity to back out; the more I thought about it, the more I wanted to hunker down and never leave the apartment again.

Arden was looking at me like she knew it. "This is too weird. Do you guys not realize how weird this is?"

"Oh, I am acutely aware," I said.

"Arden, weird is good," Phoebe chimed in. "It keeps things exciting. It keeps you *alive*."

Arden's face went soft. When she turned her gaze to me, I knew she understood; she didn't necessarily agree and she still wasn't completely on board, but she could see the difference in Phoebe. She knew why I had to do this.

It would've been nice if it didn't take *this* to make Phoebe feel alive. I wished I could've managed it on my own.

Eight

I didn't bother setting an alarm. Six-thirty on the dot, Phoebe pounded on my bedroom door, shouting that she'd made coffee and would start taking bags downstairs. I stared at my ceiling in the dark, stomach churning.

What the hell am I doing?

I dragged myself out of bed, the thought following me around the apartment like a ghost. I took a scorching shower, half expecting the question to show up written in steam on the mirror. Skin red and raw, auburn hair stuck to my face, I studied my reflection, waiting for something wrong to jump out. A new tattoo or piercing, horns, anything that might indicate this was a dream.

For months I'd expected to wake up from a nightmare. I wouldn't hold my breath this time.

Phoebe pranced around the living room dressed in black cut-offs, fishnets, and an oversized Ethel Cain tee. Her happiness made it seem even more like a dream, a sweeter one I wasn't so keen to wake up from.

Noah and Arden helped take our bags downstairs, and the four of us stood on the sidewalk under the pink sunrise. A chill perfumed the air, thick and sweet.

"I feel like we're sending you off to college," Noah said, bleary-eyed in an old hoodie and plaid pajama bottoms. Beside him, Arden stood in a sundress and slippers, eyes red.

"Are you crying?" I asked.

"This is emotional!" Arden replied defensively. "You guys are setting forth! Taking steps forward! A new adventure!"

I glanced at Phoebe, wondering if she understood the subliminal message there: *Your dad would love this.*

Dad lived for adventure, having spent his twenties working the lights for various punk bands, traveling the world. It's how he met our mother, a singer terrified of commitment who couldn't stay away from the sweet roadie. He fell hard. Waited for her every time she left him high and dry. Both pregnancies were accidental, but the second one opened her eyes to how much she didn't want this, and after Phoebe was born, she left permanently, and Dad got a stable job working the lights at a venue in Providence.

I used to ask if he missed adventures. *This is an adventure,* he'd reply as he gestured to our backyard where Phoebe chased fireflies. It was so corny, but he meant it. He was just as taken with fatherhood as he'd been by foreign countries.

There were only so many ways to express how much you miss someone. I cried into my pillow, sold my childhood home, avoided certain roads; suddenly, this trip felt less like running away and more like a homage. He spent years driving down these roads, seeing these sights. We'd stumbled into the most remarkably appropriate way to celebrate Dad and, hopefully, bring ourselves back to life a little bit.

Phoebe was already buzzing like a live wire. I'd get there.

"So, this is happening," Noah said, looking between Arden and me. "We are letting this happen?"

She nodded curtly. "We are."

"Because . . . ?"

"Stop being such a worrywart." She looped an arm around my shoulders, pulling me in. "Vi has everything under control. Right?"

"Always."

Phoebe's sharp intake of breath snapped us all to attention as Dex's car swung around the corner and cruised toward us, pulling into the fire lane.

"You owe me ten bucks," Phoebe said, casting Noah a smug grin. He rolled his eyes and reached into his hoodie pocket, withdrawing several bills.

"Seriously?" I said. Arden whacked his arm.

"Don't make bets with teenagers."

Phoebe pocketed the money and turned her attention to Dex's car. He stepped out, donned in his standard uniform of a crisp button-up and snug trousers, as well as a pair of black Ray-Bans. My small spark of excitement was snuffed out by an overwhelming burst of anxiety.

"Morning," I said, lifting my hand in a timid wave. Dex rounded the front of his car, stopping short when Phoebe bolted toward him.

"You made it!"

His brow furrowed. "Was that in question?"

"Kind of."

Impassive as ever, Dex turned to me, gesturing to the pile at my feet. "Is that everything?"

"That's everything."

With a stiff nod, he effortlessly plucked up several bags at once. For as pristine as his outfit was, everything else remained contrastingly unkempt; thick hair fisted out of his unshaven face, eyes laden with dark circles. Clearly, he got about as much sleep last night as I did.

What the hell are we doing?

Dex didn't seem conflicted, despite the obvious sleep deprivation. There was no fidgeting, darting eyes, or wringing of hands. He opened the trunk of his car—out rather than up, and Phoebe made him demonstrate twice before that muscle in his jaw ticked—and laid the bags out neatly. His shirt strained against his shoulders as he leaned in to adjust the bags, a single curl falling over his forehead like he was a goddamn Austen hero.

"You're staring," Arden hissed in my ear.

I snapped around. "Hmm?"

"No."

"What?"

"*No.*"

"I wasn't staring."

"Nope. No."

"I was appreciating the fit of his shirt. Kudos to his tailor, or whatever."

She grabbed my arm and dragged me several paces away from the group. "You haven't looked at anyone since Shawn. Every time Noah and I try to set you up, you brush it off. '*I'm too busy. Work is a nightmare. Phoebe.*' And that's fine! Everyone needs time to move on after a breakup," she said, keeping her voice low. I crossed my arms, unwilling to entertain whatever ridiculous notion she was about to throw down. "But out of everyone on the planet who deserves your attention, that guy is not related to them, or friends with them, or acquainted in any way shape or form with them."

"Arden."

She pointed right in my face. "Don't use that tone with me. I'm being serious."

"You're being dramatic."

"You were staring!"

"He's nice to look at when his mouth is shut."

She huffed, definitely fending off a smile. "Just be careful," she murmured, eyes shining.

I dropped the combative stance. Her misplaced concern had everything to do with us embarking on this strange adventure without her. For so long, I'd held her like a crutch, unable to stand on my own. I stepped forward and wrapped her in my arms.

"You guys are everything to me. How am I supposed to let you go?" Arden murmured.

"Don't bother. We'll talk every night."

She choked on a laugh, burying her face in my hair. "God. I'm gonna miss you. I had myself convinced this wouldn't happen."

"Me, too." I squeezed her tighter, eyes burning as I breathed in her Tom Ford perfume. If I hugged her hard enough, it would transfer to me, and I could hold on to her a little while longer. "Don't let your mom take you wedding dress shopping until I get back."

"No way. I need my maid of honor's stamp of approval."

I placed a hand over my heart and Arden shot me a watery smile, leaning in to rest her head on my shoulder. "We'll be okay," I said. "I'm embracing optimism again."

"Well, duh. You wouldn't be doing any of this if you weren't a dirty optimist." Her smile tipped into genuine territory. "I'm proud of you."

I rolled my eyes and gently shoved her, as if I wasn't genuinely touched or on the verge of a breakdown. She'd said those words to me so many times over the last year, but this felt like the first time I could *feel* them. I'd dipped my toe in water expecting a shock of cold and found something damn close to warmth. It only took a potentially catastrophic choice, but at least it was mine, and at least I had my sister on my side. For the first time in a long time, I was proud of myself too.

Noah walked over and slung an arm around my shoulders, drawing me in. "You sure about this?" he asked. "I could fake a medical emergency if you want to bail."

I snorted. "I'm good. This is something I have to do."

He gave me a reassuring little squeeze. "The offer stands."

"In general, or . . . ?"

"Yeah. Six years from now, I'll drop to the floor and fake appendicitis if you ask me to."

Couldn't have picked a better one for Arden.

Dex shut the trunk and leaned against it, arms crossed, waiting out the rest of the goodbyes. Phoebe let Arden squeeze her hard, rolling her eyes as Arden whispered something in her ear, and then offered Noah a fist bump.

"Dex. If that is your real name," Arden said. Dex turned to her, eyebrows raised. "If anything happens to either of them. If they experience any sort of physical or mental harm. If they come home worse off in any way, shape, or form. I will murder you."

Said with a smile. I expected nothing less.

"Fair enough," Dex said and made his way around the car to the driver's side. Phoebe darted after him, closing herself in the back seat without a second glance in our direction.

"I can't tell if he's joking or if he agrees that's a fair punishment," Noah mused. Arden glanced at me, smiling.

"Either way, brownie points."

I gave them each another hug, holding my breath, bracing

for that moment I'd startle awake in bed and it would be ten months ago and all of this would have been a terrible dream. The sidewalk remained steady underfoot. Fluffy white clouds crawled across the blue overhead. A breeze swept through and my hair flew directly into my eyeball.

Not a dream.

I scraped my hair out of my face and moved toward Dex's car. Phoebe wound down the window, a huge grin taking over her face.

"Vi, come on," she said, gesturing wildly for me to get in the car. "I made a playlist!"

I got in.

"Ready?" Dex asked, casting me a quick glance. I felt a lot of things in this car, and ready wasn't one of them, but I forced myself to nod. His eyes flicked to the rearview mirror, silently repeating the question to Phoebe, and she saluted.

I can call it off, I thought.

Phoebe sent me a bright smile from the back seat. I kept my mouth shut.

Nine

It took approximately one mile for my insides to riot.

I'd never been the most impulsive person. Where my dad and Phoebe bounced around wherever their hearts desired, I preferred to mosey down a certain path, time, plan. Not so much that I was incapable of straying for fun, but enough that I took time to weigh the options before moving forward. The first time I ever careened off-path was nine months ago in a hospital hallway, a strenuous and isolating decision that wasn't really a choice at all. Phoebe was mine from the moment my dad told me I'd have a sister—I raised her alongside him, watched that tiny bundle of energy grow into a beautiful, hilarious human I would've done anything for even before our world fell apart. When I agreed to take in Phoebe, I knew I was dismantling the rest of it. I lost Shawn, I lost stability, and for a long time, it felt like I lost my sister.

And here she was, orchestrating perhaps the most significant mistake of my life with a smile.

I cut Dex a wary glance. He seemed cool, calm, like a bored cabdriver, and it made me more insecure about everything. How was he so aggressively fine with this? Strangers on an almost three-thousand-mile journey across the country in a car—it would take at least a week to get there, and Phoebe had a list of stops she was campaigning for, and good *lord,* what were we *doing.*

Oh, this was bad. In my desperation to cheer up my sister, I let her steer us right off the ledge of a cliff. I would die in a crumpled heap before breaking Phoebe's heart. That didn't make me a decent guardian—it made me a coward.

"So, I have this idea," Phoebe said, popping up between the center console. I gasped out loud, my heart making a decent attempt to separate from my chest. Dex glanced at me, brows knitting together.

"You good?" he said. I rubbed my chest.

"What kind of idea?"

"Weeell," Phoebe said, dragging the word out long enough for Dex's fingers to tighten against the wheel, "I think by the time we've been on the road a couple hours, we're gonna need a break, right? And what better way to take a break than with cotton candy and roller coasters?" Dex was already shaking his head, but Phoebe remained unruffled. "Coney Island is basically on our route! I've always wanted to go! It's literally my dream."

"We're not stopping four hours into the drive," Dex deadpanned. "Especially for Coney Island."

"Excuse you, Coney Island is amazing."

"You just said you've never been."

"My dad went all the time when he was a kid," she said, narrowing her eyes at him. "He used to tell us stories about cutting school to go to Coney Island with his friends. He was supposed to take me someday."

My heavy heart could've crashed right through the bottom of Dex's car. "Bee—"

"Don't," she snapped. I dropped my gaze to my lap, stung. "This isn't a pity thing. I'm not trying to manipulate him into stopping. I'm being opportunistic. We're driving right through New York, right? So, this is my chance to go to Coney Island." She drew back into her seat, folding her arms over her chest. "Please."

My hands were bloody from Phoebe's barbed wire attitude, yet her suggestion of Coney Island sang to me. For our dad, sure, but also the fact that a four-hour trip was considerably more palatable than a week; I could survive four hours to Brooklyn and make the decision to turn around, or keep going for the next four hours. A coping mechanism from those first days after losing my dad, repurposed for a new mountain to climb. Back then, I'd lie in bed and think, *I just have to make it until morning.*

I took a steadier breath. *Four hours.*

"Coney Island's a good idea," I said to Dex. Phoebe scoffed, mistaking this as ass-kissing. "I think you're the kind of guy who could use a corn dog."

"I'd prefer if you didn't think about what kind of guy I am."

"How am I not supposed to think about you? You're five inches away from me."

"Do you think about the people around you in the grocery store?"

"Yeah? All the time."

Phoebe popped up between us again. "Sometimes we come up with bizarro backstories for them," she said, grinning. Immediately, the air didn't seem so stifling. "We made our dad pee his pants once."

"See?" I tossed Dex a victorious smile. "It's normal."

"This doesn't have to be a bonding moment," he replied, keeping his eyes locked on the road. "We can be three people traveling together. End of."

I studied his profile for a moment, taking in the way his dark hair curled over his ear and his stubble snaked down his throat. A profile worthy of being sculpted by Michelangelo himself. I knew so little about this man, but I knew he was once sick with love and it had nowhere to go, literally stamped and returned. I felt that so hard. All the love I had for my dad swirling around like storm clouds without rain. All the love I had for my sister, thrown back in my face.

I had that feeling, an inkling we were the same somehow. He must've felt it, too. Otherwise, he wouldn't have offered a bit of comfort when I fell apart in front of him; not after what brought us together.

"But we're not," I said. His hands flexed against the wheel.

"We're friends," Phoebe piped up, punching his shoulder for emphasis.

"We're not friends."

"Why would you invite us on a road trip if we're not friends?"

"You invited yourself." His phone buzzed in the cupholder, the screen flashing with a call from *Mom*. He ignored the call and flipped it over, screen facing down. "If we were on a plane, you wouldn't make small talk with the other passengers."

"Yes, I would. That's so normal," I interjected. "But we're not on a plane. We're traveling across the country together in a car and you're telling me we shouldn't get to know each other even a little?"

"It would be better if we didn't," he replied. I shifted to face him, crossing my arms.

"Sounds like something a murderer would say."

"I just think it would be easier on everyone if we kept it simple."

"No offense, but that's stupid," Phoebe said. "Nothing about this is simple."

"It could be, if we let it."

"What's so complicated about family history and favorite foods?"

Dex bristled, his shoulders nearly reaching his ears. "I don't see the point in small talk."

"The point is we're here, together, and we shouldn't be strangers," I said, wondering what it would take to pry open his head and take a look inside. No one was *this* closed off. Especially not someone who wrote a letter like the one that put us on this journey in the first place. "We know nothing about you, other than your name and that you work for a sketchy nonprofit—"

He scowled. "Sketchy?"

"—and you were on board to let me and my fourteen-year-old sister tag along on this trip. That's weird. You're *weird*."

"As opposed to you, the normal woman who reads strangers' mail and stalks them."

I glared at the side of his face until he sent a fleeting glance my way, our eyes meeting for a fraction of a second before he turned back to the road. His jaw ticked.

"This is fun," Phoebe said, grinning. "Also, I have to pee."

Dex swiveled to look at her. "We haven't even made it to the highway."

She shrugged. "I had a lot of coffee."

He sighed, looking as if he regretted every decision he'd made that led to this moment, the first hint that we were on the same side. Part of me wanted to reach for him, commiserate somehow. But maybe the act of merely existing beside him in the absurdity was enough. Maybe it had to be, for now.

Coney Island turned out to be the sort of place that looked, in real life, like it had popped out of my head. I'd never been, only heard stories from my dad, but as we made our way down the boardwalk with the scent of fried dough and salt in the air, the rush of rides overhead, overflowing garbage cans, throngs of people with huge smiles on their faces—it was exactly right. And from the grin on Phoebe's face, she thought so too.

She talked the whole way there. Yammering about everything from the cows in a pasture on the side of the highway to her reasoning for including a Carly Rae Jepson song on her road trip playlist. It was the most I'd heard my sister's voice in so long. Every once in a while, she'd look at me, eyes alight, and it would transport me to a time before our world shattered, when she adored me and confided in me and our dad would've been the one in the driver's seat.

"Oh my god," Phoebe repeated for the twentieth time in as many seconds. She clapped her hands to her cheeks, eyes wide as she took it all in. Sand crunched underfoot, the quiet rush of rides and patrons' squeals filling the air. "What do we do first? I want a corn dog. But I want to ride something. I want to win a Squirtle, one of the big ones. Oh my god, do you *smell* that?"

"Take a breath, Bee," I said, stifling a laugh. She inhaled sharply, and then took a deeper, slower breath. "We'll do it all."

Her face split into a bright smile. She was happy, overflowing with it. I couldn't break down in the middle of the boardwalk, so I'd hold it in until later, when I could lock myself away in a bathroom and cry in the shower like normal. Only this time, the tears would be joyful. Mostly.

"What first?" She spun to Dex, whose expression remained stony and distant, making no secret of his disapproval. "Rides? Food? Games?"

"This is your stop, not mine."

"But you're here."

"So is she." He jerked his chin in my direction.

"I'm not asking Vi because I know what she'll say." She put on a mildly insulting Valley Girl accent: "'Rides first, otherwise you'll throw up.' She always says things like 'otherwise.'"

"A normal word," I said, looking to Dex for support. He offered none. "And it's true. You can't eat before you ride that."

I pointed to the terrifying ride composed of metal orbs slingshotting people around. My stomach soured just looking at it. If Phoebe rode that one, I'd have a panic attack, but I couldn't ask her not to because then she would out of spite.

"I think you'd puke regardless," Dex replied, eyeing the ride uneasily.

"You guys are so boring." Phoebe lifted our dad's Polaroid camera, hung securely around her neck, and snapped a photo of us. Dex swore loud enough for several nearby mothers to shoot him dirty looks. "Oh my god, Vi. I found your unphotogenic soulmate."

I rolled my eyes. "Let's just go."

We rode a roller coaster first, one Phoebe promised didn't have a loop but did. Then we rode something called the Coney Clipper that was sort of fun, if you're into swinging back and forth with your stomach in your throat. Dex made up excuses to pass on the first two and ordered a milkshake while we were gone to secure his inability to ride anything else. I would've been annoyed if I wasn't jealous he thought of it first.

The world was still spinning from the last ride as we approached a giant metal contraption sending its riders somersaulting overhead, the screams louder than anything we'd encountered. My throat tightened, hands went clammy; as Phoebe darted for the end of the line, I had to pause to keep from toppling sideways.

"You look pale," Dex said. "This is your limit?"

I narrowed my eyes at him. "My limit for what, exactly?"

"Your desperate attempts to please her."

"That's not—What are you even—That is so—" The little smirk pulling at the corner of his lips pulled me up short, brain turning to static. *Danger.* I couldn't read this as flirty teasing just because the guy had a face Old Hollywood would fawn over; Dex was cold and abrasive and, most important, spoken for. Any attraction could easily be ignored, so long as he kept up the asshole thing.

Smirking wasn't allowed. Period.

"Shut up," I said. The smirk twitched, as if an actual smile might be possible. I blinked away, overheating under the blazing sun, and continued over to Phoebe. "You want to ride this?"

"Yep," she said, scraping her pink hair into a nubby ponytail. "Dying to."

"Don't say that out loud. The universe might take it seriously."

"The universe owes me and it knows it. Come on."

Anxiety roared in my chest. "You want to ride it right now?"

"Obviously."

"No, yeah. But, you know, we could ride it later. Grand-finale-type deal."

"You're such a baby." She turned to Dex. "You wanna ride it with me?"

The smirk officially left the building. "What? Why me?"

"Violet's too chicken," she said. Dex glanced at the ride, face ashen. "And you haven't ridden anything yet."

"I, uh." He cleared his throat. "What's this called?"

"Zenobia."

"What does that mean?"

"Who cares?"

"I liked what Violet said about the grand finale. I think that's a good idea."

"Oh my god." Phoebe removed the camera from around her neck, handing it off to me. "I can ride it alone. Didn't realize I was road-tripping with a bunch of babies."

"That thing is insane, Phoebe," I said defensively. "Who's to say it's even safe?"

"Coney Island," she replied. I faltered. "Dude, it's fine. I don't care. Plus, you can get a picture of me riding it."

Relief swept through me. "Yes. I can do that."

Dex and I veered off, taking a seat on a conveniently placed bench beside an even more conveniently placed trash can: perfect for anyone exiting Zenobia who needed to empty the contents of their stomachs.

"It's safe, right?" I said, watching Phoebe inch closer to the head of the line. "Like, I know this place has been around forever and the ride wouldn't be here if it wasn't safe, but still. Phoebe's small. What if the straps are loose and she slips through?"

"She won't." Dex rested his elbow on the back of the bench, glancing toward the game booths. Sweat glistened along the tendons of his neck, shoulders pulling taut against the fabric of his white button-up. He'd rolled the sleeves to his elbows, showcasing a gorgeous tattoo of winding piano keys down the base of his forearm, dangling his arms and hands in front of me like a desert mirage. I dropped my gaze to my lap to shut down the inappropriate thoughts stampeding their way into my head. "There hasn't been an incident here since the seventies. She'll be fine."

I smiled, pushing down the odd burst of fondness I felt over his research.

"We didn't get to do this much. The amusement park thing. The closest we got was the local fair and even then I had to push myself to keep up with her. She's always been braver than I am. Zenobia, though, is a lot. I'd never ride that." I paused, watching giddy strangers pass by. A group of teenagers. A couple with that obvious fresh love glow. A father with his young daughter on his shoulders. "Our dad would've been up there with her."

Dex remained quiet. This was too personal for his taste, but I needed to say it out loud, offer someone else this vision of my dad, like that would keep him here somehow.

Sidestepping the heaviness, I added, "But at least I can admit I'm afraid."

Dex's jaw clenched. "I'm not an amusement park guy."

"Shocking. With the button-up and leather shoes, you fit in so well," I said. He combed his fingers through his hair, ignoring this. "What kind of guy *are* you? Or is that too personal?"

"What does it matter?"

"You are currently chauffeuring my fourteen-year-old sister and me across the country," I reminded him. He tilted his head slightly, acknowledging my point. I went on, "It's fine if you don't want to be friends. But until we're back in Boston, we're gonna be civil. Civility requires the bare minimum and the bare minimum here is a conversation."

"Look around," he said. "We took a detour four hours into the trip. I am obviously at your mercy."

My cheeks burned under the Brooklyn sun and Dex's sharp gaze. I forced a smile and said, "If that were true, having a conversation with you wouldn't feel like trying to talk down one of my third graders."

The smirk briefly reappeared, sending a not-unpleasant buzz down my limbs. I cleared my throat and glanced toward the line, ensuring Phoebe was still there.

"Why third grade?" Dex asked. I looked at him, eyebrows raised. He'd yet to volunteer any information about himself, but information about me was fair game, apparently.

"It's a good age. They're old enough to read, too old for bath-room accidents and nose picking."

"Ah." He climbed to his feet. "I'm gonna grab a water. Do you want one?"

"Yes please."

I watched him go, breathing in the stench of buttery pop-corn. He returned with three waters, casting the Zenobia line a quick glance, realizing Phoebe had only moved forward two paces. I thanked him, ignoring the strange fizzle in my chest over the third bottle, presumably for my sister.

"I guess I understand why third grade," he said. I didn't real-ize we were picking up where we left off. "It's the elementary thing that stumps me."

I grinned. "You're not a kid person? But you're *so* good with them."

His thumb scraped at the label of his water. "I like kids. I work with kids. But I have no interest in taking a major role in molding their minds."

"I get it. It's definitely not for the faint of heart," I said, to which he widened his eyes as if to say *No shit*. "I didn't know I wanted to teach until Phoebe. I helped raise her. I helped teach her how to read. I witnessed her milestones and I got to feel the same pride my dad felt . . . It was magical. I realized how much I loved guiding her and watching her learn and it snowballed from there."

"That's touching," he said. "How often do you get sick?"

"Not that often."

"I need numbers."

"Oh, sorry. I left the graph at home."

"Is it constant? I went out with a children's librarian once and she said she was perpetually congested. She sounded like a cartoon mouse."

My laugh surprised us both; I'd been previously unaware Dex was capable of pleasant conversation, let alone humor, and his eyes sparked as if he liked the sound of it before he blinked away, taking a pull from his water. Life had been a bit too touch and go for my three things to carry weight lately, and now a new list took up the empty space: Three Things I Like About Dex. He bought Phoebe a water bottle without prompting. He researched pit stops even if he didn't want to take them. He showed remote interest in my job and, vaguely, me.

Maybe it wasn't much, but it calmed the storm inside me. If I could keep adding to the list, this trip might not be a catastrophic mistake.

"Sounds like a her problem," I said with a smile. "I get one or two colds throughout the school year."

"That's one or two too many."

"You're full of it."

"Haven't had a cold in four years."

"Full. Of. It."

"I got food poisoning last year. No colds, though."

"Like, we need to get the *Guinness Book* people on the phone. No one has ever been so full of it before."

An ache pinched at my cheek—I was still smiling. I couldn't remember the last time I'd carried on a conversation with a steady smile, but the amusement lighting up Dex's neutral expression was so much more interesting than sadness.

"Weak reference," he said. "No one talks about the *Guinness Book* anymore."

"Third graders do," I pointed out. The corners of his mouth twitched into something dangerously close to a real smile. "There are few things third graders care about more than the *Guinness Book of World Records.*"

"You need to spend more time with people your own age."

"You probably do too. How else would you get conned by a fourteen-year-old?"

He scratched at his cheek and the audible scrape sent a little zip down my spine. "Fair enough," he conceded. I cast Phoebe a quick glance—she'd moved forward another pace, now three people away from the ride—and then shifted on the bench to face Dex.

"So, why Sequest?" I asked. I hadn't realized how relaxed he'd become until it was sapped out of him, every muscle in his body seeming to tighten at once. "You were asking me about work. I figured it was fair game."

He wouldn't even look at me, his gaze fixed on Zenobia as its riders' screams filled the air. I'd ruined this somehow. We were vibing, maybe even bonding, and a simple question about work burned down what little progress I'd made. It took a second for my brain to remind me what exactly Sequest did (assuming it wasn't a front for anything illegal), and my stomach dropped.

"Wait, shit." I winced. "You don't have to answer that if it has to do with, like, your identity." He looked at me, his expression flat. "Or sexuality. I mean, I'm bisexual, so, you know. Safe space. But it's none of my business."

He tipped his head back, letting the sun kiss his skin. "Nice save."

"I am nothing if not a wreck. You know this about me," I replied. Across the way, Phoebe stepped up to the attendant with a bright smile. "Ugh. Tell me again that she'll be okay."

"She'll be okay," he said. "Physically. Mentally, I don't see how she could ever recover."

I laughed again and bumped his elbow with mine. "Look at you making a joke."

"Wasn't joking."

I turned back to Phoebe, weighing Dad's camera in my

hands. Before stepping up to the ride entrance, she glanced over and waved, reminding me of the excitable little girl who used to cling to my leg for an hour when I returned home from college.

"Nah," I said, lifting the camera to my eye to capture the moment. "She'll be fine."

Ten

The GPS announced we'd reached our destination, but the heart-shaped sign arching over the stony driveway was saying otherwise.

Pocono Woods Couples Resort, it proclaimed. *Where lovers love to love!*

I turned to Dex, wincing as the leather gripped my sunburned legs. He stared at the sign.

"So," I said. Phoebe tittered in the back seat, surrounded by a moat of prizes, empty bags of cotton candy, and kettle corn. "Do you want to explain why you decided we should stay at a couples resort in the Poconos?"

"I didn't," he said.

"Did you plug the wrong address into the GPS?"

"No."

He pulled out his phone, squinting at the brightness. It was after seven, the sun sinking behind the trees, and we were exhausted from two and a half hours in the car after a day at Coney Island. If I didn't have access to a hot shower and a pillowy bed in the next fifteen minutes, I couldn't be held responsible for the monster possessing my body for the foreseeable future.

"Dex."

"I did not book us a couples resort," he repeated through gritted teeth.

"This might be the best day of my life," Phoebe said.

Dex lifted his gaze from his phone to the sign, flicking between the two. "I'm going to kill him," he said calmly. "Excuse me."

He climbed out of the car, bringing the phone to his ear. Phoebe popped up through the center console, grinning. "Imagine how many people have had sex here," she said. I winced and turned down her playlist so I could hear the stones crunching under Dex's shoes.

"Stop."

"All the spermy sheets."

"Oh, *gross.*" I shoved Phoebe to the back seat and she fell on her side, laughing. Outside, Dex paced until whoever was on the other side of the phone answered.

"Why the fuck am I at a couples resort, Gavin?" His voice echoed up into the surrounding trees. "This is the in you had at a hotel? Are you fucking serious?"

"Gavin," Phoebe echoed. "Isn't that the guy who called you?"

"Yeah," I said, thinking of the strange phone call I'd received during which Dex's friend interrogated me about my criminal record and my whereabouts during various political atrocities over the last decade before casually admitting to burning down his own dorm room. That dude had led us *here.* "Apparently, Dex takes advice from a dude who committed quote-unquote 'light arson.'"

Phoebe laughed. Everything about the situation immediately lightened. Her happiness was a lifeboat—even when things seemed irreversibly bad, we remained afloat.

Dex scrubbed a hand down his face, his body tense like a spring on the brink of snapping. His shirt had come untucked from his pants, yet remained miraculously wrinkle-free after Coney Island *and* the drive since. Still intimidating—but I found myself opening windows I'd intended to keep locked with him. Our conversation on that bench triggered a temptation to pick his brain about everything from the odd-shaped water tower we passed on the highway, to how healthy his relationship was with his parents, to how much he'd told his friends about our trip. I *wanted* to know him, I realized, and I wanted him to *want* to know me. I tried not to read into it—I simply liked being liked.

Dex's eyes snagged mine across the dirt drive. His expression shifted imperceptibly and he turned his back to the car, moving several paces away. I rolled my eyes. As if eavesdropping was our biggest concern right now.

When he returned, he grumbled something under his breath and put the car in drive, bumping down the driveway instead of turning around.

"So," I said. His fingers tightened against the steering wheel. "Your friend has an in?"

"Yes."

"An in here?" Phoebe pressed gleefully.

"His aunt knows the owner."

"Very cool. Very chill." I crossed my legs, angling toward him. "So, you're fine with this. Us staying at a couples hotel. In the Poconos. Some might say the honeymoon capital of the world."

"We're not staying here," he said, shooting me a dirty look. "I paid for the rooms. I'm getting a refund and we'll find someplace else to stay."

"According to Google," Phoebe said, appearing between us,

"there are eleven other couples resorts in the Poconos. We can take our pick!"

The hotel emerged in all its glory—an expansive log cabin painted bubblegum pink with various topiaries of mythical creatures (unicorns and mermaids and centaurs, oh my!) and beautiful gardens surrounding the area. A practical joke. I could hear my dad laughing.

"Again," I said as Phoebe whipped out Dad's camera to snap a photo of the topiary garden, "your friend has an in *here*?"

"I don't know," Dex said.

The décor inside was tamer: Dark wood floors and high ceilings helped tone down the garishness of the pink crystal chandelier and floral mosaic fireplace. Dex approached the reception desk, where a woman in a pink jumpsuit with teased hair waited, beaming.

"Hello, sweethearts!" she crowed, clasping her hands together as if the mere sight of a man and woman standing next to each other made her swoon. When she noticed Phoebe, she blinked several times in quick succession, and then glanced around the room like she might spot a hidden camera behind a bedazzled palm tree. "We don't usually have children here."

Dex withdrew his wallet. "I need to cancel a reservation."

"Cancel?" the woman repeated. "I'm sorry. I don't understand what's happening."

"A refund, ideally. It's under 'Dexter.'"

"Refund?" Shaking her head, she turned to the computer, typing frantically. "A reservation for tonight? We need twenty-four hours' notice to provide a refund." Dex glowered, and I swore I could see sweat beading on her forehead. "It's policy. I'm sorry."

"Policy," Dex repeated. I stepped in front of him before he could unleash hell on this poor woman.

"Hi," I said, offering a smile. "Sorry about him. He gets cranky before bed. So, here's what happened." I leaned against the desk, donning my best parent-teacher conference voice. "A friend recommended your lovely establishment, but he happened to leave out the fact that it's a couples hotel. You can imagine our confusion."

The woman laughed nervously. "Yes, I imagine it was quite a surprise."

"We're exhausted. On our way to Oregon, been driving since Boston," I told her, and her eyes lit up.

"A road trip! How wonderful! What's in Oregon?"

"It's a long story." I lowered my voice, adding, "Our dad just died."

Her hand flew to her mouth. "Oh. I'm so sorry."

"Thanks." I sighed, wishing this wasn't the second time I'd done the dead dad bit in less than two weeks. To be honest, Dad would have encouraged it, but it still felt sort of slimy. "It's been rough. My sister, Phoebe—the one taking a picture of the taxidermied bear dressed like Dolly Parton?—she's been taking it hard, but the trip is helping. Anyway, I'm just trying to say that we're tired and sad and this is a *huge* misunderstanding."

"Of course, of course." The woman looked between us, biting her lip. "You know, you've been through so much. I'll refund the reservation, no problem."

I placed a hand over my heart. "Oh my gosh. Thank you so much."

"I'd hate for you to get back on the road when you're so tired, though," she said. "Why don't you take the room, anyway? On the house."

"No," Dex said, taking a step backward. "Thanks."

"Uh, hello? We will absolutely take it," I cut in, meeting his incredulous gaze. "We're not passing on a free room."

"A free room here. In this hotel."

"Who cares if everything is pink and heart shaped? Have a little whimsy in your heart."

Phoebe snorted. Dex clenched his jaw so hard, I expected to hear a tooth crack.

"We'll take it," I said to the receptionist, who beamed again. "But, uh, is that one room? As in one bed?"

"The reservation was for one room."

"I reserved two," Dex said. She shrank back. "Two rooms."

"I'm sorry. There must have been a mistake."

"Well, we can pay for another room," I said, bumping Dex's arm with my shoulder. The woman shrank even more.

"We're all booked up this weekend, unfortunately."

I threw on another smile. "It's fine. It'll be fine," I said. "Thank you for being so accommodating."

"Enjoy your stay!" She hesitated. "Maybe keep the child out of the courtyard past ten?"

My eyes widened. Dex coughed.

"Oh." I laughed uncomfortably. "Yeah, we'll, uh. We'll do that. Thanks."

"Oh my god," Phoebe whispered, grabbing my arm as Dex finished checking in. I steered her away from the desk, cheeks burning. "I wanna go to the nighttime orgy in the courtyard!"

"Stop. That can't be what it is."

"What else would it be?"

An orgy, almost definitely. Out loud, I said, "Book club, maybe."

She tossed me a dubious look. "Yeah, okay. Let's all go read smut in the dark."

"Don't say 'smut.'"

Dex appeared at my side, the dark half-moons beneath his eyes draining the life out of him. "You go ahead. I'll get the bags."

"We can help with the bags," Phoebe chirped, posture straightening. "We're not helpless ladies with brittle bones."

"Speak for yourself," I muttered, resisting the urge to massage my lower back. Every part of my body ached after spending half the day exploring Coney Island and the other half in a car. The free hotel room was certainly enticing, but the more selfish truth was I couldn't force myself back into the car. Besides, Phoebe loved it here. We could survive a night in lovey-dovey hell.

The three of us collected our bags and headed up to the room, admiring framed vintage photographs of various weddings. It was my favorite detail thus far, even before Phoebe gasped and snapped a Polaroid of vintage lesbians.

Dex stopped in front of a lilac door and offered my sister the room key adorned with a pink leather heart, leaning his shoulder against the jamb to watch her struggle before reaching over to flip it the right way. She laughed. Something in my chest constricted, pulling tight. Any semblance of good feelings disappeared upon entering our room to find mirrored ceilings and a heart-shaped bed. Our horrified expressions bounced right back at us.

"Oh my god," I said, letting my bags tumble to the floor. Phoebe's sunburned cheeks flushed a deep maroon.

"Okay, this isn't funny anymore."

"Who wants to sleep in a heart-shaped bed?" I looked to Dex, who'd had a lot of answers thus far. He came up short this time. "Shape-wise. It doesn't make sense."

"No one is disagreeing with you," Dex said. He shut his eyes, exhaustion emanating from his very being. "You guys can take the bed. I'll sleep on the floor."

"Yeah, I'm not sleeping in a heart-shaped bed under a mirror ceiling with my sister," Phoebe replied. I nodded.

"Uncrossable lines."

He heaved a huge sigh, shoulders sagging. "I'll get blankets."

I watched him slump out of the room, something pinching deep beneath my rib cage. Guilting the woman at the front desk into giving us a free room wasn't my most shining moment. The next closest hotel was probably a short drive, and then Dex and I wouldn't be sentenced to a night on the floor.

"Can I shower first?" Phoebe asked, snapping me out of my daze. She'd dumped the contents of her bag across the bed, the vibrant red duvet overwhelmed by black. "Someone puked on Zenobia and they didn't get any on me but it *feels* like it's on me, you know?"

I waved her off. "Go ahead."

She grabbed a handful of black from the bed and darted into the bathroom. "Oooh! A heart-shaped tub!"

I smiled, sinking onto the edge of the bed. Sitting didn't help the ache in my back or the exhaustion plucking at me like strings of a marionette, but it gave the illusion of rest. I drew my phone out for the first time since Coney Island. Forty-three unread texts from Arden. Mustering whatever energy I had left, I called her.

"Hey!" she shouted mid-ring. I winced.

"Ow."

"Sorry. Hey. Hi." She cleared her throat, gathering herself. "I've been losing my mind, a little bit. You've been MIA."

"I sent you pictures from Coney Island."

"But you didn't reply to any of my texts. You *said* nothing. And that, my friend, says *everything*."

I rubbed my stinging eyes. "Does it?"

"Obviously not," she said. "I have no idea what's going on. You cut me out of the loop."

"We've been gone for like twelve hours," I said, prompting a huff. "We go longer without contact when you and Noah take your anniversary trips."

"That is so not the same thing. Just tell me how it's going. I'm dying, Vi."

"It's fine." I paused, glancing at the mirrored ceiling. My lifeless eyes stared back, complete with flat hair and sunburned cheeks. "I mean, it's exhausting and my back is fucked from driving for so long. I got whiplash from a roller coaster. And we're spending the night in a couples hotel that may or may not be hosting an orgy."

A solid ten seconds of silence followed this. "You're fucking with me."

"I never joke about orgies."

Before she could spiral, I filled her in on the details as Phoebe's voice drifted in from the bathroom, singing a song I didn't know. In this unfamiliar hotel room with a stranger staring at me in the mirrored ceiling, my best friend and my sister kept me tethered to the ground. I was okay. And not only that, but my dad was out there somewhere watching us embark on this journey.

"So . . ." Arden trailed off, her voice dipping with uncertainty. "You're staying? And you're cool with it?"

I let out a breath, watching my reflection in the mirror blink slowly. "Yeah."

"Thank god." I swore I could hear her collapse onto her bed, springs creaking underneath the relief. "I kept picturing you in that car like a hostage. You're so stubborn."

I smiled and leaned on my elbows, legs crossed, ready for an Arden Rant.

"Stubborn," she repeated emphatically, and I knew she was gesturing with as much gusto. "And honestly? Thoughtless."

"Thoughtless!"

"It's one thing to investigate a letter. Find the writer, return it, deal with a few consequences. Like, yeah, I was all in, too. But that wasn't enough for you. You had to throw in a cross-country road trip with a total stranger. Because of the stubbornity!"

"That's not a word," I pointed out. Even while calling me batshit crazy for going on this trip, Arden had handled me with care until now: Life couldn't be normal until she unleashed her unfiltered opinions about my life, and here, finally, the dam broke.

"It's as good as!" she shouted with conviction. I clapped a hand over my mouth to stifle a laugh. "I thought you were out of your mind! Certifiable! I asked Noah if we should step in and put a stop to the madness. But he was all, 'Nah, let's see how it goes.' As if it was nothing. As if your life isn't nightmarishly intertwined with mine. What an insult. He's on my list too."

"How long is your list?"

"Stop *enjoying* this," she snapped. "It's not funny. I was sick. I thought *you* were sick. I thought I was indulging a sick person's whims."

"It's not *not* true," I said. She growled. "Let me have it, Arden. I deserve it."

"I can hear you smiling."

"I'm not. I'm cowering. I'm curled up in the fetal position, near tears. Please don't yell at me. I can't take it."

"I wish Dex *was* a murderer," she grumbled. I rolled onto my back, smiling at my reflection. Slightly more familiar, like someone I knew in a past life. Like maybe I could know her in this one.

The rant went on for another ten minutes, but I put an end to it when Phoebe returned. Her cheeks were rosy, both from the sun and the shower, and she wore pajama shorts, a tank top, and hotel-supplied slippers two sizes too big for her feet. She gushed about the water pressure and the heart-shaped tub for a solid three minutes and then passed out against the dozen throw pillows decorating the bed. Had to be the first time she fell asleep at a decent time . . . well, ever.

Then, I cried in the shower, more out of relief and exhaustion than grief. By the time I emerged—clean, moisturized, and comfy in shorts and a big tee—Dex had returned and set up two makeshift beds on opposite sides of the room with thick, soft-looking blankets that definitely didn't come from the five-dollar throw bin.

"Hey," I said, keeping my voice low. Dex didn't bother looking up from where he rummaged through his bag. "Thanks for getting blankets."

He grunted, probably pissed that I insisted we take this room and sleep on the floor rather than driving a mile to the next hotel.

"Dex." I winced against the silence. "You're mad."

"I'm not mad."

"You're so mad. You're stabbing me with your mind right now."

He stood up and faced me. I expected daggers, something similar to that day we showed up at Sequest, but there was no anger there; he simply looked exhausted.

"I'm not mad," he repeated, keeping his voice low with Phoebe sleeping a few feet away. "I'm done."

My heart dunked into my stomach. "What?"

"It's too much." He wiped a hand over his face. "I'm thinking we head back to Boston first thing."

"No." The word flew out of me in a gasp. "Dex, we can't."

"This was a mistake. Look at where we are right now."

"It's funny," I said. I inhaled slowly, trying to get a handle on the panic rising up my chest. Phoebe was sleeping next to us and if she woke up to the sound of Dex's doubt . . . if she woke up in the morning to find out the rug had been wrenched out from under her for the second time in nine months . . . I couldn't let it happen. I wouldn't. "Just because things aren't going according to plan doesn't mean it's a mistake."

He let out a humorless laugh. "What plan?"

"What about Catalina?" I asked desperately. *What about Phoebe?* I couldn't ask. Or worse, *What about* me?

"It's too much," he repeated, and I wondered if my sister and I had managed to finish off this already-broken man.

"I know it's a lot. We're a lot." I swallowed, casting Phoebe a sidelong glance. She looked so peaceful, pink hair fanned over her cheek, her breathing soft and steady. "But she needs this. And considering you agreed to do this, I think you need it too."

"This is crazy," he said. "It's crazy that we're doing this. We're out of our fucking minds, Violet."

"Maybe. But we're already here."

"It's not too late to turn around."

My mantra of the past twenty-four hours echoed in my mind: *I can call it off.* I forced myself to shake my head and said, "Please."

His jaw ticked. "I'm too tired to deal with this right now," he muttered, turning away from me. He squatted down in front of his bag, resuming his rifling. "We'll talk in the morning."

I swallowed the urge to argue. It had been a long day, a longer week, and I was so tired, I could feel it in my bones. I understood Dex's hesitation—my own had been plaguing me since we left, and it took everything in me to fight against turning around.

But I had to keep us on the road for Phoebe. Hopefully with some rest and distance from the day, Dex would change his mind.

I plunked down on the pile of blankets nearest to the bed. They were softer than anticipated, but very much not a bed. I stretched out and pulled a Sherpa throw up to my chin. My reflection blinked at me in the darkening room, humidity from the shower drifting in with a hint of lavender soap. I heard the zipper of Dex's bag, and his soft *Excuse me* as he stepped over my legs on his way to the bathroom. I shut my eyes, waiting for my sore, fatigued body to shut down until morning, and then immediately checked my phone.

7:41 P.M. Bedtimes don't exist on road trips, surely.

The squeak of the faucet caught my attention. God, it was quiet enough to hear the splash of water in the sink—unwittingly, I imagined Dex bent over it, shirtless, washing away the ire of the last two hours. Twelve hours. Month. I decided it was okay to imagine Dex shirtless because I was overtired and, okay, it had been almost a year since I'd been in proximity of a shirtless someone with the type of hands that told you they could destroy your entire world with the flick of a wrist.

The faucet squeaked off and I squeezed my eyes shut, willing myself to fall asleep before I heard something I couldn't unhear. But then the shower was on, drowning out anything that might be happening in the bathroom, and I shifted in the blankets in an attempt at a comfortable position. My back *killed*. With a groan, I shoved off the throw and crawled to my luggage, digging out the jumbo bottle of ibuprofen I'd packed. I took two and meandered over to the window, gazing at the gardens below.

No view of the courtyard. Curiosity scratched up my insides and my brain took off in favor of the distraction, coming up with wild scenarios of what could be going on down there. All were in the same vein as an orgy.

The shower shut off. I grimaced and padded to my blankets, unwilling to face him again tonight. Dex slipped out of the bathroom, unleashing the scent of his soap—a heady medley of citrus and cedar, the sort of clean scent you want to bury your face in and breathe until you're made up of it.

Nope. It wasn't late enough to warrant thoughts like *that*.

I remained still, taking in the dull glow of Dex's phone across the room. I wondered if he was working, or maybe doom-scrolling like a normal person. I stared until he shut the screen off with a sigh. I took the opportunity to check my phone again. 9:23 P.M.

I must've fallen asleep for a minute or two, because I certainly hadn't been staring at Dex for an hour.

Dex's phone illuminated once again, and I watched him reach for it. Our eyes met in the mirrored ceiling, barely more than acquaintances lying on the floor of an extraordinarily pink hotel room, and I couldn't help the laugh bubbling up my neck.

"Did I wake you?" he asked quietly, letting his phone dim. I flipped mine over, leaving my side of the room completely dark.

"I wasn't asleep." I hesitated, listening to Phoebe's quiet snores. "I'm sorry I made us stay."

"Don't be."

"We're sleeping on the floor because of me. And I am feeling every second of it."

He leaned up on his elbows, the shadow of him shifting. "Do you want another blanket?"

"I'm good. Thanks, though."

His phone lit up again. He flipped it over, leaving the rest of the room in the same stark darkness. "I should've double-checked the accommodations. That's on me," he said, using the sort of voice I associated with face-to-face conversations at 2 A.M. Soft and secret. "I'm sorry."

"Don't be," I replied. "It's really funny."

"It's not funny."

"There's an orgy in the courtyard right now. It's *hilarious*."

"It's not an orgy."

"Do you know that for sure? Like you asked the lady and she explicitly told you it's not?"

"No. I used basic logic and common sense."

"What else could it be?"

"I cannot articulate how little I care."

"How do you not care? I can't stop thinking about it. I might go see," I said without thinking. But saying it out loud, I realized it was true. My curiosity had won out and I needed to see for myself what the hell was going on in the courtyard.

"Please don't," Dex said.

"Not to participate. I just want to see. That sounds bad. Not in a voyeuristic way."

"Jesus."

"It's morbid curiosity."

"Go to sleep."

"I don't think I can. I can't *not* know."

"And what will you do if it is an orgy?"

"Be scarred for life. But at least I'll know."

"Maybe you should heed the advice you were given."

I sat up, staring at his dark blob of a reflection. "She said it to the teenager, not us. Come on. Let's go see."

"When did I get involved in this?"

A great question. Now that I'd involved him, though, I wanted him to be. And it almost certainly had nothing to do with the shirtless fantasy. "You told Arden you'd protect me."

He scoffed. "I did not."

"It was implied. Physical or mental harm, remember? This is one, if not both."

"I'm sorry, are you planning on getting *involved* in the orgy?" I climbed to my feet, veering for my sandals set neatly by the door—Dex must've tidied while I was in the shower because I'd definitely kicked them in opposite directions. "Violet," he growled. "God*dammit*."

I slipped into the hallway, the pink floral wallpaper and fluorescent lighting blinding after an hour in the dark. This place could've been dreamed up by a six-year-old. That or it was a rejected set from *Barbie*. I blinked hard, growing used to the brightness, just as the door opened behind me.

"You're a piece of work," Dex muttered, squinting under the lights in a heather gray T-shirt and dark sweatpants. I'd never seen him like this—casual, intimately so. This man who held himself so tightly together, unraveled and unashamed. For the first time since we met, he wasn't Benji Dexter of Love Letter fame; he was simply Dex. I liked it.

"I knew you cared."

Ignoring this, he shuffled to the elevator. I lagged behind, trying to get a handle on the sudden dryness in my throat. I tried to think of three things, but on the ride downstairs, Dex sighed and leaned a shoulder against the wall, and I noticed the slope of his bicep, as well as a tattoo just above his elbow. I stared, transfixed—someone's handwriting, impossible to transcribe without being right on top of it.

Great. Now I was thinking about being on top of Dex.

The doors slid open, revealing a vacant lobby. Twinkling lights lit up the gardens through the windows, and the moment we stepped outside, soft music swept in with the breeze. The thought of soundtracking an orgy nearly made me lose it. Together, we crept across the lawn, sticking close to the building. The music grew louder until shadows opened up to a slate patio with grand stone pillars and, beyond it, fountains enclosed the courtyard where dozens of people lounged on the grass, facing an enormous screen.

An enormous screen projecting a film in which a woman in a feather boa was absolutely railed from behind.

All my thoughts were overrun by the image of this woman with a beehive and the man working behind her with the mother of all porn-staches. I tore my gaze from the scene to look at Dex, who appeared as thunderstruck as I felt.

"Is that a projector?" he asked.

"Oh my god. It's a porn movie night," I said. Snapping out of the daze, he grabbed my arm and tugged me behind a stone pillar, blocking us from view. "They're having a porn movie night."

"There are so many people. It must be open to the public, not just guests," he murmured thoughtfully. My stomach gave a giddy lurch.

"Oh my *god*."

"We have to leave."

"Wait, wait. Did you see the movie? It has to be from the seventies. Vintage porno, Dex."

"Violet, we have to go."

"This is amazing. I can't believe you tried to talk me out of coming down here," I whispered as he wrapped his fingers around my wrist and dragged me from the courtyard. The giddiness dimmed, unable to compete with the warmth of Dex's hand against my skin—my entire body broke out in a sweat.

When was the last time I'd been touched? From my body's reaction, you'd think the answer was never. Not once.

In the lobby, Dex released my wrist and the fog cleared. I blamed the porn for getting me all hot and bothered. Maybe I needed to get laid—though definitely not by the dude driving my sister and me across the country. He was simply *there,* existing while gorgeous. Who wouldn't have an inappropriate thought or two?

"So," I said as we made our way into the elevator. Dex tugged a hand through his hair and hit our floor number. "Do we consider that an orgy?"

He shook his head and my every vein buzzed to life as he began to laugh. Slowly. Just a crack at first, the slightest exhale slipping into a catch, and then he broke. Shoulders shaking, he bent forward, pressing his head against the wall, the sound of his laughter bouncing off the metal. It seemed like the sort of magic that only passes through once every decade, a rare comet. I alone bore witness to the most remarkable thing in Poconos history.

Then he snorted and I lost my shit right along with him.

Eleven

The route led us to a sixty-foot bear. And by route, I meant Phoebe.

An unforgiving sun cast the world in the dense heat that made existing outside air-conditioning excruciating, yet the three of us stood in crunchy grass, sticky with sweat, squinting up at a wooden rendering of Yogi Bear. I wasn't sure why we were here. Yogi was before Phoebe's time, and she'd never been one for cartoons. Then again, it seemed like the kind of thing our dad would get a kick out of. Maybe that was reason enough.

"So," I said. Phoebe's expression was frozen somewhere between disappointment and irritation. "Is it everything you hoped it would be?"

"I don't know what I was hoping for," she replied. "But nope."

"He's pretty big," I offered.

She made a face. "I mean. Sure."

"He's a world record holder. That's cool."

"I'm underwhelmed."

Dex said, "It looks like he's doing a Nazi salute."

Phoebe laughed. I wheeled around, fixing him with a look. "He's *waving*," I said. He shrugged blithely, a bead of sweat working its way from his temple, arcing down his jawline.

"Right." His dark eyes pierced me in place before shifting to my sister and quickly back again. I blinked away as he asked, "We done?"

Phoebe looked at Dex, her eyes going soft, lip beginning to jut. His expression remained impressively neutral.

"No," he said.

"But this sucked!" she cried.

"You picked it."

"I want to trade it in for something else."

"We're already here. You can't trade it in."

"Please?"

"No."

"I won't make you listen to any more of my playlists." Phoebe threw on a dazzling smile, sweetening the deal. "We can ride the rest of the way in silence. Or you can listen to boring podcasts, if that's what you're into."

I bit the inside of my cheek, anticipating the wrinkle in his brow. "I don't listen to podcasts," he said stiffly.

Phoebe brushed a sweaty piece of hair out of her face. "Audiobooks, then."

He walked away. Phoebe deflated, eyes dimming, looking more like the kid I'd take out for ice cream after she scraped her knee than the surly teen who rolled her eyes when I said *good morning*. My palms itched with that familiar Phoebe-pleaser habit.

"Hey, go stand next to Yogi so I can take a picture."

She sneered. "Why?"

"Because it's fun." She rolled her eyes. "And Dad would think it's hilarious."

"Dad thought *Two and a Half Men* was hilarious," she muttered.

I waved this off. "Yeah, he had a terrible sense of humor. Just go. I'll grab the camera."

She let out a dramatic groan and stomped toward Yogi, grass audibly crunching. I smiled, despite the sweat dripping down my butt crack. Dex stood by the car tapping away on his phone with a grim expression behind his Ray-Bans, the back of his button-up soaked through.

"Ready?" he asked as I approached. I leaned a shoulder against the metal and nearly cried out; I peeled myself off, rubbing at the burn.

Dex's attention remained on his phone.

"Hey," I said. My reflection blinked back at me in his sunglasses; it looked like I'd just finished running a marathon. "Don't you think—"

"No."

"Come on, man, you know Yogi sucks."

"I could've told you that an hour ago," he said flatly. "Oh, wait. I did."

This might've been true, but I had no recollection of it. I'd spent a lot of time tuning him out considering he spoke exclusively in grunts and complaints. And then he proved that to be patently untrue, and the tuning out turned into something more like oblivion, where rather than listening to a single word out of his mouth, I stared at the faint lines by his eyes, remembering what it was like to watch him earn them.

Something had shifted in that elevator. We'd laughed until we cried, missing our floor twice before finally stumbling to our room. Dex's face seemed frozen in that smile and I'd stared, drinking it in. In the morning, I'd wondered if it was a dream, but as we checked out, Dex leaned against the pink desk and smiled right at me.

"That felt so fucking good," he'd said softly, like a secret. It set my every vein aflame. And we got back on the road without a mention of the hesitation he broached last night.

So we were friends. Ish. In the friends realm, or somewhere in that vicinity.

Dex glanced down the road, the tendons in his neck pulling taut, shiny with sweat. I averted my gaze, focusing on Phoebe as she squatted down to inspect something in the grass.

I withdrew my phone from my shorts, his words lighting a fire in my gut. I squinted at the dark screen, attempting to tap it awake, but the glare from the sun made it impossible. "Come here," I said, beckoning Dex. He looked at me, expression stony. "I need you. Your size, I mean. Height."

Heat ripped up my neck, sizzling my cheeks. The sun had gotten to me. Ignoring the embarrassing drivel, Dex stepped forward—he smelled fresh, as if damp from a shower instead of sweat. His form blocked most of the gleam so I could at least punch in my code. Still, I had to lean in close to make out anything clearly. In the middle of mistyping "cool things near me" in the search box, Dex's hand curled over the top of my phone to shield it further, his veins spiking like the inner workings of an umbrella. I had to reread the typo-ridden search to remind myself what the hell I was doing.

I'd always been a sucker for hands.

"Hey!" Phoebe's voice cut through the rustling leaves and chirping insects. Dex and I swiveled to find her standing near Yogi, hands up in a what-the-hell gesture. "Are you taking a picture or not?"

I reached through the open window to grab Dad's camera from the back seat. "Compromise," I said again, glancing at

Dex. "Maybe nothing's around here, but there must be something along the route. Take a wrong turn by the world's largest spool of thread."

"She's not interested in Yogi but sure, a spool of thread."

"I'm open to suggestions."

He lifted one shoulder in a shrug. I took it as a win.

The moment Dad's camera spat out the Polaroid, Phoebe darted over, huffing and red-faced.

"Air-conditioning," she gasped.

"What she said," Dex agreed.

A few hours and a looped playlist later, we made it to the hotel in Toledo. Not a smidge of pink to be found.

Phoebe and I shared a suite with two queen beds and a view of the parking lot, while Dex had a room to himself on an entirely different floor, apparently having anticipated needing space when he made the reservation. With glorious air-conditioning and a bed fluffy enough to keep memories of the floor at bay, I couldn't complain. But Phoebe could.

"This is so *boring*," she moaned. Her hair was damp from a dip in the pool downstairs; I'd let her go while I showered, suppressing a panic attack as I imagined her getting kidnapped at a Hilton. (Arden talked me down until Phoebe returned forty minutes later.)

"Watch TV," I said from under the covers, fully tucked in at 8 P.M.

"There's nothing to watch."

"Order a movie."

"They'll charge Dex."

"So?"

"There aren't any movies I want to watch, anyway," she

mumbled. I snuggled farther into the stiff pillow, inhaling the generic detergent; it wasn't a thousand fluffy Sherpa blankets laid out by a moody companion, but it would suffice. "Ugh. I should've stayed at the pool longer, but Dex said I shouldn't leave you alone for that long."

My eyes snapped open. "Dex was at the pool?"

"Yeah." She was lying in bed, legs crossed, inspecting her chipped nail polish. "I thought maybe he'd be up for a swim. He was."

I sat up, blinking. "You invited him? And he went?"

She shot me an annoyed look. "Yeah? We're friends."

I tried to imagine my dad's face if he knew Phoebe's only friend was a thirty-one-year-old man we met through mail fraud. Something told me he wouldn't find it as funny as everything else.

"I can't imagine Dex swimming," I said. Then another wave of shirtless Dex fantasies thundered through my brain—the lean muscles in his back, his olive skin, that little bit of hair I glimpsed when he unbuttoned his collar. Cheeks warm, I mentally slapped myself for the bad thoughts in general, but especially with Phoebe ten feet away. "Did he wear one of those nineteen-fifties bathing suits?"

"He told me he almost drowned in a pool when he was a kid. His brother saved his life."

"He told you that?"

"Yes." She shot me another look. "We're *friends*."

"Does Dex know you're friends?" I asked, and she cracked a smile.

"He has a soft spot for me," she said, stretching her legs to cross them at her ankles. "Just kids in general, probably. I mean, he works with kids for a living. Supposedly."

I smiled. "Supposedly."

"The more I get to know him, the easier it is to see." Her voice grew a bit softer and her index finger dug at the nail polish of her thumbnail. "The guy who wrote the letter and broke so bad that he just, like, reprogrammed his entire world."

Something in my chest twisted. "Yeah."

"Do you think he still loves her? Catalina?"

Whatever twisted in my chest pulled taut. I rubbed at my solar plexus, blinking furiously. "Oh. Uh, I don't know."

"I mean, would he go through all this if he didn't?"

"Maybe. I don't know."

"I wonder if she's single. I wonder if she was as broken as he was."

"It seemed like a pretty intense breakup, so," I muttered. I felt her look over, but I rolled onto my back and stared hard at the ceiling.

"Have you thought about dating again?" she asked, startling a laugh out of me.

"What? No." I twisted around, taking in the innocent curiosity in her expression. I didn't trust it. "Why would you ask me that?"

"I don't know," she said. "It's been a while, is all."

"You don't know that. Arden tries to set me up all the time."

"*Tries.*"

"It doesn't matter," I said, lying back and folding my arms over my chest. "I have other things to worry about. Dating isn't a priority."

"Right." Bitterness dug into Phoebe's tone. "Whatever."

She grabbed the remote off the nightstand between our beds and turned on the TV, filling the room with the laughter of a studio audience. I listened to her flip through the channels, biting back a complaint because that's what she wanted. I'd annoyed her. I didn't even know *how*. She opened up a crack and I said the wrong thing; it was so exhausting, the consistent failure. I was almost tempted to try out Dex's apathy since that seemed to work wonders on her.

Three things: *A bed to sleep in, shirtless Dex fantasies.*

The fantasies counted as two things because they were so fucking good.

Phoebe paused the channel surfing on Bill Murray's voice. I recognized the movie in less than a heartbeat. I snapped upright, eyes filling.

"*Caddyshack,*" she murmured, lowering the remote to her lap. I swallowed hard, blinking to clear my blurry vision.

"God. He watched this, what? Twice a year?" I said.

"At *least.*"

"He wanted to name you Spackler."

"I've never known a more annoying man."

I laughed and swiped at my eyes quickly, hoping she wouldn't notice. In my periphery, I noticed her do the same, and my heart squeezed tight. I asked, "Remember when he lost a bet and almost got Bill Murray's face tattooed on his ass?"

"Yes." She glanced at me, her smile lighting up the room. "I don't think there was a bet. I think he just wanted that tattoo."

"You might be onto something."

Her smile faded and she turned her attention to the screen, teeth digging into her bottom lip. "Do you think . . ." She paused, curling her hands into tight fists. "Do you think he'd be mad at me?"

"What?" My ears buzzed, almost like she'd shouted the words through a megaphone. "Why would he be mad?"

"For everything I did," she said softly. "Since he died."

"No," I said and got to my feet. "Out of everyone in the world, he would get it. He gets it. Phoebe, there's nothing either of us could do that would change how he felt about us." I approached her bedside and brushed a piece of hair behind her ear. My blood seemed to warm when she didn't flinch away. "And that goes for me, too. Hate to break it to you, but there's nothing you can do that will make me love you less. You break an asshole's nose and I love you even harder."

She sniffled, keeping her eyes on the movie. "Whatever."

To lighten the load, I pinched her cheek. "My Bumble Bee."

"Stop." She jerked away, a small smile piercing through the darkness. "You're so annoying."

"I am my father's daughter."

She shifted, drawing her legs underneath her. "He wouldn't have let us do this, though," she said. "This trip."

"He would've realized the letter wasn't for us and moved on with his day," I replied. She nodded, accepting this, and then perked up as the scene on-screen changed.

"Oh, wait. This is the best part."

She scooched over, silently inviting me to sit beside her. Maybe it was another step forward preceding a dozen steps back, or maybe it was simply my sister reaching out. Either way, I sat.

Twelve

Phoebe and I were, first and foremost, Ocean State girlies. We needed the beach.

"Not a beach," Dex said, his Ray-Bans showcasing the glare of sunshine, sand, and families parked across the coastline of Lake Michigan with umbrellas and floaties. He'd been grumbling about the pit stop since we outvoted him at the hotel breakfast buffet.

"Close enough," Phoebe replied. She stripped down to her striped one-piece and bolted for the water. Dex watched, wrinkling his nose in disgust.

"She's going to *swim*?"

I peeled off my shirt and tossed it in the sand. "Dude, it's ninety degrees," I said, adjusting my bikini top. He slowly turned, my body reflected in the lenses. My face went hot. "You should swim, too. It's good for you."

"Pass," he said. I rolled my eyes and shoved my shorts down to my ankles. He turned away, folding his arms tightly over his chest. "It's filthy, you know."

"Filthy, you say."

"The Great Lakes in general are incredibly polluted."

"Tell me more."

That muscle in his jaw jumped and a flicker of satisfaction sparked to life in my chest—I loved getting a rise out of him. "Don't let me stop you," he said stiffly. I sauntered off, grinning over my shoulder.

"Wouldn't dream of it."

It *wasn't* the beach, at least not like I knew it. Coarse sand squished between my toes, and the calm wake rolling in to greet me had nothing on breaking waves, but something about the air smelled the same, even if it lacked salt. I followed Phoebe into the water, bracing against the chill as goose bumps ripped down my limbs.

"Fuck, that's cold," I said as the water lapped at my belly. Phoebe floated on her back, the sun warming her face.

"You get used to it quick."

"I've never been in a lake before."

"Me neither. It's nice, not having to worry about sharks or jellyfish."

"Are there no jellyfish in lakes?" We shared a quizzical look. "No, you're right. I think."

She straightened, pink hair slick against her temples as she cupped her hands around her mouth and shouted, "DEX! COME HERE!"

"Jesus," I said. "Was that necessary?"

She ignored me, watching Dex lift a hand to rub his eyes beneath his sunglasses and then slowly move toward us, taking care to keep a safe distance between himself and the water.

"What," he said.

"Are there lake jellyfish? No, right?"

"If I say yes, can we leave?"

"Dex."

He sighed heavily and pulled his phone out of his pocket. His brow pinched and he bit the corner of his lip as he typed, and I loved that he was googling this ridiculous thing for my sister instead of telling her to fuck off, like I might've thought he would a few days ago.

"Yes," he answered, lifting his gaze from his phone. Phoebe froze.

"Wait, really? Or are you just saying that?"

"There are freshwater jellyfish in Lake Michigan." He slipped his phone into his pocket and placed his hands on his hips, regarding the water with disdain. "You about done?"

Phoebe sank to her shoulders, eyes wide as she scanned the lake for any sign of something resembling a jellyfish. I spotted a plastic bag down the shore a ways, and hoped it didn't make its way over.

"Freshwater jellyfish," she repeated in horror. I nodded.

"Yeah. The world is kind of a nightmare."

"They don't sting," Dex offered. She looked at him, her eyebrows flying upward.

"Really?"

"Apparently."

She considered this, running a hand over the water. "Huh. I wonder if that means there are freshwater sharks, too."

I immediately drew my knees to my chest. "Definitely not. Right? No?"

We both looked to Dex. He let out an aggrieved sigh and once again reached for his phone.

"This is fun," Phoebe said, sending me a wide smile. I couldn't help smiling back.

"No sharks," Dex reported.

I relaxed, dissolving into the water with renewed enthusiasm.

Phoebe shot me a grin. "How many more things do you think we could get him to look up?"

I considered this. "At least three."

"Hey, Dex!" she shouted. "What about turtles? Are there turtles in Lake Michigan?"

His shoulders rose and fell.

"I don't know," Phoebe said, watching as he consulted his phone a third time. "I kind of think he'd look up anything we asked."

"Lots of turtles," Dex told us. "Including snapping turtles."

"Nope." I shot toward the sand. "Sorry. No."

Hot on my heels, Phoebe said, "No, yeah, I was done any-way."

We kicked up sand on the way past Dex and his satisfied little smirk.

"Stop looking at me like that."

"I can't help it. You swam in Lake Michigan." Dex shud-dered, flexing his hands against the wheel. In the back seat, Phoebe dozed, face tinged pink from the sun. "We should stop at an ER to get you guys tested."

"Fuck off," I said with a laugh. He glanced over and I saw my own grin in his Ray-Bans before I noticed the corner of his mouth tipping upward. "God forbid you enjoy a day at the beach."

"Not a beach."

"It wasn't the ocean, but it was a beach."

"It wasn't the ocean and, therefore, shouldn't count as a beach."

"Sand, sky, water."

"That's the criteria to qualify as a beach in Violet-land?"

"Yes, dick, it is." I laughed again, brushing a knuckle against my aching cheek. The smiling was out of control. "Would you swim at a Dex-land qualified beach?"

"Depends," he answered with only a beat's hesitation. I shifted in my seat, facing him. Three and a half hours in a car, plus a pit stop at the beach, and his shirt remained perfectly pressed, though his stubble was a bit more pronounced than his typical five o'clock shadow. I decided it was a good length on him, and, just for a second, I let myself imagine what it would feel like to drag my hands across it. My fingernails. My lips.

Nope. Second over.

"On?" I pressed. He brushed his index finger over his top lip and I watched, mesmerized. Damn those hands.

"Rip currents."

"Rip currents?" I tilted my head. "That's . . . logical. I guess."

"It is logical," he said decisively. I narrowed my eyes, watching him rub his lip once more before returning his hand to the wheel.

"You can swim, right? I mean, you swam in the hotel pool with Phoebe, so I know you can. But she did say you almost drowned when you were a kid."

He turned sharply toward me. "She told you that?"

"It was a weird night. We watched our dad's favorite movie," I said. His fingers drummed against the wheel and he turned his attention to the road.

"I can swim," he muttered. "I've even been known to enjoy a day at the beach."

I pressed my lips together, my cheeks feeling like they might split open if I let myself smile again. "I can't imagine you at the beach."

"You literally—" He cut himself off with a cough.

I let out a sharp laugh, pointing in his face. "Ha! So you admit it's a beach!"

"I didn't say that."

"You were totally going to say it."

"I like the beach," he said casually, sidestepping his wrongness. Didn't matter. I'd be riding this high for the rest of the day. "I grew up near the beach."

He so rarely volunteered information about himself, I took a solid ten seconds to map out a response. "You did?" I needed to know more. Everything, even. "Us too. Where did you grow up?"

"Uh." He glanced at me quickly, perhaps having revealed this fact unwittingly. "Mattapoisett."

"Warwick," I said, pointing to myself. "Not too far, actually."

"No. Not too far." He adjusted his grip on the wheel, casting me a sidelong glance. "Why Boston, then? The Harbor is about as much a beach as Lake Michigan."

"I met a guy."

"Ah."

"And then I got a job. And it made sense for a long time."

"But it doesn't anymore."

I flinched and rubbed my nose. "I didn't say that," I mumbled, glancing at Phoebe. She was still napping, a hoodie bunched up under her head for a pillow. "It's complicated."

"In what way?"

"Why are we even talking about this? Let's circle back to whether or not you know how to swim."

"Because of Phoebe?" he guessed. I swallowed tightly.

"Obviously because of Phoebe."

"She didn't want to move to Boston?"

"I shouldn't have let her move to Boston." The words flew

out before I'd fully comprehended them. I exhaled sharply and glanced over my shoulder to ensure she hadn't woken up. She looked so peaceful, unaware of the turmoil ripping through my brain. "Shit. I didn't mean to say that out loud."

He said nothing, keeping his attention on the road. I toyed with a thread hanging from my shorts and counted to twenty before the word-vomit rose up my throat.

"She had a life," I whispered. "I think I really fucked up, taking her to Boston. Neither of us could stand staying at our dad's, but there were other options. I shouldn't have . . . I think I fucked up."

"You were grieving."

"Yeah, okay, but I was in charge of a teenager, so I didn't have the luxury of grieving, you know? I should've pushed it down and focused on her. It wasn't my turn to grieve."

His knuckles went white against the wheel. I wouldn't have noticed if I wasn't staring at his hands.

"I took her away from her life and now she's miserable, and she hates me for it. She hates me."

"She doesn't hate you."

"Well, she should." I squeezed my eyes shut and scrubbed my hands down my face. "I'm sorry. I'm doing that thing again, where I unload shit on you. I don't know why I do it."

"I asked," he said. I dropped my hands, staring hard at the side of his face. His stubble snaking down to his neck, a lock of hair curling around the arm of his glasses.

It should've been criminal, how gorgeous he was.

"She said you're friends," I said. He shrugged. "Are we friends?"

"Is that what this is?"

His soft tone sent something molten slithering through my insides. I took a shallow breath and replied, "I don't know."

He reached up, tugging his fingers through his hair. "I don't think you fucked up, moving her to Boston," he said. A zip of hope soared through my chest. I'd heard virtually the same thing a hundred times over from a hundred different mouths over the last year. Somehow it meant more, here, now, from *this* mouth.

"You don't?" I asked.

"I think you need to talk about this with her."

I pantomimed throwing up with my hand. "Have you ever tried having a serious conversation with a fourteen-year-old?"

"Yes," he said. "It's my job."

"Oh, right. Sorry. Your 'job.'" I threw up air quotes with my fingers and he shot me a perplexed look. "Maybe you should talk to her about this, then."

"I have," he replied. My jaw dropped. "I'm better at keeping secrets than she is."

"Why does she talk to you?" I asked. "She won't talk to me. Why does she talk to you but not me?"

"Why are you talking to me, not her?" he countered. I rolled my eyes and shifted to face away from him.

"*'Why are you talking to me, not her?'*" I echoed in an excessively whiny voice. "That's you."

He snorted. "Uncanny."

All annoyance evaporated at once. I could make him laugh again, and maybe things wouldn't be so bad.

"Hey," I said. He looked over, and even though I couldn't see his eyes, I felt the weight of them pressing in on me. "*Can* you swim?"

"Yes." He smiled. My breath snagged in my throat. "I'm the kind of person who almost drowns and makes a point to become a really good swimmer."

"He's not that good," Phoebe murmured from the back seat. "He held his nose when he jumped in the pool."

In the battle between horror that Phoebe was awake and delight over this new revelation, delight won out. I fell into hysterics.

"I did not," Dex said indignantly.

"You totally did."

I bonked my head into the window, giggling. "We should get him one of those nose plugs kids use when they're learning to swim."

Phoebe snorted, and then laughed outright. "Some floaties for his wittle arms."

"Maybe we'll get a kiddie pool for you to practice in."

"Hilarious," he said flatly. "You know, some people don't know how to swim, and they would find this incredibly insulting. And obnoxious."

Phoebe and I lost our shit.

I didn't intend to take my sister to a gay bar in Chicago. It's just that intention means very little when teenagers are involved.

"It's not the best thing in the world," Arden said, raising her voice over the pulsing music. Elbows on the table, I had my phone clamped to one ear, my hand over the other to hear my best friend reassure me that I wasn't the worst guardian on the planet. But with two women on the dance floor dry humping to Celine Dion as Phoebe sat beside me looking on with wide-eyed elation, Arden's words lacked a certain gravitas. "But is it the worst? No."

"It's not great," I maintained. Over at the bar, Dex waited for our drinks, arms crossed, expression stony. I counted a dozen sets of eyes locked on him.

"Maybe not. But is Phoebe happy?"

"Yes."

"Is she drinking?"

"No."

"Then I don't see the problem."

The problem wasn't necessarily the gay bar, but my inability to guide Phoebe in a way that mattered. She took hold of the wheel in our dad's hospital room and had been steering ever since; I may have been her official guardian as far as the state was concerned, yet I had less power over Phoebe than TikTok. She played me, every day. Worse, I let her. When we got to the hotel and she began lamenting about how bored she was, and how the sun hadn't even set yet, and we were the most boring people on earth for having nothing to do in a city like this, I gave in. She wasn't wrong, exactly, but that's not why I threw on my sneakers and led her down the hall to Dex's room to inform him we were heading out.

She hadn't hinted at it and I hadn't asked, but I knew in my gut Phoebe had heard me talking to Dex. How I believed I fucked up, that she hated me, that she had a right to. Our dad wasn't perfect, and he probably messed up millions of times. He never said it out loud, though. Not within earshot. I didn't have it together like him. I slipped up, admitting my faults and fears in front of Phoebe and proceeded to do nothing to fix them. The mortification burned.

I might not have Phoebe's respect, but I could win her over by letting her do whatever she wanted. And tonight, she wanted this.

"No, yeah," I said, swapping my phone to my other ear. Beside me, Phoebe was scrolling through the restaurant's app that connected to the speakers, picking songs to add to the queue. "That's what matters, I guess."

"You're not bad at this," Arden insisted. I made a face. At the bar, a large man covered in tattoos sidled up to Dex, and several people drooped in visible disappointment.

"I'm not *good* at it."

"Well, you've been doing it less than a year. Nobody who's had their first kid for under a year is good at it."

I opened my mouth and snapped it shut. "Huh."

"Boom! Wisdom."

"Okay, you ruined it a little."

She laughed. At the bar, Dex also laughed at something the tattooed man said, and my stomach dropped so violently, I gasped. The music drowned out the sound, but Phoebe glanced at me, brow furrowing.

"Wow," I said. "Dex is getting hit on at the bar and I think he's into it."

Phoebe stretched up in her seat to get a better view. Arden said, "Oh my god. It's like he's human or something."

I swallowed, unable to tear my eyes from the bar. The bartender set our drinks in front of Dex, who remained focused on the tattooed dude, his expression content for the first time since I knocked on his door an hour ago.

"I should go," I said. Arden replied in less than a beat.

"What's wrong?"

"What? Nothing. I'm at a gay bar in Chicago. How could anything be wrong?"

"You're doing the thing."

"What thing?"

"The thing when you're sad but you don't want anyone to know you're sad, so you overcompensate with enthusiasm."

I cleared my throat. "Oh, you know what? I think the bar is going through a tunnel."

"Violet!"

I made an obnoxious crackling sound and hung up, marginally cheered by Phoebe laughing through her nose. I'd pay for hanging up on Arden, but for now, I needed to avoid the third degree.

Diverting my focus from the bar, I watched Phoebe scan the vicinity for the tenth time since we arrived. The place itself was cool, lots of exposed brick and timber with bright accents in the lights and artwork. It seemed to balance on a tightrope between bar and nightclub, definitely the kind of place I would've frequented in college, or even today if I was both single and looking for Something. A partner, good times, a break.

I stole another glance at the bar just in time to see a bartender emerge from the back and unleash a scream that had everyone in the vicinity whipping around as she flew over to Dex and threw her arms around him.

"Wow," Phoebe said. "So he's, like, *known* here."

I'd realized this earlier, when the bouncer recognized Dex and allowed us immediate entry. I'd made several attempts to interrogate him, but he changed the subject or excused himself from the table each time. Now, he was caught in a hug with a hot lesbian bartender, and he clutched her like she was so much more than that.

What was up with this guy? My mind's version of him morphed into something new each time his vault of secrets cracked open: perpetually angry asshole with a sketchy job; the guy who follows you to an orgy and laughs until he cries in the elevator; beloved former patron of a Chicago gay bar. I couldn't keep up.

"Hey." Phoebe shoved my arm and jerked her chin at Dex. "Go see what that's about."

"No," I said, scowling. She scowled right back.

"Why?"

"I'm not leaving you alone in a bar." Laughter drifted over from across the room and I recognized the rusty creak of Dex's. I slumped in my seat, folding my arms tight. "And it's none of my business."

"Since when has that ever stopped you?" she replied. "You can't not be curious. Dex is like a hero here."

"He is not," I said, just as someone burst through the doors with a loud whoop, heading straight for the growing group at the bar. "What the hell?"

"This is crazy," Phoebe said. "It's almost like Dex used to be fun."

A surprising stab of protectiveness erupted in my chest. "Dex is fun."

"In an unfun way, sure. Maybe he went to college here or something. Did he go to college, do you think?"

I had no idea. The gap of knowledge sent a cool rush through my blood. I could only shrug in response.

"So weird," she murmured. "He's like a different person. Is this the real him? Was he a guy who had fun in gay bars before he dumped Catalina?" She shook her head, her tone quiet and thoughtful. "A broken heart doesn't do this, does it? Change you like that?"

"No," I said softly, watching as they passed Dex around as if he was the prodigal son. Phoebe made a decent point; broken hearts do a lot of damage, but I'd never seen one calcify the way Dex's seemed to, especially considering the evidence indicating he hadn't always been apathetic and cold. The more time we spent together, the easier it was to spot the whispers of his past self. And somehow in a gay bar in Chicago, a scream broke through.

It took ten minutes for Dex to excuse himself and return with our drinks. He sat across from us and took a sip of water, taking a leisurely look around the room. Phoebe and I stared expectantly.

"It's pretty loud," he stated.

Phoebe rolled her eyes and reached for her water. I practically dove for my mojito. My rioting brain needed to be snuffed out for the night.

"What was that about?" I asked.

Dex avoided eye contact. "What?"

"That." I jerked my chin toward the bar, where the hot bartender and several others ogled us. "You're known here."

"I asked if you've ever been to Chicago and you said, 'A couple times,'" Phoebe pointed out. "You liar."

He bristled. "I didn't think it mattered."

"Of course it matters! If you've been to Chicago like it looks like you've been to Chicago, you know all the cool places." She paused, stirring her drink with her straw. "Well, some. You're not that cool."

He slugged down more water, his dark expression a far cry from the unmistakable joy he'd emitted at the bar. The dude was so closed off, he refused to tell us he had at one point (Clearly? Presumably?) lived in Chicago even though we were in Chicago. It stung, him keeping us at arm's length. I'd overshared my little heart out. Not necessarily to put us on even ground after reading the letter, but it couldn't have hurt to show him I had baggage too. Now, I realized it didn't seem to help either.

"Be honest," Phoebe said, shooting Dex a wry smile. "Did you used to be fun?"

"I used to be a lot of things," he muttered. "This is Bree's place."

"And Bree is . . ."

"Behind the bar."

Phoebe bent over to bonk her head on the table. "You are the most annoying person in the world, oh my god. Stop being evasive for once in your goddamn life." Dex looked at her, his eyebrows inching upward. "I promise no one cares if you used to live in Chicago, or if you have friends, or if you have the ability to actually smile. The broody douchebag thing is getting old, man. You're almost fifty."

"I'm thirty-one," he reminded her. She let out strangled moan and lifted her head, fixing him with the flattest look imaginable.

"That's too old for the bullshit."

I sipped my drink, unsure of whether I wanted to agree with Phoebe or defend Dex, and then someone crashed into my chair, sending my mojito down the front of my T-shirt. I jumped to my feet, chair clattering, the cold zipping down to my bones.

"Shit!" I gasped at the same time Dex growled, "What the fuck?"

"Sorry, sorry!" A group of twentysomething girls decked out in lacy veils and penis-shaped jewelry giggled their way past. Of course a gay bar would be their ideal choice for a bachelorette party. I let the irritation burn, if only because the copper mug had kept my drink too cold.

"Bitches," Phoebe said. One of the girls hiccuped, eyes widening, and hurried off. "How self-absorbed do you have to be to have your bachelorette party at a gay bar?"

"Maybe she was bi," I said, pinching my shirt and pulling the damp cloth farther from my skin.

"Those were the most sexually repressed girls I've ever seen," Phoebe replied, looking to Dex for support. "Obviously straight."

"Fuckers," Dex muttered. When he turned to me, his eyes dropped to my drenched shirt and immediately to the ceiling. "You, uh." He coughed. "You good?"

I glanced at my shirt to find my bra on full display. "Oh, awesome." Phoebe took a look at me and snickered into her water. "Are we almost ready to go?"

"What?" Phoebe nearly dropped her drink. "We just got here!"

"Yeah, but I think busting the tits out before midnight is frowned upon in most establishments."

"Change your shirt!"

"All my shirts are at the hotel."

"Come on," Dex said gruffly, pointedly staring over my shoulder. "I have a shirt in the car."

Something significant bloomed in my chest, and I focused on the sprig of relief, deciding it was safest. "Cool, thanks. Come on, Phoebe."

She scowled. "Why do I have to go?"

"I'm not leaving you alone in a bar."

Her scowl deepened. Dex said, "Come with me."

Phoebe's sour face disappeared in a flash of light, and she hopped to her feet without protest. I gave Dex a searching look and he tipped his head slightly, indicating I should follow as well. He led us to the bar where the woman he'd hugged waited for us with a luminous smile.

"This is Bree," Dex said. Her smile only widened at his deadpan delivery and she reached over the bar to shake both our hands. Bree was shorter than both of us, but carried herself in such a way that she seemed tall. Her dark brown skin was dewy, glowing, and tattoos snaked down both arms. "This is Violet and Phoebe."

"Bree Calloway," she said, looking between Phoebe and me. "It's very nice to meet you. I've heard a lot."

My eyes cut to Dex. "Really?"

"From our friend, Gavin," Bree clarified. "Would you believe I've put up with Dex's shit for like fifteen years and he couldn't be bothered to fill me in?"

"Fifteen years?" Phoebe's eyes widened. "That's longer than I've been alive."

"Let's pretend you didn't say that so I don't have to kick you out of my bar."

Dex rapped his knuckles on the counter. "Can you watch her for a sec? We need to get a clean shirt from the car."

Bree flashed me a grin. "I'm such a gentleman. I didn't even look."

I couldn't help laughing, even as a tiny rush of anxiety blew through me at the thought of leaving Phoebe alone with a virtual stranger, charming as she may be. I touched Phoebe's shoulder as she parked herself on one of the stools. "Are you good?"

"I'm awesome. Bree, is there anything frozen I can legally drink?"

"Kid, I've got mocktails on mocktails. What's your poison? Strawberry? Cherry? I'm a pineapple gal, myself."

Dex's fingers wrapped around my upper arm, gently tugging me toward the exit. I kept glancing over my shoulder, watching Phoebe beaming in Bree's presence. I wasn't sure I'd ever seen her posture so perfect.

"I hope I didn't overstep," Dex said quietly, his fingers gently squeezing my arm. My pulse synced up with the thumping bass in the speakers. "Bree is one of my closest friends. I don't trust anyone more than I trust her. Phoebe is safe with her. I promise."

It meant something to me that Dex cared for Phoebe and me enough to follow us out into the city after hours of driving when all he wanted to do was sleep. His unshakable trust meant even more.

"I trust you," I said, surprised by just how much I meant it. He kept his hand on my arm until we were outside. The air had cooled with the sinking sun, sending a chill to my bones. I shivered and tugged at my damp T-shirt, holding it as far from my skin as it would stretch. Dex had parked his car nearby on a bustling street, passersby bumping us unapologetically until Dex was growling deep in his throat. I pretended not to be turned on by the sound.

Dex swung the trunk open and rifled around for a moment before emerging with a folded, perfectly pressed gray button-up. I bit back a smile and said, "I shouldn't be surprised you keep spare shirts in your car."

"I keep clean shirts in my car," he amended, handing it off to me. The fabric was softer than it looked, like silk under my fingertips. "For this exact reason."

"Do women often get drinks spilled on their boobs in your presence?"

That muscle in his jaw jumped. "Can we get back to the bar? You can—Jesus!"

I'd tugged my wet shirt over my head in the middle of his sentence, unable to take the stench of rum anymore. Dex immediately grabbed my waist, his hand hot and rough against the soft skin, and tugged me closer to the car, blocking me from view of the sidewalk.

"What are you doing?" he demanded.

I laughed shortly, wishing I couldn't still feel his handprint burned into my skin. "What's the big deal? You saw me in a bathing suit yesterday."

"The entirety of Chicago didn't."

I studied him, locking on the rosy flush inching up his neck, his hands now clenched at his sides. He was attracted to me and he *hated* it. Blinding euphoria engulfed me—I almost giggled out loud. Suddenly, it wasn't inappropriate or unfair for me to fantasize about Dex, it was normal. We were two hot adults on a road trip together. Of course thoughts would crop up.

I smiled and slipped his shirt on, deftly buttoning it from the bottom. "One time I posed nude for an art class," I told him. He turned sharply toward me, keeping his eyes trained on my face.

"Really."

"Mm-hmm. So there are at least twenty nude portraits of me in existence."

Something flared in his eyes, almost certainly recognizing why I was screwing with him. I took my time with the last buttons, biting my cheek to fend off a shit-eating grin, and then he leaned a shoulder against the car and lowered his gaze.

His eyes traveled down my body, his shirt hanging loosely from my frame, the flippy skirt showing off my legs, back up again. Lingering.

Fire engulfed me.

"You wanna know something funny?" he said.

I threw on a smile, as if his lazy perusal of my body hadn't turned me on more than my ex-boyfriend ever had. "You're going to tell me something funny? Oh, absolutely."

He shut the trunk of the car and brushed past me. "I posed nude for an art class too."

"Liar." I grinned, following him down the sidewalk. The bar sign flickered in the distance. "You're lying, right? You have to tell me if you're lying."

He smiled in a way that told me he relished my curiosity and could stoke it until it crackled into a consuming blaze, leaving nothing but ash. But *god,* that smile.

I'd let him.

Thirteen

We left the bar thirty minutes before midnight. Head swirling from half a mojito and the sharp scent of Dex's shirt, I walked to the hotel in a daze, listening to my sister prattle on about how awesome Bree was, the community of it all, how crazy that Dex was a part of it. My head was swimming and every inch of my skin felt tender, bruised. It had been a long night.

Bree did most of the talking. She moved to Massachusetts from London at fifteen, earning attention from classmates as the worldly newbie and obvious lesbian. I watched Phoebe hang on every word as Bree told us about the bullying she endured and her struggles finding a safe place for herself, and I nearly lost my breath when Phoebe admitted she'd been dealing with the same thing at her new school. My sister was being bullied. Twelve meetings with Principal Chambers and only the last one hinted at anything close to this revelation. And considering the way Dex avoided my eyes, I was the only one out of the loop.

I'd spent a lot of time grappling with my bisexuality in high school, but I wasn't bullied. No one called me names. No one even really knew. I remembered the look on Phoebe's face when we came out to each other, like we were members of the same club, and now she looked at Bree with admiration, something so much more than simple camaraderie.

I wasn't enough in *any* way for her. And I hated myself for thinking such a shitty, selfish thing, especially when Bree and Phoebe were opening up and I was warping it in a what-about-me-ism I'd regret tomorrow, but I could feel myself hitting a low. My sister was going through hell, asking everyone but me for help, and it wrecked me.

Shoving down the pointless hurt feelings and unfair thoughts, I'd listened to Bree shift the topic to Dex. How the two fell into a friendship in detention and spent the rest of high school attached at the hip, then proceeded to attend the same local community college.

Floodgates didn't burst, but Bree unleashed a trickle of secrets: Dex finished his degree at Northeastern, and after graduation they moved to Chicago with a few friends, spending nearly two years in an apartment with a view of Lake Michigan. It was easy to see their deep bond when Dex allowed himself to retaliate Bree's teasing, and it filled my chest with a fizzy sort of feeling, like I'd drunk a gallon of Diet Coke.

Phoebe steered the conversation back to Bree's life in Chicago, and Bree seemed to have limitless patience, answering my sister's questions with such an easy confidence; I couldn't remember ever feeling that sure of myself, even at my best, but I recognized the spark in Phoebe's eyes like it had once been directed at me. Bree and Phoebe ended up in a rapid-fire back-and-forth with Dex chiming in every so often. I felt myself fading. By the time we reached our hotel, I was an inch tall and ready to cry my eyes out in the shower. Dex veered for his room, casting me one last look over his shoulder like he knew something was off. In our room, Phoebe spent another twenty minutes gushing over her new hero before passing out in bed.

Was it easier for parents? Or harder? Dealing with a child slipping out of reach because it's the kid's job to hate and grow and rebel and conquer. Parents intercept and guide. But siblings? *Sisters?* Maybe I would've been able to guide Phoebe in a way that mattered before I was the one obligated to. Ever since, I'd straddled those roles—sister, guardian—never quite inhabiting either. Phoebe needed me and I just watched.

Once Phoebe was asleep, I closed myself in the bathroom, pressing my forehead against the cool wood of the door, trying to breathe through the pain. The pain of failure and selfishness. The pain of missing my little sister who used to beg me to read to her before bed. The pain of missing my dad, who would've held me tight and told me tomorrow was a new day.

God, I missed him. The grief hit like crashing waves, another, then another, pulling me under. This happened, sometimes. I held on to the grief for too long and it blew up in an all-consuming way, overriding everything. I'd collapse to the floor and cry until I was dry heaving and I'd stay there, too tired to drag myself to my bed. I knew it would kill him to see me like that. For anyone to see me like that. And it would be mortifying to admit out loud in therapy that, almost a year later, grief still paralyzed me.

I sat on the floor of the shower, hugging my knees to my chest. Vision blurry. Head static. Breaths slow, staggered. The skin on my face felt tight even as warm water flowed down it, the quiet rush acting as white noise to ease the pulsing in my ears.

Pathetic.

I didn't have the luxury of passing out in the shower, so I forced myself to stand and shut off the water. My legs wobbled as I wrapped a towel around myself, skin raw, fingertips pruned. I wiped steam from the mirror and my cloudy reflection stared back, red eyes empty, aged a decade in a year.

And yet I'd grow. I'd probably get old, wrinkled, gray, and my dad never would.

But that was a breakdown for another time, so I dried off and pulled on my pajamas, my tired limbs fighting each step through the hotel room. Phoebe snored peacefully, face buried in the pillow. My bed remained pristinely made, almost stiff. I stood beside it, knowing I would stare at the ceiling until the sun rose.

A soft knock came from the door. It was nearing 2:00 A.M. I shuffled over, knowing it would be Dex even before I opened it and found him standing there in a black T-shirt and sweatpants. His face, his presence, landed like a rescue plane touching down in a desert. Salvation, or something close to it.

If he noticed hints of my shower meltdown, he didn't show it. He pressed a palm to the doorframe, leaning on it, and said, "Do you want a drink?"

Tears pricked my eyes again.

"God, yes, please," I replied. "But I don't know if I can leave Phoebe?"

"Twenty minutes." That Diet Coke feeling from earlier returned, taking over my gut as he persuaded me to spend time with him. "Put the Do Not Disturb sign up. She'll be fine."

I nodded. I knew she was out for the night, but I left a note anyway.

A few patrons sat around the hotel bar, none of them paying mind to the exhausted someones clad in pajamas. I bent forward to rest my head against the cool linoleum table as Dex got us drinks. I'd mumbled something about strawberry margaritas on the elevator ride down, the first drink I had on my twenty-first birthday made by my dad. It became a comfort drink, one I only turned to on really great days, or really lousy ones. When I turned my head and caught sight of Dex returning with two strawberry margaritas, I wondered which this night would turn out to be.

"Thank you," I said, sitting up as he set the glasses down. He sat across from me, eyes snagging mine. "For the drink and . . . this."

"Couldn't sleep." His fingers danced along the stem of his glass. "I figured you couldn't, either."

I reached for my margarita, squirming slightly. "Why?"

"You were weird at the bar."

"Was I that obvious?"

"No." His brow furrowed and he averted his gaze across the room. "I just noticed."

A warmth rose up my neck and I tucked a damp strand of hair behind my ear. To be noticed by him seemed like an extraordinary thing, a rare sort of occurrence that shifted the world off its axis.

A bit breathless, I blurted, "Bree's really nice. I like her a lot."

"She's something," he said and took a long pull from his drink. "She liked you too. And Phoebe."

"Phoebe adored her. She's everything she wants to be."

He looked at me, and I knew he understood.

"It's nothing," I said, waving off the shame and hurt feelings before he had the chance to offer wisdom or, worse, judgment. Because really, how awful was I for a stab of jealousy over my sister admiring someone else? Pathetic, selfish, cruel, small. Our mom bailed before Phoebe was out of premature onesies and our dad was dead; I should've welcomed any and all role models. "It got to me tonight. Whatever. I don't want to talk about it."

Dex nodded, running his finger along the rim of his glass. I watched it work its way around twice before crossing my legs and taking another sip of my drink.

"It's supposed to rain tomorrow," he said.

"What?"

"A storm." His flippant tone didn't sound ingenuine, but I knew him by now. "It's supposed to be pretty bad, I guess. High wind advisory."

"What is this? What are you doing?"

"Small talk. You like small talk."

"You don't."

He shrugged. Like it was no skin off his back to take part in something he hated, for me.

"You never answered me, you know," I said. His gaze grew more intense. "What do you consider us? Friends? Acquaintances? Am I the girl who fucked you over and you're counting the days until you never have to see me again?"

He smirked. "I invited you out for a drink."

"That doesn't mean anything."

"Violet." The way he said my name burned its way into my brain. "I like you."

"Good." I swallowed, but my throat had gone dry so I took a swig of my margarita. "It's just that with most people, I can tell. You're impossible to read."

"We wouldn't be here if I didn't."

"Here in the hotel bar? Or here in Chicago?"

He bit the corner of his lip and I was too tired, too tipsy, too captivated to not wonder how it would feel to have Dex's teeth sink into my lip, my shoulder, my thighs. *I like you,* I imagined him murmuring into my skin after each bite.

"You don't think they're mutually exclusive?" he asked lowly, leaning in over the table. I could feel my breath coming quicker—

I hoped he couldn't see my breasts heaving like a Regency heroine's.

"I think you like me more than you did when you agreed to this trip," I told him.

"I know you better," he said. "More to like."

I sat back in my chair, the compliment warming me to my blood. "Oh."

"Is that surprising?"

"A year ago, no." I dropped my gaze to the table. "I haven't felt very likable lately."

"Really?" He sounded surprised. "You're so fucking refreshing. You wear you heart on your sleeve in a way that's both admirable and terrifying." My pounding pulse blurred my vision with each beat. *You're so fucking refreshing.* I'd carry that with me for the rest of my life. "You yell at strangers in their place of work and try to seduce them into giving you personal intel."

My laugh transitioned into a groan. "God. I can't believe I did that. We should never talk about it again, starting now."

"That dress," he went on.

I crumpled up a napkin and threw it at him, and he laughed. My blood hit a boiling point. "Desperation makes you do crazy things."

His smile dimmed a few watts and he reached for his drink. "Oh, I'm aware."

I winced, thinking of the letter that brought us together in the first place. How devastated he must've been when he wrote it. The damage it did to never hear back. The fallout. Everything up to now, right this second.

"What happened?" I asked, the words slipping out unwittingly. "With you and Catalina?"

Dex gulped his drink, wincing. Was I asking too much of him? Here we were on a trip to return a letter he'd written to her and I hardly knew anything about their relationship aside from what I'd (possibly illegally) read in said letter. I didn't necessarily feel entitled to the information, but it did seem odd that Dex remained so protective of it when he was the one insisting it was over.

"Doesn't matter," he said, wiping his face clear of emotion. I sighed into another sip of my drink, disappointed in myself for even feeling disappointed. "Why do you think Sequest is sketchy?"

I laughed, prompting the line between his brows to deepen. "Because you drive a Mercedes? And you're paying for this entire trip? 'Money isn't an issue'?"

"That would make me sketchy, not Sequest."

"Well, you work there."

"Technically, yes."

"That's what I mean." I pointed at him. "*Sketchy.*"

He hid his smile behind the last sip of his margarita. When he offered to get us more, I agreed without hesitation, checking my phone to see if Phoebe had woken up, demanding to know why I'd gone out with Dex without her.

She hadn't.

When Dex returned, I steeled myself for the return of the brick wall and said, "Do I get to ask you something now?"

"You found out a lot about me tonight."

"Nobody cares that you used to live in Chicago," I said, which wasn't true, but it made him laugh, so my heart did a little flip. "Did you actually pose for an art class?"

He sank in his seat, hands flat on the table. The corner of his mouth quirked. "Yeah."

My face broke into a grin. "Oh my god. *Why?*"

"My brother dared me."

"You did something because someone dared you to?"

"I did something because my brother dared me to." He

traced the rim of his glass again, his mouth tipping in a smile. "When we were kids, he figured out I'd do pretty much anything to make him laugh and I never knew peace again."

"I wouldn't know anything about that," I deadpanned. His smile widened briefly, but then he gulped down some of his drink, a complicated sort of emotion flickering in his eyes. I refused to let him put that wall back up, not tonight. "Did you get any phone numbers? After the class?"

"Seven."

"Oh, you got me beat! I got five." I sat back in my chair and shook my head solemnly. "I guess you look better naked than I do."

He let his elbow rest on the back of his chair, eyes dark under the dim lights. "I can't imagine that's true."

A hundred degrees in a Midwest summer couldn't compare to this. An inferno spread through my body. I was half tempted to glance down and confirm my body remained intact rather than crumbling to ash around the legs of my chair.

I'd been under the impression we'd spend the rest of the trip aware of the mutual attraction and leave it at that, considering we were on our way to the woman he believed to be the love of his life. But Dex was throwing out the plan in favor of . . . what, exactly?

Fun?

A warm body until reuniting with the one he really wanted?

Blowing off steam after a shitty day? Week? *Year?*

Honestly, I should've been thrilled at the prospect; hot person, no strings, the best way to ease into the dating endeavor after being stagnant for so long. Dex would be good, too, if those hands were any indication. Low stakes, high reward.

But as Dex's eyes pinned me across the table, *low stakes* seemed like the last term I'd use to describe us.

I blinked away, throat bobbing. We were the last ones left in the bar, and I had no idea when that happened.

"It's late," I said, pushing out of my chair. "It's really late. Do hotel bars have last call? Because if so, we're probably cutting it close."

I reached for my margarita, dumping the rest down my throat in hopes it might dull the feeling of Dex's eyes boring into the side of my head.

I couldn't deny that I wanted him. Was sort of desperate for him, considering the amount of shirtless fantasies I'd indulged in, and all the staring at his hands. There were no consequences for admiring from a respectful distance. Making our way to the elevator with a handful of inches between us, I realized maybe the distance itself was a consequence. A necessary one, but it was so hard to remember why when Dex's eyes were on me.

Our footsteps echoed up into the ceiling of the empty lobby. We paused at the elevators, Dex hitting the call button.

"When was the last time you did this?" he asked. I must've been gaping at him because he felt the need to clarify: "Went out."

"Went out," I repeated. "Like, with a person?"

"As opposed to . . . ?"

I cleared my throat. "I don't know. A while," I mumbled, reaching up to rub my burning nose. "It's not something I can do."

"Because of Phoebe?"

I bit my lip as the doors opened up, shuffling inside, and when they slid shut, the air inside went with them. I leaned against the wall, dizzier than I had any right to be after two margaritas. Dex hit our floor number and leaned against the wall opposite, facing me, waiting for an answer.

"I mean, yeah. But also, I'm not exactly the ideal partner right now," I said, earning a flat look in return.

"Come on," he said. "Earlier, I listed a bunch of reasons why you're awesome."

I looked at him for a moment, feeling the weight of yet another compliment before tucking it away.

"It's not an easy pill to swallow," I explained, my voice softening as the elevator shifted underneath us. "Me having a fourteen-year-old at home."

"Who cares?"

"Who wouldn't?"

"You expect me to believe that someone is going to look at you," he said, emphasizing this like it was the be-all and end-all, "and decide the deal-breaker is your sister?"

"Believe it," I replied. "It happened."

His expression shifted into the impassive mask I hadn't seen much of lately. "Tell me," he said quietly, and that muscle in his jaw ticked.

He's angry, I thought almost wondrously.

"I was with someone when my dad died. Shawn. We lived together. We weren't engaged, but we were there. We looked at rings. And then . . ." I leaned my head back, bonking it against the metal, and shrugged. "He couldn't handle it."

"He couldn't handle it," Dex repeated, no longer attempting to hide the disgust.

"At first we—Phoebe and me—we couldn't stomach going back to Dad's, so she slept on the couch of our apartment," I said, eyes locked on our distorted reflections in the metal walls. "He started pushing me to take her back to my dad's within, like, a day and a half. And when I did, the calls and texts got fewer and farther between, and then he came from Boston one night to break up with me in person. Said it was too much, he didn't sign on for it."

"Christ," Dex muttered. "What a coward."

I didn't mention the delayed response I had to the breakup. How autopilot kept me moving until I was brushing my teeth three months later and the ache hit, a blinding pain, a visceral emptiness, a new sort of grief befriending the loss. I thought I would marry Shawn and he bailed on our life so easily, as if he had a bag packed the whole time. It was a lot to handle, Dad dying and my guardianship of Phoebe—a not-insignificant part of me understood why Shawn left. So many people in my life called him a coward, but sometimes I couldn't help wondering if I should've given him an out.

"Vi." My head snapped up, meeting Dex's dark eyes under the fluorescent elevator lights. Something about him calling me *Vi* tied up my insides like a balloon animal, all twisted and ready to pop. "That guy was an asshole. You didn't deserve that, and neither did Phoebe. But that's not how every person will react to your situation."

We were closer. When had I left my wall? I'd assumed it was the only thing keeping me upright.

"Maybe," I said softly "Doesn't really matter."

"No?"

I could smell him. The sharp scent of his soap mingling with the sweetness of strawberry and tequila. I wished I could curate a cologne of exactly this, his scent right now.

"Since when do you care about my personal life?" I whispered. I could reach out and touch him, could see the pulse thrumming in his throat.

"I care," he murmured. His eyes dipped to my mouth and stuck there. "It's easy to care when it's you."

My blood went molten and every thought in my head winked

out completely. I reached for him, cupping his face with my hands, letting the coarse stubble scratch my palms. Dex's eyes fell shut, letting out a jagged breath, and his arm slipped around my waist, dragging me against him. His touch burned through my shirt. I was on fire, surely.

Our noses brushed. I couldn't breathe.

I lost every ounce of self-control in my body and pulled his face the rest of the way. His lips and mine touched, just barely; it couldn't be considered a kiss, but electricity pulsed through my live-wire veins, solar flares popping in my lips, and where his beard tickled my chin, and my lower back where his fingers dug in like he still had one last shred of the self-control I'd lost. Showoff. I pushed up on my toes, pressing harder, and his mouth tipped open for me, that first real taste pitching me down a rabbit hole.

The elevator might as well have come crashing down—it was world-bending, the pressure of him against me, the slide of his tongue, the delicious scrape of his stubble, the lingering taste of strawberry. He pinned me against the wall, a low, desperate groan coming from his throat. And I was there, too, grabbing at him, gasping into his mouth as a rough hand slid up my shirt and drew across the underside of my breast, tantalizingly slow.

"Fuck," he rasped against my mouth, and pulled away slightly, skating his lips across my jaw, down to my neck. His hand shifted, thumb brushing over my nipple, and I arched into him, so wildly satisfied that he'd flown past my expectations already.

He bared his teeth against my neck and I dropped my fingers to his shoulders, nails digging in through his T-shirt. "Fuck," he said again. Keeping one hand working over my breast, Dex slid the other down over my ass to my thigh, below the hem of my pajama shorts. His fingers curled around and hiked my leg up, and I nearly blacked out at the feeling of our hips gnashing, him hard grinding against the blinding pressure between my legs. He moaned into my neck, shifting away and into me again. My head fell against the metal, fingers so tight against his shoulders, they might bruise. I was close already.

His mouth returned to mine, a short taste before moving in deeper, slower, the sharp scrape of his chin stoking the fire as his hips ground against mine again, harder. I moved my hips in tandem, desperate for more. There was so little fabric between us, I could *almost* feel everything. I wanted it all. Wanted his skin against mine, him inside me, impossibly close, closer than any upright position would allow.

He shifted, hand flexing against my leg as he angled me closer, and I dragged my hands down to his hips to show him exactly what I needed. We panted into each other's mouths, unable to keep up the kiss when this felt so fucking *good.*

The elevator chimed, cutting into the breathy silence, and the doors slid open. Dex was off me in a flash. I blinked several times, dazed, unable to return the smile of the drunk man stumbling into the elevator from the lobby. Apparently, we'd missed our stop.

"Heyo," the man said gruffly, eyes sliding between us. "Good nights all around, yeah?"

Dex cleared his throat and hit the button for our floor again. I brushed my fingers over my beestung lips; the buzz remained. I looked at Dex, but he avoided my eyes.

When we finally stepped onto our floor, I stole another glance at Dex. He still wouldn't look my way, fists clenched at his sides. Her name flashed in the space between us.

Catalina.

We were on our way to hand deliver a love letter written by a man who couldn't even *talk* about her and I was dry humping him in an elevator. I was going to hell, for sure. But Dex was right there with me—with all the compliments and the soft smiles and the sweet words, he was every bit as much to blame. We wanted each other. We gave in. That had to mean he wasn't pining for her, right? Or was I simply a doomed optimist?

Dex slowed as we approached our rooms, his directly across from mine. He turned to me, allowing an unfiltered look of his bitten lips, his unkempt hair made messier by my fingers. "Violet," he said, keeping his tone neutral. No more *Vi*.

"It's cool," I blurted, throwing on a trusty fake smile, but it felt wrong. I never realized how unabashedly real I'd been with Dex until now.

He rubbed the back of his neck and glanced down the hall. "I don't want you to think—"

"I'm not thinking!" I stepped away from him. "There could not be any less thinking in this building tonight."

"Violet—"

"It's fine. It's the curse of the strawberry margarita. Mistakes are made. We pretend it never happened in the morning."

For a horrifying five seconds, I hoped he would protest. Tell me it wasn't a mistake, he couldn't pretend, that it felt as monumental to him as it did for me. There was something here, there *had* to be. But of course he didn't argue. He had someone we were on our way to, who I'd vowed to help him reconcile with.

My eyes stung. "It never happened," I added softly.

Dex nodded stiffly. "It's better this way."

"Cool, yeah. Agreed." I fumbled for my room key, turning my back to him. "Well, good night."

I didn't give him a chance to respond.

It was better that way.

Fourteen

It only took four hours in the front seat for Phoebe to take it upon herself to update the route.

"I'm older, now," she'd said, as if talking about years passing. "I've changed."

Dex, surprisingly acquiescent, allowed her to peruse what I assumed was a very detailed spreadsheet on his phone. A mistake, seeing as she immediately got bored and began snooping. She tittered over his home screen being organized in alphabetical order, and the fact that the only apps he had were Spotify (Premium) and *Mario Kart* (she downloaded it and friended herself from his account). Every time he got a text, she read it aloud, along with who it was from and her own commentary ("BG Brad says, 'Sounds cool.' What does the BG stand for? Big Gay Brad?").

I spent four hours in the back seat pretending to sleep, pretending not to listen to Phoebe teasing Dex, or the soft rhythm of Dex's fingers drumming the wheel along to a Sonic Youth song, or their conversation about which fast-food restaurant had the best fries, or Dex threatening to throw Phoebe's phone out the window when she added "Blue (Da Ba Dee)" to the road trip playlist and her unrestrained laughter in response. An easiness existed between them—the bewilderment I felt about it was overwhelmed by blistering relief. Phoebe sounded light and cheerful. Like a *kid*. And as much as I wanted her to sound that way when she talked to me, that she sounded that way at all was a tremendous step forward.

I contemplated this with my eyes shut. I contemplated a lot of things, like the look Phoebe gave me when I told her to take the front so I could nap, as if she knew I was full to the brim with shit, or no matter how many times I swished mouthwash around my mouth this morning, I could still taste strawberry. How every so often, in the midst of an extended silence, Phoebe would giggle, and I'd sneak a peek, wondering what I'd missed, and Dex's eyes would meet mine in the rearview mirror, anticipating it. And when I shut my eyes again, he didn't call me out.

I wasn't mad, like he thought. I'd skipped the breakfast buffet to steal a whopping thirty minutes of sleep and then retreated to the back seat because close proximity seemed impossible, and I hadn't said a word to him, but it wasn't bitterness or even embarrassment. I just felt really, really stupid.

I had a crush. Because that's what it was, the very definition of the weight bearing down on my lungs when Dex's eyes met mine, the inevitable plunge resulting in irreparable brokenness— spirits, hopes, heart. I hadn't felt this dopey since middle school. Shawn and I met through a mutual friend and we were just . . . together. No tension, no pining, no sick swirling sensation thundering through my gut at the mere thought of him. I would've married the man, but now I had to question whether or not I had felt *anything* for him, even at our best.

A depressing thought, though not nearly as depressing as the realization that struck somewhere around 4 A.M.: Phoebe's goal for this trip was a happily ever after, and it wasn't supposed to include me. Here I'd been making eyes at Dex and doing unspeakable things in public elevators, basically throwing middle fingers in the air. Did I believe I held the ability to dismantle the plan? No. Dex made it clear that what happened between us was a mistake. But the what-ifs came charging in: *What if we'd slept together and Phoebe woke up before I got back to the room? What if he left a mark on me, or vice versa, and she put two and two together? What if a pervy elevator attendant posted the footage on YouTube and someone sent it to Phoebe?*

I'd jeopardized my own happiness, but jeopardizing Phoebe's hit so much harder. I hated myself.

"Your mom is calling," Phoebe said, turning down the unfamiliar song blasting from the speakers. I inched an eye open, noting the tension in Dex's shoulders and the pointed silence as he reached over to ignore the call. "Why won't you talk to your mom?"

Wind whistled through the window. When Dex answered, his voice had chilled. "I will talk to her. Later."

"You've ignored, like, six calls since we left Boston."

"Remember when we weren't getting to know each other? That was fun, right?"

"I know it's none of my business, but as someone who would kill to have parents pestering me with phone calls, maybe you should, like, answer."

I squeezed my eyes shut.

"You have Violet," Dex said. "That's something."

She huffed. "Right. Because that's the same thing."

The sting was immediately overshadowed by Dex's words: "You're such an asshole."

"I'm an asshole?" Phoebe repeated. I kept my eyes shut, but everything in me screamed to sit up and defend my sister.

"Yeah, you are. You're lucky she hasn't thrown you out on the side of the highway."

"It's sister stuff. You wouldn't get it."

"It's sister stuff when you treat her like shit for asking a question?"

"Pot calling the kettle black much?" She resorted to grumbling, so I knew she'd turned up the attitude to eleven. "You're a million times worse than me."

"I don't matter to her," he replied. A tightness gripped my throat—I couldn't swallow. "You are her sister and you fight her on every little thing. Fuck, man. Don't you think she's tired?"

"That's not . . ." Phoebe growled under her breath. "My dad died. I have a right to be pissed."

"You're not the only one who lost him."

Something about this simple statement rearranged my insides. I'd spent the last nine months shoving my own grief aside to abide my sister's, and it hadn't helped anyone: Phoebe was still angry and I was a wreck. What would our life look like if I'd felt everything upfront instead of putting on a pathetic façade that ruined us both? I didn't want to think about it.

"I know," Phoebe mumbled. "I know, okay? Sometimes I hear myself being a dick and I want to stop but I can't. And she just . . . She didn't have to take me. At the hospital, there was this counselor lady and at one point, she took Violet outside to talk about her options. About me. She could either take me or send me to Oklahoma to live with our great-aunt. And Violet didn't even hesitate. Like, it wasn't a choice at all. It's just how it *was*. Even though it fucked up her entire life. And I can't stop being a bitch. She *should* throw me out on the highway."

I had to shift onto my side and press my face into the leather so I wouldn't start loudly sobbing in the back seat. It wasn't surprising that Phoebe felt this way—I'd suspected all along the transition was harder on her than it was on me, but hearing her say it out loud demolished me. More than anything, I wished she felt comfortable saying these things to me. But Dex knew I was awake and he poked her anyway, as if he wanted me to hear it. As if he knew I needed to.

There was so much Phoebe and I had to say to each other. I had no idea how to start.

"I think that she hasn't is proof she understands. You don't mean it," he said quietly. This must've been how he sounded when he spoke to the kids he worked with, reminiscent of the gentle voice I used with my students when they had a hard time with a lesson. "You're a kid—you're dealing with an impossible situation the best you can."

"I hope this isn't my best," Phoebe muttered.

He snorted. "There's always tomorrow."

A tear slipped out. How many tomorrows would it take for Phoebe to open up to me the way she had with Dex? Was it possible? Sometimes I wanted to shake her and scream, *We're in this together!* Not the most optimistic of thoughts, but I figured my unfailing ability to hold it in had to count for something.

"You're not gonna tell Violet I said all that, are you?" Phoebe asked.

"Nope."

"Because you guys were getting pretty real yesterday," she went on casually.

Dex cleared his throat. "Not really."

"Dude, she spilled her guts. It was kinda gross." The shutter of her camera cut into the moment. Dex cursed under his breath. Phoebe went on, "Maybe you should tell me what happened with you and Catalina, so we're even. Mutually assured destruction or whatever."

"That's not what mutually assured destruction is."

"Maybe you should tell me anyway." His silence prompted a defeated sigh from Phoebe. "Just . . . don't tell Vi. Please?"

"There's this thing I do where I mind my own business. It's a revolutionary approach to the world, but . . ."

Phoebe groaned, shifting into laughter. "You're such a dork. I thought you were an asshole like me."

"It'll come back if you make me stop at another Waffle House," he said, and she laughed again.

"Blasphemy! Waffle House is amazing!"

"Maybe to someone with extremely low standards."

"You're an extremely low standard."

Their heated debate lasted until the next gas stop. I kept my face hidden in the seat until the tears dried.

"So." Arden looked at me like she wasn't so much clairvoyant as being fed intel by a PI. "You're in love with him."

My phone clattered to the floor. I scrambled for it, giving our hotel room a quick scan even though Phoebe had gone with Dex to get dinner down the street. "God," I said, sinking into the edge of the plush bed. "What? No. That's so—What if Phoebe was here when you said that? What would she think?"

"I knew you wouldn't talk to me unless she was out of earshot," she replied. She must've propped her phone up because she was lounging on her couch, arms crossed, resembling a hard-assed therapist. "I know you. I knew what was up the second you got weird last night."

I rubbed my nose. "I didn't get weird."

"You mentioned someone hitting on Dex and I heard your heart break in real time."

"Bullshit."

"Tell me you're not in love with him," she challenged. "I dare you. Right now."

"I'm not in love with him," I said easily. Her eyes narrowed. "I may have a crush."

"Sure."

"And he may have asked me to get a drink with him last night."

She blinked twice, eyebrows slowly rising. "Sure . . ."

"And we may have made out and dry humped a little in an elevator."

Her lips parted. In the background, a throat cleared and Noah said, "So, I'm gonna go."

I winced. "Hey, Noah."

"Hey, Vi. Happy humping or whatever."

I buried my face in my palm. "It's stupid, is the thing. And I *hate* feeling stupid."

"I know you do," Arden said, her tone taking a sympathetic dip. "It doesn't have to be, though. Dex isn't a bad guy." She paused. "Right? I feel like I don't know enough about him to say."

"He's not a bad guy. He's actually . . ." I exhaled, lifting my gaze to my best friend. I'd only just gotten her rants back, and now the sympathy was making a comeback. I was hoping I'd make it at least forty-eight hours, but my reckless heart had other ideas. "It doesn't matter because what he really is, is off-limits."

"Nice," Noah said. Arden shot him a look. "Sorry, sorry. I'm going."

"He's not technically off-limits," Arden said, returning her gaze to me. "Did he write a love letter that would make Shakespeare proud? Yes. Is he on his way to hand deliver it to the woman he wrote it for? Also yes. But if he's dry humping you in an elevator, things clearly aren't as cut and dried as we thought."

My mind drifted without permission, landing on memories

of Dex's hands, Dex's tongue, his desperate groan as he pinned me against the wall.

"Oh my god," Arden said, snapping me out of my head. "You *are* in love with him, aren't you?"

"No." I rolled my shoulders and composed my sunburned face. "I'm not. And I'm going to will myself out of my pointless crush."

"Really."

"Yep. I started making a list of reasons why I shouldn't like him."

"Oh, boy," she murmured, studying me like a bug under a cup. "You're too far gone, I think."

Ignoring this, I dove in. "He's a clean freak. Dude would have a conniption if he walked through my apartment and saw the counter covered in used plastic forks and the colony of fruit flies in the bathroom. 'Why are they in the bathroom?' he'd ask. How am I supposed to answer that?"

Slowly, Arden covered her mouth with her hand. I plowed on.

"He doesn't like junk food. How pretentious do you have to be to not eat a Twinkie I bought for you out of the goodness of my heart? I should hate him for that alone."

"But you don't," Arden pointed out.

"Well, maybe he has a thing about sugar." I squeezed my eyes shut. "Oh god."

"'Maybe he has a thing about sugar,'" Arden repeated grimly. "Violet. Sweetheart. Love of my life."

"It's so bad." I looked at her, eyes swimming. "What do I *do*?"

Her expression softened. "Vi," she said. "I don't think there's anything you can do. It's already done."

"No, it's not." I waved a finger at the screen of my phone. "It's not. Because we agreed it never happened. So it can't be done because *logic*."

The softness in her expression disappeared. I'd said too much.

"What?" Her lip twitched, seconds away from bared teeth, ready to go for the nearest throat.

"Hmm?"

"You agreed it never happened?"

"Who?"

"I told him." Arden sucked in a sharp breath, face pinching with rage. "I told him if he returned you worse off in *any* way—"

"I'm not! I'm fine! Because it never happened, so we're good!"

She slumped against the couch. "I hate that I'm not there. Not because I want to hurt Dex. I do, obviously. But I want to be there for you. As in, in the same room."

"I know," I said quietly. "You've been in the same room as me all year and I don't know what I would've done without you. But we can't always be in the same room, you know? I can't rely on you so much."

For a split second, I thought she might take offense, as if I didn't appreciate how heroic she'd been over the course of our friendship—this last year put her in the running for a Nobel Prize, as far as I was concerned. Accepting help is one thing, but being completely helpless is another. I was sick of being unable to function without my best friend.

I needed her. I always would.

"I know," she said, swiping at her eyes. "God, you're healing. I'm so proud of you."

I huffed. "Healing. Right."

"Your dad would be proud, too."

My heart heaved, crashing clumsily into my rib cage. "I haven't done anything," I whispered. "Like, I know he's proud of me regardless, but—"

"Vi." She widened her eyes. "He always wanted you to do what you wanted to do and be what you wanted to be. And here you are, finally."

"Finally?"

"This isn't just for Phoebe. It's for you. You're coming back to life. You're laughing. You're exploring new cities. You're falling in love. You're stepping out of your comfort zone in every possible way," she explained, and my vision blurred. "I thought you were crazy, going on this trip. But I'm watching you blossom, babe. And for the first time since we met, you know you deserve it."

I didn't think this could be considered blossoming, considering the amount of times I'd reached for the pack of TUMS in my luggage. Falling for Dex was the worst-case scenario, other than the true crime ending Arden originally imagined. But I *did* feel different. These last few days, all the miles between here and home, something inside me changed for the better. All I really knew was that it was easier to reach for the good memories of my dad, and each day seemed to awaken a happier version of Phoebe, and I'd found something with Dex I wanted to keep.

Maybe not a blossom, but at the very least, I wasn't buried under six feet of soil anymore.

Later, once I'd promised Arden I'd keep her updated on all things crush-related and listened to a ten-minute rant about her mother's pushiness about wedding plans, Phoebe returned with a huge smile on her face, and a box of leftovers for me.

"It was so good," she shouted from the bathroom as I practically unhinged my jaw to eat half of the still-warm burger in one bite. "I couldn't decide between the burger and the chicken and waffles, so Dex let me get both. The chicken and waffles were amazing, but that might be the best burger I've ever had in my life. I was like, 'We have to get Vi one.' And Dex was like, 'Yeah.'"

I moaned into the burger. Phoebe emerged from the bathroom, hair pinned out of her face, now wearing her swimsuit with a pair of shorts.

"Right?" she said, beaming. "Dex said maybe we could go back for breakfast before we leave tomorrow. Or will you still be avoiding him then?"

I took my time chewing another bite, studying a loose thread in the carpet intently. "I'm not avoiding him," I said. I didn't need to look at her to know she rolled her eyes. "We should get breakfast tomorrow. And maybe we should consider moving to Nebraska, home of the best fucking burger I've ever eaten in my life."

She giggled and plunked down on the edge of the bed beside me, swiping a fry from the box in my lap. "We were gonna get ice cream, too, but we were so full, we couldn't. Maybe tomorrow."

"Maybe." Phoebe pulled her phone out of her pocket, her smile widening as she looked at the screen. I polished off my burger, anticipating her next giggle before it happened. "What are you laughing at?"

She set her phone down and looked at me, eyes bright, cheeks rosy from the sun and probably how hard she was smiling. "Dex let me join one of Sequest's Discord servers. And it's Sequest, so it's legit. No weirdos. They have a bunch of them for different demographics or whatever. This one is for fourteen- and fifteen-year-olds. It's basically just a bunch of gay kids sending memes to each other and ranting about how shitty school is. It's awesome."

"That's . . ." I swallowed hard. "That is awesome."

"There's this one girl, Mae. Her mom died a week after Dad.

She's so cool and we like a lot of the same music, except she's super into screamo, which is like . . ." She rolled her eyes, pulling a face. "But anyway, she wants to hang out when we get back home. Do you think I could? Dex knows her, so she's for sure not a creep."

"Yeah." I blinked hard and forced a smile. "Of course you can."

"Yeah?" Her eyes lit up. *Everything* lit up. "Oh my god, I can't wait. Maybe she could sleep over soon-ish?" She hesitated, scrunching up her nose. "I'd have to fix my room first. It's still full of boxes."

She was sprinting toward that new normal everyone told us would arrive and it knocked the wind from my lungs. I'd nearly given up on hoping for better days, let alone that Phoebe would choose to share them with me.

"First thing," I said, emotion swelling in my throat. "First thing when we get back, we'll fix up your room. We can even paint, if you want."

She leaned her shoulder into mine. "Thanks, Vi," she said and stole another fry. "Wanna go swimming? The pool here is so nice. You can just sit on the edge if you want to wait the thirty minutes after eating. I know you're weird about that."

"It's not weird. It's science."

"It's an urban legend." She swiped yet another fry and hopped to her feet. "Come on."

"Okay," I said. "I have to get changed. I'll meet you there."

She offered a little salute and left. The moment the door shut behind her, I shut my eyes and focused on my breathing so I wouldn't cry. Then I got up, got dressed, and went down the hall to Dex's room.

"I saw you buy those fucking floaties at the gas station," he was saying as he opened the door. "So, no, I don't want to—" His mouth snapped shut at the sight of me, eyes widening.

And I couldn't say anything, so I stepped forward and wrapped my arms around him in a crushing hug.

He didn't stiffen, like I thought he might. Didn't push me away gently and tell me it was a bad idea for us to be this close. Once the bolt of shock passed, his hand found my back, rubbing soft circles between my shoulder blades.

"Vi," he murmured.

"Thank you," I said into his shirt. "Phoebe told me what you did. She's making friends, and she's making plans. Things to look forward to when the trip is done. You have no idea, Dex. You have no idea."

His other hand cradled the back of my head and I squeezed my eyes shut, pretending just for a moment that I'd get to be held like this by him every day.

"I should've mentioned it to you first. I was going to."

I forced myself to step away, swallowing hard as his hands fell to his sides. His eyes swept over my face, full of some emotion I couldn't quite read. "I get it. You knew I'd be okay with it, especially after I told you how I feel about moving her to Boston."

"She likes Boston. She just needs a community of kids her own age, away from school."

"I should've thought of that." I rubbed my eyes. "I should've taken her to the YMCA or something."

He made a face. "She wouldn't do that."

"Right. She'd hate that."

"I figured this was more her style. And these kids . . ." He let out a breath, his expression shifting into a reverence that twisted my organs in a knot. "Every one of them is in a similar situation. And they're good kids, Vi. They were handed a shit hand, just like you and Phoebe."

I wanted to kiss him. No, I wanted to shove him in his hotel room and drop to my knees and make him feel good because he *deserved* it. This man cared so much, despite how hard he pretended he didn't. He offered to drive home the teenager who opened his mail because she had a blister, and he humored her grief-stricken sister with the patience of a saint, and he devoted his life to making the lives of LGBTQ+ youth easier.

He wasn't an asshole. Not even close.

"Anyway," I said, so I wouldn't move in closer, "I just wanted to say thank you. And invite you to swim, but you already answered that one."

He scratched the back of his neck, offering a sheepish smile. "She snuck some of those kid floaties into the snacks we bought at the gas station earlier, thinking I didn't notice. She's a piece of work."

"She's the best." I smiled and took a step backward, inclining my head in invitation. He followed without hesitation, letting the door shut behind him. "You're wearing the floaties."

"I'd rather drown myself."

He fell in beside me. I'd missed him, I realized. I felt at home beside him and it had been so long since I felt anything, anywhere. Why did it have to be him?

We stopped in front of the elevator. Dex coughed.

"Stairs," I blurted, and he was nodding before the word fully left my lips. "We should take the stairs."

Fifteen

I hated nature, but not nearly as much as Dex did.

"Fuck," he said, stumbling over a tree root. Regaining his balance, he threw it a dirty look. "How much farther?"

A mosquito buzzed insistently around my head and a bead of sweat slid between my boobs. Up ahead, Phoebe shouted over her shoulder, "Half a mile!"

Phoebe wasn't the outdoorsy type, but our dad was. He loved camping and fishing and hiked every worthwhile trail in the Northeast. I figured a hike in the gorgeous Medicine Bow-Routt National Forest was a homage to him, so I ignored my burning hatred for the supposed great outdoors, put on a sports bra, and feigned enthusiasm. Meanwhile, Dex spent the last two miles grumbling under his breath and scowling at birdsong.

My heart hummed with fondness.

I ignored that too.

"You okay?" I asked him, slowing my pace so he could catch up. He nodded, swiping a hand across his sweaty forehead. Instead of his usual uniform, he'd opted for a white tee, shorts, sneakers, and his Ray-Bans. Several times, I'd deliberately allowed him in front of me so I could commit every angle to memory.

"I hate this."

"Shocker."

"Hiking," he added belatedly. "I hate hiking. It's pointless."

"I think there's supposed to be a pretty amazing view at the end," I replied, to which he rolled his eyes.

"There are hundreds of photographs at our disposal. We don't have to work so hard for it."

"You're such a whiner," I said. "I had no idea."

"I'm not whining."

"I don't like this any more than you do," I said, lowering my voice even though Phoebe charged ahead, out of earshot. "But it's a beautiful day. The sun's out. We're in Wyoming and it's gorgeous. Not much to complain about."

On cue, a mosquito landed on my arm and I slapped it hard enough for the sound to echo through the surrounding trees. Dex looked at me, my own thinly veiled skepticism reflecting back in his sunglasses.

"Right."

We kept moving. Phoebe wheeled around, eyes alight, and exclaimed, "Guys, look at the hole in that tree! It's shaped like a heart."

My face broke into a smile, watching as she lifted Dad's camera and snapped a photo. Then I glanced at Dex to find him already facing me, and I could feel his eyes beneath the dark lenses.

We made it another few feet before Dex let out a sharp sound—something in the realm of a shriek—and flailed, hands blurry as he swiped at himself, flinging off his sunglasses in the process. Phoebe appeared beside me to watch with her mouth hanging open.

"Oh my god," she said. "What *happened*?"

"There was . . ." Chest heaving, he scanned the ground as he rubbed at his arm. "Spider."

Phoebe snickered. A flush swept up his neck, staining his cheeks.

"Wow. That made this whole thing worth it," she said, turning to continue down the trail. I bent to retrieve Dex's Ray-Bans, now missing a lens.

"What a fucking calamity," he groused as I handed him the glasses. I half expected him to toss them in the woods, but he hooked them from the collar of his shirt to deal with later.

"So," I said. "Flying and spiders."

He clenched his jaw and kept moving. "It's not funny."

"I'm not laughing at you. I'm curious. I've never seen you so vulnerable." *Outside an elevator,* I didn't add.

"I walked through a spiderweb with a huge-ass spider in it and it was gross. The end."

"You shrieked," I pointed out. He picked up the pace and I had to jog to keep up, careful to avoid tree roots or loose stones. "Imagine if there were flying spiders. That would be your worst nightmare."

He shot me a dark look. "This is you not laughing at me?"

"Sorry." He slowed slightly and I managed to catch my breath. "It's not bad to be scared of things, Dex. Tell him, Phoebe."

"Yeah." She didn't even turn. "Fear is in the eye of the beholder or whatever."

"Beauty. Beauty is in the eye of the beholder."

She considered this. "I like mine better."

At the end of the trail, we were treated to a view of a piercing blue lake and a wide open sky. Phoebe snapped a picture of the view, and then forced all of us together, holding the camera at arm's length to take a selfie. Dex even smiled. We ended up staying for nearly two hours, drinking in the sunshine and telling stories about other beautiful views we'd seen. Phoebe and I reminisced about a trip we took with our dad to Acadia National Park. Dex let it slip that he'd been to Greece and Phoebe and I proceeded to sing the entirety of "Mamma Mia." It felt like discovering a new appreciation for nature, at least until a swarm of gnats descended on us and we headed back down the trail.

Phoebe hummed an unfamiliar tune, leading the way. Dex and I stayed together, close enough that every few steps our hands or elbows brushed.

"You're quiet," he said. I glanced at him, finding his eyes locked on me, and I wondered what percentage of my rapid heart rate had to do with the cardio.

"I'm not always talking."

"No," he allowed. "But this silence seems louder than most."

He probably thought I harbored hurt feelings over the elevator, despite having dumped every bit of water under the bridge.

"I'm thinking," I said. He tilted his head as if to say, *Go on.* "She seems different, doesn't she?"

He tore his gaze from me to regard Phoebe curiously. "Less bite, maybe."

"Is this a turning point? Or am I naïve for thinking that?" I exhaled and palmed a handful of sweaty hair out of my face. "I know grief isn't linear. But is this the part where it stops being so exhausting?"

"I don't know."

"It feels different," I told him, my voice low. "Kids bounce back quicker, right? That's proven by science?"

He smiled, almost indulging. "Sure."

"Don't do that."

"What am I doing?"

"That." I waved my hand at his face. "It's condescending."

"My face is condescending?" he asked, not sounding entirely surprised. I doubted it was the first time he'd heard it.

"Very."

"I'm not trying to be condescending," he said. "It's interesting to hear how your brain works."

I froze, a twig crunching under my foot. Dex paused, swiveling to face me.

"What does that mean?" I asked, my voice quiet. Something about his tone dug under my skin, or maybe I was simply desperate for an excuse to feel anything other than fondness for this man. Maybe I wanted an excuse to drain the water from under that bridge.

"You're an optimist."

He said it so plainly, the same way someone would say the sky was blue. I was taken aback by how easily he came to that conclusion when I'd spent the last year grappling with my slippery beliefs until all I had was reciting three measly things to keep my head above water.

"What does that have to do with anything?" I challenged. *Hurt me,* I begged silently. *Hurt me now so it doesn't hurt so much later.*

"I'm not insulting you," he said quietly, snuffing out the emotions roiling in my chest. "It's admirable, Violet. Not many people can retain that sort of optimism, especially in grief."

I studied him for a moment. "Right. And you're the pessimist."

"I'm nothing. Life sucks most of the time," he said. "That's just how it is. I try not to think about it so I don't go out of my mind."

I inhaled sharply. This man who'd flinched when we found out where he went to college was now admitting a devastating truth that surely stemmed deeper, Marianas Trench deep, protected by booby traps. But he'd said it out loud. To me.

I stepped toward him. "I'm not an optimist because I'm impervious to negative emotions." Overhead, birds twittered and tree branches creaked in the wind. Dex's shoulders sank in a small exhale, his eyes so much warmer in this light. "It's a survival tactic. I *have* to look on the bright side. I have to believe things get better or else what's the point? I don't want to live in a universe where everything sucks and only gets worse forever, the end."

"Sounds like our universe to me."

"Except it's not! Twenty minutes ago you and Phoebe laughed over a dumb joke on top of a mountain. For a minute, things were good."

"For a minute," he said, widening his eyes.

"Yeah, and there will be a thousand more like it this week. Billions in our lifetime," I said, watching as his eyes softened. "Things get fucked, but there's always something good. Even if it's just another minute."

"Is that enough?" he asked softly.

I shrugged. "It has to be."

He stared at me for a long moment. "You're dangerous."

"Because I haven't let life beat me into hopelessness?"

"You make me want to be an optimist."

He was already turning as he said it, following Phoebe's speck in the distance. My mouth went dry. Damn him for coming up with a string of words that would tie my heart up for good—someday maybe I'd be senile, but I would remember those words. I'd remember the reverent look on his face. And I understood the danger he mentioned, the curse that plagued optimists for all their days.

Hope. It spilled over, rushing around me in a steady, uncontrollable current. There was no stopping it with Dex existing beside me. Maybe there was no stopping it at all.

"Maybe," Phoebe said gravely back in our room at the inn, hands on her hips after our fourth consecutive tick check, "there was something seriously wrong with Dad."

"Oh, there was definitely something wrong with him," I agreed. I shuddered at the thought of those bloodsucking creepy crawlies lurking in the woods, ready to strike at any moment, whereas Dad, fearless or out of his mind, laughed anytime he plucked one off his skin like it was a dandelion seed. *A fellow traveler,* he'd say. Real-life vampires, more like.

"Like, that was so fun," Phoebe went on, shuffling over to her bed. She sat at the edge and stripped off her socks, giving her feet another glance. "I would spend all day outside. But the ticks. I don't think it's worth it."

"All bugs, really."

"Nah, I can deal with most bugs. Remember that plastic terrarium thing I got for Christmas that one year? I'd fill it with grass and dirt and twigs and catch bugs?" She smiled at the memory. "Grasshoppers and beetles, mostly. The occasional salamander. That was so cool."

"Yeah, until you ran at me with a cricket in your hands," I replied, though the warmth of recollecting wrapped its way around my heart too.

She cackled. "Remember the one that escaped and jumped right on you?"

"I wish I could forget. It scarred me for life."

Phoebe beamed with the sort of pride only a little sibling could conjure at the expense of their older sister and fell back against the comforter, arms splayed. "Thanks for doing it," she said after a moment. It shouldn't have been so shocking, those words coming out of her mouth, but they sent a bolt through my body and I dropped the T-shirt I'd planned to change into. "The hike," she added, eyes fixed on the ceiling. "I know you hate pretty much all things nature, so you know, I appreciate that you went and didn't complain the whole time."

I swallowed hard. Embarrassingly enough, I'd fantasized about Phoebe saying things like this to me during restless nights: something as innocent as a smile, at first, and then the optimist in me would reach further for *thank you*s or a *you're not as terrible at this as you think. I love you,* I figured, was out of the question in a world without our dad.

This had to be a product of the conversation I'd overheard in the car. All day, I'd fought to keep it in the back of my mind, knowing full well if I gave it too much thought, a canyon would open inside my chest. But now, I couldn't deny how much it meant to hear Dex defend me and, even more, to hear Phoebe agree with him. She didn't hate me. It wasn't fair to her, what a revelation this felt like for me. Of course she was angry at the world and taking it out on the only person left. Still, after nine months of wishing at my bedroom ceiling for a sliver of kindness from my sister, *revelation* seemed like an understatement.

And now here she was thanking me, unprompted. Tears rushed to my eyes and I bent to grab my T-shirt, giving myself a moment to get it together.

"No problem," I said, hoping she couldn't detect the hitch in my tone. She pursed her lips, sliding her feet up the bed until her knees pointed to the ceiling.

"Dex hated it."

I choked out a laugh. "Yeah. He did."

"I feel kinda bad," she said. "We've only been doing stuff I want to do."

"Dex would rather pull a tooth without novocaine than admit he wants something," I replied unwittingly. I flinched as Phoebe turned her head to look at me and busied myself with folding my shirt. "And anyway, this is your trip. We want you to do all the things you want to do. When are we gonna get the chance to hike in Wyoming again?"

"It's *our* trip." She sat up, hugging her knees to her chest. "All of us. It's not fun if I'm just, like, dragging you guys from place to place and you're rolling your eyes at each other like parents when their eight-year-old watches the same movie over and over."

"That's not what we're doing."

"I just—" She cut herself off with a sigh. "I want everyone to enjoy it, you know?"

I sat down, sinking into the mattress, clutching my shirt to my chest. "We are," I said emphatically. "I mean, I can't speak for Dex, but he was laughing on that mountain. That's gotta count for something, right?"

She let her chin rest on her knee. "Maybe."

"I'm enjoying this," I told her. "I know it's not what you want to hear, but seeing you have fun is fun for me. Genuinely. I hate the outdoors and that hike today was the best. I had fun. I had fun at Coney Island and I had fun at the gay bar. Fun is the last thing I expected from this trip, but it's the most persistent feeling so far."

She pressed her lips in a line, trying not to smile. "You're so boring."

I shrugged. "I know."

"I was thinking about it," she said, then paused. I waited for her to continue with the thought, but she left her words hanging in the room between us.

"Me being boring?" I prompted.

Her mouth quirked into a small smile. I wondered if the thrill would dim eventually, or if the last nine months had permanently warped our relationship into these arbitrary give-and-takes. Fourteen years of my heart existing outside my body, this tiny toddler trailing behind me like a shadow growing into her own person and still wanting to follow me. Until the day of our dad's accident, Phoebe texted me every day about her life and her friends, asking me to come home so we could see a movie or go to the mall. I'd taken it for granted. It would break me to mourn my relationship with my sister. It broke me to realize I may have been doing it all along.

"No," she said. "I was thinking about how we've only been doing stuff I want to do, so I did a little research. Did you know there's a meteor shower happening right now?"

A year ago, I would have. I would have plugged the date into my calendar months in advance, driven down to the beach so there wouldn't be light pollution, and spent a few hours lying on my back, counting the blink-and-you'll-miss-it stars soaring across the sky. Arden would tag along sometimes, and Shawn too if he felt like making the trip, but my dad always made a huge deal of it. It was a little thing, something I'd taken an interest in since a high school astronomy class. Things had been so upside down lately, I hadn't taken the time to even look at the sky, let alone research upcoming meteor showers.

"No," I said quietly. "I had no idea."

Phoebe bit her lip. "I know you're probably sick of outside, but I thought we could check it out. I mean, it's Wyoming. Big open sky and all that."

"Do you mean 'big sky state'? Because that's Montana."

"Nah, I'm pretty sure it's Wyoming." She cheesed a grin. "You wanna?"

After the post-gay-bar meltdown and especially after the

conversation I overheard in the car, my sister reaching out meant everything to me. I'd spent months concocting tiny joyful moments like grabbing her favorite pastry on my way home from work or remembering which songs she'd been enjoying lately and playing them in the car in the hopes they would mean something to Phoebe, only for her to turn around and offer me the same thing. I knew the courage it took to go there. And maybe for her this wasn't a step forward, or even all that meaningful—maybe I was looking too hard at something with an honest face, but *dammit,* that's who I was. An optimist, constantly seeking the bright side. Just like our dad.

"Yeah," I said. "Of course. Let's go."

Phoebe hopped up, a few pieces of hair coming loose from her short ponytail. "Cool. I already checked the weather. I know you're big on the visibility," she mentioned, making her way over to her shoes piled haphazardly by the door.

"I'm not 'big on' visibility. You can't see without it."

"Uh-huh." She pulled on her shoes and waited by the door for me to do the same. "So, are we inviting Dex? Is this a thing we think he'd like?"

God, I hoped not. The thought of Dex caring about meteor showers would be too endearing for me to handle in my current state.

"No idea," I replied. "I don't care either way."

She eyed me for a moment, lips in a tight line. Then she smiled and threw open the door. "You totally do."

"What? What does that mean?" I spluttered, following her out into the dimly lit hallway. Initially, I'd been surprised by Dex's choice of a smaller country inn, but I'd since decided I preferred the busy wallpaper and vanilla-scented candles to the corporate hotels.

Phoebe moseyed down the hall, casting a glance at the rusty vintage bicycle hung on the wall. "This is what you do. When you say you don't care, you're usually, like, losing your mind from how much you care. It's not a bad thing. It's just who you are. You care and you want everyone else to care too," she said, stopping in front of Dex's door.

I rubbed my sternum. "You don't *have* to do this."

"No, that's not what I'm saying. I want to do this. But how many times did you suggest having my birthday party at the planetarium?"

"Too many, apparently."

"Way too many." She rapped her knuckles against the door. "Don't feel bad if he's like, 'Why would I waste time looking at the sky?' I already made him spend too much time outside today."

I snorted at the uncanny Dex impression as the door opened. Phoebe straightened up with a salesman's smile, practically shouting the word, "Hi!"

My brain stumbled at the sight of him in a heather gray tee and jeans, hair damp and wild, droplets of water dotting his shoulders. The scent of his soap struck and, as if trained by Pavlov himself, I could've sworn I tasted strawberries.

"Christ," Dex said. "Not another gay bar."

"There's a meteor shower," Phoebe announced. His gaze shifted over her shoulder to me, surely clocking the blush. Hey, I might've gotten a sunburn on top of that mountain. He couldn't know I was still thinking about the elevator.

"Perseids," he said with a nod.

He knew it by name.

Oblivious to the turmoil screwing with my entire world, Phoebe bounced on her heels. "Wanna see it with us?"

His eyes snagged mine. My haywire brain was pelting me with a myriad of shit, so I had no idea what he saw there that softened the slight tightness in his eyes. "You go ahead. I've spent too much time outside today."

"Loser," Phoebe replied fondly and walked away. I toyed with the zipper of my hoodie, taking a small step after her.

"You should come," I said. Dex leaned against the doorframe, seeming impossibly open for the first time, as if he'd taken down every wall and booby trap since we split off to our own rooms an hour ago. "You know it by name."

"It's not a one-night-only thing," he pointed out. I bit my lip, glancing down the hall to where Phoebe was waiting, texting with a small smile.

"Was this you?" I couldn't bring myself to look at him. "I heard you guys in the car. Did you suggest this as a way for her to be nicer to me?"

"No," he said. Grudgingly, I met his gaze and something inside my chest constricted under that softness, like I'd found myself standing in quicksand. "Her idea of nice was getting you a Twinkie at the gas station."

"I have a thing about snack cakes, so that *was* nice."

"Vi." He smiled, the corners of his eyes crinkling. I couldn't breathe. "Go hang out with your sister."

"I've had nine months of hanging out with my sister," I reminded him.

He tilted his head, eyes practically scoring my skin. "Not really."

Not like this, he meant, with Phoebe happy and willing. So much of her enthusiasm over the course of our trip was sparked by Dex, but tonight she'd planned around me. The two of us. He didn't want to intrude and the simple kindness had me melting.

I sent another glance Phoebe's way—so engrossed in her

phone, she wouldn't notice if someone knocked her down the stairs—and then stepped into Dex, pressing a chaste kiss to his sandpaper cheek. He sucked in a breath, stilling, and when I pulled back, his eyes were shut.

"You're sweet," I whispered, taking a shuffling step backward so I wouldn't twine my fingers in his shirt. He swallowed, keeping his eyes shut. "Who would've thought?"

"Don't tell anybody," he murmured. "It'll ruin my street cred."

"The street cred you acquired at Chicago gay bars?"

An impish smile tugged at the corner of his mouth and his eyes slid open, so full and bright I had to wonder if we were on the same page, somehow. If he was feeling this too. "My reputation among Chicago gay bars is impeccable," he said. "They love a six-one bisexual over there."

Dex held things so close to the chest, every snippet of information he offered was deliberate, thoroughly examined from every angle. He only told people what he wanted them to know. His honesty felt like more than trust. I wanted to explore this feeling, dig my fingers in and figure our relationship out once and for all, but Phoebe's voice broke through the moment.

"Can we hurry this up? I wanna see a meteor."

Regret, or something close to it, flickered in Dex's eyes. I took an unsteady breath and another step backward. "Are you sure you don't want to come?"

He jerked his chin in Phoebe's direction. "Go."

I tore myself away, a little bit dizzy, and met Phoebe at the end of the hall. She pocketed her phone, eyes narrow as they zipped over my shoulder to Dex.

"Were you guys talking about me?"

I forced a smile. "Of course. You are the center of the universe."

She wrinkled her nose at me and swept around the corner to the staircase. I hesitated, casting a glance over my shoulder to Dex; when our eyes met, his throat worked, but he remained in the doorway, a hand braced against the frame.

You make me want to be an optimist, he'd said.

I couldn't pretend anymore. Whatever this was existed solidly between us, taking up too much space—we needed to clear the air, really talk about what happened in the elevator and how we felt about it because pretending it had never happened wasn't better. I wanted him. It was pretty clear he wanted me. We had to discuss what it meant.

Just not tonight.

Phoebe and I made our way outside, a warm breeze curling around us as we collected a blanket from Dex's car and laid it out on the lawn, watching the sun slice a strip of deep orange into the sky overhead. The shadows crept in slowly, overtaking the rest of the daylight. Stars burst forth like pinpricks in the darkness. Out here, the sky was so clear and open, I was sure I'd never seen so much of it at once.

As we waited, Phoebe started telling me about more of her new friends from the Sequest server. About something funny that happened during cross-country a month ago. About how she woke up in the middle of the night and couldn't get back to sleep so she and Dex played *Mario Kart* on their phones, texting each other insults when the other won. Maybe it was easier for her to talk under the veil of night, or maybe she really *was* doing better and more willing to let me in as a result. I'd take it either way. It wouldn't matter if we didn't see a single meteor—I'd be fine listening to my sister's voice for the rest of the night.

Some time later, when we did see one streak across the sky, Phoebe gasped and grabbed onto my arm, shaking me with excitement. So much had been taken from us, so much we willingly let go. Now, though, Phoebe scooted closer to me, vibrating with anticipation, and we kept our eyes on the sky waiting for another meteor. There was no guarantee we'd see one, but I had a good feeling.

Sixteen

In the morning, Phoebe steered us to a viral chicken sandwich she just *had* to try. Within twenty minutes of eating it, she was heaving on the side of the highway.

"I think I'm dying," she moaned. Dex had managed to find a cabin rental close by and dropped us off before heading into town to find a pharmacy. I had no idea how long he'd been gone, but Phoebe had been throwing up pretty much the entire time.

"Food poisoning will do that," I said, rubbing soft circles between her shoulder blades. She lifted her head out of the toilet to look at me, eyes red and watery, her face a ghostly white.

"It will?"

"What? No. It will make you feel like you're dying. You are not actually dying."

She groaned and fell sideways against the penny tile, curling into the fetal position. "I'm never trusting TikTok again."

"Probably smart." I plunked down beside her and resumed rubbing her back. "Do you want some water? Or anything?"

"No. Need to stay horizontal, I think." She sniffled. "I'm sorry I'm ruining the trip."

"You're not."

"Who knows how long this will last? Dex will probably leave without us."

"He's not going to leave without us."

"We shouldn't have taken so many detours. He's gonna be so mad."

"He's not mad. He's getting you medicine right now."

She whimpered, pressing her palms into her eyes. "Are you sure I'm not dying?"

I scooted closer, leaning my back against the wall, and settled her head on my lap. She looked up at me with miserable eyes and an ominous greenish hue to her skin. "I'm sure," I said softly, brushing her sweaty bangs out of her eyes. "I promise you are not dying, Bee."

She expelled a sharp breath. I braced for her to scramble up and over to the toilet, but she remained still. "Do you think he was scared?" she whispered. Her breaths quickened. "When he saw the truck, did Dad know?"

A tear slipped down my cheek before I realized I was crying.

"I can't stop wondering about it. What he was thinking when it happened." She squeezed her eyes shut. "I think about it all the time and . . . and you don't want to talk about it."

"Phoebe," I gasped, feeling like she'd plunged a hand straight through my chest.

Her lip trembled. "I hope he wasn't scared. I hope he didn't know." Her eyes snapped open and she lurched for the toilet. I moved up on my knees to hold back her hair, a huge knot forming in my throat, tears flowing.

What the hell was I supposed to say to that? Phoebe voiced the thoughts I had on my worst nights; knowing she thought them too wrecked me. Unleashing them at her most vulnerable made sense, in a way, as if she decided she couldn't feel worse so she might as well delve into the deepest pits of her mind. It had been a long time since I dipped my toes into those. Hearing Phoebe go there hurt worse than any physical pain I'd felt in my life. I had no idea what to say. I wanted to help her without making it worse. I wanted her to know I understood without seeming preachy. I didn't want her to have those thoughts, period.

Sometimes, I hated my dad for dying. On days like this, I was sure I'd never forgive him for it.

A soft knock on the door snapped me out of my head. I took a deep breath and resumed rubbing Phoebe's back. "Come in."

Dex pushed the door open, making a point to not look at my sister. "Uh," he said, wincing at the unholy sounds. He held up a plastic CVS bag. "Anti-nausea meds, Saltines, and Pedialyte."

I forced a smile. "Thanks."

"Are you . . ." His brow furrowed as he looked at me and I fought the urge to wipe my eyes. "Everything good?"

"Obviously not," Phoebe wailed, her voice echoing in the toilet bowl. "I'm dying."

"Well, yeah," Dex replied. "You ate something called the Mega Chicken Volcano."

"Don't say its name."

"Anything I can do?"

"Build a time machine."

The corner of his mouth pulled up, but then his eyes shifted to me, seeming to ask a question: *Are you okay?* I gave a quick nod, turning my attention to Phoebe, who flushed the toilet and lay back down, burying her face in my stomach.

"I'm right out here if you need anything," Dex said. I waved him off. He'd done more than enough with that trip to the pharmacy and, as Phoebe's guardian, it was my responsibility to handle the gross stuff. She hadn't gotten sick the entire time we'd lived together—I never thought to be grateful for it, but I sure as hell was now.

I brushed my hand over Phoebe's hair, smoothing it in a slow, comforting pattern like Dad used to do when we were sick. She let out a slow breath, reaching up to wipe her forehead.

"I'm sorry," she murmured, eyelids fluttering. "This is so gross."

"Don't apologize. It's not that gross."

She pinched my side. "Don't lie."

I leaned my head against the wall, smiling. "I teach third grade, Bee. This is far from the first time I've dealt with a little vomit."

"A shit ton," she mumbled. I kept smoothing her hair and she snuggled closer to me, a little bit of pink returning to her cheeks. "So maybe we shouldn't stop at that place with the burger that has cinnamon rolls for buns."

"Maybe not."

"Thank you." Her voice went quiet, honeylike. "For staying, Vi."

I bent over, pressing a soft kiss to her sweaty temple. "Always."

I meant it, although I certainly meant it less when the next wave hit. After what felt like hours, Phoebe settled down and insisted on a makeshift bed in the bathroom for easy access. I laid out every blanket from the back of Dex's car, hoping they would be enough cushion to minimize the hard, cold tile, and she zonked out immediately.

I showered in the second bathroom, emerging in pajama shorts and a tank top, hair damp around my shoulders. I found Dex in the quaint kitchen, gazing out the window over the sink, both hands braced on the butcher block counter. After the day of misery, I couldn't fault myself for taking a moment to drink him in—the fitted black T-shirt and sweatpants, the ropy muscles of his arms, the slope of his shoulder blades, his messy hair curling at the base of his neck.

"Hey," I said.

He turned, eyes dipping to my bare legs and back to my face in a blink. "Hey. How's she doing?"

"Sleeping finally. I'm hoping the worst is over."

"Did she have any Pedialyte? She really needs to stay hydrated."

I tried to push away the warm, gooey feeling. "A little," I said, toying with the hem of my shorts. "I'll check on her in a bit and make sure she has some more."

He nodded, satisfied with this. "I, uh, got us a pizza. I don't know if you have an appetite after today, but it's there."

"Maybe later." I smiled. "Thank you. For everything."

He made a face. "You don't need to thank me."

"You found us a place to hunker down, got Phoebe medicine, and got me dinner. You're amazing." The words slipped out, unwitting. Dex blinked twice and dropped his head, shoving his hands in the pockets of his sweats.

"Violet," he said, almost a warning. Because apparently now I couldn't even say thank you. Pushing down the sting of rejection, I turned on my heel and headed into the living room. The cabin was quaint, eight hundred square feet of rustic log walls and a huge, encroaching stone fireplace. I paused, staring into the depths of it, wondering what it was like here in the winter, snow on the ground outside and a fire crackling, warming the whole cabin. I imagined three stockings hung from the mantel and enough twinkly lights to illuminate the state of Wyoming.

I shook the thought from my head and folded my arms tightly, veering for the couch. I sank into it—it was worn, too soft, and my back would kill if I sat there for more than twenty minutes, but then Dex appeared in the doorway and I pressed myself farther into the cushions, feet planted firmly on the floor.

"You were crying," he said quietly. I exhaled, scrubbing my hands over my face.

"Yeah. She was . . . she said some stuff. About our dad," I explained, dropping my hands to my lap. "It broke my heart."

"You wanna talk about it?"

"God, no. I want to be distracted. You up for the job?"

It took a beat for the words to land, for both of us. I hadn't meant it in a suggestive way, but it sure sounded like I did, and my blood sizzled to a boiling point. Dex cleared his throat.

"Television," I blurted, gesturing wildly to the ancient box in the corner of the room. "TV is a great distraction. One of the best."

His face broke into a smile and he shook his head, coughing out a laugh. I couldn't help joining in. We were being silly. I couldn't figure out if we were pretending too hard or not hard enough.

Our laughter put a pinprick in the tension, enough for us to sideline the rest and eat the entire pizza while watching reruns of *The Office*. It was so delightfully mundane. The sort of unremarkable night that maybe once would've been easily forgotten, but now I knew to hold on to it with both hands. What a privilege it was to be bored and boring. We were alive at the same time, on opposite ends of the couch. I could've lived in this moment with him forever.

I checked on Phoebe in twenty-minute intervals and by midnight, it seemed like the storm had officially passed and she was out for the night. When I returned to the living room, the end credits were playing and Dex had slumped farther down the couch, long legs crossed at the ankles, eyelids heavy.

"What's the update?" He'd made a point to ask after each check-in and I tried my best not to melt into a puddle of goo.

"Still sleeping," I reported. "But now she's facing away from the toilet."

"Good sign."

"I thought so."

"What do you think? Are we done for the night?" He was already reaching for the remote. I could've stayed up with him longer, but that might have led to waking up tangled on the couch and the resulting complications, so I forced myself to nod even as I plopped down in my spot. He shut off the television, snapping us into silence. "I hate that show," he mumbled, folding his arms over his chest.

I gasped. "What?"

"The most overrated series of all time."

"You're the most overrated of all time!" I cried. "*The Office* is classic. Steve Carell deserved an Emmy. I'll die on that hill."

"Have fun with that," he said, his eyes slipping shut. I leaned my head against the couch, admiring the slope of his nose, the sharp jut of his jaw, his dark hair curling over the top of his ear, his eyelashes long enough to fan across his cheeks.

"Okay," I said. "What would you watch, then?"

He hummed thoughtfully. "I'm not a big TV guy. I'd rather watch a movie."

Another tidbit unlocked. I wanted to unravel everything about him, right here on this couch. "What's your favorite movie?"

"*Magnolia,*" he answered without hesitation. "Fuckin' masterpiece."

"Is that Paul Thomas Anderson?" He opened his eyes, regarding me with muted surprise. I smiled and added, "*Phantom Thread.* Fuckin' masterpiece."

He groaned, shutting his eyes again. "You're wrecking me, woman."

My heart banged against my rib cage twice, three times. I licked my lips, unable to draw in a sufficient breath. "Why?"

"You know why."

"Do I?" I stared, rapt, as he opened his eyes, keeping them focused on the ceiling. "Does that mean we're not pretending it never happened anymore?"

He let out a small sigh. "Violet."

I raised my hands innocently. "Hey, you're the one who brought it up."

"I don't think I did."

"Okay, well." I took as deep a breath as my struggling lungs would allow. "I think we should talk about it because it did happen and it was . . ."

I trailed off as his eyes cut to me. The dull lamp behind me cast long shadows around us, framing his head, and he was so much more beautiful than he ever was as an intimidating stranger. I pitied anyone on the street whose eye he caught—they'd miss out on the things that made him shine like this.

"It was really fucking good," he finished for me, his voice low, ragged. I felt it somewhere deep and untouched. A want so foreign, I was sure I was the first to ever feel it—or second, considering the look in Dex's eyes.

"Yeah," I exhaled. "I haven't stopped thinking about it."

He swallowed. "I can't stop. It's on a constant replay in my brain."

"That's good. I was a little worried I was alone there."

"Not alone. I am very present."

"Are you?"

He broke away, leaning his head back against the couch. "I shouldn't be. But yeah. I really am."

"How present?" I asked softly, eyes roving over his face. That muscle in his jaw jumped predictably—I could read him in ways I never dreamed possible the day we met. So tightly wound, valiantly holding himself back from the things he wanted. God, I wanted to see him come undone again.

"Violet."

His voice was a warning. Something about him tonight, only a cushion between us on the couch, the deep scent of timber and cinnamon surrounding us—he had me. I couldn't look away. He opened his eyes, meeting mine in the dull glow shining through the skylight. The sensation of falling gripped me, room spinning, but Dex remained still, stoic, his eyes so dark, something flaring deep within them that sent a ripple of electricity through me.

I felt like a deer caught in a staring contest with an oncoming truck.

He unfolded his arms slowly, placing one hand on the cushion between us, the other on his thigh. My eyes dropped with the movement. I inhaled sharply at the outline of him through his sweatpants, the hardness obvious against the thin fabric, and *fuck,* that ache between my legs returned with a vengeance. Maybe we were both still keyed up from the elevator. Maybe it had been just as long for him as it had been for me.

What are you thinking of doing to me? I thought, lifting my eyes back to his. *I'd let you.*

He let out a jagged breath and I wondered if he was a mind reader or if the desperation was written all over my face: *Touch me, fuck me, hold me, break me. I'd take it all and say thank you.*

I placed a hand on the cushion, close to his, accepting the invitation to this strange game of Chicken. My other hand, seemingly of its own volition, drifted to my stomach. Dex's gaze slid down slowly as my chest rose in heady breaths, to my fingers twitching with the urge to move. He swallowed, snapping his eyes back to mine.

Then he moved the hand on his thigh to his erection, adjusting himself with a pained expression, and I wondered what hurt more: the need or the want. The pressure building between my own thighs grew blinding. We needed relief.

It never happened, my brain whispered as my hand drifted lower, toying with the string of my pajama shorts. Dex watched me, rapt, inhaling sharply as my hand slipped under the waistband. I was wetter than I could ever remember being and at the first brush of contact, an involuntary sound scraped from my throat. Immediately, any semblance of hesitation disappeared, overwhelmed by the need to come with his eyes on me. I looked at him, breathing hard, fingers working exactly where I needed them, imagining they were his. His lips parted as he watched me and then he squeezed his eyes shut, so briefly, and reached into his pants.

Stars filled my vision. He groaned at the first slide of his hand, and the second, and I synced up my movements with his, that slow, precise maneuver that would probably be considered making love if he were inside me. But he was, wasn't he? He'd overtaken everything, filling my head with a constant fog, and now here we were. Inevitable.

In the quiet room, our sounds were obscene. Skin against wet skin, bitten moans, the couch whining against our soft movements. We each kept a hand on the cushion. It didn't take long for me to reach the point of gasping, of fractured, slippery movements anticipating relief. It landed like a detonation, rocking through my whole body, overwhelming every thought, limb, cell. The noises coming from me were unfamiliar. This *feeling* was unfamiliar. I'd had plenty of orgasms, and yet coming on my own fingers with Dex's eyes locked on me was the most intense experience of my life. I couldn't help reaching across the cushion, my fingers wrapping around his wrist, nails digging in as I rode out the release, and then he bent forward with a guttural groan.

Our heavy breathing soundtracked over the silence. I swallowed hard, dizzy, staring at the side of Dex's head as his movements slowed to a statuesque stillness. My fingers were tight around his wrist.

Could we pretend *this* never happened?

Slowly, Dex withdrew his hand from my grip and climbed to his feet. "See you in the morning," he murmured without looking at me and moved toward the bedroom, the door softly clicking shut behind him.

I'd expected this and still, my hopeful heart sank. He wasn't mine to touch, to watch, to turn on, to keep. And I just kept reaching, hoping he might reach back.

But he *did*. Each time I plucked up the nerve to push a little harder, he pulled me right in, at least until reality dawned. Dex didn't seem like the type for games, so the logical answer was guilt. Catalina was states away, closer to him than she'd been in years, and he kept looking at me. *I'll love you forever,* his letter said. We wouldn't be here if that wasn't true.

I had to stop holding on to this man whose heart belonged to someone else. I needed to accept things as they were instead of wishing they were something else, something better. I was beginning to wonder how thin the line was between *hope* and *hopeless*. I sat there for a little too long, waiting, and I imagined Dex on the other side of the bedroom door doing the same thing.

I went upstairs.

Seventeen

Wyoming boasted the most beautiful scenery we'd witnessed so far, which was the perfect excuse to avoid looking at Dex.

Phoebe remained wobbly in the morning, but by the afternoon she'd downed four slices of peanut butter toast and loudly complained about how gross Pedialyte was, so we felt okay piling into the car for the long drive to Idaho. I'd spent a solid five minutes in front of the bathroom mirror, debating the patheticism of another few hours pretending to sleep in the back seat and decided against it. The color had returned to Phoebe's face, her mood bright and cheery, and I refused to put a damper on it. I contributed to the conversation like everything was just peachy, and I pointedly avoided looking at Dex.

He didn't look at me either. His attention had become a solid, physical thing. I felt it as if it were a heavy pressure bearing down on my shoulders and now that it was missing, I had to walk carefully as to not drift away in the wind.

"We should make this an annual trip," Phoebe said about an

hour down Interstate 80. I turned fully in my seat, fixing her with an incredulous look. "Not going to see Catalina. I just mean the trip in general. We should travel more."

"On Dex's dime," I said.

She beamed. "Exactly."

"It's a nice thought," Dex said. "But I'm never driving again after this, so you're out of luck."

I rolled my eyes. "You're so annoying. I've offered to drive a million times."

He grumbled something unintelligible under his breath. Phoebe popped up through the center console and said, "He doesn't trust you with the Benz."

"I don't give a shit about the car," he muttered.

"Says the guy who vacuums it every morning," I said.

Phoebe looked around, eyes widening. "Oh my god. You do?"

"No," Dex said through gritted teeth.

She slapped her hand down on the console. "You're a freak!"

"That's not very nice, Phoebe," I said diplomatically. "It could be a sickness."

"Fuck off," Dex snapped. "You two are the messiest people I've ever met. You eat an apple and produce crumbs. I don't know how you do it."

"It's a gift," Phoebe said. "Also, I like cinnamon sugar on my apples. I can't eat them any other way."

"Except Honeycrisp." I glanced at her and her eyes lit up. "You love Honeycrisp apples."

"I do love Honeycrisp apples." She sighed wistfully. "Our grocery store never has them. They have Red Delicious. Who likes Red Delicious?" She paused, taking a moment to regard Dex suspiciously. "I bet you do."

"That," he said, "is the worst thing you've ever said to me."

She threw her head back, laughing. "And I say a *lot* of terrible things to you."

In my periphery, I watched him adjust his grip on the wheel and I did not think about what those hands did last night. "The grocery store near my place has Honeycrisp apples," he mentioned. "I'll bring you some."

I spun in my seat to look at him for the first time since last night: his stubble more pronounced than I'd ever seen it, the shadows under his eyes revealing he got about as much sleep as I did. He was making plans to see us when this was over, as if things wouldn't be irreversibly different. If all went well with Catalina, he might not even come back to Boston.

The thought turned my stomach over. I sank in my seat, breathing hard to steady my spinning mind.

"Can we . . ." I swallowed over a dry patch in my throat. "Can we stop? For a second."

The weight of Dex's eyes returned and I hated the relief of it. "Are you okay?" Dex asked sharply. Phoebe's clammy hand clamped over my forehead.

"She's warm," she confirmed. I batted her hand away. "Oh man. Did I do this? Is food poisoning contagious?"

"I'm not sick. I just need to stop for a sec."

Dex took the next exit to the closest gas station. Once parked, I pushed the door open and ducked my head against the warm wind, letting fresh air fill my lungs. Phoebe's jelly sandals appeared in my vision and when I lifted my head, I was met by concern etched in her features.

"I'm okay," I assured her. She shifted her weight, giving the parking lot a scan.

"There are a bunch of bushes if you have to puke. I wouldn't do it in the bathroom."

"I'm not going to puke." I was pretty sure. "But thanks, Bee."

Dex got out of the car to join her, giving her shoulder a squeeze. "Here," he said, offering her some cash. "Grab some water, Dramamine, and a granola bar."

Phoebe nodded, seeming relieved to have a task, and darted for the entrance. I shut my eyes, the dizziness setting in as the weight of Dex's gaze returned.

"Vi," he said quietly.

"It's okay. I'm okay." I rubbed the space between my brows and then dropped my hand, finally meeting his eyes. He squatted in front of me, too close, and words tumbled out before I could help it. "I'm sorry about last night."

His expression shuttered slightly. "You're sorry."

"I heard you when you said it's better for us to not . . . whatever. But I keep . . ." I blew out a frustrated breath. "I don't want things to be weird between us. I don't want to not talk to you. But I also don't want to keep getting caught up like we did last night when that's not what you want. You must realize I have feelings for you. It's not fair. Rip off the Band-Aid. I promise I can take it."

He studied my face for a long moment. "You think I don't want you?"

"I . . ." I furrowed my brow. "I touched you and you left, Dex."

"You touched me and I came."

Heat ripped up my neck. "That's—" I huffed out a breath, dizzy for an entirely new reason. "You're confusing me."

He scrubbed a hand down his face. "I'm sorry. I wasn't expecting this."

"This," I echoed softly. *I wasn't expecting you,* he meant. His eyes searched mine, his conflict so obvious, it felt like a living thing screaming between us.

"I'm trying so hard to focus on what I need to do while what I want is getting louder. And then that goddamn letter," he said, his voice rough. "What am I supposed to do, Vi?"

The wind whispered Catalina's name, her presence haunting from miles away. The way Dex looked at me made the idea of him being hung up on her almost silly, but his insistence that we keep our distance said otherwise. I wanted to believe he was in this. I couldn't trust my optimistic heart.

"I don't know," I whispered. His throat bobbed and his finger brushed my bare shin. It landed like a punch. "So, we . . . yeah. All settled?"

Another brush, this time his knuckle scorching a circle into the side of my knee. "I have no idea what I'm doing here," he murmured. "I look at you and I can't get a hold of myself."

"Oh." I swallowed hard, watching his knuckle drag up the skin of my thigh and back down again. "Well. Maybe we give in, just once. We get it out of our system and . . ." Eyes locked, he shook his head before the full thought left my lips. "No, yeah. Bad idea."

"That's not something I can do," he said. "*Once.*"

I inhaled sharply. His eyes dipped to my mouth. I remembered what it was like to kiss him, how the world crashed to a halt to accommodate the moment, how it felt deeper than fucking anyone else.

I caught a glimpse of something pink over his shoulder and recoiled, my foot jabbing him in the ribs. "Phoebe!" I exclaimed as he doubled over in a groan. Phoebe approached, eyes narrow as she took us in. "I may have incapacitated Dex. Accidentally."

"Okay," she said, sliding her gaze between us. He stood up, rubbing his side. "You good, man?"

"Did you get everything?"

She held a plastic bag aloft. "Yup. I also got Gatorade, 'cause

I thought you might be dehydrated," she said, moving toward me. "And some donuts in case your blood sugar's low. I don't know if that's a thing if you're not diabetic, but I was covering the bases."

"Thanks, Bee," I said, my bruised heart melting into a puddle in my chest. She handed me the Gatorade. It was the lemonade flavor she always made fun of me for getting because it looked like pee.

Phoebe swiveled to Dex, pulling a pair of neon green plastic sunglasses out of the bag. "Here you go."

He stared at them. "What is that."

"Your new sunglasses." She moved up on her toes to slip them on him, biting back a grin. "Wow. You look *cool.*"

He turned his gaze to me, a glare from the sun bouncing off the neon frame.

"Gorgeous," I said.

His jaw flexed. "We ready?" He rounded the front of the car without waiting for an answer.

"Good call on the sunglasses," I said, shooting Phoebe a smile. She eyed me for a moment and for a split second, a spike of anxiety drilled its way behind my ribs, certain she'd figured out my feelings for Dex. But then her face softened into a smile and she produced two more pairs from the bag, neon purple and neon pink.

Somehow, Wyoming looked even better through a lilac hue.

Eighteen

"**I**s that it?" Phoebe leaned in, practically pressing her nose up to the glass of the bakery. "It looks sort of like it."

I tilted my head for a new angle of the pastry. The window display was full of desserts, most of which were topped with chocolate or fruit, definitely not what my sister dragged me out of bed at 6 A.M. to track down.

"I think that's a chocolate croissant," I said. She threw her head back in a groan. A man jogging down the sidewalk in short shorts shot us a strange look on his way by.

"I hate this. Why can't Google ever tell the truth? I'll be all, 'Hey, Google, where's the nearest public bathroom?' And it'll be like, 'Here's an ad for toilet seats. Wet your pants, pussy.'"

I choked on a laugh. "Phoebe."

"It's not funny." She glared at Mama Sheridan's bakery, folding her arms over her chest. I looped my arm around her shoulders, gently guiding her away in case Mama Sheridan herself emerged to square up. "There's supposed to be an Italian bakery here. I looked it up. Why can't Dex like something normal, like cinnamon rolls?"

"Well, that would be too easy. He's not an easy guy."

She cut me a look and I dug my fingernails into my palm in an effort to keep my face composed. "Maybe it's, like, a hole-in-the-wall place. We should ask around. Someone must know."

"Yeah," I agreed. She charged forward with renewed purpose, head held high.

I'd been confused since she shook me awake for a mission: finding Dex's favorite pastry, something Sicilian called *granita con brioche.* Apparently his grandmother used to make them. When I'd asked how she managed to coax the information out of him, she rolled her eyes and reminded me they were friends.

Maybe if I wasn't so busy blowing past the flimsy boundaries we set, I could've been friends with him too.

We made our way down the sidewalk of a Main Street on the outskirts of Rock Spring, Wyoming. After driving for nearly eight hours yesterday, Dex was exhausted and grumpy, so I'd suggested stopping for the night instead of trying to make it to Idaho. The motel we ended up at only had one room available—two queens—so Phoebe and I shared a bed while Dex crashed in the other, everyone out before seven.

I didn't mind the extra stop. It bought more time before the inevitable.

Phoebe and I asked several locals about the alleged Italian bakery and none of them knew what we were talking about. She grew more frustrated, growling under her breath in a way that would make Dex proud.

"I don't understand," she grumbled, tapping her phone furiously. "It says it's here. It says it's open. So where is it? Where the fuck is it?"

"Maybe we should just . . ." I trailed off when she shot me her dirtiest look. "Sorry."

"It's *annoying*."

"It is, yeah."

She rolled her eyes. "Of course."

"Of course what?"

"Nothing. What were you gonna say? 'Let's just get something from the regular bakery and go back to the motel'? Sure. Whatever." She brushed past me, stomping down the sidewalk. Flummoxed, I jogged to catch up.

"What was that?" I asked. She ignored me, cheeks flushed. "Phoebe."

"Nothing."

"What is going on?"

"I'm mad!" she yelled, wheeling around. I stumbled to a stop, my stomach lurching at the return of her glower, her raised voice, the apparent derision she felt toward me. "Oh, wait, that's right. That's an unfamiliar emotion to you."

I blinked several times in quick succession, a preemptive stinging sensation radiating through my body. "What does that mean?"

"Nothing bothers you these days. Everything is A-fucking-plus all the time." She sniffed and glanced away to hide the glassiness in her eyes. "You're not you anymore. And not even in, like, the 'dad died so we're different' way. From the second you had to take me in, it's been different. You and me. It's wrong."

I took a shaky breath, ignoring the looks we'd begun to garner from strangers moving around us on the sidewalk. "I'm trying, Phoebe," I said. "What is it you want from me? What are the magic words you want me to say? Because I've been searching for months, and I give up. Nothing I say is ever the right thing for you."

"Because it's bullshit!" she shouted, and a tear slipped down her cheek. "It's all fake bullshit you pulled from a parenting book you shouldn't have even had to read. I want to know what you think, not fucking Wanda Knows Fuck All M.D."

"Okay, fair enough." I swallowed hard, taking a small step closer to her. "But can't you just say that to me instead of yelling it on a public sidewalk?"

She kept glaring. The tears in her eyes sparkled under the sun. "This is what I'm talking about. A year ago, you wouldn't be asking me not to yell in public, you'd fight back. Yell at me! Call me a bitch! Punch me in the face! I deserve it!"

"Stop." I moved in closer but she took two big steps backward, bumping into the brick building behind us. "Phoebe, talk to me. Please talk to me. I know I always say the wrong thing, but I am begging you to just talk to me."

"You wanna know why I talk to Dex?" She raised her chin, swallowing hard. "He's real with me. He doesn't bother trying to spare my feelings. He says what he means, all the time."

"I'm real with you."

"On this trip, yeah. You have been. Because you get to act like a normal twenty-six-year-old instead of being cooped up in that stupid apartment with me."

I rubbed my burning eyes. "What's wrong with the apartment?"

"Nothing! Oh my god!" Tears streamed down her face. "Why can't you just admit that I ruined your life?"

I recoiled, feeling like she'd ripped my heart out of my chest and thrown it across the street. "What?"

"I'm sick of you pretending I didn't. Pretending everything is fine." She gulped in a breath and wiped at her eyes. "Shawn left because of me. You were gonna get married. You were happy. And then suddenly you had to take me in and he left."

"Bee—"

"Don't, okay? I need you to stop being, like, 'No, it's okay! Everything's okay!' Because it's not. It hasn't been since Dad died. Since that lady asked if you would take custody of me or if I'd go to Aunt Cindy's and you didn't even *hesitate*. You didn't think about what it would do to your life. Sometimes I wish you'd just give up and send me to Aunt Cindy so we could at least be us again. Now, all I do is make everything harder and worse. Just hate me out loud."

"Phoebe, *no*." I moved forward, taking her face in my hands so she couldn't break eye contact. My vision swam, but she looked up at me with something like hope sparking there. "You are the only reason I'm still standing. You are my reason to wake up in the morning."

"But Shawn—"

"Fuck Shawn."

"You were going to marry him!"

"And it would've been the biggest mistake of my life. Don't think about him. He's not worth it."

"Okay, yeah, he sucks," she agreed, voice trembling. I wiped her tears with my thumbs. "But I still ruined your life."

"Nope."

"You're too young to be stuck with me! You should be out partying!"

"I don't want to party. Sounds like a nightmare."

"*I'm* the nightmare. I've treated you like shit for a year."

"So?"

She blinked up at me, her expression blank. "What do you mean, 'So'?"

"You think I shouldn't love you because you treat me like shit sometimes? I shouldn't want you around?" I tilted my head, gazing at my sister, filled with so much frustration, so much sadness, so much *love*. I should've told her every single day how much she meant to me. I would from here on out. I was still learning how to do this, would probably never fully get the hang of being Phoebe's guardian. But I was her sister, always. "Phoebe, you are the most important person in my life. I love you so much. *So* much. No matter what."

She sniffled, more tears falling. "But it shouldn't be like this."

"I know. It shouldn't. But it is."

She squeezed her eyes shut. "I'm sorry I'm such a bitch."

I moved in, hugging her so tightly, I probably cut off her circulation. She held me just as hard. "You're fourteen and your life kinda sucks right now," I said, planting a kiss on her head. "It's justified."

She crumbled completely, sobbing into my T-shirt. "I miss him so much," she cried. I let my cheek rest on the crown of her head, running my hand up and down her back like our dad used to do when we were sad.

"I know. I do, too."

"I'm so sorry, Vi."

"I'm sorry, too, Bee. I'm so, so sorry." I kissed her head again, squeezing her tighter. "We're always us. I know things got messed up for a while, but we're still us, I promise."

She nodded and I felt her shoulders relax as she melted into me, as if for the first time in a year, I'd finally managed to take some of the weight she'd been carrying.

We stayed for a few more minutes before Phoebe playfully shoved me and said we'd embarrassed ourselves enough. On the walk to the motel, we stopped in Mama Sheridan's and she told us the Italian bakery was on a *different* Main Street and people made the same mistake all the time—an annoying end to the mission, but Phoebe seemed content with the box of baked goods Mama Sheridan sent us away with for free because she could tell we'd been crying. Over the course of the trip, I'd watched my sister's growth in real time, but as she bounced down the sidewalk—pieces of pink hair spilling out of her nubby ponytail, her face clear and open and calm—I knew a corner had finally been turned.

She'd spent the last year convinced I resented her. I'd spent the last year convinced she resented me. It built a wall between us, and I regretted chickening out at every opportunity to knock it down. I should've forced that talk a long time ago. I should've done a lot of things. But I was beginning to understand the grace everyone told me to award myself: Grief is fickle, overwhelming, rude, uncomfortable, and, frankly, impossible. We both lost our dad, we both lost the lives we'd grown comfortable in, and we had to start fresh. With a fourteen-year-old to take care of, I'd done my best. But now that Phoebe and I had spilled our guts, the world felt easier to navigate. Phoebe didn't want to be anywhere else. She didn't resent me. She didn't need me to be perfect, she just needed me to be open and honest. I'd tried so hard to hide my pain, convinced it was a weakness. But Phoebe breaking down on the sidewalk was a showcase of bravery. If she could pluck up the courage to tell me the truth, so could I. I'd do better.

When we got back to the motel, Dex was sitting on the edge of his pristinely made bed, his hair damp from a shower, elbows on his knees as he typed something into his phone. He glanced up, immediately clocking the signs of our breakdown.

"Hey," he said, training his face into that neutral expression. Phoebe rolled over the bed we'd slept in, offering the box of baked goods.

"We got stuff!" She opened it, rifling through the treats, and Dex looked to me. His eyes were full of what felt like the same fondness that was pulsing through my veins. I sent him a small smile and sat next to Phoebe. "We tried going to this Italian bakery to get your brioche, but it didn't exist. So, we settled. Didn't know what you'd want, so we got pretty much everything."

"Thanks." He plucked a flaky cinnamon roll from the box. "I appreciate the effort."

"It was so much effort," Phoebe said and housed a cheese Danish in two bites. Hopping to her feet, she let out a garbled "Shower" and disappeared into the bathroom.

Dex's eyes returned to me. He hadn't taken a bite.

"You hate cinnamon rolls, don't you?" I said.

His mouth quirked on one side. "I'll eat it."

"Of course you will." Because my sister had gotten it for him, the same way he wore the green sunglasses she got him at the gas station. He knew that when Phoebe took the time to do something for someone, it mattered.

"Everything okay?" he asked, lowering his voice even as the shower squeaked on in the bathroom.

I nodded, fingers toying with the hem of my skirt. "Yeah. I took your advice, actually, and talked to Phoebe."

"How'd that go?"

"It wasn't so bad."

He dropped his gaze to the cinnamon roll in his hand. "Good. That's good, Vi."

"I think we're gonna be okay," I whispered. He met my eyes, allowing a full smile to light up his face like the sun painting the branches of trees in the woods. The corners of his eyes wrinkled with the beginnings of crow's-feet, a slight indent dug into one cheek that couldn't quite be considered a dimple, and his front teeth sported the teensiest space between them. I'd once thought he was intimidatingly handsome, but seeing him relaxed and maybe just a little bit happy, he was the most beautiful man in the world.

"I always knew that," he said. I shut my eyes, the warmth of this statement swallowing me whole.

My conversation with Phoebe had opened my eyes to how withdrawn I'd become with everyone in my life, even Arden, who'd practically been fused to my side since freshman year of college. I didn't want to be that way. I wanted to say what I meant, feel what I felt, and stop letting the fear of reaction influence my words. I couldn't hold in the truth just because it would tug at Arden's concern, or let Phoebe talk back because she'd hate me if I grounded her, and I wouldn't sit here with Dex and pretend whatever happened between us didn't impact me at all.

"You have to stop saying things that make me want to kiss you," I said softly.

"Considering how long I've wanted to kiss you . . ." he said. "This entire time—Fuck, Vi—it's not something I can just turn off."

I swallowed hard. "But you said—"

"I know what I said. I meant it."

"You sure about that?"

He let out a sound, half laugh, half pure exasperation. "Obviously not."

I plucked the cinnamon roll out of his grasp and took a bite. He watched me, his expression full of conflict.

"I didn't expect this to happen," he added, lowering his voice. "Given . . ."

I flinched away, the unspoken end of that sentence landing heavier than the silence: *Given we're on our way to the love of my life*. I wanted him in a way that physically ached, but I wouldn't stand in the way of Dex and Catalina's happily ever after. As long as that was what they wanted.

My brain kept reaching for assurance that this thing between us was real. It felt real when his eyes were on me. When I said something so ridiculous that it dragged a full-bodied laugh out of him. When he let himself flirt with me and then let it slip into the most unabashedly romantic words anyone had ever said to me. I wanted to believe in him, but how could I when we were still on our way to the woman he'd said he would love forever?

"Maybe we just . . . keep our distance," I said.

He looked away. "Maybe."

"It's not long until Oregon. Once you see Catalina, things will be clearer, I bet."

His eyes snapped to me. "What does she have to do with this?"

"Um." I blinked. "Everything?"

He dropped his head into his hands and groaned. "Fuck. Okay. Violet, I have to tell you something."

My stomach dropped. "Okay?" I said and put the cinnamon roll in the box to free up my hands. When Dex looked at me, there was something so hauntingly familiar in his expression, I gasped out loud. "Oh my god. She's dead. She's dead, isn't she? That's why you said giving her the letter was pointless."

"What?" He scowled. "No. Cat's not . . . No."

I placed my hand over my racing heart. "Okay, Jesus. What was I supposed to think? You look like someone died. What is happening here?"

"This has always been about closure," he said. "I needed this letter gone. Cat deserves it—she deserves that closure. That's the point. I needed it done so we could both move on with our lives." He swallowed, eyes roving my face. "I'm not about to tell you what you deserve. You can decide that on your own. But I'm not worth much of anything with this hanging over my head. I wanted it done before I let myself feel anything for you. Vi, I like you," he said, and my next breath snagged in my throat. "I like being around you—and I don't like being around anyone anymore."

Our knees brushed. I pressed in harder, a reminder I felt the same way, that he already knew. "This means something to me," he said earnestly. Warmth radiated in my chest, my whole body awash with relief. He had no intention of reconciling with Catalina. He wanted me. "At this point, I can take or leave the closure. I could turn around and go back to Boston and be okay with that, as long as you were there and you were looking at me like this. Meeting you and meeting Phoebe . . . that's what made this trip worth anything to me."

I stood, needing to be closer. He opened his knees for me, I stepped between them, my hands brushing over his shoulders, his hands finding my hips. I wanted to kiss him—the elevator felt like so long ago, and now we could relish, unhurried and real—but he pressed his face into my stomach, his arms looping around to hold me, and *oh*, this was better. To be held by him. To let the electricity simmer in a warm glow. To inhale the crisp scent of his soap, to feel his hot breath through my T-shirt, to wrap him up in my arms and bury my face in his hair.

I could so easily fall in love with him. I was halfway there.

When Phoebe emerged from the bathroom, Dex and I had returned to our respective beds and finished the cinnamon roll. She sat beside me and held up her hands.

"So, hear me out."

"Uh-oh," I said.

"I think we should take a detour," she continued, shifting her focus to Dex. He regarded her impassively. "Utah's close, right?"

"Utah?" I raised my eyebrows. "What's in Utah?"

"There's this wildlife sanctuary for exotic animals and you can meet elephants and giraffes."

Immediately, I turned to Dex and said, "We should go to Utah."

Phoebe held out her fist and I bumped it. Dex looked between us, unamused. "That's a pretty big detour."

"A *worthwhile* detour." She shot him a charming grin. "Come on, Dex. This is a once-in-a-lifetime opportunity and it's *so* much better than Yogi."

"You picked Yogi," he reminded her. "You want to add another two days to the trip?"

Phoebe glanced at me, her confidence slipping. But that number didn't scare me. I looked at Dex, thinking of spending two more days wrapped around him, and when he looked at me, I knew he was thinking the same thing.

"Fine," he said. "But we're listening to one of my playlists on the way."

Nineteen

"I'm not sure how I feel about this," Arden said, her voice impeded by the rain pelting the windshield. I hadn't meant to slack on updates, but after my heart-to-heart with Phoebe and this thing growing between Dex and me, I'd forgotten to answer more than a few of Arden's texts. This morning, I woke up to: IF YOU DON'T ANSWER IN THE NEXT TEN MINUTES I AM REPORTING YOU AND PHOEBE AS MISSING PER-SONS!!! Of course, she hadn't accounted for the time difference, and we'd all overslept and had to rush to make checkout, so I didn't end up calling until two hours later from the highway.

Her relief trumped her anger, although I could tell she wasn't thrilled to be on speaker. No way could I try to explain what was happening with Dex in the car with him and my sister; even if I spoke in code, Phoebe would figure it out. She was too clever for her own good.

"It's only two more days," I replied.

"No, I mean you guys meeting elephants without me."

Phoebe laughed. "You should go there for your honeymoon."

"Is it bad that I don't hate that idea?"

"Well, Noah hates sand and you hate swimming in open water," I said. "It makes sense in a very specific to you way."

"Hey, Noah!" she shouted, not bothering to lean away from her phone for our benefit. In the driver's seat, Dex flinched. "How do you feel about Utah?"

I could just barely make out Noah's response: "Uh, pro?"

"Interesting," she said, returning her attention to us. "I could get him on board, I think."

"Noah would go anywhere you asked," Phoebe pointed out. Dex glanced at me, so briefly I wouldn't have noticed if I hadn't spent a majority of the last eighty miles staring at him. My heart fluttered.

"He would," Arden agreed. "But it's our *honeymoon*. He should enjoy it, too, and you know he would spend the whole time complaining about the smell."

I looked at Dex and said, "He has a weird thing about zoos."

"The smell or the institution?" he replied.

Phoebe snorted. "You'd think the institution, but no. He hates the poop."

"It's not just the poop," Arden said. "It's all the poop. Multi-species poop."

"Great band name," Phoebe quipped.

"I can't make him deal with multispecies poop on our honeymoon." Arden sighed. "So, it sucks that you guys are doing this magical thing without me. I hate you a tiny bit."

"Sorry." I reached for the bag of gas station goodies stashed at my feet, rifling around for snacks. I came up with a package of powdered donuts and tore them open. "Be glad I vetoed Phoebe's Mall of America suggestion."

Arden gasped. "I'm *dying* to go to Mall of America!"

Dex made a face. I smiled and said, "Dex thinks Mall of America sucks."

"You suck!" Arden cried.

He shrugged. "There are better places."

"Than the biggest mall in the world?"

I had to bite my cheek to keep from laughing at Dex's eye roll. "He thinks you have bad taste. And that you need better life goals."

"That's . . ." Arden paused. "That's nice, actually. It sounds mean, but it's like telling someone they need higher expectations. Dex thinks I'm worth more than Mall of America."

"A cockroach is worth more than Mall of America," he muttered.

I couldn't stifle my laugh that time.

It was honestly embarrassing, how taken I was with this man. My mind had whirred to life, concocting scenarios where we were partners, he liked my friends, and he brought takeout to the apartment and played *Mario Kart* with Phoebe while I dozed on his shoulder. Quiet, domestic scenarios. A future. And then he would discreetly brush my hand or my thigh and I'd be ripped into the blissful present, and I'd remind myself to appreciate it. Here on a highway in Utah, Dex caught my eye and smiled a small, secret smile. He didn't care that I wanted to talk to Arden. He adored Phoebe. It felt like he adored *me* and that meant he was willing to tolerate anything he deemed unpleasant.

If I asked him to take me to Mall of America, he would. He'd complain, but he'd do it.

Before hanging up, Arden asked me to take her off speaker. Softly, she asked, "Are you okay?"

"Yeah," I answered honestly. "Things are really, really good."

She inhaled sharply. "Oh, you slept with him."

"No." I cleared my throat, casting a quick glance over my shoulder at Phoebe. She'd lost interest in Arden, now grinning at her phone. "Not even a little."

"Oh, you did *something*."

"Something isn't *that*."

"What did you do?"

"Nothing." I cleared my throat again. Dex chuckled, probably reading into this fluently. "Stuff. It's cool."

"It's cool?" Arden repeated, sounding surprised. "So, we're no longer pretending it never happened?"

"It happened."

"Are you two . . ." Her voice rose an octave, excitement bleeding in. "Is this a thing? Are you going to come back from this trip with a boyfriend?"

I studied the side of Dex's face until he glanced over and smiled. "I don't know," I said. "Maybe. I hope so."

"I will never forgive you for calling me from the car. How are we supposed to have this conversation right now?"

"We'll have it tonight."

"Will we?"

I hesitated, a warm flush rising up my neck. "Um. I don't know?"

"You know," she said, and I could hear her smirk. I tried to laugh it off, but Dex's eyes bounced back to me, twinkling as if he could hear the salacious undertone of every word.

Once we got to the wildlife refuge, I watched Phoebe's entire being light up as she fed a giraffe. I got to pet an elephant. We laughed until we cried when an elephant swiped Dex's sunglasses off his face. And still, the whole time, I was aware of *him* more than anything.

He grinned when Phoebe fed the giraffes and took a Polaroid with our dad's camera when she met the elephants. He smiled fondly when I asked a tenth question in a row to the man giving us a tour. He laughed just as hard when the elephant stole his glasses and told it to *keep them, please, you're doing me a favor*. His dirty grin when I caught him checking me out on the way back to the car.

You know, Arden said with such conviction. From the look in his eye, Dex did, too.

It took Phoebe forever to go to sleep. Any other night, I'd have cried in the shower over her enthusiastic suggestion of watching a movie with me. Tonight was not that night.

We made it about three-quarters through a second movie before Phoebe crashed. I threw on a dark green Reformation dress I snagged for a hundred bucks on ThredUp, double-checked that I remembered deodorant after my shower, and slipped out of the room.

The fluorescent lighting was harsh after such a dreary day. I padded down the hall to Dex's room, focusing on the brightness rather than my nerves rattling like a loose screen door. We hadn't made definitive plans, nothing out loud. But considering the amount of loaded looks we'd shared, I figured I had an open invitation.

Something unspooled in my chest at the sight of him when he answered my knock: his soft smile, his shirt unbuttoned at the collar and the sleeves rolled to his elbows, feet bare against the plush carpet. I had to resist the urge to step right up to him and bury my face in his neck.

"Hey," he said, opening the door wider for me. His room was identical to ours, although it had one queen bed and a slightly different painting of a landscape.

"Sorry it's late," I said. "Phoebe wanted to watch a movie and then she wanted to watch *another* movie." I hesitated, noting his smirk. "Not that we had plans or anything."

His smirk graduated into a smile. "We had plans."

I swallowed down the frenzy of fireworks bursting in my throat. "Yeah. We did."

He got us each a bottle of water from the minifridge and we sat at the edge of the bed, knees pressed together, angled toward each other. Tension hung like smoke, but I was glad neither of us initiated anything. As good as I knew it would feel, now that I was here, all I really wanted to do was hang out with him.

He'd become one of my favorite people so quickly. It was dizzying.

"I was a little worried you'd be asleep when I got here," I told him. He smiled, his thumb scraping at the label on his water. "I almost fell asleep during *Mr. Deeds* and that's one of my all-time favorite movies. It was such a long day. Not bad, just long."

"I used to like driving," he said, and I snorted. "I used to go for long drives to wind down. Now, I get behind the wheel and I'm instantly furious."

"Just let me drive!"

"I don't want you to drive. You deserve a break."

A loud buzzing filled my head. Our eyes locked. "So do you," I said quietly.

I felt his smile in my gut. "You can drive tomorrow," he agreed, just as quiet. "And I will stare at you the entire way to Idaho. I won't be subtle."

My heart did some sort of kickflip. Rubbing my chest, I said, "I think you were actually born to be a passenger princess. It's your calling."

"What does that mean?"

"Phoebe keeps texting it to me. I'm ninety percent sure it's not an insult." He snorted and I felt myself glowing. "I really don't mind. Driving, I mean. We still have the whole way home."

His smile widened. "Maybe we'll take the southern route. Hit every Waffle House along the way."

"Crazy that you'd voluntarily deal with us longer than necessary." I bumped his shoulder with mine. "You like us."

"I do."

"No complaints?"

"Very few."

"Well, now you have to tell me."

"The Twinkies."

I gasped. "Those were gifts! Out of the kindness of my heart!"

"Anything else. Literally anything else, Vi."

"Fine. Next time you're getting a Moon Pie."

"What the hell is a Moon Pie?"

"It has marshmallow in it." He pulled a disgusted face and I laughed. "Tell me what else you like," I urged, leaning in closer. His eyes drifted from my face down the slope of my neck, catching himself before dropping any lower. "I want to know you. You know so much about me."

"What do you want to know?" he asked.

"What's your favorite food?"

He didn't even hesitate. "Pad Thai."

"Favorite color."

His eyes dipped to my dress's neckline. "Right now, green."

Heat burned up my neck. "Stop."

"This." He took a lazy perusal of my body, and every part of me buzzed to life. "Yeah. That's my favorite."

"Such a charmer." I pushed a piece of hair behind my ear and his eyes snapped to the movement. "Do you have any embarrassing hobbies? Like, truly embarrassing."

"Every few months I'm overwhelmed by the desire to learn how to play the harmonica."

That startled a laugh out of me. "What? Why?"

"When I transferred to Northeastern, I moved into a dorm

with two guys. Gavin and Denny. Gav insisted the best way to bond was to form a band. For three guys with no musical prowess, he assigned us what he deemed the easiest instruments. I got the harmonica. Denny got the kazoo. Gav obviously gave himself the triangle."

"Of course he did."

He smiled, that not-dimple digging into his cheek. "Maybe it's the nostalgia that gets me reaching for the old plastic harmonica he bought at the dollar store."

"You still have it," I said wondrously, though I'd come to realize Dex was a sentimental guy when it came to the people he loved.

"I do. And I'm just as terrible now as I was the day he gave it to me."

"That's so funny." I rubbed my nose, hesitating before adding, "My dad played the harmonica."

His eyes widened. "You're kidding."

"He was a roadie in the nineties. He learned a lot of useless shit from bands."

He nodded slowly, letting this information simmer. "Gonna have to pick up the harmonica when we get home. For your dad." He set his water bottle down on the floor between his feet, his focus never leaving me. "What else?"

I couldn't breathe. My lungs collapsed under the weight of Dex casually vowing to honor my dad. "Hmm?"

"You were asking me questions."

"Oh." My brain fuzzed between static and coherent thoughts. "Right. Um." I swallowed hard, my gaze slipping from his face to his open collar, sticking on the bit of chest hair visible. "God. This would be easier if you didn't look like that."

"What would be easier?"

"Thinking."

"Ah." His knee pressed harder into mine and I felt myself lean closer to him, as if drawn by a magnet. "So, you understand what I've been dealing with."

A soft laugh whooshed out of me. "It's different. You're . . ." I waved my hand at his face and he caught it, bringing it down to the bedspread. "Gorgeous. I didn't even shave my legs."

He laughed and my stomach swooped at the sound. "Vi. I don't care."

"I know." He'd seen me at some truly low points and stayed anyway. I mattered to him, in any state. "You're so different than I thought you were."

"You just . . ." His throat bobbed and his eyes fell to my lips. "You woke me up. I'm half convinced I was sleepwalking until you showed up."

"Oh." I scooted closer, closer, until my forehead touched his and I could draw his hand into my lap, holding it with both of mine. Somehow, Dex had managed to articulate this feeling. "Yeah. Awake."

"I am so fucking awake."

"Me too."

He cupped my jaw, soft and reverent, tipping my head back until our mouths brushed. A taste, and then he pressed in deeper, his breaths coming quick and sharp in time with my own. I parted my lips, needing more of him, and it still wasn't enough, so I dropped his hand and anchored myself with his shoulders, pushing myself up and over to straddle his lap.

"Is this okay?" I whispered as his hazy eyes roamed the low neckline of my dress.

"God. Yes." He leaned in, pressing a hot, open-mouthed kiss to my neck. I arched against him, reveling in the sensation of his tongue brushing over my skin, the softness of his hair slipping through my fingers, the friction of him through his pants. "Do whatever you want to me. Please."

My laugh snagged in my throat as his hands moved over my breasts, feeling me through the thin fabric. A pathetic sound ground out of my throat and he immediately pressed kisses to the underside of my jaw, my cheek, my lips. If the elevator had been a frenzy, this was controlled chaos; we'd fall into a passionate rhythm, all tongues and panting breaths and grinding hips, and one of us would force patience. Him stilling my hips with a tight groan. Me breaking away to remember to breathe.

When his hands slipped under my dress, I gasped even before he lifted me up to lay me on the bed. He knelt between my legs, his fingers tracing an agonizing line up from my ankle. "Do you have any idea how hard it is to focus on the road when you're in those little skirts?" he murmured, brushing his thumb across the inside of my knee and sending a bolt of lightning through my body. "Unreal. It's unreal."

"Didn't know I was so distracting," I said, voice catching on a whine as his touch brushed upward.

"Right here." His fingers lingered at the sensitive inner skin of my thigh. "You cross your legs and your skirt slips up. I can't believe you haven't caught me staring."

"Dex." My own fingers wrapped around his wrist, urging him closer.

"I can't stop looking."

"*Dex.*" He tore his gaze up, his tongue swiping across his bottom lip. "Touch me."

He was such a good listener. So attentive to every detail. I didn't fully appreciate that trait until he obliged my demand without hesitation, reaching up my dress, fingers hooking the waistband of my underwear, dragging them down my legs. I squirmed, watching his brow furrow with concentration as his hands cupped my thighs, scraping over them deliciously, and then farther to brush his thumbs over my hip bones. I shut my eyes, trying to control my breathing.

"God," he mumbled, and then his mouth was on my thigh, a soft kiss, a gentle bite. I cried out and reached down to tangle my fingers in his hair so he wouldn't get any crazy ideas, like stopping. "Patience is a virtue, you know."

"What's virtue?" I replied breathlessly, and he laughed into my skin.

The ache building between my legs graduated into something close to pain and when Dex finally brushed a featherlight finger over me, I bucked against him and let out a moan. He didn't laugh. Didn't tease me. He applied more pressure, abandoning his post at the hickey on my thigh to give me his full attention. *He wants to know what I like,* I thought just as he ran his fingers across the slickness and my mind winked out entirely.

"Fuck," he exhaled. His fingers moved the same path, almost experimentally. My breaths were jagged, unsteady. Spots impeded my vision.

"Dex, please." I gasped at another brush of his fingers. "This is really embarrassing, but I'm going to come and I don't want to come like this. This is great. It's unbelievable. But I need your fingers or you need to fuck me or *something.*"

He blinked up at me, his cheeks flushed, the haze in his eyes clearing slightly. "You're going to come?"

"Yes."

"Why is that embarrassing?"

"We haven't even done anything yet." I tried to take a steadier breath. "It's been a long time since I was with anyone."

"Okay," he said, and he ducked his head between my legs. My mind lagged, catching up as his mouth opened up against me, and we both moaned at the slide of his tongue. "Christ," he said, angling my body closer. "This is all I've thought about for weeks."

My fingers fisted his hair, probably too hard. I had no control. "Oh my god."

"You taste like a fucking dream."

I couldn't pinpoint whether his words tipped me over the edge, or his fingers joining the swirl of his tongue. Blinding pleasure rushed in from all sides. I was vaguely aware of my own sounds—a mix of garbled words and whimpers—and as I came down, I realized my grip on Dex's hair had inched too far past rough, holding him against me. I tried to catch my breath, exhaled a soft apology and released him, but he grunted his disapproval and dipped another finger inside me.

"Dex," I gasped, my body jolting.

"One more minute. Can I have another minute?" His tongue melted against me and my head fell back. "Please, Vi?"

"Yes."

"Grab my hair again. Just like—*Yeah*."

I gripped him hard and he rewarded me with a deep groan, his mouth and fingers syncing up in a devastating rhythm, practically devouring me. I'd never experienced this sort of pleasure. Dex loved this, it was so apparent in his sounds. And when I managed a glance down at him, I could see it in his face, how good this was for him, too, and I fell apart again, crying out at the ceiling.

Dex crawled up my boneless body, kissing me gently, tasting like me, and I reached for the buttons of his shirt, working them quickly. He let me push it off his shoulders and run my hands down his chest; my wildest fantasies couldn't compare. And I wanted his skin, so I shifted to pull my dress over my head, tossing it over the side of the bed, relishing the flare in his eyes upon realizing I wasn't wearing a bra. Immediately, his hands came over my breasts, followed by his mouth. The soft suction paired with the guttural groan he let out, reveling, sent a spike of pleasure right through me. Was I that pent-up? Or was this the effect Dex had on me?

"Perfect," he murmured. Goosebumps rose under his tongue. "You're perfect."

"You already made me come twice. I don't think I'm the perfect one," I said, slipping my hands to his pants. He was so hard, so patient. I took a moment to feel him, running my hand over him, and he pressed his forehead to my shoulder. "Do you have a condom?"

"Yeah." He swallowed hard. "Yeah. I got some at the gas station earlier."

"Thank god."

He kissed the space between my breasts and rolled off me, shuffling over to his bag. I sat up, naked, flushed and breathless, and when he looked at me, he tipped his head back and ran a hand down his face.

"Perfect," he said again.

He returned with a condom and peeled his pants off before climbing over me. I tore open the foil wrapper, my breath coming in hot bursts as he moved down my body, lavishing it with wet kisses and soft bites, sucking the skin under my breast until the pressure was almost too much and I scratched at his shoulders, begging him to let me put the condom on him.

I looked up at him, a little spiral of thrill setting in at the darkness in his eyes, watching me roll the condom down his length. "You sure?" I whispered.

He nodded, cradling my jaw with his hand. "Are you?"

"Yes."

He settled over me, taking another moment to just look. *I can't stop looking,* he'd said. I knew what he meant. And as he pushed inside me, I let myself watch him. The muscles in his neck and shoulders pulling taut, his brow pinching, his eyes roving mine, first in search of discomfort and then a softness edging in as he began to move and I wrapped myself in him, pulling him close, pressing my face into his neck, breathing him in, tasting the salt on his skin, muffling my sounds until I couldn't hold back anymore and pulled his face to mine. His mouth opened, his tongue sliding over mine. I could taste his sounds, could feel them deep in my gut. My nails dug into his back and he hissed out a "*Fuck, Vi, yes.*" I lifted my hips for him and he hiked my leg up like he had in the elevator, angling to get deeper.

Vocabulary no longer existed. Just our sounds, our hands, the place where our bodies met, the wet wonderful slide of it. Another orgasm tore through me and I grabbed at Dex, my body out of control as it chased the pleasure, and he worked me through it, sweat beading on his forehead. When he came undone, he groaned my name and nearly bent me in half, his hips jerking into me hard, out of his control, and I held him, whispering in his ear that it was so good, he felt so good.

We fell together, breathing each other's air, hands absentmindedly stroking each other, his shoulders, my hair, his cheek, my hip. I kept my limbs wound around him so he wouldn't go, but he didn't try to. He pressed his face into my neck, letting out the smallest sigh when I brushed my fingers through his hair.

"I have the bizarre urge to thank you," I said.

He chuckled lightly and rolled onto his side. I went with him, attached like a barnacle. "The pleasure was all mine."

"Liar." He laughed again and I buried my grin in his chest. "I love your laugh."

He brushed his fingers through my hair, a slow pattern, and my eyes fell shut, snuggling farther into him. "You said you want to know me," he murmured. "I want that too. Sometimes it's just hard to get the words out."

"I know," I said softly, brushing my fingertips across his stomach. "Take all the time you need."

His lips pressed firmly to the top of my head, once, twice. My every atom hummed. He said, "You smell so good. It makes me dizzy."

"That's good?"

"Mm-hmm."

I dragged my fingers up and down the line of his stomach, watching his breath quicken, as I said, "You smell good, too."

"I smell like you, now," he replied. I felt him smile against my hair. "How long can you stay?"

"We have time," I said. He exhaled slowly, holding me closer. "Yeah. We have time."

Twenty

I wasn't ready to leave Utah, so I cashed in a detour. We spent another day exploring Provo before heading to a rental Dex had found near the Idaho border. We ordered takeout and watched a movie (Phoebe's pick of *Saw* had Dex complaining incessantly while I watched from behind a pillow), and once I was sure Phoebe was asleep, I snuck down the hall to Dex's room.

If Phoebe was suspicious, she didn't let on. She seemed thrilled that I had chosen a detour, and she even discovered a lookout with an amazing view she wanted us to visit along the way. Now, though, it seemed like the route was merely a suggestion, not necessarily meant to be followed.

Oregon loomed, too close for comfort. The stakes felt higher. Phoebe still believed in a happily ever after. I was half in love with Dex. And he seemed to be on the same page, but I couldn't help the fear popping into my brain like a monster in a haunted house: Dex taking one look at Catalina and snapping into the mindset he'd been in when he wrote that letter. *You're everything, Cat. I'll love you forever.* We went on this trip because he *needed* her to have those words. His dedication to handing over that letter meant something and I was pretty sure it wasn't just closure.

But then he'd kiss me. He'd whisper sweet words into my neck, my stomach, between my thighs. He let me catch him looking in the car, miles-long traffic spent in a staring contest. He made sure the rental had three bedrooms and he let me cling to him all night. And in the morning, after slow, sleepy sex, he told me he wanted to make breakfast, and it felt like he'd offered me the world rather than some scrambled eggs.

"Did we know he could cook?" Phoebe asked, shooting the kitchen entryway a wary look, as if Dex had been swapped out for a clone overnight.

"Nope," I said, my eyes locked on the arched path leading into the kitchen. Every once in a while, Dex would drift into frame, whisking something.

"We've had every meal with him for the last week and he didn't think to mention it? What else can he cook? Is it just breakfast or have we been missing out on everything?" She shifted on the couch to face me, her expression turning serious. "Vi. What if he can *bake*?"

I imagined Dex in an apron and immediately shoved the thought away. Too inappropriate with my sister's eyes on me.

"There's so much we don't know about him," she said. "He keeps the weirdest things secret. Why couldn't we know he lived in Chicago? Why didn't he tell us he could cook? How is he so rich? What sort of monster says 'neither' when you ask if they're a dog or cat person?"

A tiny wave of unease lapped at my mind. I didn't know the answers, either, and if I asked, I couldn't guarantee he'd offer them. *Sometimes it's just hard to get the words out.* I'd told him to take all the time he needed and I meant it, but that didn't make it easier to exist on the outside of a locked door.

"He was screwing with you on the dog or cat question," I said and she made a dubious face. "He's a private person, Bee. Give him time."

"Hmm." She reached for the remote and switched the TV on. "Whatever."

I watched her flip through the channels as the thick scent of bacon barreled in from the kitchen. The rental was a quaint Cape Cod–style house with a large garden, only a short ride to the lookout Phoebe wanted to visit. I'd thought the house was a bit underwhelming, but now I had to appreciate the compartmentalized floor plan.

"Be right back," I said, hopping to my feet. Phoebe nodded, eyes locked on the screen. When I entered the kitchen, Dex was tending a sizzling pan on the stove and steam screamed from a waffle maker on the counter. Three plates littered the marble island, dressed with sliced strawberries. "Wow," I said. "This is impressive."

Dex glanced over his shoulder. "Is it?"

"You're like Gordon Ramsay or something." He turned his attention to the bacon, flipping it with tongs. I made my way over, leaning into his shoulder. "Phoebe's aghast. She can't believe you didn't tell us you can cook."

"She didn't ask."

"So, this isn't a fluke."

"A fluke?"

"You didn't learn how to make one meal and bust it out whenever you need to impress?"

"There was a box of instant waffle mix in the cupboard. I wouldn't call that impressive."

I smiled, watching his hands as he adjusted the burner. "You would do numbers as a social media chef."

He snorted.

"No, seriously," I said. He glanced at me, eyes alight with the warmth of a smoldering campfire. "You're hot. You've got that dry sense of humor the kids are into these days."

"The kids?" he repeated, pulling a face.

"In an alternate universe," I went on, poking his arm, "you would've made a great chef."

He was quiet for a moment, moving the bacon around the pan. "My mom is a chef."

I looked up at him, breath catching. "Really?"

"She worked a lot. We didn't see much of her. My brother and I sort of trained ourselves to wake up at midnight when she got home from the restaurant, and she'd make us scrambled eggs or pancakes or grilled cheese sandwiches."

"That sounds nice."

"It was."

I didn't want to push my luck, but I was greedy. "What about your dad?"

"He died when I was six. I don't remember much about him." He cleared his throat. "I just had my mom. And my brother."

My legs turned to jelly and I leaned against the counter for support, unwilling to put all my weight on him. "Oh," I whispered, eyes stinging. I ached for both of us; all this time I'd wondered what drew me to Dex, or him to us, and here it was. We were the same.

He reached for me, his hand squeezing my shoulder gently, a silent plea to let it go. He'd gotten the words out, but that was as far as he could go right now. I pressed my face into his arm, nodding. *All the time you need.*

"I can't picture you as a kid," I murmured. "What were you like?"

"I was different."

"Different like you didn't vacuum your car every day?"

"I was more . . . reckless. Selfish. Happy." He shut the burner off and stepped away to deal with the waffle maker. "You wake up one day and the things you care about most are gone. Everything is obsolete in their absence. It's not easy anymore."

I squeezed my eyes shut. He may as well have punched me in the gut. "You have things," I said. "You have friends who trick you into going to couples hotels. You have a job helping kids. You must find that a teensy bit rewarding. I mean, as long as it's your actual job."

"It's not sketchy." He carefully divided the waffles across the three plates, avoiding my eyes.

"You have a fourteen-year-old who is, like, obsessed with you," I continued, the tension in my veins ebbing at the slight quirk of his lips. "And a hot elementary school teacher who is also obsessed with you."

His lips pulled into a real smile. I could've floated to the ceiling. "Likewise," he said. "But I don't need the . . ." He gestured vaguely. "I'm okay with who I am."

But who did you used to be? I wondered, watching him drop his attention to the plates. *Weren't you the one insisting time is the only thing that helps wounds like these?*

As he walked over to the stove to grab the pan of bacon, he paused to press a kiss to my forehead. "I can hear your mind working," he said quietly, giving my hip a slight squeeze. "You'll drive yourself crazy."

"Right," I replied, forcing a smile. "I'm the one who's driving."

He forced a smile right back.

The lookout near the border of Idaho wasn't the first view to take my breath away on this trip, but it was the first I got to take in with Dex's hand on the small of my back.

A guardrail stood between us and a rocky slope leading down to a canyon with a deep blue body of water nestled inside, surrounded by evergreens. Somewhere overhead, a hawk cried. The air was crisp, clean, full of florals and grass. It took Phoebe a solid minute to lift Dad's camera.

"Good call, Bee," I said. A few others had pulled over to take in the view, snapping pictures with their phones. "This is really beautiful."

"And we didn't have to hike five miles to see it," Dex added. "Gold star."

I smacked his stomach and he laughed loudly, the sound echoing into the cavern. Phoebe swiveled to look at us, eyebrows flying up. I took a step away from him, warmth rushing to my cheeks, and it turned into a blaze when she snapped a Polaroid of the two of us standing there.

"We should go somewhere you wanna go, Dex," she said, lowering the camera.

"Isn't that what this whole thing is?" he replied.

She shrugged with one shoulder. "Sure. Theoretically." Dex and I exchanged a look. Clearly, we weren't as subtle as we thought. "But I've picked most of the detours. Vi picked one. You haven't picked any. It's your turn."

"Pass." He folded his arms, his button-up pulling taut across his back. I had to tear my eyes away before Phoebe caught me. "Are we done?"

Phoebe rolled her eyes with her whole body. "We just got here."

"We saw it. It's great. You took a picture. Let's go."

He headed to the car. She shot me a look. "Can you hold

him off? I wanna get another picture. I don't want the guardrail in it."

"Sure. But don't climb over. It's there for a reason."

"When my therapist calls later, I'm going to kick off with how idiotic my sister thinks I am."

We shared a smile. I followed Dex to the car, where he leaned against the passenger door, head back to let the sun warm his face. "Hey," I said. "Quit being a grump. You're killing the mood."

He jerked his chin toward the lookout. "Think she knows?"

"Maybe," I allowed, glancing over my shoulder. Phoebe stretched over the guardrail, this time with her phone, keeping both feet firmly planted on the ground. "She's perceptive. Chances are, she's known for a while."

His eyes dipped to me, almost black even under the midday sun.

"About me," I tacked on belatedly. "I haven't been very stealthy since Chicago. But we all know you're a vault."

He winced and looked away. "I'm trying, Vi."

"I know. I'm not saying—"

"You are so *brave*," he said emphatically. When his eyes met mine, I recognized a flicker of impatience I hadn't seen since Boston, and the reemergence put an ache in my gut. "You feel things out loud. You can't keep it in. You'll shout your problems at a stranger on the street."

"So by brave, you mean unbalanced."

He pulled a hand through his hair and I tried not to think about how those curls felt between my fingers. "You're open in a way I'm not. I'm not like that. And sometimes you look at me like I'm missing a piece because of it."

I sucked in a breath. "Dex. I don't think that. Of course I don't think that."

"A week ago, you did," he said. I bit my lip, unable to dispute this. "Maybe I am. Fuck." He raised his hands to his face, dragging them down. "This is why I didn't want to do this."

Every bit of air rushed out of my lungs. "Do what?"

"You are so fucking good, Vi. I'm—I'm nowhere near you."

I stepped away, head spinning. "You're seriously doing this *now*? Now that we've had sex and I'm half in love with you, you're gonna pull this?"

His breathing quickened. "Violet."

"You're right about one thing," I said. "I'm brave, you're not. Because this is what you do. It's what you did with Catalina, right?"

His jaw flexed. "Don't."

"You got low and when she tried to be there for you, you pushed her away?"

"*Don't.*"

"When should I expect your letter?"

"You have no idea what you're talking about," he snapped, stepping toward me. "From the second we met, I have never given any indication that my life was perfect. I'm a fucking mess. That's not a secret. And then you show up and make your mess just as obvious. You spill it everywhere you go. You're telling me everything changed for you in Chicago? I've been fucked out of my head since you walked into Sequest in that dress." He looked up at the sky, throat bobbing. "And I thought *maybe*. Maybe because you're messed up, too, this could work. I want it so bad, Vi. It's you. I had myself convinced I liked being alone and now I miss you when you're in the next room. I think about going back to Boston and being with you. Letting you and Phoebe loose in my apartment to put some life and color into it. I want to wake up and see hints of you, even if you're not next to me."

Emotional whiplash grabbed me by the throat. I'd thought

he was ending this. Maybe he meant to. But he didn't want that—he wanted me, a future together, and the only thing standing in the way was his own brain. He couldn't get a grip. And he wouldn't tell me *why*.

"I want that too. Why can't you let yourself have something?"

His shoulders rose in a breath and then his eyes shifted over my shoulder, his pinched expression smoothing into pure horror, and he took off running. I wheeled around in time to see a shock of pink slipping down the cliff and Dex diving down after her.

Twenty-one

"It's fine," Phoebe said for the tenth time in as many seconds. "I'm fine."

I still couldn't catch my breath. My heart was somewhere in the dirt by Dex's car. "You're bleeding," I said, voice trembling. Everything was trembling. I would've thought we were having an earthquake if the kind stranger tending to Phoebe's wounds wasn't applying medicine with steady hands.

"I skinned my knees. It's fine." She looked over her shoulder. "Dex, tell her I'm fine."

"You're not fine. You're bleeding."

"Skinned knees! God."

I sat back on my heels, seeing spots. Still dazed. Still paralyzed with the terror of watching my sister fall off a cliff and Dex following without hesitation. People screamed, gasped, jumped into action to help. For the longest second in world history, I couldn't move. I saw the teachers' lounge. I saw the ICU. I saw a nurse unplugging my father. I saw Phoebe, broken and lifeless, and Dex right beside her.

No, I'd thought as I forced myself forward. *No no no no no.*

They didn't fall far. Dex managed to grab hold of Phoebe and maneuver their bodies so he took the brunt of the hit, landing on a shallow ledge two feet down. A few of the others who'd stopped to look at the view helped them back up. The moment they were safe on solid ground, I'd vomited.

But they were okay, save for some bumps and blood. They were okay.

I glanced up at Dex, trying to meet his eye. He remained focused on Phoebe, his arms hanging limply at his sides. For the first time since we'd met, his shirt was wrinkled, stained with dirt.

The stranger finished cleaning Phoebe's knees and covered them with Band-Aids. She stood up, a little wobbly on her feet, our dad's camera grasped tightly in her hands.

"I'm okay," she said again, extending a hand to me. I took it, letting her help me up. "I'm sorry. I didn't mean to scare you. Or make you throw up. I know how much you hate throwing up."

I rubbed my eyes. "I'm just . . ."

"I'm fine."

"Adrenaline."

"Huh?"

"You feel fine right now because adrenaline is pumping through your veins." I dropped my hand to look at Phoebe, eyes sweeping over for something broken, out of place. "Once you calm down, something might be wrong."

"I'm fine," she insisted. "Dex is the one who's hurt."

I whipped around. He'd brushed off the stranger with the first aid kit, standing away from the thinning crowd. He narrowed his eyes and said, "No, I'm not."

"Are you hurt?"

"No."

"He's not moving his arm," Phoebe pointed out. "His left one. He landed on it."

"I'm fine."

I made my way over, reaching for his arm. "Let me see."

"No," he growled, but he made no attempt to hold it out of my reach, immediately proving Phoebe right. His hand was purple, knuckles bloody, and when I carefully unbuttoned his shirt sleeve and pushed it up, his arm had swollen to the size of an eggplant.

"Oh my god."

"It's a scratch."

"Your arm is broken, you maniac."

"What?" Phoebe darted over, her eyes zipping to Dex's arm held aloft in my delicate grasp. "Oh my—" She dry heaved. "Gross! What the hell? It's like *127 Hours*!"

Ignoring her, I looked at Dex and said, "We have to go to the hospital."

He gave the surrounding area an apathetic scan, ignoring several onlookers gaping in our direction. "It's not that bad."

"Don't be an idiot." My eyes burned. "But you are. You are such an idiot."

"Vi."

"I'm sorry I said you're not brave." I squeezed my eyes shut. "You saved Phoebe. She could've died and you . . . You didn't even hesitate. You just went and you saved her. I'm so sorry, Dex."

He stepped into me, wrapping me in a tight hug. I took a shaky breath, pressing my face into his neck. "Everything's okay, baby," he said. "I'm sorry, too." He pulled back, bending to meet my gaze. "We'll go to the hospital. We'll be there for like six hours, but we'll go. Are you good to drive?"

I blinked, his black hole eyes dragging me in. "Hmm?"

"Right," he said. "I can drive. Let's go."

Phoebe looked at me and raised her eyebrows. "Yeah, *baby*, let's go."

It made sense for hospitals to smell the same, like how walking into an unfamiliar high school transports you to fifteen with too much to prove. The moment we walked through the doors of the emergency room, I was on the brink of a meltdown. That sickly muddle of antiseptic and cleaning agent clawed at my throat, stomped my lungs, and brought unwelcome memories screaming back.

Phoebe sobbing.

Nurses tiptoeing.

My lousy optimism holding out until the moment the heart monitor flatlined.

The last time I was in a hospital, my world ended. And now, sitting in a stiff chair in an off-white waiting room, a tank of tropical fish embedded in the wall across the way, I just wanted my dad. He would know what to say. He'd ease my mind with a joke. He'd reassure me that just because something bad happened once didn't mean it would happen every single time, and he'd say it in a way that made it impossible not to believe him. My twin optimist.

A flash snapped me out of my head. Phoebe lowered the camera, offering a sheepish smile. "Sorry. I wanted a picture of the fish," she said. I looked around the empty waiting room, eyes snagging on the nurse behind the counter who'd recorded Dex's information when we arrived. He'd taken his time checking in, making sure I was comfortable in this waiting room that smelled like my worst memory, ignoring his own pain to abide mine. That was nearly two hours ago.

"Should I . . ." I swallowed, willing the nurse to meet my gaze. Maybe she forgot we were here and she would rush to give us an update. *No news is good news,* my dad would've said. That always seemed like crap to me. "It's been a long time. I should ask about Dex."

"Don't," Phoebe said. I turned to her, fingernails digging into the arms of my chair.

"Why?"

"Because it's pointless." She lifted the camera to her eye, looking around the waiting room through the lens. "First of all, we're not family so they won't tell us anything. And two: He's fine."

"You don't know that."

"His arm is broken, Vi." She put the camera in her lap and sat back, eyes lifting to meet mine. "It takes at least an hour for x-rays. Another hour to put the cast on. And there's probably, like, two hours of waiting in between. We've been waiting a long time because it takes a long time."

My precious voice of reason. I could've burst into tears for the third time today. "Yeah. You're right."

She shifted in her chair to face me, folding her legs pretzel-style. "So," she said, "when were you gonna tell me?"

The topic had cropped up several times, once in the car and a few more as we camped out in the waiting room with nothing but a TV hooked up in the corner playing a weather broadcast on repeat. She let it go each time. Now, though, determination sparked in her eyes and I knew I wouldn't be so lucky.

"I don't know, Bee. We don't even know what it is, yet. If it's anything."

"It's obviously *something* if he's calling you 'baby.'"

"*Something* isn't necessarily . . ." I waved my hand, searching for the right word. I landed on: "Meaningful."

"Okay, well, that's bullshit," she said. "You're losing your mind over a broken arm. That's meaningful behavior right there."

I sank in my seat, glancing up at the TV screen. Storm warnings. "Okay, that's not the right word. But I don't think he knows what he wants."

"Seriously? Violet, that dude has been obsessed with you this whole time."

"What? No."

"Uh, yeah."

Dex's words swirled around my brain: *I've been fucked out of my head since you showed up at Sequest in that dress.*

"Well, just because we have feelings for each other doesn't mean it will work out," I said.

She scowled. "Ew. Don't treat me like a kid whose parents are getting divorced." She leaned in a little, her eyes searching mine. "I knew you guys liked each other. It was only a matter of time before one of you did something about it."

"You knew?" I raised my eyebrows. "And you didn't . . . care? I thought you were team Catalina."

"I mean, sure. But I don't know Catalina. I know *you*. And I'm not stupid. When I saw all the vibes between you guys it was like, okay, yeah, this is happening."

I swallowed. "Yeah."

"That's a *good* thing. Don't sound so doomed."

"What if it is doomed?" I worried my bottom lip with my teeth. "What if he sabotages it like he did with Catalina?"

"He won't."

"You can't know that."

"He's the kind of guy who almost drowns and learns how to swim really well," she explained, smiling so warmly it twisted my heart. "He'll make new mistakes, but he won't make that one."

I exhaled for what felt like the first time since watching Phoebe and Dex tumble over the side of that cliff. At some point, my sister had lapped me in emotional maturity. Something to grapple with another day.

"Thanks," I said softly.

She grinned. "It's purely selfish. I really want Dex to stick around."

A real smile tugged at my mouth. "Me too."

A few minutes later, a nurse emerged from down the hall, coming straight for us. We scrambled to our feet. "Are you here with Mr. Dexter?" she asked, looking between us.

"Yes," I said. "Is he okay?"

"He's fine. You can come on back."

We followed her down the same hallway, our footsteps echoing off the linoleum floor. At the very end of the hall, a line of cots were separated by curtains, and Dex sat on the first, now wearing a white T-shirt, his arm adorned in a white elbow-length cast. When he noticed us approaching, a huge grin spread across his face.

"Oh my god," Phoebe said, grabbing my arm. "He's high."

"Hey!" he exclaimed, his voice bouncing off the walls. Phoebe immediately hopped up on the bed next to him, fixing her face into a starry-eyed expression.

"My hero!"

"I'm broken," he reported with a grin. "Twice."

"His arm is broken and his wrist is fractured," the nurse explained, checking one of the machines Dex was hooked up to. I drifted over to the bed, running my hand up his shoulder and into his hair. He leaned into me at once. "He'll have the cast for six to eight weeks. All in all, he's incredibly lucky. People have died falling from that lookout."

My blood went cold. Dex hummed something that sounded like "Call Me Maybe" into my shoulder.

"But he's okay?" Phoebe asked. "Nothing permanent? No concussion?"

"He's fine." The nurse smiled. "I'll be back in a few minutes to check the heart monitor. If it's still normal, you guys will be all set to go."

"What if it's not normal?" I asked, eyes wide.

"It's protocol. I promise you, he is just fine."

I sank onto the edge of the cot, pressed against Dex, letting his scent overtake everything else. "Are you okay?" I murmured, combing my fingers through his hair. He nodded against me. "Does it hurt?"

"Not anymore."

"Morphine?" Phoebe guessed. Dex chuckled.

"More like. More please."

She guffawed. "This is so fun. Let's ask him personal questions and see if he's high enough to answer. Hey, Dex, why do you have so much money?"

"Menace," he muttered, pulling away from me. "You're a bad person. Taking advantage of someone who just risked their life to save yours."

"I wouldn't have died," she said, waving this off. "Probably."

I rubbed a hand down my face. "Did you guys know it's one o'clock? This has been the longest day of my life and it's nowhere near done."

"Where's the closest hotel?" Dex asked. "We'll check in. I'll sleep until tomorrow and you guys can grab dinner or something."

"We can't leave you alone when you're this high."

"I've been higher."

Phoebe's eyes lit up. I cut in before she could pounce. "I already checked nearby hotels. There's a Holiday Inn down the road, but you're not a Holiday Inn guy," I said, at which he grimaced, confirming this. "There's a cool lodge not too far from here. I think you'll like it."

"You know what I just realized?" Phoebe said. "This was Dex's detour. Nice one, man!"

"I'll kill you," he replied and she fell over laughing. I kept brushing my fingers through Dex's hair, listening to the sound of Phoebe's laughter. For the first time in hours, the tidal wave of my mind shrank to ripples.

Three things: *Them, them, them.*

The nurse returned. As predicted, Dex's heart rhythm was normal, so he was given the okay to leave. He wobbled on his feet and I held his arm, steadying him. Phoebe snapped a photo.

"Christ," he muttered. I bit my lip in a small smile. "Can we go? I'm sick of this place."

"Do you have everything?" I asked.

He rubbed his eyes. "Uh. My shirt and stuff is in that chair."

I made sure he was steady before grabbing his crumpled shirt from the wooden rocker in the corner. Phoebe bounced on her heels, poking Dex's elbow. "How long do you think we're staying? Because there's a sushi place not far from here—"

"You want to eat sushi in a landlocked state? Do you have a death wish?"

I shook the shirt out so I could fold it and his wallet, car keys, and a card flew out, clattering at my feet. I bent to pick them up, Dex's unsmiling face staring back at me, and I grinned at how predictable his license photo was, as if it was such a nuisance to take. As I stood, my eyes stuck on the name.

August William Dexter.

"I'll take you to a great sushi place when we get back to Boston," Dex said.

"Does it have a conveyor belt?" Phoebe asked.

"No."

"Pass."

I stared at the name, waiting for it to break apart and reconstruct into what I knew to be true. His name was Benji. He hated it, so he went by Dex. I shut my eyes, breathing hard, remembering the disgust in his eyes when I asked if he was Benji Dexter. He'd never answered, I realized. The only other time I used that name, he'd said *Don't call me that*.

"Can I sign your cast?" Phoebe asked, inspecting Dex's arm closely. He nodded, hair flopping over his forehead.

"Sure."

I could've been standing on that cliffside, watching Phoebe and Dex spill over. A visceral sucker punch and the paralysis that followed. A solid beat of *nothing*.

"What color? I have markers in the car. Ooh! I have stickers too!"

"You're not putting stickers on my cast."

The world ebbing back into focus. Something huge and sharp clawed its way out from inside my chest.

Phoebe's voice sounded farther away, almost like an echo. "Please?"

My hand shook as I inspected the license for a mistake. Dex's sour face and a name that didn't belong to him. I had slept beside this man. I had woken up with him. I had no idea who he was.

"What kind of stickers?" Dex asked. Phoebe let out a maniacal laugh and snatched the keys from my shaking hand, bolting down the hallway. He turned to me. "Well, that's not a great sign. Are you . . . Vi? What's wrong?"

"What, um . . ." I blinked hard, brandishing his license, watching the color drain from his face. "Is your name August?"

He lifted his hand and immediately dropped it back to his side, squirming as if he'd forgotten how to stand. "Violet."

I tried to take a steady breath but it was more like a gasp. "What the hell is going on?"

He walked backward until his knees hit the bed and he sank down, dropping his head into his hand. "I can't believe this is happening when I'm on morphine," he moaned.

"Dex." I blinked hard, trying to right this topsy-turvy universe I'd stumbled into. "I'm coming up with a lot of scary scenarios in my head, so I need you to talk. Tell me I'm being ridiculous. Tell me *something*." My mind grasped for logical explanations. "Sometimes a zebra is a horse, right? So, Benji's a nickname. That's why there's no record of you online."

He looked at me, eyes swimming in misery. "Violet."

"It's either that or you're some kind of con man. Is that why you have so much money? You're a criminal mastermind?" My fingers tightened around the soft fabric of his rumpled shirt. "Maybe Catalina has no idea who you are. Maybe nobody does."

"Violet," he said, clearer now, as if I'd shocked the morphine out of his system. "My name is August. Benji is my brother. He died a year and a half ago."

I sat down on the floor, burying my face in a shirt that smelled like Dex, only he wasn't Dex. Everything was upside down.

"I was going to tell you," he said. "I tried. I just—I don't talk about him. It's too much. He was my best friend and I'm still so fucking lost. I was going to tell you before we got to Bend."

"I don't understand." My voice came out soft, muffled by the shirt.

"Cat was the love of Benji's life." He was breathing hard. I could tell he hated this, but I didn't tell him it was okay, that he could take his time. Not this time. "They broke up a few weeks before it happened. He obviously sent the letter sometime in between. I don't know why it took so long for the post office to return it. I . . . I don't know. When you showed up at Sequest and said his name, it felt like something broke inside me."

I heard the groan of the cot as he stood, soft steps against the tile floor. He didn't touch me, but I could feel him right there in front of me.

"It didn't matter then, who I was," he said quietly. "I didn't expect you to come back. I didn't expect Phoebe to come up with this plan, or convince us to follow through on it."

I raised my head, glaring at him through burning eyes. "Think very carefully about the next words out of your mouth because if you even *think* about putting this on Phoebe, no amount of morphine on earth will help you."

"No! No, that's—I didn't mean it like that." He swallowed hard, his uninjured hand trembling as he raked his fingers through his hair. "I'm just saying this whole thing caught us off guard. The trip, you and me . . . it wasn't supposed to be like this."

"But it is. It's been like this for days. For *weeks*."

"I haven't talked about him since he died. It's been almost two years and I can barely get the words out."

"That's not an excuse," I said feebly, through an unbearable pang of sympathy. I spent nine months without the luxury of living in grief, setting it aside to take care of my sister. I didn't have a choice. Dex made his choices. He lied to me, and to Phoebe, for weeks. It felt the cruelest joke, to have something good dangled in front of me only to discover it was a mirage.

"I'm not trying to excuse what I did. I'm trying to explain." Dex let out a jagged breath. "You have every right to be mad. But I've never lied to you, Violet. Everything I told you. Every moment we had since this started was real."

"Every moment was under the umbrella of a lie. That's not real, *August*. It's bullshit."

He groaned, ducking his head in his hand. "This went so much better in my head. I wish I wasn't high."

I stared at him, a tear slipping out. I couldn't begin to wrap my head around this, but I hated how much sense it made. Pieces snapping into place in every mysterious corner of the puzzle. Phoebe's words regarding Dex's joy at the bar swept through the chaos in my mind: *A broken heart doesn't do this.* In retrospect, the truth felt obvious. Grief, on the other hand, had a ruthless tendency to stalk, reap, destroy. I'd looked at him and had the thought that we were the same, and it still didn't click. I felt like a fool.

Part of me wanted to book a flight back to Boston. Another wanted to reach for him because his grief was so familiar. *Familiar,* I quickly reminded myself, *but not the same.* Even at my worst, those nights I couldn't drag myself into bed, staring at the ceiling from the floor with tears streaming to my ears, begging the universe for one more minute with my dad so he could reassure me that I wasn't fucking everything up for Phoebe, I never would've allowed someone to spend weeks at my side, in my bed, in every nook and cranny of my brain, without letting them first know who I was. I'd clawed my way through hell while hoisting Phoebe above my head. I did that. And Dex let himself drown rather than tell me the truth. He let me drown with him.

His dark eyes found mine, willing me to hear him out, as if a million moments didn't exist between our meeting and now where he could have come clean. I realized now that he'd tried in that Wyoming hotel room, all the talk about closure while letting me believe this trip was inspired by a broken heart. Catalina wasn't a heartbroken woman, but a woman destroyed, and we were in possession of the last words the man she loved would ever say to her. All this time I'd spent wondering if Dex was in love with her or what kind of mistakes he'd made . . . how fucking shallow. If only he'd been honest from the start—I would've done everything the same, only now it wouldn't be warped like plastic in the sun.

With effort, I pushed myself to my feet. "Phoebe's waiting," I mumbled, heading for the hall.

"Violet, come on," he said. I quickened my pace, sneakers squeaking. "You can't walk away. We haven't settled anything."

"I'm trying to wrap my head around this. Around you *lying* to me this whole time."

"A name is a name!" He caught my arm and I wheeled around to face him, fire burning its way up my neck. "It's not who I am. You know who I am."

I wrenched my arm out of his grasp. "I know what you want me to know. This whole time, I thought you were someone else and you were fine with that."

"What do you want me to say? I'm sorry that when three strangers came searching for my dead brother, I didn't tell them he overdosed in a fucking bar?"

Another gut punch. "No. God. I'm sorry. I just—I need to not look at you for, like, forty seconds."

I kept walking. He kept up. "I tried so hard to stay away. I didn't want anything to happen between us until you knew, but you're so incredible and when I realized you wanted me . . . Fuck, Vi, I couldn't resist. I'm so sorry," he said, a note of anguish rising in his tone. "You said you want to know me. I'll tell you whatever you want to know. I'll give you a long-form interview if that's what you need. I'll do it."

He was saying the magic words for the Violet I was two weeks ago, three days ago, an hour ago. I'd wanted him to *want* me to know these things about him, not barter them in an attempt to smooth over the jagged edges of grief when I was already bleeding.

I pushed through the double doors into the waiting room where Phoebe was distracted by the tropical fish, one of the sticker books she'd gotten to decorate her Polaroids clutched in her hand. I slowed, far enough away so she couldn't hear, and looked at Dex. "I can't do this right now."

His shoulders sank in an exhale. "Violet."

"I'm so sorry about your brother." My voice broke, a real wave of tears unleashing at the shine in his eyes. "I get the grief. You know I do. I could've been there for you, if you let me. But right now, I have nothing else for you. I was honest with you. I trusted you. And you didn't even tell me your name."

I wiped my eyes and left him standing at the doors. Phoebe glanced up as I approached, her face falling as she took me in, and even further when her eyes snapped over my shoulder to Dex.

"Is everything okay?"

"We have to talk," I said briskly, heading for the exit. "Let's go."

The doors opened, the crisp sunshine violent. Dirt cracked under our shoes as we made our way across the parking lot. My head pounded, eyes burning, my heart so heavy I couldn't remember what it felt like to fit comfortably inside my chest. Phoebe kept shooting glances at me and over her shoulder, waiting for one of us to explain. I gave myself the walk to the car; a few more seconds of Phoebe's happiness before we ripped the rug out from under her. It wasn't fair. And I hated myself for putting Phoebe in the position to lose someone else she cared about.

It wasn't supposed to be like this, Dex had said.

I remembered leaving the hospital after my dad died, how I existed outside of my body, autopilot taking over. Now, I'd do anything for a semblance of separation from the ache. I felt every step, every breath, every agonizing thought that seemed to contradict the last.

Dex duped me into trusting him and I let him.

Was I supposed to cut him slack because he was grieving?

What he did was wrong and unfair and betrayed every bit of trust we'd cultivated, but *fuck,* where would I be if I didn't have Phoebe and Arden when Dad died? Would I be broken enough to do what he'd done? Was it even a question when I'd been broken enough to take a cross-country road trip with a complete stranger?

But the lying was inexcusable, especially with Phoebe involved.

God. Phoebe.

She was going to be heartbroken. She was going to be angry.

Would she blame me? I couldn't blame her if she did. I hadn't been careful enough.

How fucking naïve was I to believe I'd finally done something right? Phoebe's smiles and laughter egged me on and I bent, not caring if I broke as long as she was happy. It never occurred to me that she might end up broken, too, but it should have. I was the guardian. I was supposed to look at it from every angle before setting forth, and I failed. I let Phoebe down. Again.

I needed to let Dex explain for four hours straight so maybe this wouldn't seem so irreparable. I needed to never see his face again.

His grief was uglier than mine; that didn't mean I should leave.

This last thought was unwelcome logic in the sea of hurt and anger. I didn't want to think about this in a nuanced way. Not with Phoebe looking at me with shining eyes as if she already knew this little universe we'd created together, the three of us, was gone. Dex became integral so quickly. Phoebe opened up to him and he helped her through the insurmountable grief I'd never managed to scale. My pathetic, optimistic soul had reached for him, twining with his as he slowly let me in, unaware that the foundation we were building on was a lie.

The floor may have fallen out from under me, but Phoebe was still standing, and I needed to be okay for her right now. I needed to hold myself together long enough to map out our next move now that Dex wasn't Dex, but he was still injured and heavily medicated. I needed to explain this situation to Phoebe calmly and retain the ability to answer whatever questions she'd have. I just needed another second. A breath. One last moment in a place where life didn't feel so impossible.

I was tempted to let Dex explain it to Phoebe. Maybe with the words coming out of his mouth, she'd see him as the villain and me as a fellow victim. But I didn't want to run from the hard things anymore. I wanted to be honest. I needed to be someone she could trust, even when everything fell apart. I needed to reassure her that it was her and me, us, forever. Dex couldn't take that away.

I wiped a stray tear from my cheek and faced Phoebe when we reached the car. She hugged the sticker book to her chest, chewing her bottom lip, waiting for me to explain. She didn't look to Dex for answers this time. I took a breath, my eyes meeting his over Phoebe's head as he trailed behind, and he looked every bit as broken as the bones beneath his cast. *How did we get here?* I thought desperately. *How do we go back?*

I'd trusted him. With myself *and* my sister. His grief clouded his judgment and now here we were, over two thousand miles from home, strangers.

Twenty-two

BEND, OR

It rained all the way to Bend.

Another minute in Dex's presence felt unbearable, let alone ten hours. I wanted nothing more than to drop everything and go home to cry on my best friend's shoulder, but Phoebe was quick to point out that we couldn't in good conscience leave Dex alone, at least not while he was medicated. I nearly put my foot down—I was almost positive Phoebe would let me. But I'd go to the end of the earth and back if it meant one more second with my dad, and I hoped if anyone was ever in the position to hand a gift like that to me, they wouldn't hesitate. So I would do this for Catalina, and for Benji.

It was nice to focus my screaming mind on something simple and reliable like the highway rather than obsessively combing through the last two weeks with retrospect's fine teeth. I did my best to keep it at bay. Just road and rain for miles. Snapshots from the hospital parking lot crept in periodically, taunting me. Phoebe looking exactly her age, so small and innocent. The look on her face when I forced out the words: *Dex's name is August. Benji was his brother.* Her expression crumbling, stuck on one word.

"Was," she'd repeated softly, and Dex squeezed his eyes shut and turned his back to us.

Our tight-knit little trio, fractured in a matter of minutes. For a second there, I really thought we'd found something permanent. I thought we'd found *everything*.

If Phoebe was angry at either of us, she didn't show it. Once we were on the road after picking up Dex's prescription, she plugged in her phone to play one of her mixes and immediately dipped a toe in conversation. I did my best to tune them out, tried not to zero in on the soft scratch of Dex's voice. They kept the volume low, topics innocuous. My eyes never strayed to the rearview mirror unless merging. Rain pounded down from the pewter sky. I could feel his eyes on me.

He didn't try to speak to me. I was equal parts relieved and furious.

I breathed easier once they fell asleep. The dull roar of rain acted as white noise to drown out my thoughts, my feelings, the steady breaths of Dex sleeping in the back seat. My dad used to tell me his favorite part of traveling was the quiet, and I never understood it until now. I felt him with me as the highway struck Oregon, and somehow, my spirit rose.

Phoebe and Dex were still sleeping when a road sign welcomed us to Bend sometime after 1 A.M. I pulled over, tearing up as I searched nearby hotels on my phone. This should've been the finish line, but nothing felt done, and as angry as I was, a part of me wasn't ready for the drive to end. I needed more time, so maybe it was a good thing that we had to wait until daylight to show up on Catalina's doorstep with ghosts from her past, especially now that I knew this wasn't a simple heartbreak, but catastrophic grief torn open and left to rot. Meeting Catalina was never going to be easy. Now, it seemed impossible.

We checked into the hotel, moving like zombies. Bend was

supposed to be a new beginning: We were going to take our time on the drive back east and once we got home, we were supposed to start a life, not whatever this new, splintered existence was standing on opposite ends of the hotel lobby.

Phoebe's eyes tracked me when I emerged from the bathroom, my skin red and raw from another shower breakdown. My limbs ached. My brain buzzed with exhaustion. I knew she had questions, but I was in no shape to answer them; I'd been awake for twenty-four hours and it all caught up at once. I could barely hold my eyes open as I crawled into the bed closest to me.

"Vi," Phoebe said. I buried my face in the pillow, squeezing my eyes shut. "Are you okay?"

"Mm-hmm."

"I know it's a lot to take in. I feel like I should've known. Like, when I went to Sequest that day and he told me to call him Dex . . . I don't know. It looked like he was in pain." She paused, taking a shaky breath. "He *was* in pain."

"Phoebe," I said into the pillow. "I'm so tired."

"I googled him," she blurted. "August Dexter. He's one of the founders of Stall."

My brain seemed to jerk awake as if electric-shocked. I rolled over, meeting her wide eyes. "The dating app?"

"It was him and Bree, and a couple of their college friends. How insane is that?"

Dex was a co-founder of one of the country's leading hookup apps. I stared at Phoebe, my mind swimming hard to keep up with this information.

"He resigned last year," she told me. "According to *Forbes,* they bought his share for, like, a billion dollars. Just kidding. It didn't say the amount."

I returned my face to the pillow, releasing an anguished groan. "Phoebe. This is none of our business."

"Dex wants us to know. He was going to tell us everything."

"I'm having a hard time believing anything he says right now."

"Okay, yeah, it was bad to let us think he was Benji," she admitted. "But you know what else is bad? Opening someone's mail."

"Oh, so *now* that's a thing you care about."

I felt her sit beside me, the sweet scent of her coconut shampoo more like a warm blanket thrown over my shoulders. "It's not like he's a different person," she said, a note of caution in her tone. "He's exactly like us. He's just trying to get through it. But it's different because when Dad died, we had each other. We had Arden and Noah. Dex didn't let himself have anyone. That kind of loneliness fucks with your head. He lost his *brother.*"

I turned my head to meet her eyes. Her teeth worried her bottom lip, fingers scratching at her own nail polish.

"I know," I said. "I need time. I need space. But I'm . . . we're not done with him."

Her shoulders sank in relief, and I realized my sister would've let Dex go if I asked her to. My beautiful, selfless girl. She'd grown so much, with Dex playing a not-insignificant role. I'd be lying if I said I hadn't contemplated how to keep him in her life without touching mine, but merely imagining it was painful. I wasn't done with him, I couldn't be. I just hadn't figured out *how.*

In the hours since the revelation, I'd grappled with whether or not a case of mistaken identity could be considered a betrayal, landing in a frustrating gray area. A complicated situation made trickier by grief. I couldn't blame Dex for holding back in the beginning, but once the trip was on the table, he should've explained. He should've come clean before anything happened between us. I would've hated him if I wasn't neck-deep in my own debilitating loss.

Grief fucks you up. It's fickle and stagnant and overwhelming and it never ends, no matter how far you think you've gotten from it. It's just there, forever.

Dex lost his brother and dismantled his entire life in the months that followed, doing everything in his power to put distance between himself and the grief, and then we showed up with a fresh wave to knock him to his knees. It broke my heart to consider the amount of pain he was in the day we'd come to Sequest with the letter, or since. How much pain does someone have to be in to be physically unable to say a name out loud, even if they're desperate to?

Phoebe lay down beside me, looping her arm through mine. "I'm glad," she said. "I thought . . . I don't know. I thought maybe you'd hate him forever."

"After everything, this whole year, I'd never hold someone's grief against them," I told her. "He wasn't trying to trick us. I know there was nothing malicious about what he did, at least not deliberately."

"He's a sad boy," she said, resting her head against mine. "And we're sad girls. Match made in heaven."

"I'm still mad." I shut my eyes. "Or maybe not mad. It's hard to sort through my emotions right now. I don't know what I am. My brain and my heart and my body are all . . . disconnected."

"I kept thinking maybe I should be mad, but then I thought . . ." Phoebe swallowed, inhaling sharply. "I don't know what I'd do if I lost you. It's my worst nightmare. And Dex is living it."

Tears sprang to my eyes and I pulled her in closer. Phoebe roughly swiped at her cheek. "I'm here, Bee," I said through the tightness in my throat. I couldn't speak on Dex's pain, could barely make it through my own, but she was opening up to me, asking for reassurance. This, at the very least, I could give her. "I love you. I'm not going anywhere. You know that, right?"

She let out a shaky breath and nodded, holding my arm tighter. She was my world. The brightest spot that illuminated even the darkest of days. And if I thought too hard about the possibility of Dex losing that, I'd fall apart again.

"I just wish it was different," she whispered. "I thought it was different."

This trip had cut through the awfulness wrapped around our world, giving us a chance to breathe for the first time since September. For almost two weeks, existing felt easier. We weren't backsliding to slammed doors and rolled eyes, but a majority of the good surrounding us had drained.

"I did too," I said. "Maybe it still could be."

Our breathing slowed, my eyes grew heavier.

"Vi?"

"Yeah?"

"Do you think . . ." She took a small breath. "Maybe we shouldn't go tomorrow? Like, if we were overstepping before, this is insane. It doesn't feel right."

"No," I murmured. "You're right. It's not our place."

"What if she's made all this progress and getting this letter ruins it?"

"Dex knows her. I trust him." I paused, surprised at how easily these words slipped out. I couldn't pinpoint if it was a knee-jerk reaction or if the trust transcended his mistake. I quickly amended: "I trust him with this. If this was going to break her, we wouldn't be here right now."

"Yeah." She snuggled in closer, her voice softer, slower. "If someone showed up with a letter from Dad, it would be every-thing."

Yeah, I thought as the darkness closed in. *It would.*

"Don't ever let me stay up for over twenty-four hours again," I groaned into my coffee. Phoebe tittered, bringing her own cup to her lips. "This feels like the worst hangover of my life. But worse."

"Getting old sounds terrible."

"No, it's great. It's the best. As long as you don't make any sudden movements or stay up past nine."

She laughed, her voice giving life to the nearly empty hotel dining room. We'd slept in and took our time padding around our room getting ready for the day, only making the effort to go downstairs for sustenance after I texted Dex telling him to go ahead to Catalina's without us. I hadn't heard back from him, but he'd mentioned he wasn't a big texter, so I tried not to read into it.

Maybe it was anticlimactic to make the trip to Oregon only to miss out on the end result, but now we knew exactly what this trip meant to Dex and to Catalina—Benji's last words to the love of his life were in that letter. We'd never had a right to read them. A mistake of cataclysmic proportions. But we were here because of that mistake. We found Dex and now we'd found Catalina, and hopefully bringing her the letter would give them both a semblance of peace. We weren't entitled to take part, so we loaded our plates at the brunch buffet to keep our minds off it.

"Remember when Dad threw his back out before his forti-eth birthday?" Phoebe said around a mouthful of scrambled eggs. I nodded, propping my chin up with my hand. My head felt like a bowling ball balancing on a golf tee. "And I spent like a week waiting on him? That's gonna be us by September."

"You shut your mouth."

"I'm gonna have to get you a little bell."

"Hilarious."

"You'll only have me for a few years, though. Once I go to college, we'll have to invest in Life Alert."

I plucked a blueberry off my plate and threw it across the table at her. She dodged it with another laugh. "I'm not elderly," I said. "I am merely suffering from two weeks spent in a car with a dude I thought was another dude."

"Is it terminal?" she asked gravely. I snorted. "You know, the whole mistaken identity thing is kind of on you. I figured you would've done a background check."

"I told Arden I did. It was the only way to get her off my back."

"She's gonna kill you."

I knew this. I'd been deliberately vague in my text update this morning and Arden had texted five times since. "I'm trying not to think about it. Or anything, really." I stabbed a home fry with my fork and pointed it at Phoebe. "How are you doing with all of this? You still good?"

"Yeah." She shrugged. "I might try to con him out of, like, twenty grand, but I haven't decided yet."

"You could probably get him to pay for college."

"And a master's."

"Throw in a doctorate."

"Culinary school when I realize my life isn't where I want it to be."

"He'll personally fund your first photography exhibition when you're thirty."

"Twenty-five," she amended, shooting me a sly grin. "While I'm still young."

I rolled my eyes, taking a moment to bask in the euphoria of goofing off with my sister. As upside down as the rest of the world was, I had her.

"Piece of work," I muttered.

She beamed, shoveling a heaping forkful of pancakes into her mouth. Her eyes caught something over my shoulder and her expression dimmed. "Um," she said, jerking her chin in the direction of the lobby. I anticipated Dex's presence before my eyes found him in the arched entrance of the dining room, standing with his back facing us in a black T-shirt and blue jeans. My heart squeezed painfully in my chest, watching as he dragged a hand over his face up into his hair and squared his shoulders. He turned.

For a moment, we stared at each other. He swallowed hard. I resisted the urge to lift my hands to my face to make sure my head still sat in place on my shoulders.

He hadn't gone to Catalina's. His shoulders were tight with anxiety, his brow in a permanent furrow, eyes heavy and dark; this was a man, burdened. A man grieving. Alone.

I pushed out of my chair and moved toward him. His eyes tracked me across the room.

"You can't do this," I said, making a point to leave a good amount of space between us. If I smelled him right now, game over. "You've come too far to give up."

"I can't do this alone." He shook his head sharply, squeezing his eyes shut. "I *can't*."

"Yes, you can." My hand twitched at my side, desperate to reach for him. That Phoebe and I hadn't checked out of our room and Ubered to the airport hinted at something in the forgiveness realm, but neither of us had broached the topic and today wasn't about us, anyway. "This has never been about Phoebe and me, Dex. It has nothing to do with us."

"That didn't matter when you were opening my dead brother's mail." My instinct to defend Phoebe kicked in, but his words bore no bite, no venom, and then he was groaning, rubbing his eyes roughly. "Fuck. I'm sorry," he rasped, and my stomach tanked. He sounded wrecked. "I fucked everything up and now I'm losing my mind. I'm sorry. I am. I know I screwed up and you're gonna leave and I'll deserve it, but please do this for me." He stepped closer, eyes bloodshot and shining. My dad used to hug us when we cried, telling us to *just say when,* and he'd hold on until then. I wanted to do that for Dex, to hold him until the pain went away, even now. "I need you. I don't know when it started, but I need you with me for this. I have been alone for so long, I forgot what it was like to have a hand to hold. You and Phoebe are the only reason I'm here. You carried me. I can't do this without you. I don't want to."

I couldn't catch my breath. A tear slipped down my cheek. "Dex . . ."

"We'll go." Phoebe appeared at my side with that determined look on her face. When she cast me a quick glance, her eyes were swimming. "That's what we do, right? We're here for each other, even through the messy shit."

Dex swallowed thickly. The fog of uncertainty in his eyes told me I wasn't the same person I was in Boston; I could tell Phoebe no and feel all right about doing it, even if she refused to speak to me for a day or two. For the first time since Dad died, I was running the show. And right now, a surge of pride radiated through my chest watching my sister stand by Dex, unflinching and solid. I knew the pain and despair, the echoes of loneliness, the urge to push everyone away because if the person I believed to be the love of my life walked out when I was at my lowest, who could possibly stay?

"We'll go," I agreed. Dex's expression crumpled, just for a

second, and then he stepped into me, pressing a soft kiss to my forehead.

"Thank you." He pulled away to squeeze Phoebe's shoulder. "Thank you."

"Don't thank us, idiot," she replied. "We're all messes here."

Catalina lived in a quaint ranch with a cherry blossom tree in the front yard. The three of us stood on the sidewalk, a breeze winding the floral summer scent around us.

"It's her dad's house," Dex said without prompting. "She moved here after everything. I haven't . . . It's been a long time since I saw her. Or spoke to her. Too long."

His nerves were contagious—beside me, Phoebe bounced on her heels, nearly chewing a hole in her lip. She'd put so much thought into her striped tee and denim shorts while we were getting ready, forgoing makeup. I wondered how she pictured this day before reality caught up to us. Admittedly, I'd never wanted to think about Catalina as anything other than a name on an envelope, so I hadn't thought about this at all.

But now, with Catalina merely feet away, I took charge. "Come on," I said. Phoebe shot a panicked look at Dex. His eyes fell from the house to me, clouded with doubt. I couldn't imagine the chaos raging in his head right now and there was nothing I could do to deter it, but I reached for him anyway, sliding my hand up his back, encouraging. His throat worked, the tension seeming to drain a bit.

Together, we walked up the porch steps. Dex hesitated before ringing the doorbell. *You are so brave and you have no idea,* I thought, watching him roll his shoulders, anxiously picking at his cast as the door swung open.

Catalina was beautiful—dark curls tumbling over her shoulders, full lips, curves showcased in a wrap dress. Immediately, I lumped her in the same category as Dex: the intimidating, almost scary sort of beautiful. And then her face broke into a grin, and she could've been a little kid.

"Dex," she said and burst forward, throwing her arms around him. He lifted her up until her bare feet dangled and she let out a wet laugh. "You look *terrible*."

"I feel worse." He set her down and she beamed, her hands sliding down his arms until meeting the cast.

"What happened?"

"Broken arm. It's fine."

"Bree didn't say anything about a broken arm." She crossed her arms, still smiling. "She told me you were coming."

"I figured."

"She didn't say why."

He tugged a hand through his hair and gestured to us. Her eyes followed. "Violet and Phoebe. They live in the old apartment."

"Ah." She smiled tightly. This, it seemed, wasn't new information either. "Come on in."

Once we were inside, Catalina disappeared to the kitchen to get Phoebe water. I didn't think Phoebe needed water, she was simply giving Catalina an excuse to breathe for a second. I focused on other things, like the soft leather of the couch and the river rock fireplace with a mantel full of framed photos. On the wall by the front door was a colorful, almost abstract painting of a boy with short hair and a nose ring, a space between his front teeth. I knew, even before Dex's expression broke at the sight of it, it was Benji.

Catalina returned with a glass, placing it in front of Phoebe.

She sat on the couch across from us, folding her hands in her lap. I stared at her, half dazed that this was the same woman we'd read about in a letter. It seemed like forever ago.

"How's work?" she asked, focusing her attention on Dex.

He shrugged. "Fine."

"Does Mary miss me?"

He reached up to rub his neck, the corner of his mouth twitching upward. "Of course. Everyone does."

Catalina smiled, glancing at Phoebe and me. "You know, it's funny. Nobody ever thought Ben should work with kids. He had the dirtiest mouth—I once kept track of how many F-bombs he dropped in a day and it was, like, two hundred," she told us. Phoebe straightened at the casual mention of Benji. Dex kept his expression painfully neutral. "We always joked about how they should swap careers. Ben was better suited for the corporate billionaire app thing and Dex has always been great with kids . . ." Catalina's smile slipped. "I still can't believe you stepped in like that. I mean, I can. He loved Sequest so much and you'd do anything for him. But still."

Dex cleared his throat, squirming in his seat. "Cat."

"Sorry, sorry." Her voice wobbled as she waved her hands. "I'm doing that thing where I dive into the deep shit and you've been here two minutes."

Phoebe's hands were trembling in her lap, so I reached over, holding on for dear life.

Dex's fingers drummed the side of his cast. "There's a lot of deep shit, Cat. It's hard to avoid."

She let out a sigh. "Okay, then. Rip off the Band-Aid. I know it's not will stuff. Your mom dealt with that when she visited."

Dex furrowed his brow. "She visited you?"

"Yes, August. Christ. Call your mom once in a while. She's worried about you."

"I'm fine."

"Are you?"

He dragged a hand down his face, his shoulders drooping. "I'm sorry I haven't been in touch."

Catalina's face softened. "From what I hear, you haven't been in touch with anyone, so I don't take it personally," she said. "He's why you're here, right? He has to be. He's the only one who would get you out here."

He withdrew the letter from his pocket, the red stamp visible over the fold. Phoebe's grip tightened against my hand. "This showed up at the apartment. I don't know what the hell is going on with the postal service that they're return-to-sendering a dead man's mail, but that's how it played out."

Catalina stared at the letter. Her hand shook as she reached for it. I had the urge to beg her forgiveness, and from the way Phoebe's breath shook beside me, I knew she felt the same.

"They opened it," Dex added, maybe seeing Phoebe's and my stricken expressions. "But if they hadn't, I wouldn't be here."

A rush of gratitude swept through me at the reassurance that he wanted us here. That we belonged here, in a way. Catalina's shining eyes turned to Phoebe and me on the couch, holding the letter over her heart. And I knew for certain Phoebe had done the right thing when she opened it.

"Did you read it?" Catalina asked, turning to Dex.

"No," he said quietly. He turned his cast over, studying the stickers Phoebe had pasted all over it. "From what they told me, it's important. It . . . it would've been important if it was a fucking grocery list."

Her lip wobbled as she turned the envelope over, handling it like it was the most precious thing. To her, it was.

"I feel like . . ." Catalina wiped her eyes and dried her hand on her dress before returning it to the letter. "I feel like I should not want to read it, you know? This is the last thing. I'll never have anything else. And it's going to destroy me. I know it is. He never needed the last word unless he had something really good to say."

Dex shut his eyes, wincing.

"I'm going to . . ." Catalina stood, cradling the letter to her chest. "I have no idea. I haven't decided yet. But make yourselves at home."

With that, she shuffled out of the room. Dex stared after her with an expression I could only describe as haunted. I saw it nearly every time I passed a mirror, and the familiarity ached.

"Hey," I said. "Do you guys want some privacy? It might be easier without an audience, you know?"

"I want you here," Dex murmured without looking up. Phoebe looked between us, chewing her lip. "Cat will be grateful for the distraction. It's fine."

"August." His eyes snapped to me, fingers curling into his palm. "The hard part is over. Now you need to go in there and have a real conversation with her, without us. She deserves that much."

He stared at me, all those fractured feelings shining through. It meant something to me, the way he'd allowed me to witness the deepest pits of his soul from the moment I discovered his name. He meant it when he said he'd been honest with me, and if I asked him to stand under a spotlight and monologue his side of the story from beginning to end, he would. He wanted me to know him. I already did.

"You're right," he said. He climbed to his feet, taking a slow breath. "Don't leave. Please."

"We're here," I promised.

"You don't have to be." He stared at the doorway, eyes hazy.

"After this, I mean. I don't want you to think you're obligated to stay or forgive me. I'm not an easy person to care about. No hard feelings."

He was gone before his words made their impact. All this time, I'd had the thought that Dex and I were the same, and here he was repackaging the saddest thoughts I'd had about myself, dropping them at my feet, like he was damaged goods that should be cast aside. But he wasn't damaged to me. All those broken pieces snapped together in a mosaic masterpiece, beautiful and raw.

Left alone in Catalina's living room, Phoebe and I didn't look at each other, didn't speak. We let ourselves out, taking refuge on the porch swing. Overhead, the sky was a crisp, cloudless blue. The grass swayed in a warm breeze. It wasn't our grief, but when my sister buried her face in my shoulder, choking up, it could've been.

By the time Dex came to find us, frogs and crickets had begun chirping in the grass, and his eyes were red.

Catalina invited us to stay for dinner so earnestly, we couldn't say no. We grilled and ate burgers on the cobbled patio as dragonflies zipped over our heads. The afternoon sun was relentless, but we sat out there for hours listening to stories about Benji Dexter, the man who'd brought us together. He was a talented artist always sporting acrylic paint on his hands. He and Cat were friends growing up, but they didn't fall in love until their struggling twenties, sharing a shoebox apartment outside city limits, him freshly transitioned and finding comfort in working at Sequest, her working at the library, meeting up for lunch every day on a bench equal distance between their jobs. As a big believer in the grand gesture, he would try to one-up him-self after every fight—Catalina cringed as she recounted a flash mob years after the fad died out.

They were going to get married, though they weren't offi-cially engaged. It was simply a fact everyone around them knew. But Benji lived with depression and occasionally went through phases of mania, during which he would self-destruct and push away the people close to him. *I wish I hadn't left,* Catalina said with a sad smile. *But he told me to. It sounds so stupid, now.*

His death was a cosmically unfair accident on a Thursday night. Benji had told friends that when he died, he didn't want it to be a drag, so there was no official funeral, only a meetup at his favorite lighthouse where the people who loved him toasted to him and cried together and spread his ashes. *Gav got a mouthful of him,* Dex said, cracking a smile. *Ben wouldn't have had it any other way.*

It seemed strange to posthumously meet the person who shaped the last month of our lives. Phoebe and I sat rapt through the stories, the memories, the tears shed. Benji was a special person, his loss catastrophic. And when Phoebe launched into a story about our dad, Catalina and Dex leaned in, hanging on every word. We would keep them alive like this. My dad could've been right there, standing over my shoulder. As the stories began to slow and the air cooled, I caught Dex's eye over the glass-topped table. Now that I'd been formally introduced to Benji, it felt easier to understand the wreckage he'd left behind and how it led to Dex's inability to face his past. The bravery it took for Dex to make the choices that led him here took my breath away—he couldn't say Benji's name out loud, but he chose to take this trip, to sit alongside Phoebe and me in our own grief, to keep going. He'd been fighting so hard for so long, alone.

Eventually, Phoebe and I said goodbye to Catalina, intending to give her and Dex some privacy, but he ducked his head and followed us out, everything about him weighed down by exhaustion. I hadn't recognized the grief for what it was, but in retrospect only the most catastrophic losses could dismantle a world the way it had for Dex, and for Phoebe and me. It was all over him. I wished I'd looked a little bit closer.

A soft breeze rolled in, sending cherry blossom petals dancing around our feet as we made our way to the car. I watched them settle, a sense of impending doom pressing in, either from the glances Phoebe kept shooting Dex or the way he couldn't seem to lift his gaze from the ground. *This is over,* I thought, but I couldn't put my finger on what exactly was ending.

"You okay?" Phoebe asked, nudging Dex's elbow with her own. "That was a *lot.*"

He nodded. "Yeah."

"Yeah it was a lot or yeah you're okay?"

"I think . . ." He slowed to a stop and I curled my fingers into my palms, bracing for the end of his sentence. His eyes met mine under the golden hour sun. I could see him, read him, feel the weight he was carrying like it was my own. I *knew* him. He would never be a stranger. "I think," he continued, voice low, "you guys should go home."

The words landed somewhere deep in my gut, sharp with shame as if he'd grabbed me by the shoulders and shouted *Gotcha!* instead of handing over something I was supposed to give him.

"What?" Phoebe said, sounding so small. "But . . . no. No, we're supposed to be in this together. You can't just decide on your own. That's not how it works."

Dex dragged a hand down his face. "I'm sorry."

"You're *sorry*?"

"I am." He dropped his hand, meeting her eyes, and then

mine. "I never wanted to hurt either of you. You trusted me, you let me into your world, and I fucked it up."

"You lost your brother!" Phoebe wheeled around to look at me, eyes wild. "We talked about it, right? He wasn't trying to hurt us. We know that."

"But I did," Dex said quietly. "I did hurt you. Whatever my intentions were can't erase that."

"Stop talking to me like I'm one of the kids at Sequest!" Phoebe spat, blinking back tears. "You're not my therapist. You're my best friend."

His voice cracked: "Phoebe."

"You're punishing yourself on our behalf!" she cried. "You can't do that!"

Eyes stinging, I reached for her and she let me wrap my arm around her shoulders. She softened against me, the blaze of rage and turmoil in her eyes dulling. This was more along the lines of what I expected in the hospital parking lot, this desperation to hang on to something disappearing before her eyes. I felt every bit as undone, but I held her tight. Nothing I said right now would reassure her, I could only show up for her and her feelings.

"You said you weren't done with him," she said, willing me to fix this somehow. "We aren't done. You said that."

"Let's hear him out so we can make good on it."

"Fine." She steeled herself as she turned to Dex, everything about her stiff except her eyes, which sparkled with tears. "Talk."

His anguish was obvious, his expression pinched as if it weighed him down to the point of physical, terrible pain. For weeks he'd donned an impassive mask, unwilling to let us see this side of him. "I'm not giving up. I'm not bailing on you," he said. His eyes met mine, full of heated determination, and it felt like he'd dug his fingers into a raw nerve. A crush of dizzying thoughts descended. He was going to fight for us. He hadn't fought for anything in two years and he was going to fight for us. For me. "I want to fix this. I *need* to fix it, if it's possible. But all this time I've been stuck in my head . . . I hurt just about everyone I care about. There's so much I have to make right."

The current of thoughts winked out in lieu of a dawning realization. "You're staying."

He sniffed, fingers toying with the edge of his cast. "For a little while, yeah. This is something I have to do."

Everything about this situation hurt, but this was good. Dex wasn't burying his head in the sand. He was looking us in the eyes and apologizing. He explained what he was doing and why. Straightforward and honest, the best way to build a foundation of trust. Dex was taking responsibility for what he'd done—or hadn't done—one step at a time. He was fighting, for us and himself.

I wondered what, exactly, Cat said to him when they were alone. I needed to shake her hand or buy her a drink.

Beside me, Phoebe relaxed.

"I know it's bad timing," Dex said. "And I'm throwing out the plan."

She smiled wanly. "What plan?"

"There's a flight leaving at eight. You'd be home in the morning."

I pressed my fingers into my eyes, fending off the bizarre urge to laugh. Nearly two weeks spent crossing the country, undone in eight hours or less. What absolute *nonsense.*

"Is this really something you need to do?" Phoebe studied him closely, arms crossed. "Or are you pushing us away?"

"I'm not."

"Because a couple hours ago, you were all, 'Leave me in the dust, alone and miserable and too stubborn for my own—'"

"I want you both in my life," he interrupted, his voice steady and firm. "If you'll have me, that's what I want. For all the shit that's up in the air right now, this is something I am sure about."

How foolish I'd been, thinking love was something that could pause halfway. How bittersweet for this realization to sink in now that we were parting ways for a while, a warmth like sunshine slipping through my fingers. I wanted to close it in my fists and somehow trap the light without extinguishing it.

"I don't want to leave if you need us," Phoebe insisted. I brushed a piece of hair behind her ear, offering a small smile.

"You can be there for someone without actually *being* there." I made a point to meet Dex's eyes. "We're here. However he needs us to be."

The corner of his mouth twitched and for the first time, I truly understood how much it meant for him to feel even a hint of joy. All those tiny moments at the beginning of the trip, thrilled over the slightest smile—I'd had no idea just how significant they were. And I was so fucking grateful he let himself open up to Phoebe and me instead of shutting us out like he did with everyone else.

"Okay, well, my being there for you will be kicking your ass in *Mario Kart*," Phoebe said.

"If you say it out loud enough times, it might become true," Dex countered. His voice was thick. My breath snagged in my throat, missing him already.

Phoebe glanced between us, smiling. "We're gonna be okay, though," she said with authority, reminding me so much of our dad. Reminding me so much of *me*. "All of us."

"Of course we are," I replied, giving her a squeeze. She squeezed back and then slipped away, heading toward the car.

"But if you think you're not getting us Voodoo Donuts before we leave Oregon, you are sadly mistaken," she called over her shoulder.

"I'm not driving three hours for donuts," Dex said, and she hooted, turning to walk backward.

"You looked it up!" She ducked into the car, shutting the door behind her and immediately peering wide-eyed through the window, not bothering to pretend she wouldn't eavesdrop. I expected nothing less.

Dex looked at me, shaking his head slightly. "I have so much I want to say to you. I don't know where to start."

"It's been a long day. You don't have to say anything right now."

"I don't want you to think I'm pushing you away. Or that I don't care. I do. I care so much, Vi. I—" He exhaled sharply, shaking his head again. "I meant what I said. I want you in my life."

"I know you do."

"But I need to fix things with Cat. She's my family." He glanced at the house. "I don't know how long I'll stay. Bree and Gav are gonna fly out in a few days. We haven't all been together since the lighthouse. We thought we'd do something to honor Benji."

I knew better than anyone how important it was to hang on to the people you loved in the black hole of grief and now, finally, Dex would allow that for himself.

"That's what you've been doing this whole time, right?" I said. "Your job, this trip . . . Everything was for Benji."

Wind circled us, picking up a few stray petals and grass clippings. Our eyes locked.

"Not everything," he murmured. "I'm so sorry, Vi."

"I know." I stepped closer to him, my fingers tangling with his. "I haven't mapped out my feelings yet, but . . . God, I get it.

I do. People do stupid shit when they're grieving. I'm a prime example. Look at where we are right now. Look at what we've done." His shoulders sank in a slow exhale and I squeezed his hand. "You did something for Phoebe and me that I can never even begin to thank you for. You think you're not easy to care about, but you made it impossible not to. It's so easy to stand here and think about how crazy we were to do any of this and still believe with all my heart that it was the *best*. I'd do it all again."

He nodded tightly, eyes shining. "Me too."

"But I need some time to . . . to wrap my head around this."

"Yeah. I get that."

"This isn't me walking away."

"This isn't me telling you to."

The warmth spread through me, wrapping a hand around my heart, holding it delicately. "So, you'll stay. I'll go. And we'll be okay," I said. His fingers squeezed mine.

"We'll be okay," he agreed, and somehow it didn't feel like goodbye.

Twenty-three

"You know what?" Arden said, putting her hands on her hips as we faced the wall of paint colors. "My bathroom has been looking a little drab. A nice sunshiny yellow would look great."

"Nope." I smacked her hand as she reached for the swatches. "We're here for me."

"But—"

"Noah told me to tackle you if necessary."

She narrowed her eyes. "I don't need to be tackled. I have a modicum of self-control."

"Then use it," I replied. Her fingers twitched. "You have a problem."

She shot the samples an imploring look. "They're just so pretty."

"This is why I told you not to come." I reached for a swatch of soft blue greens. Phoebe and I were on a DIY kick after painting her bedroom and building various IKEA purchases. Our apartment was a work in progress, but every day we discussed new ideas of how to make it home: a vase of fresh flowers by the door, framed photos, nonplastic cutlery, fresh paint for each room. Six months ago, it might've felt like a Band-Aid solution. Now, though, the relief Phoebe and I felt when we walked through our door made it all worthwhile.

"I'll behave," Arden said, waving me off. "But you did invite me. Your bad, maybe."

"Right. Sorry. I won't tell you the next time I'm in the market for paint samples."

She crossed her arms and immediately uncrossed them, dropping them to her sides. "I do have a problem," she muttered. "I wanted to be an interior designer when I was a kid. My parents wanted me to be a pharmacist. I'm not built for pharmaceuticals."

"You're a great pharmacist," I reminded her. "And you like your job. People are mean about their houses, Arden. Remember when Noah wanted that chenille couch?"

She shuddered. "No, yeah. You're not wrong. I'll help you paint and hope it scratches that itch."

"Counting on it."

We collected a few more swatches and I successfully removed Arden from the premises without a gallon of Sunshine, a portable grill, or, inexplicably, a snow blower. I settled into the passenger seat of her Kia, briefly balking at the way my knees hit the glove box and the empty water bottles littering the floor. Two weeks since Dex dropped us off at the airport in Oregon and I still expected the tidiness of his car every time I got into one. Last night, I'd had the mind-numbing realization that we'd been home longer than we'd traveled. I'd had him, *really* had him, for days. I missed him so much it was hard to breathe.

Coming home felt different than I'd expected it to. The strangest muddle of relief and discomfort, like I'd forgotten something vital and now I had to learn how to exist without it.

But I found it easier to breathe when Phoebe let her head rest on my shoulder on the plane or when she let me carry her bag through the airport. Arden picked us up in her pajamas, her expression pinched with concern considering the vague text I'd sent: Can you pick us up from the airport at 10am? Everything is fine. I thought she might allow us the drive before diving into the interrogation, but she refused to leave the parking lot until we explained. She was so furious about my background check lie, she didn't speak the entire ride home and slammed her apartment door once we got there. I spent the length of a shower drafting an apology, but by the time I emerged, Arden and Noah were on the couch with Phoebe, Polaroids littering the coffee table. Arden stood and hugged me at once.

"You're not mad anymore?" I'd asked, voice raw from a mini shower breakdown. She'd squeezed me tighter.

"Not at you," she'd said. "I'm going to break his other arm."

But she couldn't stay mad at Dex either. I wasn't sure if it was the Benji of it all or the undeniable joy Phoebe radiated as she talked about him that softened Arden to the point of whispering that she had a good feeling everything was going to work out for the three of us. With nearly three thousand miles between Dex and me, it was hard to feel optimistic about it, but I managed.

Whenever I felt too far from him, I perused the Polaroids Phoebe and I had pinned to the wall of our living room. Every photo she'd taken on the road trip, so much life in each one. My favorite was the three of us at the end of our hike, disgusting and sweaty and happy. I sent Dex a photo of the finished wall and he'd responded a few minutes later: *I miss you both.*

He kept playing *Mario Kart* with Phoebe (sometimes I'd find myself listening to her swear through the wall with a huge grin on my face). He kept texting me, simply to let me know he was thinking about me. Gavin and Bree reached out, too, hoping to hang out when they were in Boston, all of us together. With the distance, it was easier to make sense of my feelings, and what exactly I wanted. My anger felt justified, but so did forgiveness. I would be patient for him. Understanding. I wouldn't take his shit, he wouldn't take mine, and at the end of the day, we would stay because we were both in this and we were the same.

A new life bloomed among the wreckage. I felt ready for the first time in so long.

It was a Saturday, the July sun blazing with a vengeance. It hadn't rained in over a week, so flowers drooped and grass crunched underfoot. Stepping through the doors of our building into the air-conditioning had Arden and me saying "Oh thank god" out loud.

"Hot," she said, veering for the elevator. "Heat stroke, even."

"It's not that bad. Here's some advice: Don't have a summer wedding."

She shot me a dark look over her shoulder. "I would rather die. My grandmother would *literally* die. She's lived in Alaska for the last six years."

Upstairs, we let ourselves into my apartment, and the relief from the AC hit tenfold. *Home,* I thought, even as I tripped over the backpack I bought Phoebe last week that she hadn't bothered to move. I didn't mind a bit of mess. I'd gotten into the habit of washing dishes immediately after using them and taking out the trash before it bred fruit flies, but I liked the clutter on our new coffee table, half-read books and film canisters. Growing up, our house was always sort of messy, mostly because we were having too much fun to clean. I wanted that for Phoebe. I wanted it for both of us.

We weren't magically fixed, by any means: I said the wrong thing more often than not, and Phoebe still held the record for most eye rolls in a twenty-four-hour period, but I hoped—my optimism soaring—that without my internalized guilt and devastation, we could finally move forward. Phoebe had been hanging out with friends (plural!), and I'd made a point to reach out to some of the friends I hadn't seen much of in my own case of tunnel vision. Phoebe invited me to sit in on an appointment with her therapist and even though we spent the entire hour with snot running down our faces, it felt good to get some of that residual hurt out, and afterward we treated ourselves to milkshakes.

I'd spent so long running in place. Taking that trip was a decision to bolt onward, even if I hadn't realized it at the time.

"Hey!" Phoebe emerged from her room, hair freshly pink and trimmed.

"I thought you were at Mae's," I said. She wandered over, plucking a strip of samples from my grasp.

"She wasn't feeling great, so I left early."

"How'd you get home?"

"Bus."

I made a face. "Phoebe."

"It was fine! Don't lecture me. It's just a bus."

"I've taken that bus before. I've been flashed on that bus before."

She patted my shoulder. "I'm sorry to hear that. But I wasn't flashed. Arden," she said, keeping her eyes on me, "tell her I can ride the bus alone."

"You definitely shouldn't," Arden replied. "We both got flashed on that bus."

Phoebe rolled her eyes and handed the swatch back to me. "Not pink."

"I thought you liked pink," I said, pointedly staring at her hair. She reached for the other swatches and then laid them out in a row on the island, studying them with interest.

"I do like pink but I don't want a pink bathroom." She flicked one of the strips and it skidded to the floor. "I hate that yellow. I hate yellow in general."

"What!" Arden gasped. "Yellow is the happiest color!"

"Maybe that's why."

"Oh, sorry. Should we have gotten black?"

"Now *that* would be cool."

I rolled my eyes and cut in, pointing to one of the deeper shades of green. "What do we think of this one? Too much?"

"It's a little dark," Arden said. Phoebe lifted her chin defiantly.

"I like it."

"Do you actually like it or are you just screwing with Arden?"

She took a closer look at the swatch. "Nah. It's a little dark."

Arden threw up her hands. "Devil child!"

We went back and forth, flicking rejected samples away until we were left with a strip of light blues and grays. I could tell by the look on Phoebe's face that she didn't like either option much, and I could tell by Arden's that she was mentally prepping for another trip to the hardware store.

"What about wallpaper?" I suggested. Arden clapped her hands to her cheeks, eyes lighting up.

"I love that idea."

"Less boring than paint, much worse to apply," Phoebe said thoughtfully. "I'm in."

"Great." I collected the swatches and handed them off to Arden to squirrel away in her hidden stash. I said to my sister, "Find a couple you like and order samples."

"Aye, aye," Phoebe said with a salute and dove over the side of the coach, landing with a groan. "Fuck. I mean fudge. My laptop. Ow."

"Is it broken?"

"*I'm* fine, thanks for asking."

Arden grinned at me, eyes screaming with pride. She'd said the words so many times since we returned from Oregon, I had to tell her to rein it in. Now, it simply radiated off her whenever we were together. *I'm so proud of you,* over and over.

I'm proud of me too, I thought, and I didn't even have to fake it.

Noah arrived half an hour later, armed with two tote bags of groceries and we got to work on dinner. I'd offhandedly mentioned wanting to start cooking again, and he jumped at the chance to help, despite his bloated schedule—rather than our regular take-out nights, he'd suggested we make something from scratch. More often than not, it wasn't a disaster. Phoebe even joined in on occasion.

Tonight, we tried our hand at personal pizzas. And not to toot my own horn or anything, but Antonio had nothing on my cheese-to-sauce ratio.

"Oh, hey," Noah said once we were seated around the living room with plates balanced on our laps. A dining table was next on the list. "You guys are officially invited to our engagement party."

I raised my eyebrows. "Is it official if it's a verbal invitation?"

"Sure."

"You guys are having an engagement party?" Phoebe asked.

Arden nodded into a bite of pepperoni. "My mom's idea. She's planning the whole thing."

"How many prewedding parties are there? Do we have to get you a gift?"

"I don't think so."

"Seems cash-grabby to me."

"You don't have to get us anything!"

Noah placed a hand on her thigh. "It's a small get-together to celebrate our engagement," he said. "Nothing fancy."

"Except it's at Stanus Tea Room," Arden added, widening her eyes meaningfully. It was easily the most upscale restaurant this side of Massachusetts.

"Ah, St. Anus," Phoebe said. "My fave."

"Don't call it that."

"Well, maybe they should've considered what it looked like before naming it that."

"Oh my god," Noah said, a laugh creeping into his tone. "It literally is St. Anus."

"Noah!" Arden threw up her hands. "Great. Now our engagement party will forever be at St. Anus. We didn't even pick it."

"Obviously," I said, going for another bite of pizza. "You guys would pick someplace cool. A beer garden or something. Not the number one destination for straight white couples whose parents bought them vacation homes on the Cape."

Noah feigned a gag. "Beer garden sounds fun. Wish we'd thought of that."

"You should have a separate engagement party," Phoebe suggested. "One for friends, one for family."

"Not a bad idea. Although it wouldn't help with the cash-grabbiness," Noah said, shooting her a wry smile. "We'll suck it up because it means a lot to our mothers. If they start dictating where we have the wedding, that's where I'll draw the line."

"You should draw the line at them doing one annoying thing," Phoebe said without a note of irony. "It's *your* wedding. You shouldn't have to suck anything." She paused. "Well. Unless you want to."

A piece of pepperoni flew at her face and she shrieked, batting it away. Arden pointed at her. "Do not. You are a *baby*. You don't know what any of those words mean."

"I'm gonna be fifteen in two weeks." Her words sounded glum. I knew Phoebe dreaded her first birthday without Dad, but instead of plotting to overcompensate with gifts I couldn't afford, I took a breath and let her feel sad. It *was* sad. I wouldn't let her stew in sadness all day, but we would carve out a part to remember.

"That's right," Noah said. His eyes flashed to me and I tried to convey the *Be Cool* message with my eyes. "Asking for anything good?"

"I want an Xbox, but we can't really afford it."

"I was thinking about upgrading. You could have my old one."

Phoebe perked up. "Yeah?"

"Sure."

"I wonder if Dex will be back by then," she said, casting me a quick glance. "He said definitely before school starts."

A tiny thrill zipped up my chest. "When did he say that?"

"A few days ago." She plucked a piece of basil off her pizza, inspecting it thoroughly. "We text. He has good music recommendations."

My throat tightened. "Yeah, he does," I said.

"He could come over, right? For my birthday?" She looked so hopeful, it split open my chest.

"Of course he can." I shook my head, gathering my thoughts. "I miss him too."

Phoebe's eyes lit up, but she trained her face into an impressively neutral expression. Dex would be proud. "So, you guys are good?"

"We definitely need to talk, but it won't be the sort of conversation that would make me ban him from your birthday."

She bit her lip to tone down the beaming. "Do you think he'll come?"

Arden leaned in, obviously interested in the answer to this. Oblivious, Noah stuffed the rest of his pizza in his mouth.

"I don't know," I answered honestly. "I'm not sure how he feels about this apartment. It's probably similar to what we felt at our house. I don't want to push him into doing something that might hurt. Because he would come if you asked him to. You know he would."

Phoebe nodded, offering a small smile. "Yeah. I guess we'll see."

Arden and Noah stayed a while longer, chatting while I did dishes. Once they left and Phoebe retreated to her room to FaceTime with her new friends, I grabbed my phone off the counter and pulled up my text history with Dex, chewing my lip until blood bloomed on my tongue.

I hear you're coming home soon, I wrote, sending before I could think myself into a coma. Three dots appeared at once.

She is so bad at keeping secrets, he replied.

Followed by: But plans might've changed.

I sank against the couch, crestfallen. I hadn't noticed the balloon of excitement inflating in my chest until he whipped out a pin.

Too bad, I sent. And then, because the hurt was raw and I was alone and, damn it, it was true: I miss you.

I miss you too, he replied. Finding you in all the good things isn't enough.

Warmth overflowed from my chest, spilling everywhere. If it wasn't for my steady consciousness or lack of pain, I would've thought my heart exploded.

We stayed up until four texting like teenagers. I updated him on the paint situation and my concerns regarding Phoebe's birthday. Dex told me about Gavin's pointless crush on Cat, and about his fear that he'd fail to keep in touch with everyone once he was on his own again.

I didn't require a long-form interview from him. Just this.

I needed this, he told me once I admitted I could barely hold my eyes open.

It was too late to feel shame or anxiety, so I wrote: I need you.

You have me, he wrote back.

I fell asleep smiling.

Twenty-four

We stayed up talking every night.

I floated through the days, applying the wallpaper in the bathroom and shopping for Phoebe's and my school supplies, counting down until the clock ticked past eight. It became a competition, who would call first. I won more often because I'd gotten really into cheating (calling at 7:55).

There was a delicate innocence to it, the way we simply talked about our days. Dex opened up more each night, the highlights and low points of his day slipping into messier feelings I helped navigate as best I could. He did the same for me. It was such a gift to be understood. I hated that we had this thing in common, but every time Dex told me he knew exactly what I meant, something inside me came back to life.

We agreed to hold off on the deeper conversations until we were face-to-face. He hadn't given me an update on his return home, but I assumed it remained a number of days away. Until then, it was enough to know he had every intention of coming home to me.

With Phoebe's birthday next week and the anniversary of

Dad's death looming, it was nice to have a happy distraction. I kept expecting Phoebe's mood to take a turn, but she seemed okay. We'd tentatively discussed how to deal with the anniversary: ordering enough food to last the day and crying our eyes out to his favorite movies. The preplanned breakdown eased the dread slightly. I would be devastated and it would be horrible, but Phoebe and I were in it together. As for her birthday, I special-ordered a donut cake and dipped into some savings to get her a real camera. We had to find a way to live with the pain, not live *in* it. We were making progress.

I walked home with my tote bag of school supplies slung over my shoulder. The clouds overhead blended into a milky white and if I wasn't sweating through my clothes, I might've thought flurries were in the forecast. I didn't mind walking. It cleared my head and it was nice to get to know our city better. Sometimes I stopped into the bakery located an equal distance between school and home, and every time I passed the run-down café before 8 A.M., three old men sitting outside would tip their hats to me and tell me to have a great day. Boston was vast, but I'd found a quaint comfort among it.

My eyes snagged on Sequest on my way by. The Pride flag danced in the wind.

I wasn't a religious person, but I liked to believe my dad was somewhere out there, and I talked to him on occasion, when no one was around to hear. I'd started talking to Benji, too, mostly to say thank you for bringing Dex into our lives. *He only needed the last word when he had something really good to say,* Catalina said, and I had a feeling this whole thing was his last word, one more grand gesture for the road.

By the time I reached our building, the sky had darkened

and a light drizzle fell. I moseyed inside and checked the mail, letting out a breath when I got in the elevator. My phone told me it was almost four. We were in different time zones, but Dex hadn't complained about my increasingly earlier phone calls. I wondered if six was too early. Or now.

I debated it all the way to my door until the sound of voices inside snapped me out of it. Phoebe had company? Not notable, really, seeing as she'd invited a few friends over since returning from our trip, but she'd never done so without asking first. Awareness pressed in from every side as I pushed the door open. Holding my breath. Bracing for—what? A few teenagers on the couch or maybe even just Noah home early, attempting to fix the leaky sink.

Or.

I stepped inside, greeted by Phoebe's cackling laugh and a loud, plinking soundtrack to whatever game system she'd hooked up to the TV. *Mario Kart,* I recognized, and my heart jerked wildly at the sight of three heads on the couch, facing the screen. Phoebe in the middle. Noah on one end. A familiar mess of dark hair on the other.

"Dude!" Phoebe shouted, turning her controller upside down as she furiously tapped buttons. "What did I ever do to you?"

"Hit me with two red shells in a row." Dex's voice sent me into a tailspin. I caught myself on the door, the metal cool against my clammy hand. He was *here.* I blinked hard at the back of his head, expecting him to disappear in a wisp of smoke. Instead, he groaned and said, "Fuck. Blue shell."

"NO!" Phoebe wailed. He laughed, glancing over at her, catching me in his periphery. He spun around, his chest rising in a tight breath.

"You guys keep focusing on each other," Noah said, turning his controller forcefully. "And I'll keep winning. This works for me."

Dex's mouth tipped into a devastating smile, turning my mind and limbs to jelly. My tote slipped from my arm, landing with a loud thunk on the floor. Phoebe jumped and wheeled around.

"Vi!" She scrambled to pause the game. "Hey! You're home!"

Noah grinned and set his controller down, giving us his full attention. Dizziness engulfed me. I managed a slight nod, my focus never leaving the man on the far end of the couch whose hair had a teensy bit more length to it and a bit of curl, his face semirecently shaved, that easy smile tugging at his lips. Something had changed in him, maybe the same thing that had turned over inside me these last few months.

Without the tension in his shoulders or the tightness in his eyes, he seemed more at peace than I'd ever seen him.

My body was drawn to him. *I remember you,* it seemed to say.

"Is this okay?" Phoebe said. "I figured it probably would be, but—"

"Yes." My voice came out too loud, so I cleared my throat and tried again. "Of course it's okay. Hi. You're here. You're home."

Dex's smile lit something up in me. I could've produced actual light. "I'm home," he said. "Sorry it took so long."

"Oh!" Phoebe smacked her palm against her forehead. "Noah! Remember you were gonna show me that thing?"

Noah hummed and climbed to his feet. "Oh, sure. That thing."

Phoebe hurled herself over the side of the couch, bounding up to me. "I know you don't love surprises," she whispered. "But I figured this one might be okay."

I squeezed her elbow. "Thanks, Bee."

They slipped out the door, easing it shut behind them. Silence echoed. Dex stood up and rounded the couch, his gray button-up loose at the collar, jeans dark, his sleeve folded up over his cast.

"Hey," he said softly. I padded over, not stopping until he was right there and I could fling myself into his arms, knocking him back a couple steps. He lifted me up, squeezing me even tighter than I held him.

"You're here," I said into his neck. His hand brushed up my back, his fingers sliding along my nape.

"I'm here."

"I missed you so much."

Impossibly, he held me tighter. "I missed you, too, Vi. So much."

"I know we have stuff to talk about. But can we just . . ."

"Yeah. Yeah. Another minute."

In reality, it was another three and a half minutes. It felt so good to touch him again, to simply be in his presence. I could feel myself glowing, could see him glowing right back at me.

I wanted to jump his bones. Badly.

"So, we should . . ." I said, and he nodded, the fingers of his opposite hand tracing one of the countless stickers and signatures accosting his cast. I made a mental note to sign it later, after the more pressing matters.

"Yeah." He took a breath, the muscle in his jaw ticking as he met my gaze. "Violet, you have to know I regret it. Not telling you about Benji. I'm sorry."

"I know."

"I spent the last year convinced I was fine," he told me. "Because I didn't talk about him and I rarely let myself think about him. It was so bad at first, it didn't feel survivable. I needed the repression to get through the day. And then I just . . . kept at it. It worked, or it felt like it did. I ran. I kept running, thinking if

I went far enough, it wouldn't catch up. And then you came out of the blue and you wouldn't let me run anymore.

"It was terrifying, Vi. You were terrifying," he went on, shaking his head. "You felt everything so loudly. You didn't care who knew. It was intimidating, but it was also addicting. You were . . . *fascinating* to me. Someone who lost so much, who wasn't afraid to feel every second of it, and still believe in a bright side." He stepped closer to me, his hand sliding up my neck to cradle my jaw. "At first, I tried to pass it off as morbid curiosity, but the more time I spent with you, the more time I *wanted* to spend with you. I knew I needed to tell you, but I wasn't sure if I'd already taken too long to do it, or if I could do it at all in the state I was in. That letter was suffocating me. It felt like Benji was sitting on my shoulders. He was everywhere and it was too much, but it was also . . ."

"Good," I whispered, finishing his thought. "You realized it was good to have his memory around. You didn't need to repress it."

He nodded. "But that didn't make it easier. I rehearsed what I would say in the shower and I'd just end up crying like a baby, right back where I was when I found out he was gone. Like I hadn't moved an inch."

"It feels like that sometimes." I swallowed hard and placed my hand over his. "I think it's always gonna take our breath away. But we are further from it, Dex. The fact that you're talking to me about this, that you've been opening up to me, is proof of that."

He exhaled and leaned in to press his forehead against mine. "I'm sorry," he murmured. "I wish I'd told you."

"I get it." My hands moved to his shirt, making fists around the fabric. "I really do."

"And what I said at the lookout." He dragged himself back to look in my eyes. "It was pathetic and I was drowning, so I tried to push you away. I won't do that again."

I smiled. "We'll make new mistakes."

"Better ones," he promised.

"I'm going to kiss you," I said. His eyes flared. "But I want to know something first."

"Anything."

No hesitation whatsoever. I knew now he would've read off his Social Security number and his mother's maiden name if I'd asked.

"Should I call you Dex or August?" His expression softened and he pulled me in closer, his lips brushing my cheek.

"My friends started calling me Dex in college and it stuck. A lot of people in my life call me August. My family. Co-workers. Bree when I piss her off." He hesitated. "Benji."

"You don't have a preference?"

"Nah. Whatever you want."

"Maybe I'll just start calling you 'gorgeous.' Throw out the others entirely."

I felt his teeth graze my cheek as he grinned. "I do admire innovation."

I turned my head, slipping my mouth against his. A rough sound ground from his throat and he hauled me up, anchoring me with one hand on my ass; I gasped into his mouth, legs wrapping around his waist, fingers tangling in his hair as he pressed me into cool metal.

"I was gonna take my time," he said against my lips. An involuntary whine left me. "But now I'm thinking about fucking you against the door."

I nodded furiously. "I'm good with that."

As if on cue, someone knocked on the other side, rattling

against my back. Dex groaned and dropped his head to my shoulder. Pushing down the disappointment, I twisted around to look through the peephole. Arden.

"Just a sec," I murmured, squeezing Dex's shoulders. He set me down and scanned the room casually, as if he wasn't sporting an impressive hard-on. I cracked the door open, poking my head through. "What's up?"

Arden stared at me for a moment. "Are you . . . naked?"

"No."

"Is he inside you right now? I swear to god—"

"*No.*" I opened the door a bit farther to prove I was clothed. "Thanks for the heads-up, by the way."

"You mean like the heads-up you gave me when Noah was proposing?" Her face split into a grin. "I was just letting you know that Phoebe's at our place. You guys can come over when you're . . . finished."

I slammed the door. I could hear her laughing through it.

"Sorry," I said, shooting Dex a smile. He nodded, his eyes locked on something over my shoulder. I twisted. The carving: *At least tomorrow.* I moved into him, pressing up on my toes to kiss his jaw. "You didn't tell me Benji was an optimist."

"That was me, actually."

He smiled so softly, it felt as if every frayed end in my world tied itself up. I kissed him again, slower this time, taking time to memorize and relish. I would learn new things about him every day and I would show him how much it meant to me to know him.

To love him.

"And you say you don't believe in fate," I whispered. He buried his face in my hair, hand sliding over my hip. "Can I do something really quick?"

"You can do anything you want to me."

I laughed and patted his cheek, making my way over to the kitchen junk drawer. He tilted his head, watching as I brandished a Sharpie, grinning. "I want to sign your cast."

He held his arm out. I bent over it, inspecting the signatures—no one really signed their names, instead jotting little messages or jokes or insults. Phoebe doodled a little caricature of Dex, basically an angry stick figure. In the blank space beside it, I wrote: *At least tomorrow* with a little heart underneath. Dex studied it, eyes heavy.

"That message on the door saved my life some days," I whispered. "And it was you."

"I thought about it sometimes," he said quietly. "It was our thing, me and Benji. Today sucked, but at least we have tomorrow. And then I didn't care anymore." He pressed a soft kiss to my temple, lingering there. "You make me so fucking excited for tomorrow."

And that was it, wasn't it? The ultimate thing I could add to those lists of threes, the one good constant: There was always tomorrow. And then a tomorrow after that. And some days it felt like it didn't matter, you would wake up feeling the same for weeks, months, years. It was so hard to get unstuck, to even remember the sun would rise again. I'd spent nine months spiraling, caught in the miserable time loop of grief, and now, suddenly, a new day.

I was excited for tomorrow too. And the one after.

Acknowledgments

I've always followed the advice to write the book you want to read, but *Return to Sender* was the first time I ever *needed* to write something. To put all the complicated grief I was feeling down and to try to make sense of it. This is the book of my heart, and I am so immensely grateful it's the one that made my silly pipe dream come true.

This simply couldn't have happened without any of the following people:

My wonderful agent, Hannah Schofield. Thank you for your unflinching belief in me. I'll say it over and over: I couldn't do this without you, and I wouldn't want to.

My brilliant editors, Katy Nishimoto and Melanie Hayes. You casually handed over my dream and then proceeded to make it even more magical than I ever could have hoped. Your enthusiasm has never meant less than the world to me.

JP Woodham, Cindy Berman, Rebecca Berlant, Laurie McGee, Whitney Frick, and the whole team at Dial Press and Random House, including the cover designer, Cassie Vu, and the cover artist, James Weston Lewis.

Everyone at LBA and ILA, and everyone at Simon & Schuster UK.

I never would have made it out of the querying trenches without the writing community. The support, laughter, and understanding kept me afloat. And to my fellow 2026 debut authors who welcomed me with open arms: Thank you, thank you.

I could never say enough about booksellers and librarians. Thank you for all you do.

My family, far and wide. It is not lost on me how lucky I am to have all of you. Thank you for your endless support.

Mom, Samantha, and Luca: Thank you for carrying me when I needed it. I love you.

Dad.

And finally, dear reader. You are the reason any writer's dream has the chance of coming true. Thank you will never feel like enough.

RETURN TO SENDER

Stephanie Parente

Read on for an exclusive
chapter from Dex's POV

The Re-do

Sitting at my dead brother's desk, I seriously contemplated arson.

A thousand years had passed over the course of three days, and I'd found myself in a cataclysmic hell where every second was plagued by the two worst things that had ever happened to me: losing Benji a year and a half ago, and the moment that redhead stepped into Sequest. These moments were not mutually exclusive. These moments were, in fact, wound so tightly around each other that it felt almost like time had become slippery, and I'd ended up moving backward. Suddenly, the wound was fresh and I was bleeding out, and I couldn't fucking breathe.

I blamed *her*. Waltzing in here like she was doing me a kindness, a favor. That hesitant doe-eyed glitter emanating off her as she gazed at me like maybe she expected a *thank you* when it took everything in me not to fall to my knees in the lobby. I'd been okay. Or at least I'd been scraping by. I worked. I went home. I dodged calls from my mother and pacified my friends' concerns with irregular responses to texts and emails, the occasional FaceTime. I'd even humored Bree's latest scheme to keep an eye on me by letting Gav crash at my apartment for the last six weeks. Things in my life weren't good, by any means, but I'd gotten to the point where I woke up in the morning and my brain didn't reach into the dark. I'd get up and get ready for the day. I was *fine*.

And now it was fucked. All that progress in the wind because of the incompetency of the United States Postal Service and a good samaritan in a red dress.

Fuck. I had to stop thinking about the dress.

Arson was clearly the answer. I would come back in the middle of the night and douse Sequest in gasoline. A few years in prison would be preferable to my life in its current state. I'd make sure the employees were taken care of, I'd fund the rebuild myself, and I'd never have to walk into this haunted house of an office ever again, let alone think about the letter screaming at me from the desk drawer.

But if it was possible to forget, arson would be overkill. Throwing it away would suffice.

I doubled over in the chair Benji spent a small fortune on, digging the heels of my hands into my eyes until pops of color impeded the dark. I knew I had to tell someone about the letter. Gav had been watching me like a hawk since I strayed from my routine that day she showed up; instead of arriving home at 5:45, I'd gone to a bar and drunk roughly a gallon of whiskey, stumbling into my apartment sometime after dark. In the morning, I woke up with a splitting headache, a plastic mixing bowl on my nightstand, and Gav sitting by the door in a chair he'd dragged in from the living room, watching over me so I wouldn't choke on my own vomit after I passed out.

I couldn't remember crying, but from the way my eyes stung, I knew it'd happened. I'd hidden so well for over a year only to slip up on a bad day. From the way Gav looked at me, I'd confirmed every one of his worst fears.

I wanted to reassure him that I was fine, but there was no point. So I looked him in the eye and said, "Please don't tell Bree about this."

Gav was a fool in most respects, more intent on making people laugh than being taken seriously. He was the living embodiment of comedic relief, but he was also the most loyal person I knew. He cared with his whole chest; that he'd moved in with me in a pathetic attempt to watch over me was proof of it. I knew, somehow, he'd spent the night grappling with indecision, whether he should alert Bree of my meltdown or wait and see what happened in the morning.

Gav had always been a wait-and-see guy.

"Okay," he'd said quietly. Later, he pressed me to talk about it, and I did my best to reassure him that night had been a fluke on a bad day. He didn't buy it, but he'd stopped digging for answers, opting to just watch me more closely. And considering Bree hadn't showed up on my doorstep, he'd kept his word.

But it was exhausting, carrying this new aspect of the loss. A responsibility tied to it. I'd always thought you were allowed to make your way through grief at your own pace and now, suddenly, I had an obligation to face it head on. Because while this letter had found its way into my hands, it didn't belong to *me*.

But I couldn't think about Cat. Instead, I daydreamed about burning down the charity that gave my brother purpose along with the last words he'd ever written for the love of his life, and I wanted to take a pen and shove it into my ear until I hit brain.

It was a mistake, taking over Benji's job. When I stepped down from my position at Stall, I'd intended to get myself together before figuring out what came next. And then a call from my accountant confirming a tax write-off had me driving fifteen hours to Boston.

A few months before Benji died, he showed up out of the blue at my apartment in Chicago. I hated living so far away, and my debilitating fear of flying made visits few and far between. He and Cat had made the trip for Bree's annual Friendsgiving event, and then I'd driven to Massachusetts to spend Christmas at Mom's. As thrilled as I was to see Benji on a random Tuesday, I knew better than to believe he simply wanted to see his little brother.

We sat on my couch, facing a wall of windows looking out onto Lake Michigan. Benji folded his hands in his lap, eyes downcast, everything about him seeming heavy and tense.

"You know I wouldn't do this if there was another way," he'd said, his voice cracking. "I've never asked you for anything, not like this. I never wanted to be the one to need you, August. But . . ." He'd broken off, rubbing his eyes. "Sequest means everything to me. I didn't realize this was my dream until it was right in front of me and now . . . I can't lose it. These kids can't lose it. I know it's too much to ask. I know that. But I *have* to."

I'd put my hand on his shoulder and offered a smile I hoped reassured him that I *wanted* him to need me. I *wanted* to help.

I'd given him a blank check and he broke down in tears, hugging me tighter than he ever had. And when he only cashed in $10,000, I sent another donation anonymously, tacking on another couple zeros.

"You're a goddamn menace," he'd said on the phone later. He spent the rest of the call saying *thank you*.

I never meant to stay at Sequest. It was supposed to be a meeting to set up an annual donation in Benji's name. I knew I could have made a phone call, but I'd never seen it in person, this place Benji called his dream. He talked about Sequest all the time. Told me about the kids, how funny they were, how much heart they had, how significant it felt to be a safe space for them. He'd found his purpose. When I walked through the door, he was everywhere. In the colorful decor, the tangerine-scented air freshener, a painting of his hung on the wall. Behind the desk, Mary took one look at me and knew who I was.

In addition to breaking their hearts, Benji's loss had proved detrimental to Sequest; he'd been the one to talk one-on-one with the kids; they trusted him, confided in him, adored him. He made them feel safe and seen and understood. Without him, the kids weren't opening up, that is if they showed up at all, and the rest of the employees were floundering. They were in trouble, and this time, it had nothing to do with money.

It was supposed to be temporary. I was going to help them find someone I thought Benji would approve of, and help with some of the digital media that he'd been in charge of. A few days into it, I was sitting behind his desk, trying to make sense of his filing system, when Mary brought in a glum teenager. She had a pageboy haircut and a split lip. Her name was Mae.

"Mary said you're Benji's brother," she'd said, regarding me warily, arms crossed. I'd nodded. Immediately, Mae dropped her arms, everything about her softening, and she dropped into the cushy chair facing me, her eyes welling up. "I miss him so much. We all do."

"Okay," I'd replied, pushing down the instinct to retreat. She needed Benji and all she'd get was me. But here she was, trying. The least I could do was try. "Well, we have that in common. That's a start."

When she smiled, it resurrected something in my barren chest.

I was unsteady, uncertain, but the kids seemed to respect that I didn't put on a front. I was honest. I didn't speak down to them.

It had been a long time since I felt warm, but it existed in me, if only in this room to help the kids who sat in front of me. They were struggling, with their home lives, their sexualities, their identities, and that was something I understood, to an extent. It took a while to come to terms with my bisexuality—fervent denials and reassurances that I hadn't looked too long at my shirtless friend in the locker room, that I didn't fantasize about kissing him, that when we ended up hooking up, it was a drunken experiment. I spent years suppressing it, dimming myself down, and I hated myself a little bit. Bree, the hurricane that she was, tore my life into disrepair as she flagrantly showcased how great it was to embrace your queerness. She never pushed me to come out, but when I finally did, she wrapped an arm around me and said in the sweetest possible tone, *Obviously.*

Working at Sequest, I felt closer to myself. I decided it was worthwhile to stick around, even as Benji's ghost lurked in every corner and I still couldn't bring myself to refer to his office as mine. Now, though, with my head in my hands and that letter mocking me incessantly, I had regrets. If I hadn't been around, Mary wouldn't have thought twice about telling Violet the man she was looking for was gone.

She thought the letter going unsent was a bad ending. She had no fucking *idea.*

"You look like shit."

I snapped to attention, bleary eyes focusing on a pink-haired girl standing in the doorway. She smirked at me with the confidence of a self-righteous teenager, wearing a T-shirt so big it fell past her knees and Converse so dirty I couldn't tell what color they used to be. I was familiar with this sort of attitude; the kids who came to Sequest were often reserved, but many exuded an arrogant façade as a shield. It never took much to see a crack.

"Gee," I said, and her smile widened. I didn't have an appointment today, so she must've wandered in after school. Walk-ins weren't uncommon, but Mary usually handled them.

The pink-haired girl approached the desk, narrowing her eyes. "You don't remember me, do you?"

I was excellent with faces—if this kid had been here before, I'd know. I studied her for a moment, trying to pull the memory out of my brain, coming up empty. This seemed to delight her. She settled in the chair across from me, dropping her backpack on the floor at her feet, and grinned.

"I'm Phoebe," she said. The name set off an alarm in my head and I leaned back in my chair without meaning to, as if the real-ization physically shoved me backward. "Violet's sister."

This was my life now. I'd be haunted by Benji for the rest of my life, stuck in the grief like quicksand, fighting so hard to get out that I sank and sank and sank. Sand in my lungs, no way up.

"I was under the impression," I said coolly, and she only smiled harder, "that I'd never see you again."

"You'll never see Violet again," she amended. "I wasn't a part of that deal. You should've clarified because I am way more an-noying than she is."

Outside, I could hear the rain picking up, spattering the win-dow behind me. I wanted to kick this kid out of Benji's office. I wanted to walk away and never come back. I wanted to stop thinking about Violet in that dress while she looked at me like maybe I was the answer, and I wanted to stop wondering what her question was.

"So, anyway," Phoebe said, shifting in her seat to look around the room. "What does this place do? Help LGBT kids, sure, yeah, but what does that actually *mean*? Like, is it only kids who are kicked out? Or do you also help fourteen-year-old lesbians whose only parent was killed in a car accident and now they're bullied at school and pretty sure they'll never be happy again?"

She turned to me, her wide eyes cocooned in smudged black makeup. "Hypothetically."

"I don't believe for a second you're here to talk about Sequest," I said.

"Two things can be true at the same time. Am I gonna bother you about the letter? Yeah, obviously. But I'm also a queer youth in crisis, so you're kind of obligated to help me."

"What's your crisis, exactly? Are you thinking about hurting yourself or others? Are you displaced? Because if not, I'm not obligated to do anything."

"My crisis," she countered, completely unfazed, "is that I am a lesbian and I am sad. Also, I got a blister on the way here. My life is a *nightmare*."

"Wow," I said. "This might be the most serious case I've encountered."

A sharp laugh burst out of her, and she clapped her hand over her mouth, seeming startled by it, and whatever defenses I had locked in place suffered a direct hit. The first visible crack in her façade. Two things could be true: Phoebe was here to interrogate me about the letter, but she was also drowning in the loss of her father and struggling with the transition of moving with her sister to a new city, feeling utterly alone. If she was anyone else, I wouldn't have hesitated. But she'd held my brother's words in her hands and let them carry her here.

I dragged my hands down my face and let them fall in my lap. Phoebe's smile faded.

"What do you want from me?" I asked. She sat up straighter, that unsettling confidence dipping in favor of something more genuine.

"I want a re-do," she said. "Our first impression sucked. But when Violet came to see you again, she made it seem like you're not an asshole. I get why you were mad and I really am sorry we read your letter. But now . . . I don't know why, but I think we're supposed to help each other."

I let out an exasperated sound. "Come on."

"I know it sounds like bullshit. And you owe me less than nothing." She leaned forward, eyes searching mine. "I know that letter means something to you. I think maybe it means everything."

That letter was a black hole, sucking my whole life into it the harder I tried to ignore it.

"We can help each other," she said earnestly. "Please, just . . . Hear me out." When I didn't say anything, she cautiously extended her hand across Benji's desk. "Phoebe St. Clair."

I should've turned her away. This only prolonged the hell, but if I was already choking on it, what did it matter? Ben had never once turned away a kid who needed help.

I shook her hand and said, "Dex."

This was the part where I should have explained that Benji was my brother and this situation was more complicated than Phoebe ever could've anticipated when she opened that letter. Just the thought of saying those words out loud stung my throat. I could barely talk about Ben with Bree or Gav, let alone a random teenager.

I told myself it didn't matter. Phoebe would walk away from this with a satisfactory level of closure and we'd never see each other again. I wanted to believe it.

"Dex," she repeated, the small smile on her face laced with hope. And then she started talking.

A lot of kids experienced a moment where they couldn't hold in the pain anymore and it spilled out in a clumsy rush. I wasn't a therapist. My job wasn't to heal them, or even try to make them feel okay. My job was to provide support, understanding, a safe place, a fresh meal, and in some cases, aid in finding sufficient housing. To be someone they could *trust*. A government official once told me Sequest worked in small potatoes. It never felt small to me.

Phoebe started with last September. How one morning she woke up with a sore throat and went to school because she didn't want to make up a biology test, and now every day her first thought was if she'd stayed home, her dad would be alive. She told me her sister didn't hesitate to accept custody, it ultimately ruined Violet's life, and yet she pretended everything was fine for Phoebe's benefit. She explained how relieved she'd been to start fresh in Boston, but the kids at school were cruel, throwing slurs and insults at her in the hallways, and even making digs about her dad to get a rise out of her. She looked me in the eye and said she felt lost until the moment she held that letter in her hands, and then she knew exactly what she needed to do.

"Catalina deserves that letter," she said. "Maybe you think it's a sign that it never got delivered, but I don't think that's true. I think . . ." She let out a sharp breath, her eyes glassy. "I think it's supposed to be me, Dex. And Violet. We're supposed to help you with this. Why else would the letter end up with us?"

"You live in that apartment," I said. "If it showed up last year—"

"But it didn't! We were the ones who ended up with that letter and we were the ones who returned it instead of throwing it out like someone else might've." Her tone was heated, but her eyes gave her away. This girl was as desperate as I was, and this realization cut to the bone. She was just a *kid*. "I know those words by heart, Dex. I can't stop thinking about them. You poured your fucking heart into that letter and Catalina deserves to know. She deserves to know you were sorry."

I swiveled around in my chair, burying my face in my hands.

I hadn't read the letter. I had my own last words from Ben

memorized, an email that would live in my inbox until I died: *Broke my phone but I know how you get when I don't respond. Maybe I'll come crash on your couch for a bit. Boston hasn't been so good to me lately. Don't worry about me. It'll pass. Always does.*

He was gone two days later.

I'd offered to drive to Boston after he admitted he was having a hard time and he refused, claiming he had everything under control. Then he broke up with Cat on a whim, obliterating them both, and I knew I needed to get to him. But work was chaotic and I was too much of a fucking coward to get on a plane. I kept putting it off.

I wasn't there when he needed me and somehow, I was in possession of his last words to Cat. And now I knew he was *sorry*.

Fuck. I couldn't pretend there was any other resolution to this than getting that letter to Cat. Not when she was under the impression that their last words were a goodbye.

"You're right," I said, turning to face her. Her cheeks were a ruddy shade of pink, her fists gripping the arms of her chair.

"We can get the letter to her, Dex. I want to help you."

"Help me how? You wanna buy the stamp?"

She fixed me with a stern look. "You can't *mail* it."

Thunder cracked, rattling the window. Phoebe jumped, eyes widening.

"Why not?" I asked.

"Because she deserves more than that. You know she does." She leaned forward, elbows on her knees. "It's been years. You can't mail it with no explanation. She'll think you're a creep."

I lifted my gaze to the drop ceiling, trying to remember the last time I spoke to Cat in person. The lighthouse, when we all got together to celebrate Ben. I couldn't believe I'd let it go so long. She was the best of us, and she'd been handed the shittiest hand in the world, and I sure as hell hadn't made it easier.

"Fuck," I exhaled. "Fine."

"You're gonna do it?" Phoebe sounded awestruck. When I looked at her, her eyes were the size of planets. "You're going to give her the letter? In person?"

"I think I have to."

"You definitely do," she agreed with a cautious smile. "When are you gonna do it?"

"As soon as possible." I tugged a hand through my hair, considering my options. It wasn't out of the realm of possibility to fly; I'd knock myself out for the duration of the flight like I did for the Santorini trip, or London, or Sydney. The problem was when Ambien failed and I ended up spending hours in the throes of a panic attack and then vomiting, passing out, and waking up with a paramedic taking my vitals because my pulse was so erratic, it seemed like a serious medical emergency.

Who was I kidding? I wasn't flying.

I'd always liked driving; it gave me something steady to focus on and helped quiet my brain down. The only problem was driving to Oregon would provide plenty of opportunities to talk myself out of it. I needed to do this, but I had a shitty track record when it came to doing things that needed to be done.

"You look like you're thinking hard about something," Phoebe said, snapping me out of my head. I nodded through another roll of thunder. "You kind of look like you're in pain."

"I have to do this," I said. "Doesn't mean I want to."

She pursed her lips, considering this. Then she said, "I think we should go with you."

"Who should go with me where?"

"Me and Violet. We should go with you to see Catalina."

"Why?"

"Because we're a part of this."

"You are not."

"Dude, I'm the one talking you into this. You might not like it, but I'm a part of it."

I resisted an eye roll at the return of her arrogance, borderlining on delusion. This kid was on another level. She probably thought she could talk at me for an hour and wear me down.

"All right," I said, lacing my fingers behind my head. "Let's say this wasn't a half-baked absurdity that popped into a preteen's brain thirty seconds ago."

She scrunched up her face, annoyed. "I'm fourteen, you dick."

"How would it work?"

She pushed herself up so she could fold her legs under herself in the chair. "Well, Catalina is in Oregon," she said, pausing to gauge my reaction to this. I kept my expression neutral, trying not to think about Cat withdrawing from grad school and moving across the country. She'd claimed she wanted to be closer to her dad, but we all knew it helped to be as far from the scene of the crime as possible. I'd felt the same way until I walked into Sequest.

"Yes," I finally said when Phoebe refused to continue. Her eyes narrowed slightly, but she didn't question it.

"So, we get a cheap flight and hotel and spend the weekend in Oregon. Quick and painless." She winced. "Well. Quick."

A rush of wind and rain clawed at the window. I crossed my arms and said, "I don't do planes."

Her face fell. "Oh. Wait, then how are you getting there? You're gonna drop everything and drive across the country?"

"You should go," I said. Another beat of thunder struck, and I tried to ignore the pang of guilt manifesting in my gut at the crestfallen look on Phoebe's face. "Do you have a ride? You shouldn't be walking in this rain. Or with a blister."

"We are so not done here," she said.

"You sure about that?"

"Your job is helping kids, right?" She stood, staring me down fiercely. "So help me. I'm fucking miserable, Dex. Everything sucks and I keep trying to look on the bright side, but there isn't one. Or at least there wasn't until that letter showed up. It's the first thing that has made me feel anything other than depressed in nine months. I just . . . I *need* this."

"This has nothing to do with you," I reminded her.

"I don't care." She lifted her chin defiantly. "I need this, Dex. And I think my sister needs it too."

Immediately, I thought of Violet standing in the lobby in that red dress. *I like to look nice. It makes me feel good.*

I shook the memory from my head. "I find it hard to believe your sister would be on board with this."

"Violet won't care. She'll do whatever I want."

I scoffed. I didn't doubt this was true, but the fact that Phoebe was willing to exploit it so carelessly meant trouble. Those two were deep in the trenches, together, and yet they couldn't have been further apart.

I couldn't afford to care about this.

"I know that sounds bad," Phoebe said, backtracking. "But I'm not kidding when I say she needs this. Probably as much as we do. She's not happy. Violet literally used to be sunshine, and now she's just sad. All the time. And she can't even try to move on and be a normal twenty-six-year-old because she has me. She hasn't done a single thing for herself in *months*."

A flash of Violet breaking down, head in her hands. *I don't know what to do anymore,* she'd cried. *I don't know what I'm doing and it's ruining her.*

"This," I said, gritting my teeth, "has nothing to do with her, either. What are you expecting? That a week on the road will fix your problems? I promise you, it won't."

"I'm not stupid," she snapped. "I know it won't fix anything. I'm not looking for a fix. If anything, I'm looking for a Band-Aid."

"Then look somewhere else. Join a club, read a book, learn how to play an instrument. The world is full of interesting shit to focus on. Find something you like and keep at it until life doesn't feel so impossible anymore."

"Is that what you're doing?"

I didn't like the look she gave me, like she could see through to my most broken parts. Like she could see through my façade just as well as I could see through hers.

"It's what everyone's doing," I said. Phoebe's shoulders slumped and she sank down in the chair.

"I found my dad's polaroid camera," she mentioned. I tried not to think about the collection of cameras Ben had lined up on our shared dresser growing up. The walls surrounding his bed were covered in photos, most of them of us.

"That's a good start," I said quietly.

"But I don't have anything to take pictures of. Violet won't let me ride the bus alone. So, what am I supposed to do? Take pictures of our apartment? Of Violet not smiling? These aren't things I want to remember, Dex."

"You know it's not going to be like this forever, right?"

She sniffed. "But it's like this now. It's been like this for nine months. So, like, maybe it *is* going to be like this forever, if it's been this way for so long already."

"Unfortunately, in order to move on, you have to start moving," I said. She glowered at me.

"I'm trying. You're not letting me."

"And what happens if I agree to this and at the end, you feel exactly the same?" She dropped her gaze to her lap, gnawing her lip. "It's a fantasy. You're dreaming up an easy way out. There is no easy here, Phoebe."

She turned away, quickly wiping a tear from her cheek. I'd let her down, unaware she'd held me to the sort of esteem that warranted hope or disappointment. I hadn't realized just how invested she had become in that letter, in Catalina, in Benji.

"I miss feeling normal," she said softly.

"You *are* normal," I responded. "It is really fucking normal to lose someone. In fact, it's boring."

She let out a wet laugh, wiping her eyes again. "Oh, yeah. It's been *so* boring."

At first, Phoebe reminded me a bit of Benji; that chaotic energy, always on the move, passionate to a fault. Now, though, the closer I looked, the more I recognized pieces of myself I'd lost. A younger sibling who wants to terrorize and save their older sibling in equal measure, a little bit selfish, impatient, stubborn as all holy hell. She reminded me of the me I was twenty years ago, ten, three. The me I was when my brother was a phone call away.

"You look like you're about to tell me *it gets better,*" Phoebe said. I reached into one of the lower desk drawers where I kept a few multipacks of snacks. Kids were crankier after school, and I'd figured out snacks helped roughly 80 percent of the time. I tossed her a small bag of chips.

"Do I look like an optimist to you?" I replied. She tore open the bag and popped a chip in her mouth, considering me.

"No. But you did tell me it wasn't gonna be like this forever, which is pretty optimistic."

"It's realistic," I argued. "You might be sad forever. But it won't always feel like it has its hands around your throat."

She smiled wryly. "And you say you're not an optimist."

I felt myself smile too, and something in her lit up. She set the bag of chips on her knee, shifting the entirety of her focus on me.

"You seem like a reasonable person, Dex," she said.

"I hope so."

"It wouldn't be reasonable to take two random girls on a road trip across the country," she continued. "But I think you should anyway. Before you say no . . ." She swallowed, blinking rapidly. "Don't say no. Please."

I knew this feeling. That raw desperation, clawing at anything that might ease the pain, even for a second. A Band-Aid, she'd called it. I'd been seeking them out for two years. I was still stuck in it.

I couldn't bring myself to keep being the bad guy with this kid. Not today.

"Maybe," I said. Her eyes widened comically. "If this is something your sister would be comfortable with or want to do—not because she's trying to appease you—*maybe* I'd consider it."

Her face split into a bright grin. Days ago, Violet broke down in the lobby because it had been so long since she'd seen this kid smile, convinced that Benji's letter was the answer. It seemed she was right.

"Are you serious?" Phoebe let out a mystified laugh. "Oh my god, this is amazing."

"Maybe," I reminded her. She nodded and bent to unzip a front pocket of her backpack, withdrawing her phone.

"No, yeah, for sure. I'm gonna text Violet and let her know I'm here."

"She doesn't know you're here?"

"She never would've let me, so I just came by after school. Don't worry about it."

"I'm not," I said. "But she probably is."

She waved this off, focusing on her phone. "I'm not that late. Shit, my phone is dead."

"'Not that late' is still late." I grabbed a pen and a Post-it off my desk. "Do you know her number?"

Phoebe looked up at me, the first hint of regret splashing across her features. "I didn't think it would be that big of a deal. It's been, like, an hour."

"Do you know her number or not?"

She relayed the number, and I jotted it down. Briefly, I contemplated calling her myself, but I didn't want Violet to associate this particular moment with me, and I tried not to think too hard about what that meant. Instead, I told Phoebe to sit tight and headed into the lobby.

Mary was sitting at the reception desk, fingers flying across the keyboard with her eyes locked on her computer screen. She'd been Benji's favorite co-worker; they were both trans and I believed it meant the world for my brother to see someone like him who made it out on the other side, gay and happy. That first day I showed up at Sequest and she told me how sorry she was, I could *feel* how much she meant it.

"Hey, Mary," I said. She glanced over, still typing. "Sorry to interrupt."

"You're not interrupting." She pulled her hands back and spun in her chair to face me. "What's up?"

I offered her the Post-it. "Could you call Violet St. Clair and let her know Phoebe is here?"

"Sure." She studied the Post-it curiously, and then her gaze lifted to meet mine. "Anything else?"

The smile she gave me was unsettling. I rubbed my jaw and muttered, "No. Thank you."

I liked Mary. We were friendly. I didn't share things with her, so it made sense why she believed there was something different about Violet. Mary saw me that day Violet showed up on her own, and she saw me afterward.

I'd been rattled. It had been so long since I'd looked at anyone and felt something, Violet may as well have sunk her hand into my chest cavity. It was painful; not looking at her but *seeing* her. She was a stranger and yet I knew her, understood her. And when she looked at me, it felt like she understood me too, which was so fucking absurd I had to sit at Benji's desk with my head in my hands for half an hour afterward.

Mary had to ask me twice if I was okay. For once, I'd answered honestly: *I don't know.*

I tried to convince myself Violet affected me like this because she was beautiful—so fucking beautiful in a devastating way, like she'd already broken my heart. But mere beauty doesn't haunt you, and it certainly doesn't attach itself to you, hanging off your neck, fingers pressed against your windpipe so you can't breathe without thinking of pink lips and freckles.

I returned to Benji's office and Phoebe proceeded to talk for fifteen minutes, seemingly without taking breaths. I focused hard on every word, every syllable, so I wouldn't think about the imminent arrival of her sister until the moment she barreled through the door.

I scrambled to my feet, Benji's chair clattering into the wall behind me, and Phoebe looked at me like I might be crazy. Violet was soaked to the bone, clothes practically melded to her body, copper hair stuck to her cheeks. Rain dripped from her eyelashes, her chin. She was gasping, terrified, until her eyes landed on Phoebe, and I watched relief hit her like a dose of morphine. I couldn't breathe. I couldn't breathe and a part of me would've been fine with Violet's face being the last thing I saw.

I was fucked.

STEPHANIE PARENTE was born and raised in Rhode Island, always within twenty minutes of the ocean. She is a romcom enthusiast who is passionate about writing messy characters falling in love. When she's not writing her next romance, she spends most of her time reading, hiking with her rescue dog, and daydreaming.

Instagram: @etnerapwrites